Dwelling in the Dark

DAVID J. FAIRHEAD

Burning Bulb

PUBLISHING

Dwelling in the Dark
By **David J. Fairhead**

Burning Bulb Publishing
P.O. Box 4721
Bridgeport, WV 26330-4721
United States of America
www.BurningBulbPublishing.com

Cover designed by Gary Lee Vincent with the following licensed elements from Fotolia: #70732699 - spider's web. close-up © schankz.

First Edition.

Paperback Edition ISBN: 978-0692376867

Printed in the United States of America

For Denise.

Only you know where it all comes from.

CONTENTS

ACKNOWLEDGEMENTS

The author would love to thank his wife Denise L. Fairhead for her time and inspiration. Without her this collection would not have seen the light of day. Thank you to Gary Vincent of Burning Bulb Publishing for coming up with the idea for an anthology. The warmest thank you to Donald and Gloria Fairhead, my parents, for continuing to believe in me.

A big thank you to Society 13 Podcasting Network that continues to flourish with new shows, refreshing ideas and of course BADDASERY.

Kettle Whistle Radio
The Wicked Library
Mouthing Off with Chris Westrick
TBA with Mr. Pink
Red Horse Radio
Prog Squatch
9th Story Podcast

SOCIETY13NETWORK.WORDPRESS.COM

Contact David J. Fairhead on Facebook, on Twitter @Fairlydark , or via email, KETTLEWHISTLERADIO@Gmail.com.
Check out Kettle Whistle Radio on Facebook for horror, music, and an endless array of underground artists.
The poem "Over the Moonbow" appears courtesy of James Clark.

SEEING THROUGH THE DARK
BY
PAUL VICTOR WARGELIN

Perception is a dangerous trait to possess. Especially when you're a kid with an overactive imagination, an insatiable ambition, and an enthusiasm to embrace ideas that raises a questioning eyebrow from the average parent if you're lucky and fearful, confusing anger from your peers if you're not.

"Where do you get your ideas?" is the question that most writers are asked. Many roll their eyes at the ridiculousness of the question, while others answer it with a goofy punchline. Whether the writer is truly offended or slightly amused is irrelevant. Writers write to communicate and connect with readers, but there is always a line that separates them as evidenced by this question and the frequency it gets asked. People who have never experienced the fun of writing a story simply for the sake of writing one tend to be mystified by the process involved, as if it's some kind of alchemy.

Then there are those who view storytellers with suspicion and the question they tend to ask most is "Why would you even *think* of something like that?"

Translation: "What is *wrong* with you?"

David Fairhead has been asked the untranslated version of that question since we were kids, both of us being prideful and perhaps foolish in sharing our stories with schoolmates uninterested in reading anything they didn't have to read outside of an assigned textbook.

A disarming grin was the only answer David would give them, because if he spoke it aloud, the answer would disturb them more than his fiction did.

"How can you *not* think of something like that?"

David has the ability to see *through* the dark. I don't mean the shadows that fictional boogeymen hang around in, but the shroud of normalcy the average family hides behind because it's easier to continue the daily routine of jobs, school, and prime time programs than deal with the darkness of despair and deception that erodes away the quality of lives and loves. The fact that David can perceive this frightens people who just want to alleviate their stress with a harmless jump scare provided by whatever monster happens to be the flavor of the moment.

The stories in this collection dare you to stay scared much longer after you've jumped. They dare you to live with the knowledge of your childhood being ripped away without warning, your body's eventual betrayal of your health and happiness, your guilt consuming your soul, and your complacency and acceptance of injustice as long as you're safe.

As all writers aspire to be, David Fairhead is his own genre. In his fiction, he traverses the dark, finding the heart of the things that frighten us and leading us out the other side to the light without pulling any punches along the way. That light may be dim, it may be flickering, but it's there.

And it will shine upon you.

Paul Victor Wargelin
December 14, 2014

- 1 -
ADVENT OF AUTUMN

Kasey waited at the bottom of the hill for them. The sunset was at its peak of beauty on the grassy knoll. For the past three summers this was where she met the boys at the end of the school year, and spent many summer days. It became a ritual now, bonding beyond the scope of most of the children in the rural setting on the outskirts of Carlisle, Pennsylvania. The houses were strewn about the town, in tiny clusters like a child's blocks on a carpet of farm country. The surrounding mountains were far off and the urban district where the truckers stormed through town to get to the Waffle House was a bit far from Kasey's home. She lived a few miles from Main Street where the upper class lived in the newly formed Welsh Living Estates.

She sat with a handful of Black Eyed Susan's in the lap of her summer dress. This was her favorite summer outfit. She wore her blue denim hat with the oversized sunflower poking out above the brim. Because of the chill on the late summer air, she had her tight long sleeved shirt under the white sun dress. Her brown hair fell just to her shoulders, outlining her pretty little face with her big brown eyes.

The hill was just on the very back end of the Burke's farmhouse, where her friend Tommy lived with his dad and older brother Jack. Kasey could see the back yard of the house with its fencing to keep the coyotes away from the chickens. Just barely though. This little spot in the universe of theirs was a good distance from the farm house and the other houses down the rolling hill. She could not see her house from here since it was further down Corvair Lane, shielded by many trees. Most were thick maple trees that appeared to be hundreds of years old. Tommy's farmhouse shone with a soft pink hue from the sunlight peering between the mountains behind her.

"Come on. Hurry guys." She whispered softly. There was only a small window of opportunity while the sun's beams struck their meeting place with such brilliance. Also, Kasey knew that none of them wanted to be out here after dark.

She turned to look up the hill to gape at the one lone maple tree that stood at the center. The relic was wider than it was tall. A freak among its fellow giant brethren that bordered all the acres of farmland surrounding their houses. The trunk was thick with bark and fantastic for climbing as the branches hung quite low, spidering about and dense with leaves. What

1

did Jeff call it? Kasey thought. "Formidable." That's what he had said about their tree. "Our stout maple is a loner, but a formidable guy."

This had made all three of them laugh. It made sense. Jeff was the smartest of the three of them, as well as the shortest. Maybe that's why he related to this rebellious growth from the earth. Just like Jeff held himself in school, this "formidable" tree of theirs stood shorter, alone but stalwart on the hills that lay before impending mountains of this part of south western Pennsylvania. Jeff was shorter than most of the middle school kids. At fourteen, skinny as a rail, Jeff had taught himself to hold his ground at a very early age by using that smart mouth of his.

It certainly helped having Tommy as a friend of course. He looked out for Jeff, being the bigger of the two. Tommy's older brother, Jack, showed him how to workout and lift weights even when they were not helping their dad around the farm doing chores. Tommy had muscles even at thirteen, was strong enough to ride a horse, and could shoot a rifle. Wrestling with his older brother, Jack taught him how to handle himself. Tommy was a tough kid, but he loved his friends, never once raising a fist to the people he loved.

Jeff has the brains, and I have the beauty, Kasey joked to herself.

They all felt safe around one another. As long as they were, indeed, all together that is. Right now, waiting for her two friends, Kasey was getting a little uneasy.

She turned to look at the tree again. When the sun struck it on this angle, all the branches that seemed to grow more sideways than upward became visible like spider veins. The leaves became a bit invisible with the bark burning with white and orange light.

Kasey also looked for movement. None. Good.

"HEY!" Tommy's gravel laden voice made her jump before she could turn to face him. Jeff was giggling next to him.

"JERK!! How the heck did you sneak up on me from that field?" She poked his solid chest lovingly on his white Dave Blaney racecar shirt.

"Came that way." Tommy was smiling. His many freckles were more vibrant now in the late day's setting sun. His big brown curly locks seemed to appear redder in the light. "Snuck around the trees outside our own property. That's where we normally find them. Right Jeff?"

Jeff held up the plastic garbage bag, gleefully, as if he should win a prize. "Yep. Didn't think it was girls work anyway, but how do you think Tommy and I always find what we need Kasey? It's not like these things pop out of the earth! Haha… eh?"

"Shut up." Kasey turned and began to walk up the hill to their tree. "Let's get a move on. It's getting late." She glanced sidelong to the woods that bordered the open field and the hill. The boys must have been out there, she thought, and shuddered. Even in the late day she would not be running around in the surrounding woods. Not these days.

"Yea, late. Late for summer too. It's almost over." Jeff said sadly.

"Aw com'on Jeffy, don't go there yet. It's depressing." She said to him. Kasey and Tommy liked to call Jeff "Jeffy" because then all their names ended in a "Y." It was a goofy bonding thing, she knew, and was glad that the boys accepted her girly ways. She preferred the boys' company over most of the other kids in town. The three of them all lived within a mile of one another so becoming a tight little troop came naturally. The thought of summer ending and not being together with them all the time made her very sad. School had a way of breaking up friendships. She knew that, and so did Jeff. He dreaded the start of a new school year even more than she. This year he'd be in Honors classes so the chances of even seeing Tommy or Kasey around was bleak. "Why do you have to even bring it up, Jeffy." She peered over her shoulder at the smaller boy in his cargo shorts and orange tank top with the number 76 on it.

"Enough, let's do this so we can go home. I'm starting to hate this." Tommy gave Jeff a little shove forward. "Let me carry it Jeff. You carried it most of the way from the woods. Damn, I think I got poison ivy...." Tommy was looking down at his calf on his right leg.

"Poison Ivy Tommy? Really?" Jeff glared at Tommy, handing the heavy bag over to the bigger boy. "That is going to be the least of your problems if we do not take care of this....and I mean at some point *really* take care of this. It's gone on too long. We need to tell someone. You both know that."

The grimness in Jeff's voice bothered both of them. They knew Jeff was correct. It was fear that kept them in this cycle. The days of summer were carefree for most kids; there was a certain peripheral envy that the three of them dealt with when they saw other kids on the playground at Frick Park or at Telbaums Go-Kart Track. Whether it was a pickup game of softball, a pool party over at the Carlisle YMCA or summer cook out at Jeff's house (His parents owned a butcher shop, so the cookouts there were called "Crucial Barbeques") the three of them could not shake the mounting shadow that gloomed over their final innocent days of being a child. Those "Crucial Barbeques" used to attract neighbors from miles around until Jeff's dad was hitting the bottle a little too frequently and hours before the parties. Those barbeques ceased altogether when Jeff's mom left.

This envy of the summers of old cut them deeply so much so that changing back to the old carefree days was something they wanted to take back. They also knew, that telling someone would only lead to more problems. Terrifying problems that could escalate out of control.

Tommy put a hand up to shield the sun so he could see the steadfast maple tree as they approached it. Looking for movement he almost spoke aloud what he was really thinking. "Just be gone. Just disappear. End this."

A cool late summer wind blew through the lonely tree, taking Kasey's hat right off her head. Jeff had to pull the brim of his Phillies hat down tighter. "Cool breeze. Summer is really almost…."

"Enough, Jeffy. I don't want to hear it." Kasey picked up her hat, pulled the denim brim down, harnessing her hair from blowing into her adorably dimpled face. Keeping her eyes from any obstructed view was essential. It was important to have their mouths shut too. They knew they had to be at the top of their wits in this situation. As much as they wanted summer together to last forever in the past, it became evident that this particular summer needed to end.

Tommy grew uneasy, glancing all about the hill around them. He looked behind the tree, to the sides and above it too. Some branches that were still moving through the breeze had ceased. Shuffling unnaturally, some of the top branches shook and leaves flapped like paper in the wind.

"Its here." Tommy stopped. They now stood by the base of the maple. Kasey put her hand out and Jeff took it gently in his own, assuring her that she was not alone.

Tommy placed the bag down at the base of the tree and opened it. The smell within the bag wafted out briefly, forcing Tommy to turn his head. Then he looked up to meet two yellow orb's glowing down upon him from the center of the tree, where the thickest branches all met at the heart. Tommy shivered, flexing his young teen muscles in defense, knowing full well he probably did not have a chance to defend himself.

"As promised." Jeff spoke, arcing his head up to the furthermost reaches of brambles where the eyes met his. "A little late. For that we are sorry, but I could not get a hold of scraps from the butcher shop today. There would have been questions asked. Dad is not happy with me." The last bit trailed to a whisper.

Some dead twigs snapped while leaves shook. A raspy breath seemed to surround them, exhaling some type of reply to the fourteen year-old's boldness. Jeff held himself firm, stepping in front of Tommy, suddenly taking a leadership role. Kasey let out a gasp as she too met the glowing yellow orbs above.

How long do we have to endure this offering? She thought to herself, desperately wanting her summers of her past back as soon as possible. The last three months were a living nightmare. If only she could share with her mom and dad the reasons for her night terrors or more simply explain to them why, in June, when school ended, she had asked them to take her to a psychologist whom blamed her wild tales on puberty.

God, if only they had not played outside here on the hill that first night when summer began. Kasey's mind was full of regrets.

*****

Back then, in June, summer broke the school monotony on the fifteenth. Immediately, on that last half day of school, Kasey Langely sought out her brothers in arms; Jeffy and Tommy. Busses were departing, kids dispersed to various directions around the school's u-shaped driveway and even teachers were smiling while walking to their cars to start the summer.

Jeff had found her first, sneaking up on her to put his hands around her face to say the typical, "Guess who?"

"Enough Jeffy."

He released her and handed her the second half of his banana flavored ice pop. "Its Happy Summertime Jeffy! Here you go. Let's get this party started! I could've taken more ice pops from the school store but Mr. Chaney showed up for inventory, and you know how that old hippie gets about rules." He pulled his Phillies Cap out of his backpack, immediately placing it on his flat head of brown hair. "Won't need these for a while." He removed his glasses and carefully placed them into a small plastic case inside his backpack.

Tommy found them shortly. "Ritual! Go to the Formidable Tree later? Sunset? Come on it's been every summer for the past three. I'll bring my IPod and docking speakers. We can blast some Korn or Avenged Sevenfold and give the finger to the whole town from up there. Even if we can't see the whole town." Tommy was so excited. More than normal. He was whipping his backpack around on his back, looking like he felt triumphant about something. Nothing about finals week could have prompted this reaction, Kasey was sure of that about Tommy.

"Why is your cheek bruised...and ew... you're sweating like crazy. What the hell have you been doing?" Kasey scrunched up her face.

Jeff addressed the question, placing his own backpack on his shoulders again. "Oh, you didn't hear? Tommy beat up Stu Welsh about a half hour ago out back by the field. Last day of school, haha, figured he'd get away with it. And did."

"And did!" Tommy hi-fived his smaller friend.

"Well, that's dumb, and then we really should go now... you guys are so lame. But, Stu had it coming." Kasey softly jabbed Tommy in the shoulder. She would find out later that Tommy beat up Stu in her honor. Stu had referred to their friend as a two timing slut. All of them were well aware that Stu Welsh knew nothing about two timing anything. He was just a tall skinny pimply bully with rich parents.

Tommy Burke just needed the excuse to let go and beat down his old gym class rival.

"Here's to one hell of a summer!" Tommy shouted back at the emptying school while they bounced down the sidewalk and made their way to Corvair Lane.

They met up again at their tree on the hill just before sunset.

Tommy's IPod was not charged so there were no tunes, but he did manage to bring a six pack of Pabst that he stole from his older brother. His playmate cooler had the six pack swimming in a pool of ice. He knew Jack, his brother, would want to kill him when he found the beer missing but he also knew that his trump card was the fight he had today with Stu Welsh. Jack would love that story. He always hated that Welsh family since his own days of football back when he was in high school. The Burkes and the Welshes did not get along.

"Man, Tommy, do we really need that?"

"I'll have one." Jeff put his hands out as if he was to have a football hiked over to him. Tommy tossed him one. "To summer!"

They sat on the hill laying on their backs. Kasey had worn her other favorite summer dress that day. The one with the Easter Lilly prints in white throughout the yellow dress. Her head was adorned with her denim hat so that she could lay down on the grass, head and all, and not worry about bugs crawling into her hair.

The boys were having a competitive burping contest. She'd had enough. Smiling at them (no more school) when she got up to get closer to the tree behind them. It was a good climbing tree, but not in her dress. The branches started right at the height of her head so it would take a leap to get up there. Sometimes they did climb it. The boys would surely end up climbing it before the sun went down completely.

"You know I blew off Susan Tyson's party to hang with you two today. Just out of tradition." Her voice took on a teasing tone.

"Eh….what do you want with that bitch anyway… her mom owns a floral shop where they clearly overcharge everyone for some rotting carnations. Brrruuuuurrrrrrp…! But feel free to blow us off and hang out in ritzy Welsh Living Estates. Say hi to asshole Stu Welsh and his rich parents for me. " Tommy was clearly buzzing.

"Hahhaa… Oh man, I'm feeling it…" Jeff got to his feet.

"Lightweights." Kasey giggled back him. She had tasted beer once at Susan Tyson's house on a dare and did not like it.

A cracking sound above her forced her to shoot her head straight up to the center of the tree.

Something was climbing down the trunk and coming right at her! The skin was black, but meshed with the trunk so that it mimicked an approaching shadow. Two yellow eyes were fixed on her as this thing, shaped like a man, was using four limbs to climb down at her, all the while a mouth of yellow needle-like teeth released a horrible guttural sound.

She jumped back, screaming in terror. The boys were at her side immediately. This thing came out of nowhere, moving fast.

Like a monkey, this hideous creature with brackish charcoal skin, came to a stop on the last branch, crouching and glaring at the trio.

They were transfixed by this alien sight. Unable to move, they were frozen before it. It happened upon them so fast.

"What... oh God....." Jeff stared, his mouth hung to his skinny little chest.

Thin tentacles trailed from the creatures head down to its back, appearing more like a main of hair. Clearly though, it could use the tentacles for climbing, as several were wrapped around the branch above the one it crouched on. The shadowy thing peered down on them with what seemed to be a grin on its snout.

They were petrified, backing away slowly.

Then the thing spoke. "I will not hurt you. Please stay."

Black lips parted as the words dripped forth between the yellow needle-like teeth. "I can pounce on you at any given moment. Fruitless to run. Your timing was unfortunate. I'm not to be seen and was on my merry way when you children showed up." It appeared to smile at them.

"Don't hurt us." Kasey Langley's mind was losing its grip. She continued to back away, tears streaming down her cheeks.

Tommy stepped forward. "You're a monster...where did you... My father has guns. He'll come out here soon......" The words spilled forth from the boy's mouth while his shorts filled with urine.

The thing used its tentacles to rise up two branches to a higher mount. It still crouched down on its two legs while its two arms flailed about as it tried to converse. "There, feel better now that I'm further up? Proud young man. A fighter, no doubt. But I have nothing to gain by harming you. You see, I'm lost. A bit. Came out of hiding a little prematurely." Its voice was deep, raspy but with a strange echo effect that was most unsettling.

"Just let us go home." Kasey could not take her eyes off the creature.

"Little ones, have you not found yourself lost or in a place you shouldn't be? Have some mercy on me. I'm a long way from home, and alone for now. Like a curious child I grew impatient and came for a visit. Surely I'll be in some trouble for this later, but for now I'm here. And with you." It said the last part with over exuberantly condescending pleasure.

"Where did you...." Tommy started mouthing his question, never taking his eyes off the beast among the branches.

"Oh. From here. Just below your homes. Well, below quite a way down, I should say properly. You have a series of caves just beyond the mountains there..." It looked over its shoulder, motioning to the setting sun between the two mountains in the distance. "I recommend highly that children should never venture there. I spend most of my days back there, trying to tunnel back. There was an unfortunate collapse." It turned to each one of the group, eyeing them up with yellow lanterns that sunk into its skull. The skull was thinner and more elongated than a human's. The flesh seemed to appear as an exoskeleton wrapped in black licorice. The tentacles down its spine were thin, whipping about when not being used to climb.

The creature's manner of reptilian head jerks, quicker than a human, disturbed Jeff and Kasey the most. Tommy's mind was having a hard time digesting any of this.

"Please, Jeff, let's go." Kasey tugged on his shoulder. She was shaking. "None of this makes sense." Her little world was crumbling before her. All her beliefs, in God, her family, Grandma and Grandpa's house and trips to the ice cream parlor... all of those happy places were all dissipating.

I don't want to be seeing this. She thought, blinking her eyes.

"I'm real. I'm older than most humans though still considered to be a child much like yourselves. Wisdom grows with experience. Had I realized this, I would not have made the unintelligent choice of entering your realm prematurely. Oh, but we are so much older than humans. We all are. So, you should listen to me when I grant you a task. Tell no one about me, and your families will continue to live. There are more requirements." The creature was twisting about, appearing to make itself more comfortable against the trunk. Tentacles flowing from its back wrapped around the tree holding it in place so it would still have the use of its long boney black arms to convey its messages. Black clawed hands moved about as it kept its conversational tone.

"The girl wishes to run. As do you Tommy. I advise against this." Its teeth rattled.

"Just let us go. We will not talk..." Jeff was shaking but still focused enough to try to back them out of this nightmare.

"Oh, you will not talk. You see, child, I'm a hunter too. Just like Tommy and his older brother Jack. Yes, Yes. I've seen you. Been watching you in the fields gunning down deer and some lesser beasts. I'm young, so these talons of mine are small, but not small enough to wrap my claws around the trigger of your weapons. But watch this...." The creature appeared to be grinning as it wrapped its left claw of four fingers around the opposite hand, focusing on the finger.

CCRRAAAACK!

It broke the black talon off that would qualify as its index finger. Snapped it completely off! A black syrupy substance erupted, spouting a goo fountain that hit Tommy in the chest. Clearly smiling, the creature put its injured finger in its mouth.

"Ah, see. Now I can fit this little finger on a trigger. This is not, however, how we...... *I hunt.* No. Not preferential at all. I would need your brother Jack to show me how to shoot of course. And don't worry

Kasey, this will grow back." It grinned at the three of them. They stood with their jaws dropped.

Then he continued, "So....how do I convey this? I want you to hunt for me. Bring me food. Freshly killed game. And ...." The creature made odd sniffing noises through its black holes on its slightly protruding muzzle. "You, the Jeffy one. You cannot hide the scent of fresh blood that sticks to the bottom of your shoes day after day when you come home from your father's....butcher shop...you call it? No? Yes. Butcher shop. Oh I would so love some of your refuse from their cutting board. Daily please. This time, every night. Can you steal entrails? I know your type tends to use most of the meat, but I will not be too picky. I mean, when the day is over and the clouds part to reveal the moon crying above, it still ends up that this is all my fault, being here." The creature forced a smile. Its yellow teeth were growing dimmer with the failing sun beam behind the tree.

"I can do that." Jeff said, noticing the coming dark. He would say anything to wake from this nightmare or make this creature in the formidable tree, simply go away and leave them unharmed.

"How long have you been watching us?" Tommy was very scared, backing away now.

"Just a few weeks. I breached your boundary only weeks ago." The echo of the voice became lighter, less frightening.

"Why the hell don't you hunt on your own...?" Tommy asked but in his heart he really wished he had not asked the question. His palms were sweating while his teeth were chattering with fear. Kasey was hiding behind him, trying to pull him back, making him walk backwards a bit faster.

"Silly child. I do not want to be seen, any more than I have been already. Now go. It is getting dark. Your parents will worry. See you tomorrow." Then it disappeared to the further reaches of the tree, deeper into the higher leafy sections.

The three of them shared a glance and ran down the hill toward the farmhouse with nothing more on their mind but the safety of the indoors. Tommy tripped over his cooler initially, then got to his feet and outran his friends down the hill to his own house.

But really? How safe could they be from this otherworldly being? What does he mean by "our realm?" Jeff was running this through his head, fervently, scared to death that he'd never make sense out of this new found fear. While his Nike shoes kept him almost in pace with his terrified friends on the soft grass, his mind was tearing apart everything his parents had ever told him about the world around him. Monsters do exist. One lived in a tree in their neighborhood!

*****

Why couldn't we have just gone to the movies, or to that dumb party that Susan Tyson was having at the very moment that changed all three of their lives forever? Kasey was thinking about that first night and how things could have been so different. But no, we had to be out at the Formidable Tree just in time to see Gnasher and witness his being. Gnasher was the name that Jeff had given it, back in June, only a few days after that initial mistaken meeting. The name had stuck to their creepy crony almost as raw as the memory of the protruding nasty jaws haunted their every thought. Gnasher would lash out with his jaws when the creature grew tired of their whining or questions that he deemed as stupid. What made it worse was watching it eat.

Like now.

Tommy had poured the contents of the garbage bag onto the base of the tree. "Found this." The carcass of a groundhog plopped to the ground. "Jeffy couldn't swipe anything from his dad's shop today. Too many folks working in the back, right Jeffy?" Tommy was just waiting for the nasty retort from Gnasher.

Summer's faltering light flared behind the tree from the crack in the mountain range beyond. Gnasher spidered his way down. Branches bent, cracked, and gave offerings of leaves that floated down on the three children's heads. Kasey hated this part. The approach.

Yellow eyes glowed with the shadow on this side of the maple while the back end of the tree was silhouetted with sun. Gnasher lowered himself from the last of the denser branches by the long thin tentacles on its back, snatching the carcass with his two front claws while his legs dangled. Really, he was not much bigger than Tommy. Wherever in hell this creature really came from, they were pretty sure now, after spending three months with him that he was indeed a juvenile. Something familiar about his behavior gave them a little comfort. He had also made them chuckle with his tales of debauchery and the fun things he would like to do to the people they were not fond of.

He offered to eat Stu Welsh once, half kidding, or so he had claimed. Tommy almost gave the ok. Then back in July, during one of their early evening picnics of the bizarre, Gnasher had asked Kasey if it was alright to relieve itself in Susan Tyson's swimming pool when she failed to invite them all to her 4th of July party. She could not hide the smile even when Jeff elbowed her.

"I can turn the entire pool a fine smelling purple haze, if you wish. Only you three would know that the fresh grape scent was the wretched refuse of your friend at the Formidable Tree." Gnasher had teased.

Then there was that moment last week when Gnasher was so pleased with the bag of deer entrails that Jeff had brought to him that he offered to "*teach your dad a lesson Jeffy.*" The threatening guttural tone made them all shudder. It sounded pleased with itself.

Jeff was shocked when the creature revealed the secrets of his own family right in front of his friends. These were secrets he kept from his best friends and he did not appreciate his dad's abusive ways even being insinuated. A week later and he was still mad that Gnasher spoke about his father coming into his bedroom at night, after coming home from Benny's Again Bar and Grille, and smacking him around.

"He could use a smacking too? Huh Jeffy, what do you say?" The beast enticed him, clicking his claws.

"NO. No, you stay away from my house. I kept the deal. I told no one." To the shock of his friends, Jeff had stood face to face with Gnasher, glaring with bright green eyes narrowed with an anger formed deep within his own gut. The creature was mockingly hanging upside down, anchored by his two black clawed feet also supported by the mess of thin black tentacles, so that he could be almost at head height with the children. Daringly, he never stepped to the ground into their world in front of them. That would be a breach of contract. Gnasher had it easy for now, enjoying the service. Why break things up sooner than needed?

Jeff's own father frightened him more than this monster, so standing in its face with a scowl all his own really was not a challenge. Or had the monster tapped into something brewing so deep that fear had no room to play in his young mind?

Inches from the angry little boy's face, Gnasher hissed when he spoke, "And I will be leaving soon. Summer is almost over. Whether I get home or not, I will surely be punished. I doubt you'll see me, *in particular*, again, after this season you so adore. I can relate to your young minds, you see we are not so different." He was talking to them as they departed from the base of the tree. Tommy had pulled Jeff back by his shirt. The three were all backing away now. Time to go. "Fear of our elder's retribution is our commonality."

The creature continued. "I was bored, lonely and full of …exciting dreams, like you. I had to escape out my window, like you have done in the past Tommy, to go sneak on your brother and his friends out drinking in the park. Peeping in on brother Jack and those girls he so easily takes advantage of. Handsome brother Jack."

Tommy stopped, appalled by the thought of being watched that closely.

Their new summer companion went on a bit longer droning with his vibrato prattle in the dark, preparing himself for his meal. Gnasher seemed a bit too excited about some rotting flesh. Coming to his senses, Jeff was uneasy at the jubilance that this monster was purveying. He motioned for them all to move a bit quicker. And so they did. But not before his last words echoed into the coming darkness. Just as the sun was completely sunk between the mountains beyond into the pink bloody drift of the sky while the night threatened its coming, the feasting creature let loose a hideous guffaw that melded with the breeze so that only they could hear the evil cadence.

Gnasher ended with a raspy, whimsical bellow that would fade into the rolling field below the three friends. "Just want to make all this worth your while kids." It stopped talking, retreating to the top of the tree to continue its feast. They usually began the return jaunt down the hill at the point when Gnasher reached down to tug and slop at his nightly feasts. It was far too foul even to listen to. He kept their attention a bit longer this time in his gleeful advent of the feast.

"He's lonely. You think?" Tommy ventured a guess, trotting downhill.

"So he seems." Kasey did not look back, afraid to see the glowing orbs of yellow piercing the night at their backs through wilting branches. "Imagine if there are more of them like he says. What could we do? We could not keep this up."

Jeff spoke in a whisper while their sneakers sifted through the high grass at the trough of the hill, where the end of the knoll met Tommy's property. "If he is not gone by the end of the summer, I will tell people. Not my dad, but cops. I think your brother might listen, Tommy, if we can prove it to Jack."

Neither of the other two could argue with their friend. There was a firmness to his voice that commanded that this was to happen, performing the act himself in an act of stolid determination. Jeff's watery green eyes were giant pools of emotion.

A bit of anger too? Thought Kasey. She knew their friend did not like the revelation of his father brought into this melee of misadventure. Something had to give.

She pondered about her own form of diplomacy, to save them all.

This was their home. Gnasher was an obnoxious visitor from a realm that they could not even begin to understand. Hell? Was he a demon? He certainly fit the profile when Jeffy and she went online at the library, and found all sorts of information on the incubus or the female succubus, but nothing about gnomes, imps or even the Irish version of fairies really fit this profile.

Their summer "friend" was new here. Fear aside, in return, she was going to try something *new* tomorrow, in the light of the summer sun, whom she was friends with long before Gnasher.

*****

Kasey Langley woke up nice and early with the sun peeking through her upstairs window. Throwing her pink sheets aside (she insisted on being covered even on hot summer nights) she ran downstairs to meet her dad leaving for work. She kissed him, loving the smell of his work jumpsuit that he wore to the shale mine works. Her dad was not a miner, working his way out of that line into the plumber's guild, he now had a contract with the new local shale mine. Even they had to have working bathrooms to use before they went deep down underground! More mining in the area meant more work for her dad, so she was glad he was happy with the newly constructed mining digs that had popped up all around Carlisle. She just missed her dad not being around as much. Her mother was getting a bit edgy about this too. As luck would have it, more mining, more contracts, meant more work for her dad as they hired him solely for their maintenance.

"Have a good day honey.... Oh I might have a babysitting job for you next summer, so enjoy this one." He smiled, grabbed his keys and went out the door to the Johnstone Plumbing van outside.

Yea, if I have a next summer! Parents can be so oblivious to the real issues at hand, she thought. Deciding it was better to get out to her mission before mom was up (mom would know something was wrong) she grabbed a yogurt from the fridge, chowing it down quickly before running back upstairs to get dressed. She would grab a banana on her way out, with a bottle of water too. Energy to help her be on her toes, both mind and body.

Kasey glanced over at Jeff's house across the street behind overgrown shrubs that enshrouded a white picket fence. The fence was now rotten with flakes beyond repair. Jeffy's father's ramshackle ford reliant sat in the gravel of the driveway next to his work truck. The driveway was the only part of the property or house that was visible due to the overhanging trees, high grass and abundant overgrown weeds that seemed to supplant the house her friend lived in with his horrible father.

The revelation that the same man that had provided those fun "Crucial Barbeques" all those summers ago was actually a monster himself cut her heart deeply.

It made her sad to think what went on there at night. Ultimately it horrified her just how they found out too. Now she stopped at the side of her own white shingled house, just below the bedroom window where her mom was still sleeping.

Gnasher had no doubt been watching them when they were not suspecting. Looking in the windows at night, just as she peered into her own window in the safe light of day now.

She picked at the Black Eyed Susans growing below the sill, grabbing a bunch of them to create her own bouquet, and then stopped to look about. Wearing her favorite denim hat with the big sunflower on it, a cozy SRU shirt that kept her warm on the cooler summer mornings like this one (dad had aspirations that she would follow in his footsteps and go out to

Western PA and attend SRU. She had hoped to make him happy and be able to do just that) and jeans. The jeans had thick pockets. She would need the pockets today.

Thinking on her friend Susan Tyson (friend? Loosely fit term) and how she would still be sleeping in her nice new home on Sycamore Street, waking up to the smell of bacon and eggs in another hour without a care in the world except what Coach Purse to borrow from her mother today. Ridiculous. She was only thirteen. Who needs a Coach at our age? Certainly it was not material items that spurned her jealousy. Susan Tyson could still be a kid and enjoy her summer.

Here was Kasey Langely going monster hunting. This time though it was on her own specific terms.

After walking across her own well groomed yard (except where the maple roots poked through) she went a short distance further along Corvair Lane, with its cover of aged willows overhead that created a ceiling that was impenetrable by the sun. Then came Tommy's house. She walked past the mailbox, up the driveway and alongside the detached garage where the orange of the new sun shimmered on the fresh new coat of white paint that Tommy and his brother Jack had taken care of last summer for their father.

Kasey had her flip flops on (not going to let him take that away from her, not her summer shoes! I wear flip flops in the summer! Even though it would have been smarter to wear shoes that could clearly help her run faster if need be, she had thought that morning) loving the feel of the cool moist dew of the uncut grass on her ankles as she approached the slope of hill at the back of the Burke's property line. The sun was not quite hitting the Formidable Tree yet. She forced a smile, bag of breakfast in hand, freshly snatched bouquet in the other. "My own summer." No, she was determined that there was no way that some hideous demon from a nasty netherworld was going to take away her childhood. It was infecting her good memories of a safe home and warm places to covet the bad times. This had to stop.

Gnasher was a child himself. He made this clear.

Would he be nearby this morning? He clearly ventured out in the daytime too, spying on her in her garden with her mom pulling weeds in her own backyard and this was just days ago, on a hot day. He had reported that he found it amusing watching her mother and her as they tugged at weeds that stood in the way of their patch of pink Sweet Williams and lilies.

God, was he in the trees on the side of her house, or hiding behind the garden or behind the shed?

She was losing her nerve.

Gnasher also knew Tommy and his big brother went hunting, even describing big brother Jack's denim jacket with the Slayer patch on the back of it that had hypnotized him to stay among the trees until Jack's long curls of hair would move to the side again enough so he could get a better look.

"Such art you adorn, you young ones. How do your parents feel about these, hieroglyphics, you so embellish." Gnasher had made them all laugh at this snippet on that day, some weeks ago, temporarily tabling the fears of him spying on them. He had spoken of the many carvings on his own black leathery skin, resembling shanks of bark being run through with a hunting knife. These represented certain coming of age tests down below in his cavernous community.

He also spoke of how he would earn more respect before his time above ground was over. Or so he had hoped. First there would be punishment that he would face upon his return home.

Like Jeff, Tommy and Kasey herself, he had the simple curiosity of a child coming of age. Mistakes would be made. She found this endearing and decided to give this creature another chance on her terms. In the morning daylight of her own summer.

A breeze shifted the leaves above her in the maple. Looking over her shoulder to the rolling fields of the valley that engulfed their houses, now seeming so far away. The sun was up higher now beaming upon her when she sat down to eat her breakfast, waiting to see if she would be alone. Kasey had left the bouquet at the bottom of the tree trunk, wrapped in a hair ribbon she had stuck in her pocket.

Finishing the banana, she sipped her water, capped it and looked up at the tree.

"You here? Gnasher? Hello? Good morning." Keeping the quiver out of her voice she surprised herself how very little fear tingled her belly. The food had to be forced down. The idea was to keep this morning as normal as any other. Instead of sneaking up to Jeff's window or Tommy's she was paying an early visit to their new friend.

"Expected you girly. I'm more in tune with you than you'd like to know." The voice had more scratchy gravel in it, almost like her dad's when he first woke up on Saturday mornings and wanted to sleep in. Not as soothing of course.

"Good morning. Brought you a gift. Also, I have an extra piece of fruit for you. Try that yet? Good for you. Better than what you ....."

The hidden voice, up in the dense brambles cut her off. "I thank you for the flowers. Generous, though I'm quite botanically challenged. What be these of type? Pretty to you I'm sure. You seem to have many of these types in your grasp whenever you have the chance. What do they mean to you? And please, put the fruit back in your bag. I despise the smell."

"You should try. These are my favorites. Black Eyed Susans."

"Shame they would have the name of your adversary in their title. How goes it with that little bitch friend of yours? She will become a real problem for you in the years to come, Kasey Langely. Competition for boys affections, jobs, friends…oh she is a problem for this community in your future. I can smell it on you folks. Competition has already begun. I see that in your eyes. Susan Tyson has throbbings for your friend Jeffy. Not good, huh? No not good."

"Please. Enough about her. I'm here to enjoy the morning. Was curious if you'd still be here." She tried to refrain from her ill feelings of the pretty blond girl with all the privileges one could hope for at thirteen. "You know it's rude to jump to conclusions with our emotions. Especially if you call yourself a friend, *Gnasher*."

He seemed to laugh at the use of his given human name. He had told them weeks ago that they would not be able to pronounce his born name. "Friends should tell one another the truth, informing them when they are wrong, helping them achieve things that they normally deem impossible. Ssssometimesss… " The creature held on to the "S" this time, preaching, unseen above in the shelter of the thicker mesh of green above. "…the truth is hard to hear."

"Sometimes, friends just give and want nothing back. Those flowers are a gift. So you like coming out in the morning? Thought you'd be down the other way, in your cave." She forced a smile, not comfortable being alone suddenly. Gnasher's tone was changing again.

"Slowly, I am building, what is that word…a tolerance… for your sun. Prefer to be in the shade of trees. It sucks the strength from me, makes me ill. Human activity runs rampant in the light of day so I felt it essential to watch but, oh, this sun of yours is a strong adversary, so I will retreat soon, to the coolness of my home, continue my dig….. I have a report to bring home now. May save me a beating or two." There was a pause as the branches above creaked.

Oh, please do not come down now. She thought.

"Wish I could say the same for your beloved Jeffy. Only trouble, dark dealings, bad bloody things seem to happen in the night for your kind. I can see why you retreat to your homes as the night closes in. There are spirits that breach the soil, taking flight to your world that wreak havoc on the human soul. I've bared witness to the dark dwellings of these invisible spirits that enter your realm in very much the same way I did. Demons come in all shapes and sizes my little dear. Some are hungrier than others, more relentless, ruthless and cunning." Its cadence sounded like Mr. Chaney, the class guidance counselor, faking a soft pitch to provide comfort before accusing you of not "showing an effort in your future."

"Like you?" She jested. Curious all the same.

"NO. I came willingly, out of the pureness of my own need to play tricks. Win the choice over competitors from my elders. Oh the tales of tricks and the power they achieve when playing with you folk…. I could no longer resist. I was not conjured." He sounded closer, enchanted by the conversation. "These spirits...the unseen... the specters that your kind pray against in your churches... they are conjured by your own people that have turned...either by drink, passion, murderous revenge... oh and you do....hahahah... do preternaturally have some people that are born evil. Take that father of Jeffy's for instance. He pays nightly visits to several local women after drinks at that tavern, takes to the bottle, and beats your friend...."

"Stop."

"And that Welsh child from that clan that your friends over at the Burke's house.... Oh, he Aint NO GOOD. He will murder one day. Someone in this town will die because of him. Maybe a few. He is only two years away from this task in mind. Tommy should be mindful. Yes, the face behind the largest murder spree your town here has ever witnessed has short red hair, freckles, pimples and occasionally wears a backpack with his favorite athletic team. Did you know he ties tiny explosives to rodents that were meant as pets? Sadistic, oh yes." He paused, audibly gnashing his black lips on his long yellow teeth. Your Susan Tyson is no angel either..."

"Enough. We do not want your promises. We are not bad people, don't you understand that?!"

"Then tell me, girly dear, why are you here?"

Kasey thought hard about her next choice of words. "We met you in the summer. This is our time for friends, friendship in general, memories. We thought you were frightening. I mean, you are scary to look at to us you know? But you can't help how you look." She looked down at her flip flops sinking into the grass, afraid she might have offended him. "Gnasher is not the nicest of names."

"I like it." The droning exaltation of the creature's response startled the young teen.

"Jeff, as well as all of us really do not like our secrets revealed in front of others. It's not, *nice*. I had hoped you were nice. What exactly are your plans? Summer is ending, and I do not know how we can continue or (she gulped) end this relationship of ours." She scratched her scalp under her summer hat.

"You really wear that hat, Kasey Langely, because you have a fear of spider's dropping from the tree branches on to your scalp, where you received a nice little bite once, when you were very young. You remember the feeling of the pincers penetrating your five year old scalp and the crispy feeling of the dried blood on the healing wound days later."

For the most part, the creature hidden up in the branches seemed more distant, climbing up the highest points of the maple. "... you remember the feeling of the furry little beasty between your finger and thumb as it wriggled trying to free itself from your grasp when you felt it biting you

17

under your grandmother's red maple in her backyard. It struggled in your fingers, biting you again before you realized what you plucked from under your fine brown hair."

"Stop it... ugh...." That memory sickened her. "That's what I'm talking about... we do not want these memories spoken aloud, or people hurt, whatever your intentions seem to be...."

"What do spiders do, my lovely?" Gnasher was closer now, approaching from another point in the tree but still hidden. The sun was shining bright, blocking her view. Shielding her eyes, wincing against the morning light, Kasey strived to see where the creature was.

Suddenly he was dangling from the tentacles that stemmed from his entire back, easing his way to the tree trunk grabbing her offerings. Leaving the banana, but taking the flowers, like a bungee cord, Gnasher disappeared back into the bulk of branches in a shuffle.

Pondering the vague question, she stepped back. "You are not a spider."

"Thank you for the lovely flowers, and you are correct I am not. Not even close. But that was not the question Kasey Langley." She hated hearing her full name spoken as if he was emulating Mr. Chaney, the guidance counselor with the hippie hair and glasses. That silly acoustic guitar he kept in his office under his The Doors poster to win the confidence of his much younger clientele. Ridiculous. Just like a lot of folks in this dying town. At that moment she drifted, wishing her dad was here. If she were to survive this mess, she would do everything she could to go to college further west, like her dad had desired.

Wanting to leave now, she answered, "They feed on smaller bugs. Nasty, unfriendly."

"What else?"

"They spin webs...." She wrinkled her cute little nose up at the tree.

"Ahhhh, Ms. Langley, now we are going places. As I will do myself, soon. I need to go back to the cave to sleep before digging again tonight. I heard some digging on the other side last night, before day break. I think others are coming to retrieve me, which precludes the fact that I must have a story for them, right Kasey Langley? ... Oh how you hate how that young guidance counselor uses your name when you came to him about changing your dance intramurals for creative writing... awwwww, you were afraid you'd hurt your dance teacher's feelings." He was cackling annoyingly.

Shutting down her current conversation a haunting memory came to her. It was the familiar sadistic sarcasm in Gnasher's teasing and tone that opened a new revelation to her. He enjoyed this too much.

She was reminded of the story Tommy told her a couple of weeks ago, in July. Tommy was sent to Mr. Chaney's office by Principal Ramsey after his first encounter with Stu Welsh in early spring. Principal Ramsey wanted to "change Tommy's outlook and direction" thinking that Mr. Chaney could interest him in some intramurals (something that Stu Welsh would not be interested in) like the photography club.

Tommy had referred to it as community service, which made Kasey and Jeff laugh. That was exactly what it was. Certainly better than a month of detention, though Tommy had no interest in photography, and he had paid a heavy price when Stu Welsh found out and shared the knowledge that Tommy would no longer be playing football but "taking pictures of flowers after school." He also did not appreciate that Mr. Chaney called his house to talk to his father in regard to his fighting at school. This resulted in many groundings.

All of this was of course relative to growing up in the shadow of Middle School.

Kasey, while thinking back on the story, looked down to the white farmhouse below the slope of hill and could see her friend's bedroom window on the ground floor. She looked up at the tree again, not finding Gnasher. A chill ran through her back, equally disturbed now as she was the time that Tommy had shared his story.

So the trivial friction between Tommy, his father, Mr. Chaney, and pimple faced Stu Welsh only set the board for game time. No, this was not the part of Tommy's story that disturbed Kasey. It was by far the chapter of the story that came later. When all this silliness had come to a head, late one night, while Tommy was in his bed trying to fall asleep, the game had changed.

His older brother Jack's room was adjoined to Tommy's. He could hear Jack snoring while he lay awake. The humid summer air from the barely open window showed no sign of cooling down.

Tommy had said, while he lay, staring out at the approaching mist coming down the hill from the Formidable Tree, he could see the stars clearly overhead twinkling in summer brilliance. The misty fog about waist height was traveling at a great speed though there was no wind coming through the screen on his open window.

He jumped out of his sheets when two black clawed hands slapped on his sill, raising his screen next by stabbing through the frail mesh. A cold sweat ran down his back in advent of what he knew was going to show through his open window next. Something he could not handle mentally, and more than likely would never be able to sleep again in this room, this house... "Please do not show yourself in the window, in my room... in the dark. " He thought, gripping his sheets.

His throat was dry, crackling a silent plea to his brother Jack's snores on the other side of the adjoining room's door. Tommy put two hands into his mess of curly hair, shivering, as the elongated black leathery head of Gnasher appeared in his window. Yellow orbs stared into his, freezing him on his bed, back against the wall. He imagined himself pushing himself though the sheetrock of his room into the hallway and screaming for his father and brother to come rushing in. There was no way he could jump from the bed to the closed door leading to the hallway outside in time.

The only light was coming from the creature's eyes, revealing spiders, and other bugs of all sorts crawling forth from the open window. Some crept directly off of Gnasher himself, jumping from his tentacled back, down his boney shoulders onto the window sill. At one point the sill was a wave of movement that made its way down from the window, to the wall pattering its way to Tommy's bedroom floor somewhere in the dark.

Where his feet were now.

He lifted his feet, knees up to his chin, "What do you want, why are you here... you're scaring me Gnasher…. We gave you the offering." The boy shivered even as he told the story to Kasey and Jeff while they sat outside of the Smart Aid drug store. They had bought some Slurp'Icey's, trying so hard to recapture the normalcy of their youth while enduring the horrific visions that Tommy shared with them.

Mostly, both had wondered when *their* turn would come for such a nightly visit.

"All he did was talk." Tommy had continued, "He asked me about Mr. Chaney, and Welsh and if…if he should handle this for me. I only shook my head. Gnasher had growled back at me. While Tommy explained this visit, he shook at the memory of that ugly snarl with the black protruding jaws over his yellow needle teeth. "I was so scared. And then he was gone. Just gone. I put the lights on and there was no sign of the bugs or spiders, nothing. Slept in the living room. Just made sure I was up and out of the house before Jack or dad saw me there."

Kasey knew after that incident that someone needed to do something, just like Jeffy had said. They had waited too long though. Here she was now, standing before this monster that seemed to own them. She was making no progress. "You know, you really scared Tommy when you visited him at his house. You can't do that. And for what? These problems of ours….. I mean not being invited to a pool party at Susan Tyson's house is no reason for revenge, Gnasher..." She was a bit angry now, desperate to make some sense of this tenuously weird situation they found themselves in. "Maybe you should be on your way. Let us deal with our problems. Your ideas at helping a friend are….."

"A bit out of your league Kasey…Langley." The whisper seemed to be all around her like the slight breeze itself called her name. She could not take it any longer. Not without Jeff and Tommy here. Breaking into a run down the dew drenched hill, she felt the sun on the back of her neck, comforting her. Glancing over her shoulder, she saw the sun was the only thing bearing down on her. Then a pinch, a sharp pain on the back of her neck. She stopped, putting her right hand into her thin brown hair. Her fingers clasped around a soft furry object the size of a quarter. Knowing exactly what it was that she had pulled from her hair, Kasey immediately shook her hand, emitting a scream but not before the spider could bite her thumb.

If someone had caught a glimpse of her at the moment they would have thought a mad woman was loose in the Burke's field, jumping, screaming, and winging her wrist around, her hat falling from her flailing head. Some strange morning dance of terror, kicking her flip flops free so that she could be ready to really run.

The sound of a deep throated laughter waved its way down the hill as rapid as the mist that Tommy had witnessed that night, reverberated through the open field, bounding off the surrounding trees. "GOTCHA!" It said. *"This could have been so much more fun if only the three of you had just participated…. Forced me to be creative…forced my hand. "*

A bit of laughter trailed out at her back as she made her way to Jeffy's house passing Tommy's farmhouse in a frenzy. It was not safe at Tommy's, nor far enough. Jeff would know what to do, she thought. Hopefully his father had left by now. It may be time to get her own parents involved but she would wait to see what Jeff would say first. Of course, then, they would have to go to Tommy too. Possibly Jack? Possibly get the gun from Tommy's older brother?

Need to calm down, Kasey thought while hyperventilating. Need shoes first. She ran to her house wishing her dad had not left for work.

Back on Corvair Lane, she had just begun to run across her own lawn when Jeff's father's work truck was backing out of the driveway across the street. Jeff was in the passenger side as their eyes met. His big beautiful green saucer eyes were sadder than ever before. He shook his head. She did not know what this meant but turned away when his father also saw her, staring from under his big trucker hat that held down his straw-like hair and pork chop sideburns. Jeffy had on his overalls she could see, so it was possible that he was going to work with his father. She would have to seek out Tommy.

Did he tell his father? Was he taking Jeff away?

Kasey let paranoia have its way with her fever dream speeded blood pumping adrenaline to her temples. Mom? Do I tell mom?

Never had she felt so scared and alone. She should never had gone to the damned Formidable Tree by herself. There was no satisfaction to be found there. Their secret place of solitude and dreams had been stolen by a malicious presence. The only saving grace was that Gnasher promised to be leaving soon. How soon?

*****

Kasey watched TV with her mom that night, wasting her silent thoughts on trivial family issues on the Hallmark Channel. Her mother, in her nightgown, chamomile tea and cookies on a tray table, was trying to ease her daughter who had been relentless in her pacing, waiting for her father to come home.

Kasey knew she was driving her poor mother crazy. With her friends gone for the day, and what seemed most of the night too, she just waited for her father to come home. He would understand. Would he? He would at least listen.

She found Tommy earlier in the afternoon, packing the truck with Jack to go hunting for the late afternoon, and maybe some night fishing at Smeltzer's Creek down the road. There was a tone to Tommy that Kasey did not quite recognize. He also would not look her in the eyes.

Does he dare to turn his back on our situation, forgetting that it ever happened? Does he dare go on with his normal summer outings with his family and leave her and Jeff behind to pick up the pieces? She glared at him while he put tackle boxes into the truck. Jack was barking from the garage about ammunition and "a four pointer buck" he saw the day before.

Jeff had been at work all day with his dad, per Tommy. This subsided some of her fears at first. Then, Tommy had gone on to explain that Jeffy's dad was punishing him for "talking crazy," and he was to be grounded for a long while. Tommy had told her this briefly before Jack came out hauling the rifle shouting about going hunting first, fishing later when they were biting.

"Gotta go Kasey, we are going up to camp today, won't be back till after dark." Tommy fist pumped her little hand, seeing the sadness in her face, and something else. "We can catch up then…."

"Tommy…. I went to the Formidable Tree this morning…. It wasn't good." Kasey said to his back.

Tommy turned slowly, gulping. "I'm practicing my shot Kasey. Jack is going to show me some stuff. You know… so we can deal with things."

She stood there wondering what Tommy meant with his stolid stance fortified with a look of proud defiance. Had he told Jack? Were he and Jack preparing for battle? Or was he speaking in code to her only? It really just seemed like Jack was just trying to bond with his younger brother, showing him how proud he was at beating up Stu Welsh.

Jack came out of the garage, tossed a box of shells to his younger brother, "Com'on, times wasting. You will never learn to shoot, much less catch a carp." Jack looked handsome in that tough guy sense, adorned in a leather sleeved denim jacket complete with the Slayer patch. His long curls stuffed under what she assumed to be another metal band's emblem on a

22

hat labeled BLS. He was taller than Tommy, but not much bigger. "Hey Kasey Baby, where you been all my life?" He smiled, teased, stepping into the red pickup.

Tommy gave her a forced smile getting into the passenger side. That was when she convinced herself that she may never see Tommy again.

Watching Jack and Tommy drive away in their dad's truck, once again she wanted to scream, stamp her feet and plead for someone to listen. Listen to what? Madness?

Not knowing the true intentions of her friends made her wonder if they were doing this to protect her? Not likely, but possible, she thought.

Sitting with her mom on the couch she could not help but wonder if she should involve her parents. No doubt she would be sleeping on the couch tonight, as her mom usually fell asleep in front of the late show on TV most nights when dad worked late.

"Dad will be home soon." Her mother dosed, her head falling to the back of the paisley colored couch. Kasey made her way around the large living room of the house that portioned itself off into a dining room. The house had high ceilings and giant rooms. It was a farmhouse that had been built at the turn of the century. She hated how wide open things were, how every noise rebounded off the high ceiling or the yellow wallpaper. Making sure to pull down every blind on the ground floor, she turned the clasp on all the windows shut too, rechecking each one.

Lowering the volume on the TV, bringing trivial bickering between two siblings and whether or not they should tell their parents about the coyote's that were stealing chickens on the family's homestead down to a minimum. Envious of the TV family, Kasey shook her head, putting one hand on her right hip to see if her dad's pocket knife was still there.

Mom was asleep. Kasey was not going to sleep till dad got home. She would then inform him of the Formidable Tree and their new friend. Whether he would believe it or not, he certainly would listen to her and hear that someone or something was wrong out there. She knew she could be convincing with dad.

Placing one hand on the hardened lump on the back of her neck, she itched it, but only pain followed. Dad would definitely take care to listen when she showed him that, even if it is a small spider bite.

"Probably, he'll just tell me not to play out there anymore....or worse, blame Jeffy or Tommy for my new fears..." She whispered.

"Whuut honey...." Mom questioned, never opening her eyes, then fell back into a snore.

"Nothing at all." She thought about calling Tommy, and wished Jeff had a phone. She did not see their red pickup come past her house yet, and now with the shades drawn she would only be able to see headlights light up the living room as an indication that Jack and Tommy came home. It was 9:00 and he said he'd be home by dark.

Damn, she thought, this bite really hurts.

*****

She woke up to sirens in the distance, credits rolled on the ancient TV box. Her last memory was the throbbing on the back of her skinny neck. Headlights had flickered across the entire room on two separate occasions while she dozed against her will. Dad still did not come home yet. The cuckoo clock on the wall behind mom said 1:30 a.m.

Distinctly louder than the static from the TV, there was scraping on the kitchen window to her right, next to the dining room. Unmistakable, the sound came from there, like a tree in the wind brushing the pane with questions.

This time she sat up, putting her hand to her hip to pull the knife out. Making her way through the dining room, she turned left into the kitchen. Kasey had left the light on in there and every room in the house.

Gnasher said his home was underground. He must know that dad works for the shale mine works? Oh no. Her mind ran loose with renewed terror.

A shadow had moved from the window outside, rattling the bushes, causing a strand of vine to unfold down in front of the window. She jumped, but regained composure temporarily, until she saw the four fingered claw scratches on the pane accompanied by smears of crimson. When the moon hit the window from a new angle Kasey could see this was more than a smear. She now approached the sink with the window above it, unprotected by blinds. She could clearly read the words etched in red on the outside of the window.

Only bad things happen at night Kasey Langley.

*****

Her father had come home four hours after that, finding his daughter shaking at the kitchen table with his knife in hand. The comforting scent of his oil covered hands blended with old aftershave woke her from her trance. She dropped the knife, falling into her father's arms. Mom came in the kitchen screaming about police outside in the street while dad assessed the writing on the window by squinting his tired eyes.

"What?!" Seeing the blood on the windows as a threat, Kasey did not call the police nor did she wake her mother. Shock kept her plastered to the old wooden kitchen chair.

Within the hour the sun had cast its fleeting summer shimmer on a broken day in Carlisle Pennsylvania that filled certain cracks in the town with a permanent crimson stain. The glow of the flashing lights of squad cars could barely be seen now at the break of day. The morning was full of rays flowing with the sun's light through the valley between the far mountains to the north, behind the Burke's farmhouse and above the lonely maple tree.

Hours ago, sirens had broken through the normal nightly locust sounds waking most residents in the very early a.m. Those closest to the Welsh residence off of Main Street behind the Waffle House were the first to be alarmed by the sound of two gun shots echoing about Welsh Living Estates.

Mr. and Mrs. Welsh found their boy in the shed with a hole in the back of his head. Stu Welsh's body was not alone as there was another body suffering from rifle shots to the head that made the larger body impossible for anyone but a close friend or relative to identify. Blood, bits of skull and long hair had plastered to the back of the other body's denim jacket. No one but police would make it to the backyard, across the freshly groomed lawn to the tool shed beside the in-ground pool before the golden sun would be high above the upper class section of Carlisle.

Though, not too far away, down Main Street in Welsh Living Estates after a slight left on Brightwood Lane, Susan Tyson's mother was screaming a high pitched wail on her own knees. She had made her knees bloody after her initial collapse to the pavement, staring at the body of her thirteen year old daughter floating face down in the pool. The water was slightly purple.

Mrs. Tyson's early "wake up" swim was interrupted on this morning by a sight that her mind never quite processed. It was not feasible that her beautiful daughter could end up dead in their own pool. No. This was not acceptable, in the middle aged woman's mind. Reacting with a never ending bellow of pain while holding her hands to the sides of her head, hair all tied up in a tight bun, Mrs. Tyson stared into the once blue water of the pool where some of the sun's beams refracted onto the pool house windows with a shimmer.

There was Susan, still in her pink and white nighty, blond hair spread out in an alluvial fan, and a trail of crimson blended with the purple water from her slit throat that would not be seen entirely until the EMT's could retrieve the body. Since one ambulance was on its way to the Welsh residence and oddly, the other ambulance that the Carlisle Fire Department had in its service was on its way to Corvair Lane, far from Welsh Living Estates, nobody would be there to retrieve Susan Tyson's body until the entire in-ground pool was tainted with crimson clouds on the purple pool water.

Meantime on Corvair Lane, Kasey watched police dragging Jeffy's father down the driveway while he kicked and shouted obscenities until he was shoved into the back of a squad car. She stood with her dad and mom. Then her dad ran down the street toward the Burke's house. She ran after her dad when she saw that an ambulance had stopped in the Burke's driveway.

A police chief was holding the thin frame of Mr. Burke back. He was still wearing his pajamas, his gray hair disheveled. He was shouting, "It's not possible...no. Where's Jack? Where's Jack? Where's my Jack?!" Mr. Burke was hysterical, waving his hands in a frenzy.

A fourth policeman pulled up to the house and approached the swarm of uniformed cops, EMT's and Mr. Burke. "Please, Mr. Burke come with me. We think your other son is at Welsh Living Estates!"

Kasey's dad held her by the shoulders.

She could see the EMT's wheeling her friend Tommy toward the back of an ambulance escorted by a team of policemen. He was strapped down. "I didn't....I didn't!! " She could hear her friend screaming.

"Admit him. We'll assess him later. I'll send a man with you." She heard a policeman tell the EMT's.

The two friends locked eyes. She started to run to Tommy, but he looked crazed. There was a moment of recognition. He struggled against the EMT's, one cop came and held him at the shoulders. He managed to shout to Kasey, "GNASHER! Oh God Kasey, GNASHER...."

Tommy then disappeared in the back of the ambulance, the doors closed. The shouting did not cease.

Kasey pulled free from her father's grasp. Running in her tennis shoes this time, but still in her nightgown, she ran to the back of the Burke's house where more cops were taping off what appeared to be some blood stains on Tommy's bedroom window sill.

Her father chased after her, followed by some of the police.

"I need them to see. They should have been told, Jeff was right all along." Her mind was racing. Now that there were adults involved in *God Knows What*, type of investigation (whose blood was that?) she had no fear when she began to run at the top of her ability up the hill to the lone maple tree.   Something was different today at that tree. There were small shadows that normally were not visible when the sunlight blasted behind it from the north eastern valley beyond.

There was a small trail in the long grass where something had been dragged.

Her chest became heavy. Kasey's run became a trot, exhausting her last ounce of strength, she had also become aware of the thick syrupy substance that the grass was painting her ankles with.

Someone had been dragged.

She was feet away from the base of the tree, already aware that she was indeed alone now. Gnasher had kept his word. He was gone. Back home?

She could hear the men running after her through the grass when her knees buckled, unable to sustain her body from the sight before her.

The tears of shock poured down her cheeks. There was Jeffy from the torso up, but only one arm still attached, half his face ripped off, gruesomely both eyes stared straight up to the tree top. Purposely of course, his Phillies hat had been placed up on his head. The sound of flies was building on the breeze among a loose trail of entrails that ended with a single leg, still wearing a sneaker.

Kasey could hear her father's voice approach from behind her, shouting up the hill along with a dozen or so other men. She could not take her eyes away from her dead friend, whom she had loved dearly. Nor could she look away from the message carved in crimson that had been etched into the thick bark of the tree just feet above the ruined body of Jeffy.

Thank you for your generous
offering, Jeffy
I left some tricks behind for
the rest of you
and
He was right, this tree
Is indeed a formidable one

*****

It would be days before the mangled body of Mr. Chaney, the Guidance Counselor, would be found in the Langley's garage, stuffed inside three separate storage containers. Two mornings after the other bodies were discovered, it was inevitable that the police find it when they came to question Mr. Langley and Kasey herself for insight on her friend and neighbor Tommy Burke and his killing spree. No one had left the sanctity of the home for days, so they had overlooked the sight and smell in their own garage.

Practicing obstinacy, all Kasey could do was try to convince the others that Tommy would never do these things. Afraid for her own family, even though she knew she would never see Gnasher again, she never said anything about who might have torn little Jeffy apart with goring animal bites and tears. The blood trail started in Tommy's room, where one of little Jeffy's calf muscles was found under Tommy's bed. Tommy had been unconscious when the cops found him with a wound on his head. Jeff's blood was all over him, sprayed about his bedroom and dripped on the outside sill. His remains dragged to the lone maple tree.

27

The police officer in front of her had a blank face. Meaning, Kasey had no recognition of the people that interrogated her even having features. They may as well had white paper machete' faces and spoke like Charlie Brown's parents. She stared ahead, seeing nothing but the two yellow orbs, flashing in her mind. The policeman had come to see her a few times, sharing these awful details of the crime scenes to clarify if she knew anything.

She only replied with "I do not know" when asked who else could be capable?

Her father was taken in for more than just a little questioning two days after what was referred to as the Carlisle Massacre. He was now suspect, since there were no motives as to why Tommy would shoot and kill his own brother as well as the Welsh kid. As for little Susan, more blank stares and whispers were shared.

Kasey stood between the rotting stink of the garage and her house, her mother holding her by the hand. Never taking their eyes off the father and husband, the good man, being taken away in the back of the squad car, both mother and daughter ignored the cleanup crew gathering the bits and pieces of Mr. Chaney from their blue storage bins labeled "Christmas."

A large man in a jacket that said "Sheriff" sprawled on the back of it, eventually came over to them while they watched her father being driven away. The Sheriff had a kind voice, but she only saw a paper machete' face outlined by graying hairs. No one knew the truth. No one would ever believe. They were clones to her now. This one bent down to address Kasey. He smiled through his brillo sponge of a beard. She could smell his cigarette coffee breath.

"Don't speak to my daughter…" Mom choked through a dry throat and a raw face.

"Kasey Langley, your name has been brought up by your friend Tommy Burke. And one other name….."

"Gnasher." Kasey looked past the policeman.

She seemed to have said exactly what the officer was hoping she'd address. His blue eyes perked up with renewed interest. "Yes, I would like to ask you some questions Kasey, if you and your mom would please …."

"It was just Tricks." Kasey's lip quivered with sickened sadness, but her eyes locked on the officer's face for a moment, never really seeing the man nor caring for his help now. She still had her mother to think of, so silence would remain.

Turning her head over her shoulder to the Formidable Tree where the sun lit the hill gold over the long carpet of green. The tree's trunk was draped in police tape waving in the late summer breeze.

- 2 -
DEEPER

Off of route 88, just south of Pittsburgh, the sprawling array of small towns slowly turn to farm country. Plots of land were found at the end of dirt roads where some folks had their hunting cabins or modest homes where they simply spent the rest of their days. This became more prevalent towards the mountainous region of Monongahela. Commonly, the local taverns that had not changed ownership nor their rotting awnings in forty years, were always down the road a mile from any section of the mountainous region you found yourself. If you happened to traverse off of Gearing Drive, a twistingly dangerous curve that wound itself up a steep but short mountain you would find yourself one dirt road away from the Ross's cabin. The rocky road was flanked by overgrown shrubs. At any given weekend, the cabin was occupied by no more than two folks, and sometimes just one. The two brothers stayed a good part of November, meeting up per old habit's sake more so than the love they had for one another. The small green cottage was off of Gearing on their own paved Ross Drive, just past the old Calvary Cemetery after you emerged from under the graffiti covered train trestle.

Scott Ross stayed a bit longer than his younger brother Mathew, and this weekend would be no different. Unemployment allowed him such privileges on the off season when the landscaping petered out. They had no neighbors, their father had seen to that when he was still alive, picking the lot for its remoteness.

Scott did not miss his father, but was happy when Mathew would come out and stay on weekends, watching the Steelers with him, drinking beer till one or both of them were asleep on the torn up couch or green recliner inherited from their grandparent's house. Scott found himself pushing his overweight body from the recliner, knocking Straub Beer cans all about the old book shelf on his right under the front window.

"Damn." He had fallen asleep watching the new flat screen that Mathew had brought with him the last time. It appeared to be about noon from the sun's position through the trees out front. Some moths had gathered on the screen door. "Left the door open too…sheez." His stomach felt like it was full of rusty nails, clattering away, while his cotton mouth made him smack his lips. He headed across the rotting wood floor, sliding a bit on a brown and white area rug that he hated, making his way into the small kitchenette. "Really did a job last night. Ugh…" He rubbed his thin wavy hair, scratched at his beard with his bulky fingers while squinting his eyes. The beard felt like it had some solidified beer in it, if that was possible? Smelled like it too, right under his large hairy nostrils.

"Nope, Cheetos." He brushed at the crumbs of cheese curls that were left behind in his twirling mesh covering his face. Unbuttoning his brown plaid shirt to get some air, Scott began to rummage through the cabinet above the sink for Tylenol. It seemed unseasonably hot in the small cottage for November. Even with the door open all night, it felt as though it was a humid 70 degrees.

Matt's going to be here soon, place is a mess, he's gonna kill me. Scott thought to himself, checking the fridge to be sure there was still another full case of beer for the 4:00 Steeler game. Then he quickly recanted that thought. His baby brother was not even capable of killing those moths strapped to the screen door! Certainly never capable of ditching the wife for an entire weekend either. That bitch has his nuts tied these days! He could only come late on a Sunday to watch football, taking Monday off for some hunting, and then back to the hag and that twerp boy of his with the lisp.

Truthfully, his little brother sickened him.

He looked out the kitchen window facing the front yard and their road below. Poking his fingers between the old brown shutters with the green and white checkered curtains on them, he caught site of the giant fracking drill that poked up through the tops of the trees, a little less than a mile away, down the hill towards Route 88. "Could apply with them. Might have something open till next spring?" He said aloud, then belched, entertaining himself. Those gas companies seem to be busy with the mining, deep into the locals' property, paying out generous amounts on top of that! Scott found it funny that Matt referred to the giant smokestack in the distance, standing over the forest by the old mill, as The Monongahela Monster. At night it had two red lights that glowed on either side of the pipe, releasing gray smoke into the sky like it had grown a mop of hair. Matt was not fond of staying the night out in the cottage, at least not when he was alone. Plus, he had that silly skinny bitch, Megan and that useless video game addicted kid to go home to.

"Monongahela Monster, what an idiot." He rasped under his breath, snorting snot from his nostrils.

Scott had enough women in his life, so he did not find it necessary to stay with any one in particular. Taverns out here were full of women, desperate or just plain easy. Milfs were his favorite, acquiring the term from some high school kids that were drinking illegally at the Slovak Club one night. Yep, stay around long enough after hours, you'll go home with something. He smiled to himself, knowing now that bringing women home would get more difficult if he did not lose his ever protruding gut.

He found Matt's fear, of just about everything, as endearing as it was annoying. From smokestacks at night to women in bars, Matt was too domesticated. Never going over the speed limit, even when both of them knew that no cops had jurisdiction over this side of Route 88 since local budgets could not support them. Cops had to come from one township over to break up any trouble, or come in accompaniment with an ambulance call.

Convenient if you wanted to break the law, or several laws. Scott feared nothing and no one. His size, though currently overweight, was intimidating enough at 6'5". Arms like jack hammers, a voice like an angry bear; not too many folks got into his way. Those that did...

The boards were creaking from the kitchen floor threshold to the one bedroom in the back of the house as Scott made his way through. He had decided to sleep off this booming hangover till his brother pulled up the drive, then he could start all over again with some fresh beers and lightweight Matt for company.

Parting the curtains of the bedroom, he noticed the crack above in the white ceiling with the brown stains. Slow drips of water from rain in the recent past were crusting with dried brown rust that dripped from a hole in the roof somewhere. Scott remembered when they considered selling the place a couple of years ago, but they had to qualify for mind subsidence now in western Pennsylvania. He chuckled to himself, remembering Matt's disappointment when that fell through. Damn, did his little brother want to get rid of the old place.

They both had looked at it as Daddy Ross's way of saying "Nope, you aint selling hair nor hide of this old joint."

Between the curtains, Scott looked to the overgrown backyard. Tufts of high grass hung over with their own weight while weeds sprouted everywhere from an unkempt yard that parted just before the woods became thick with brush. A small trail that he and his dad shared knowledge of lay back there. A homemade track that led to piles of newly plotted heaps of dirt. Both Daddy Ross and Scott found solace in that place back there that he never shared with Matt. It was their secret place, dad and he. Scott would not have sold the place anyway. Never, once, did he have intentions of giving away the family secret, not even to his own brother who had shared absolutely no bond with Daddy Ross to begin with. Scott exhaled through his nose, blowing some more dried snot out in flakes, scoffing at Matt's fear of their father, and also how righteously so he had been to keep the distance he did. Scott turned from the window to roll onto the old bed with the squeaky springs. He was finished absorbing the sight of the old path in the backyard. Appearing dark, creepy and uninviting to most folks even in daylight, it only allured Scott Ross when he was a boy. His dad had given him the tour of that slight trail into the woods at a very young age, needing to share its secrets with someone, preferably of the same blood.

*****

"Really dad. Here." Mathew Ross heard the bump and grind of the gravel in the wheel wells of his wife's Reliant. Anxious to see his brother for the weekend (and get away from his spoiled screaming kid and nagging wife) to put a few beers in his empty gullet. Still, he never really understood why their father chose this hilltop as his refuge. Never bothered to ask the man while he was alive. Would he have, given the chance? No. Mathew was always afraid of their father, distancing himself from the man as best as he could, talking through Scott for information on when to show up at Thanksgiving, or who was going to cash dad's pension check this week?

He did love his brother though, odd as it seemed, that Scott took on the role of father after theirs passed away. Rite of passage? Mathew thought to himself. Matt worked hard at the office for the bank.

"Desk job makes the hands lazy, Matt" their father would say. With dad gone, Scott decided to keep tradition and repeated the old song refrain to him on a regular basis.

Pulling up in front of the small green cottage, parking next to Scott's red and white pickup, he rubbed the pocket of his red and black flannel searching for his Marlboro Box. Raising his thick glasses to the top of his thin stringy dirty blond hair, he sat in the car, lighting up before going up to the porch. Something was different this time. Mathew left his Steelers duffel bag in the back seat next to the pile of fishing gear.

Hot for November. He thought, pushing back the long strands of his scraggily hair. The clearing in front of the cottage was lit bright with late afternoon sun through the thinning trees. Pine needles and leaves carpeted the soft ground under his work boots. "No birds." He thought then blew smoke out through his thin gray lips. The air was still. Usually you could not hear the cars circling around Gearing Road down below. No one ever came up their own Ross Drive, not even to turn around. The brothers had it posted for no hunting only so they could take out all the turkeys themselves during the season. Tons of wild turkeys up on the mountain top and the forest below. Only the brothers would take advantage of this since there were even less folk that ever visited the Calvary Cemetery down the road. The historical site consisted of three huge crosses in a clearing and some stone markers on the ground. Not much to see.

Sort of like their own cottage before him.

Turning, he squinted his eyes to the tops of the trees down the slope he had just drove up from. There was the fracking drill in the distance and beyond that the smokestack with the red lights just becoming visible in the early orange of dusk.

"Monongahela Monster, Heh," He had a chuckle at the smokestack he so aptly named. Still, it gave him the creeps. Mathew puffed away, turning back to look at the cottage. He could use a beer, feeling somewhat uncomfortable. That old familiar pang of unease, sort of how he felt when he visited while their father was still around. Small, frail, weak and inferior to his brother even though he was the one that kept the career, had the family, carved the turkey on the holidays! Sometimes even shot the turkey.

Never could figure that out. Mathew thought on the relationship that Scott had with their dad, playing third-man-out, over him. "Feels, like he's still here." He thought. His brother was slowly turning into the hulking narrow minded, short tempered father that they both had known growing up.

"Being stupid," He whispered, then yelled, "Hey Scawtt, I'm here... what're ya' sleeping one off?" He figured he would finish his smoke first. What was the point? Scott hated when he smoked in the house anyway.

He thought about some of his first memories staying here, how his father would be up late watching Sports Channel after sending them to bed. Daddy Ross would stay up drinking, eventually sleeping on the couch. The daytime memories were good, with the fishing, turkey hunting, sometimes going out on a boat that Dad would rent. At night, all he remembered was his father's shambling shape coming down the hall to smack the shit out of him when he and Scott messed around, laughing, giggling or whacking each other with pillows. All the fun and games would end when Daddy Ross's dark shadow appeared down the hall, footfalls like bowling balls on the light wood floors. Scott never got the brunt of the man's unrelenting anger that resulted in the beatings on the back of his legs, head, ass; these moments were all for him to endure. Scott never even acknowledged it, showing no empathy. In the morning after a night of whimpering, it was never ever talked about.

The good memories were sporadic in the days of their father.

Now, standing level with the front porch, Mathew could see the shingles on the gray roof, noticing that some more were falling free since his last visit. Something else was different. There appeared to be a slanted shift in the roof above him, more so than compared to last time they were here. "Wait... what?"

From this angle he could see some pieces of wood were sticking up, pointing at the sky where part of the roof had dipped, collapsing with either water damage or some unseen interior fracture. A small spark lit in his belly, "Good, now we can finally get rid of it," he thought, any excuse to extinguish memories of the monster that his father had become. He could almost picture the man's huge form standing on the porch after crouching his bald head from under the front door, in his boxers and army jacket. Daddy Ross had developed an even more frightening appearance when his eyes and face had become jaundiced with his sickness. Still, he had managed to scoff at Mathew when he arrived saying things like, "I thought it was a weekend for the men?" or "If you didn't bring beer, then go back into town, and come back," and his favorite, "Did your wife find a real man yet? That why'yer here this weekend?" from the later years. The final years.

Mathew blinked and the memory on the porch faded.

It was worse than he thought.

Running up the moldy white chipped steps to the porch he could see some fallen beams in the living room that crushed the TV, just missing the couch. None of this was visible from outside. The screen door came off its hinges when he tugged on it, tumbling to the porch floor with a small piece of wood still attached to it. He half expected to see his brother buried, dead, on their father's couch, where he used to fall asleep. But no. He was not on the couch. The couch actually was still totally intact.

There was no preparation for the sight beyond the living room. When he stepped in front of where the kitchen threshold used to be, between the living room and the kitchen table was a deep dark hole larger than the kitchen itself had been. The hole in the center of the roof stretched to the back of the house while a sinkhole under the cottage threatened to swallow what little was left of the interior of their weekend house.

"SCAWTT!" The realization that Scott might have been in here when it happened froze his spine where he stood. The bedroom was all but gone too! Only a broken headboard lay flimsily against the wall. Between where Mathew stood and the far wall was a black hole blowing cold damp air up at him. A small sound like a breeze inside of a cavern blustered from below in the darkness. The smell of freshly broken wood, cement, and musty earth howled from its depths.

"Scott... oh no. SCAWTT!!" He heard his own voice echo down the chasm, reverberating deeper into the dark than he ever wanted to imagine himself dangling over. He pulled the cell phone out of his back pocket.

Before he could even flip the phone open, he felt the sensation of his feet sliding on dusty wood. The floor was moving, slipping underfoot, with a loud *CRACK* of wood breaking, it was taking him down, deeper, tumbling, smashing his head on a rocky slope. Black and then more black.
*****

Scott woke up to the crumbling static of his brother crashing down the opening overhead. He watched in the narrow light above as his brother's thin frame fell with the piece of flooring beneath him, letting out a yelp, then silenced as he slid down the side of rocky sand on top of piles of crumbling sheetrock and beams. The sound of his brother yelling his name initially woke him. Useless though, as he was pinned under a pile of wood and rubble on his legs. He sat, facing up, his back arched behind him where his shirt had ripped, feeling the wetness of blood pouring into the crack of his ass from the bottom of his spine.

"Dammit…. Matt. Wake up. Where are you?" Scott's eyes were adjusting. He could just barely see where his brother had landed. Matt's lanky body hung limply onto two large pieces of beam that jutted from the rocky sinkhole. The light above, where the hole sucked down half of the interior of the house, was so far up that the light it emitted was too faint to really see clearly. Matt was dangling above, across those beams, unconscious, but alive. He was wheezing on the damp air.

"Wake up Matt. Tell me you have your phone. WAKE UP you dipshit!!"

Then he did. Coughing out crumbles of dust, Mathew woke up in the most unlikely of places that he ever would imagine himself on football Sunday. "No… No….what the. Scott… you here? Oh my god. I can't see how far up I am."

"Stay still. Far as I can see you are a good fifteen feet higher than me. Bro, I can't move. Maybe you can dig in, climb up. You have a good start." Scott's voice remained calm.

Mathew was fighting panic, having to pee, on top of puking up dirt, "Oh man, we're gonna die down here… Scott, we're gonna die!" The tears streamed down his face while he put his arms tightly around the two beams that he came to rest upon.

"Your phone Matt. Do you have your phone?" Scott's deep grumbling voice echoed off the chamber of the sinkhole. "Breath, asshole. Breath."

Pushing himself up, off the metal beams, praying that they would still maintain horizontally stuck in the side of the pit, he glanced below him, away from where he heard his brother's voice. His chest stung him violently. "Ow… oh shit, man, I have broken ribs…" He started a coughing fit.

Getting a hold of himself, he cupped his mouth, spitting away dirt from his throat. A faint glow shone below him, but further away from where Scott's voice was. He could see the greenish shine of the flip phone. "OH man, it's closer to you, but must have fallen deeper. Can you see it?"

"No. SHIT! How the hell did you fall in, you goddamn idiot!" Scott was losing his temper now, realizing the situation just became desperate.

"Dunno…man, the floor gave way… How the fuck did this happen at all?!" Mathew was weeping. "Gonna die, man."

"Listen to me, you weak piece of shit… you have to try to climb. Find footing on the wall. If you can't make it up…" The hole above with the failing sun seemed miles away, "… then try to inch your way down to the phone while it's got juice, man… I'm pinned. Think my legs are broken, Matt."

This made some sense, forlorn as he could be, Mathew would try climbing further down to reach the phone. Oh, God, what if there is no signal down here? Stop it. He said to himself, not wanting to disappoint his brother, he would try to get some footing below the beams on the side of this newly formed pit.

"I can see it, I'm going to try..." Like a lightening bug on cue, the phone shut off. He had an idea where it was, so he was going to lower one of his long legs down below to see if there was footing.

"What? What was that?!" Scott's voice took on a high pitched tone that Mathew had never heard before.

"What was *what*?" Fearing that the ground below them was going to give way again, Mathew found his perch, straddling his legs around the beams tightly.

Then the light from the phone blinked its bluish green glow again. "Oh man, the light came on again. I can see it. Do you think someone is calling? I don't hear the ringer... That means we have a signal Scott."

Clenching his teeth, Scott could feel the pain in his legs begin to shoot up to his abdomen. "I can just barely see the glow.... Oh gawd...this hurts....." His throat was dry with fear, an emotion that was new to him, and he really was more uncomfortable with this new found tremble in his mind than the stinging in his legs under the rubble. "Something hit it, Matt. Something is walking around down here... I felt something walk across my legs. Get down here... you have to get me out of here!" So this is fear? Anger at this sudden flare up of emotion, he felt panicked when several pitter patters of clawed feet the size of (in his mind) a rat's, were casually walking across the rubble over his legs. Whatever it had been, something was down here with them and Scott caught a glimpse of movement by the fallen cell phone.

Several *somethings* were crawling on it, knocking it around, investigating the small foreign device.

"What do you mean, Scawwtt... what do you mean something's down here?" Looking down to where his brother's voice was coming from in the deep dark, Matt tried to avert his eyes from the location of the cell phone. He too, could hear crumbling pebbles on dirt, a strange tapping on plastic, but it was the *chittering* sound from a repugnant clicking source that tempted him to peer down below.

In the dull light of the cell phone, he could see several crab-like shapes, shimmering with metallic green, yellow and red glowing against the fading light from the small device. The *chittering* was becoming louder. These shapes were clicking aggressively, nothing like the soft cricket bows of the night; these were awful, unfathomable things creeping around in the dark, and getting closer.

"SPIDERS! Oh Scott, they're huge…. Pick up a rock, they are so close to you…. Oh shit oh shit, I can see them climbing the walls too…they're coming for me!" Stretching his neck to pray to the opening above that was so high that it seemed to be miles away. The light was way above (so out of reach even on a good climb) where the cottage had been breached from below the ground. Stinging with regret, Mathew wished he could just have been more careful when he stepped near the hole to begin with.

Descending from the sides of the chasm, dark shapes were hanging from thick strings, dangling down from all angles. The light above would catch one of the apple sized shadows, hanging like failing yo-yo's proving to be Mathew's worst fear. More of the spiders were coming from above as well, the fading light refracting off their shiny hides!

"Scott, there's more coming down from the sides…. Oh damn, man what are we going to do?" He began to whimper, looking for some words from his brother below to inspire some kind of hope in fighting back. Scott was always the strong protector.

Unless Daddy Ross was the malefactor.

Scott watched to his left as the cell phone's light went out again. Prior to that he had reached around in the piles of debris in order to find a weapon to wield. Closing his hands on a splintery piece of wood, he had a broken piece of 2x4 in his hands, ready to swing if something came close. Relying on his hearing now, he wished Matt would shut up. He had heard something different. Something scattered the spiders away from their mischief with the cell phone. The sound of rock being moved, shifting sand pebbles over shale, just to his left in the pitch black. A smell now, like rotting flesh.

He was very familiar with that scent.

"Hhhhissssssssssssss" As if the dark had a voice, it released an exhalation, deep, droning, becoming threatening.

The hairs on his neck all the way to his scalp tingled. A virgin to this *"fear"* a new emotion that now was pronouncing itself within his heart and mind only angered Scott more. *"I don't get hunted."* He snarled back at the dark.

"What… what is that….Scawwtt….what's happening… there's yellow lights…" Matt was panicking, laying on his stomach, on top of the beams trying to look down. Scott could make his outline out against the waning light above, when his eyes adjusted to the pure dark once again. Adept at adjusting his sight in the dark, he knew if he closed his eyes, after the cell went out, he could adjust his eyes a bit quicker than the couple of seconds extra needed to adjust to the dark again. He used this often when he followed one of the women home from People's Place Tavern over in New Eagle, down the road. There was no light in that parking lot when folks went to their cars too, he would be there already, fully adjusted to the dim roadside plot. Patience and motivation on top of his strength would get him what he needed in those cases when buying a drink and small talk just was not enough.

He gripped the piece of wood hard, wishing his brother would shut up so he could concentrate on the large target emerging to his left that now approached him, stomping its way down on broken wood, sheetrock and stones.

Above, Mathew watched a shape emerge from the shadows, resembling, for a split second, Daddy Ross coming from the deep of the hallway to suddenly appear in the doorway of their bedroom. Mathew's mouth sealed shut with fear.

Below, Scott was relieved that Matt's cowardice had finally silenced him so he could now concentrate on the sudden changes to their environment.

He saw the yellow lights, hovering about eight feet in the air, roughly six steps away from him, something was surely coming to a rest very near him. Scott heard the bellowed breathing trickling from the thing in the dark. The sound was more like a giggle from a throat choking on Jell-O. It was releasing the most hideous sound.

I should have my legs, I'm ready to fight…. I don't get scared, I do the scaring! He was furious that he was being played the victim by this unseen terror, then blurted out, waving the wood around in a frenzied arc, "Come closer and I'll smash you… I'll fuckin' break you down… ya' HEAR ME!!!"

To the surprise of both the men, came a reply in the dark.

"Of, coursssssss, Mr. Ross, becaussss you are the hunter, killer, preying spider of the dark, of coursssss, who are we to frighten you?"

Both men, from different perspectives could just make out the moving shadow, human in shape, spider-like in movement, it moved on two bent legs, with long arms, like tree branches that it dragged behind it. Hideously, the thing turned up its leathery head looking directly at Mathew, getting contact with his teary gray eyes, sending a shiver through the man's shaking body. Mathew let the urine pour out, looking into the bright yellow orbs the size of baseballs. This impossible creature had to be standing just over his brother now. His eyes were adjusting, but failing at the same time as the sunlight above was disappearing.

"Don't kill us. What….. Are you?" Mathew was hyperventilating. The dark was playing games with his vision, this man, this thing shaped like a very tall, elongated man seemingly had tiny limbs or tendrils hanging off its back from the top of its oval head down its tree-bark coated spine. Long arms protruded from its front very spiny with a black exoskeleton. But what was trailing off the top of its head to the tailbone?

Tentacles? What is this thing? Mathew could not contain his thoughts, losing his mind at the sight of the monstrosity, he prayed he had hit his head and this was a nightmare. Pressing hard, he closed his eyes, forgetting the spiders that were now crawling on the back of his legs or hopping around the two beams that held him, *chittering* their song angrily at him.

"Scott Rosssss. Tell your brother why you do not fear me. Why you are not cognizant of sssuch trepidationsss in the dark." The thing's voice reverberated with harsh double tonality, full of accusation and pending threats.

Familiar to both the men, someone else was in charge and had the floor, in accompaniment with their total attention.

Scott could smell the burnt brackish flesh of the beast standing over him. The last of the sunlight came through the hole reflecting off of one of the remaining windows, possibly, because Scott could now see the beast a bit clearer for the moment. The feet at the end of the boney black bent legs were immense. One clawed foot, with three talons came down next to his waist. Tentacles hung down from its head to the ground, all around the back of the tall brackish creature. Spiders were gathering around the tentacles, some hanging off of the beast, as if familiar and comforted by its presence as they had ceased their *chittering* too. Scott assumed this devil was here to collect him finally, so he listened intently, like he had when his father taught him about the family secret.

It must have huge teeth, for he could hear them clack together with each opening of its jaw to form words.

Intrigued more than frightened now, he heard his brother crying above while he paid close attention to the only show in town. He submitted to the figure that stood before him, with the authority that his father once had.

"What do you want?" Scott asked.

"Letsss see. One of you will be staying with usssss. One of the Ross brothers will be free to leave. Why? Why indeed would we allow thisss? Ssssimply, because we can. Am I correct Sssscott Rossss? Sssuch a sssurge of power when the decision is yoursss to constitute." It tiled its black oval head, blinking the yellow orbs, shrugging its shoulder as if the man knew what it was saying. All the while the multitude of tentacles whirled in limitless waving motions behind it.

The thing shifted its bright orbs upward toward Mathew, just above him, and continued, "Poor younger brother, never could win daddy's respect... never would, never will. Do we tell him, Scott? The little family secret? What is buried in the woodsss, beyond the backyard of the cottage... through the treesss, the dwindling dead brush, the dirt path through the thickets, only paved by daddy and brother Scott's workbootsss..." Clacking of jaws, wet drippings of sour saliva splashed down on Scott, it continued, "...the trail of long wispy grass and weedsss that were forced to bend and stretch, dying in one direction as the bodies were dragged to their resting place in that small clearing, where the dirt was soft."

"Scawwwt. Oh, what is it doing? What is this?" Mathew was crying out.

"Who are you?" Scott was calm, curious, sucking in his vicious tinderbox of temper. He had seen these demons in his mind since he was a small child. Daddy Ross had very different bedtime stories for him too. He had come to expect and accept their existence in the caverns of the mountainous regions of the land.

The thing looked down on the pile of wood and rock that trapped the bigger, more dangerous of the two men, then its eyes met Scott's. Now, the yellow eyes were the only light in the chasm, as the sun above dwindled. "Even now, Sssscott, you would fight me if you were able. Yes, you know me. Your family's lineage hasss alwaysss known us. Little brother was spared, incapable, pathetic, hopeless man. He would have told. Am I right? Yesss... of course I'm correct. This was why you never barbequed in the backyard of the cottage, played catch, went for hikes through the path, even though as a child Mathew begged you to take him. He wanted to go with big brother on his journeys. Daddy was always too busy. The mounds of the first dozen or so were still fresh."

"Let me go. Get this shit off of me." Scott hissed, the pain worsening from his broken body.

The thing crouched over him, its bones cracked, jaws snapped, "All intentions. You do good work. Doubled the quota of Daddy Ross, my son, except, you really need to go back to the tracksss and drag that last hooker's body back up here, and sssssoon. She will be found by authoritiesss, soon. You left her, but she sssstill livesss. Was it the cop car that drove by that ssscared you off? Fool, you know no fear! The blow to her neck paralyzed her. Only days ago. Messy by your sssstandardss, Scott. As sssssoon as you are healed, bring her, bury her, the one with the beautiful black skin, that I see in your mind. Lots of muscle, gave you a good fight... will feed our darlings for days..."

The spiders erupted from the silent blackness with that clicking and clacking chattering noise. Their exclamations were more rapid as their chirping rose in pitch from their large mandibles.

"..Oh and Ssscott, do begin to bury them a bit deeper. Your burial ground is getting a bit crowded of late." The thing started to pull at the debris covering Scott's legs. "When you heal, you will continue."

Mathew had listened to the exchange, gulping down his disgust, "Scott, what is it saying?"

"Your brother is a killer and you are meat." It replied calmly, hard at work to uncover the man's legs from the fallen debris.

The beast made a clacking sound with its jaws. Within seconds thereafter, Scott listened to the screams turn to gargles, a terrible whining in the pitch black while the sound of dozens of nail clippers opened and closed, picked and prodded, pulling apart Mathew in tiny bites.

His host was wrapping him in something he could not see, but it comforted his legs, body and mind. Soon he was raised closer to the familiar scent of the dead leaves surrounding his father's cottage. Cool November night air filled his nostrils while he was carried up the side of the sinkhole. The creature's claws biting into the dirt, clamping into the side of the cavern could not quiet the shrieking death throes of his brother being eaten alive by dozens of the denizens below.

Scott would fall asleep on his father's couch, where he was left to rest, listening to Mathew bellow for hours deep below the surface. The wailing howled to an eventual quiet whisper, melding to the damp air that blew out the top of the mouth of the pit to the ruined interior of the cottage.

Scott Ross woke to the flashing of an ambulance above him, a stretcher below him, he was being wheeled out of his father's cottage.

"He's waking." An EMT looked down at him. A policeman also looked down on him.

"Were you alone in the cabin sir?" The policeman asked, truly concerned.

"No. My brother was asleep in the bedroom." Dryly, Scott answered the officer, rubbing dirt from his beard. He felt relieved that he no longer had to hide the family secret from his brother. Those that learned the family secret would get to see the path in the backyard. Sometimes they were conscious when he buried them. They howled like his brother did for hours too. Sometimes days.

THE MOONS' CRYIN'

Some folks never listen. I told her so many times before that the garbage goes out Wednesdays. Always. Always and never. Always put it in the orange barrel before 5:00 a.m., drag the barrel up the driveway and leave it. NEVER, pull the blue recycling bin up till Wednesday after 8:00 a.m. when the dew on the grass has dried. They do not like the noise and are still active when the grass is moist with morning sweat. Rolling that noisy recycling bin disturbs the entire neighborhood too early; disrupts the gallant balance of Hope Springs. Special pickups are a new option presented to the board.

"They will not allow us to live this life we have, in this warm state of being…immaculate and safe!" I remembered yelling at Laurel every time she screwed up our pick up dates. Just like the time she retrieved mail from the mailman, Edward, himself, instead of waiting for the FUCKING bell to ring! Edward, our khaki dressed servant of the community, dropped our packages or envelopes into the waiting metal bin outside the front door foyer day after day. There is no reason to alter this situation!

"WHY do you feel the need to walk across the yard, and take the mail? Edward, the skinny mailman gets PAID and PAID *well* to drop our mail in the box!" Laurel and her open robe, and perfectly groomed regions….for all to see… Or just for Edward? That skinny *well paid* mailman.

To live this privileged life, here in the community of Hope Springs, Laurel had to know the rules. Live by them, stay on the path, or ruin it for everyone. Not this time. Not again. I've been here too long to even know why anyone would need anything else.

Movies on Thursdays. They came in directly to our TV. A choice of five. You can pick one or all. Better to spread them out or you get sick of the repetitiveness of five movies for a week. Laurel ran out the front door just yesterday (granted it was afternoon) to see if she could borrow a book from Steven across the street. He lived alone and was older than us, in his 60's. So when she ran outside, adorned in her see through white stretch pants, a thin blue blouse with straps and nothing else, you can only imagine how that must have knocked poor old white-haired Steven out of whack. I peered through the curtains to take note of the grin of greedy pleasure on his face. It had been five years since Margaret had been gone, leaving him to his lonely gawking. Steven handed Laurel the book that she had asked for, and they both looked down our street either way, making sure no one else was about. I mean after all it was a Friday afternoon! Had it been Saturday, ok, I can see being out and socializing. But fucking practically naked running around Hope Springs on a weekday afternoon?!

I swear she did it to get a rise out of me and not the kind of rise she used to give me. No use for that anymore with the Steady Gaze they prescribed me. Funny how satiated I am now, but why does she have to antagonize me by tempting neighbors?

When she came back in the front door, after bringing the damn garbage out (on the wrong day) I had confronted her. I had to confront her again, as I disciplined her in regards to her scantily dressed approach with Steven. "Rules, Laurel... you need to follow." She smiled artificially and walked in. Her blue eyes glazed with a glee that I understood. She was a bit well lit.

Saturday was coming. Block Association day. Each street in Hope Springs had their own block party and socialized with food, music and beverages of all sorts. Liquid libation, smiles, cheering children and sometimes folks had new house guests to introduce to the neighborhood. It was nice, and I did not have to keep my eye on Laurel or the kids that day. Not Saturday yet, but I was excited in advent of the coming weekend. Don't we all live for our weekends?

So five new movies would arrive. Hopefully one for the kids this time. Peter has lost all his smiles and Casey is just too damn jittery. She's more of a boy than that son of mine could ever dream to be. Sitting in his room all day, never venturing out on Block Association Day to meet the other kids or even the new kids. Annoying as all hell that Peter of mine. Sulking and salty all the time. Before he turned ten last year I would take him down to the lower shelf of land in our backyard; the closest thing to a field in Hope Springs. He had an arm. Boy could throw!! Talked some smack to me on playing for the school team. School team? "School TEAM?!?! " I says...to him.

Peter and his dumb pimpled face was under the impression that homeschool (at our PC) ended when he was old enough to go to Middle School. "Not gonna happen...ace." I says to him. "Stick to the PC and your instructional baseline classes and soon, very soon, the money will roll in when you hit fifteen. You'll have your account credited enough to surf any web site and purchase any vids and clothes you may want. Work from home...like all of us." I had told him while tossing the ball around under the shelter of our pine trees. Loved those tall pines back there, even with the thick spider webs strewn all about the tips of them.

Don't you know? After I told him about his future, Peter winged the ball at me, missing my head by mere inches. I remembered he ran back into the house from the open back door while I retrieved the ball from the neighbor's grass line. Not really supposed to do that, ya'know....upsets the balance, crossing over to your neighbor's house, I mean.

Damn Peter, he really had some fuckin aspirations. Like that time he disappeared all day to go down to the pond two blocks over. Told the dumb shit a dozen times that a PRO-JEK pond is not one to play in, around, or even nearby. He came back with a bite mark on his calf about the size of an ice cream scooper, almost the right radius too! Said a damn frog with big glowing green eyes bit him, right after it talked to him using mental telepathy and called itself Charlie!! I believed half of it. As for Peter, no more going down to the pond! He's such a little prick. I may be stuck with him but my sperm count did not go down any when he came into this world.

Casey, my little lady, now that's a butterbean of a baby girl with hope. She completes her classes before nightfall on the computer and then takes the training courses on web navigation and resource trafficking. She will be a model worker next year. Her fifteenth year. So what was I saying....oh Thursday...movie day. I would check the uploads later, but at that moment, just grabbing a cold Bisner Choice was all I had planned. Let Laurel flirt with the neighbors and the mailman. They knew better, and if they didn't, they found out harder.

The beer was so nice and cold on my throat that I forgot that I had sweat out most of my body's nutrients in the humidity of the afternoon and surely would have to hit the kitchen cabinet for our Vita-Sect A and maybe some B for good measure. The beer will drain you, but also intensifies the Steady Gaze so that less worries come your way for a good couple of hours! HAA!

Casey came outside and slapped my balding head from the back of the lounge chair, playfully trying for my attention. She wore a bikini, making me more uncomfortable than I had with my current wife showing off her thing-a-ma-jiggs to old white haired Steven the widower (six times over!) across the street.

Steven did have the best lawn mind you. Envied that, as I sat and looked at the browning patches in the backyard. Front looked good. That's all that mattered. Right? Mans' gotta tend his lawn.

"Honey, for god sakes put some clothes on! Yer ass is hangin out ...."

"Shut up dad!" She smiled through her coke bottle glasses. Dark brown hair pulled back in a long pony tail. She bent over, adjusting the chair before her. She was fixing the rubber strapped extremely out of date lounge chair. You know the kind that leaves you with red stripes on your back? Ok so not everything was up to par at Hope Springs, but they improve whatever you complain about. Usually promptly within a week.

I saw through the pines in the back yard that Edward, the Skinny Mailman was returning to his own house. Done for the day, he removed his uniform vest and sweat scarred hat and walked up the side steps to his house right behind me. No need for a currier vehicle when you only deliver to your own neighborhood! Man he made some credits!

Also caught him looking at Casey's ass. "Watch yer self-there Eddie....!" Knowing full well he could see me but not hear me, I yelled at him with a smile on my lips, spilling a good bit of pilsner on my thin white tee shirt. They supplied us with a lot of those. "What's your brother doing today?" She had a book, something about THE FUEL DISTRIBUTION centers outside of our neighborhood, outside of our life. Never could stop her from getting ahead! But books? Everything was on that PC!

"He's preparing the spiders."

Forgot, little Peter did have his uses. Tending the spider garden was a strong point.

"He still got them in his room? It's about time..."

"Please dad, he likes them more than he does us."

I looked to the neighbors' houses, very close in proximity. Some would say too close, separated by a driveway, but with no cars to wheel around the driveway, the pavement served its purpose as just that. A border. But windows still showed the face of a neb nosed kid next door looking at my pretty little girl's bosom in the hot midday sun.

"You got your boyfriend's attention again..." I got up to go in the front yard to make sure the sprinklers were ready for tomorrow. "That fat little kid next door is staring at you." And he was. Saw the kid part the curtains for a full view.

"Neil is harmless. He may not pass his courses, and refused some Gaze the other day....his mom is not happy. But for me....no worries. Poor thing's head ain't right." My daughter says.

I adored how sure of herself, Casey was. She'll do fine. Now I had a bit of hope for Peter too. As for this wife of mine, dunno. So, I left Casey so she could continue teasing the neighbor's kid (brat spread her legs for him now. She's bad but I love her tenacity) and walked up the driveway to the front yard. I passed the small shrubs to the shade of the giant maple tree in the front. This maple tree spidered out on the top so that it was looming over our lawn and house like a protector from giants. Laurel was out there, tending a small flower bed she planted with some form of roses that I knew had to go. Rose thorns would not make *them* happy. Her back was to me, knees to the lawn, head down and sunglasses holding her waft of dark hair in place. Her ass, nice and round, plumped on her heels. Thankfully, she had some shorty shorts on and a tank top. God I liked that. I was reminded why I accepted her.

"The moon's cryin'..." She rasped to the ground in a voice trembling with tears. Had she taken two days' worth of the Gaze?

"Wahhh?" I says.

She pointed over her shoulder, never looking at me. "Our moon….look."

"Oh…" I knew what she meant now. She hung a ceramic white moon on the maple that stood out like a glistening marble in a bag of mulch. Between the humidity, rain, and our sprinklers hitting it, the crescent moon that once had a nice smile staring at you, now morphed into a melty frown with ice cream-like tears. "Huh huh….sonofabitch. Looks like it is cryin a bit."

Laurel had hung it up there so many moons ago….huh huh, PUN intended!! The damn things were all over the house. She found solace in the crescent smile on ceramic, or plastic or whatever, just hanging in purple or blue, gold or in this sad case of weather beaten white ceramic. She made the mistake a month ago, when PRO-JEK (our mail-in pill service provider) lowered her milligrams of Haze and Docile Ringer by a bit, and she got boldly in my face about an old lover named James who…"was so much sweeter….and cared….and handsomer than…."

WACKADOOO!

Smacked that bitch down. The boy saw it, ran to his room, but not my Casey. She was all my blood, with the third wife. That damn Peter was falling for this one, maybe she reminded him of his mom, whoever she was?! He was provided by a Hope Springs service partner in association with PRO-JEK. Still, he loved those spiders, but definitely could not handle watching a woman get hit. I think Casey, and those stern little eyes of hers liked seeing Laurel get hit. Not to mention the learning curve. Casey went right back to her distribution studies with PRO-JEK's latest upgrade after witnessing my anger again.

I didn't like hitting Laurel in front of them, subsequently, I try my best to keep my temper. Standing behind her on the lawn at that moment I threw down another Steady Gaze from a sagging shorts pocket to ensure my temperament for conversation. She turned on her heels, looking up at me. She had unwrapped her long hair in seconds in front of me and now she pulled a scarf around her head tugging her thick dark hair from her scalp so that the rest spilled over her shoulders. Laurel then pulled her sunglasses from her blouse, where they previously dangled between her breasts, to put on her face. Makeup-less, she didn't need it, I've told her. Natural beauty. Even when she was sweaty doing outside work, her scent was alluring. I was reminded why I fell for her initially by the rock in my pants in that moment.

But damn, she had belonged to Terence Makelroy down the block, for a season or two, when they brought her into Hope Springs. He couldn't handle her. I remember Laurel all smiles and talking about her time outside and this James guy, a writer or somethin' else irrelevant. Who entertained people with books? Books? Libraries went out fifty years ago. Remember when that Napitester took out the music industry and everything was free on some inter-web thing? Nobody paid for shit like that anymore! Why would you? They pump some techno shit on Tuesdays through our in-house surround system. I didn't like it but it made Peter tap his shoes and Casey danced some weird thing she saw on some archive vid on a Music Vision station. Weird, wacky stuff. Useless. Radio? Books? Just as irrelevant in a distant bonfire as her former love, James. And Fuck that Terence Makelroy. She told me he never could fill her needs. Fill. Ha ha huh. Yea. I got her on the Haze and occasionally Steady Gaze. All she needed to be a good girl.

"I want to cook tonight." Laurel took me out of my stupor.

"Ok hun, but Sweens Finest should be by soon…. Something off that? Saw the truck down the road earlier. Also, Frozen Bulk is in two days. We still have a spillover in the basement fridge."

"Mason, please. Just to try it again. I did before…."

"BEFORE YOU HAD IT GOOD!" Oh…the Steady Gaze was kicking in from this morning! I had plopped a Haze pill into my can. I had a pill stewing in my Bisner Beer gut that was hangin over my shorts. Of course I knew I was disgusting, and could not score a piece like Laurel outside Hope Springs. This, my friends is what I'm talking about.

I smiled, offering her my hand to lift her up. "Come on, I feel good, you look great, let's go in and make Edward the Mailman and old gray haired Steven over their across the street, jealous."

She forced a smile. I'd be forcing a bit more on her in no time if she did not hit her Steady Gaze. Before we even got into the bedroom that night I slipped a Haze into her tea, and rode her into happiness. Ok, well, at least she had a smile on her face when she passed out the second time around.

******

The birds!! Four a.m. and THERE THEY GO!! Loud as hell. Spiders must have been active in the night, taking out the nests more than usual throughout the neighborhood. Another hour before sun up and then I could take my walk. Birds get louder every year. I know this cause I had grown old in Hope Springs, and compared to the vids I've seen of other communities, I know we have it better. Just these loud goddamned mornings is what I got to deal with. So be it.

I knew about Laurel's ex-lover James, a guy on the outside, early on. Caught myself in jealous delusions in the morning some days. There was a day when we were alone for a bit, no kids around, and we had some beers out on the back porch. Laurel's almond shaped eyes were longing for attention, staring out past our giant willow trees between the pines, I could not help to wonder what bleakness was going on in that head. The trees dominated our view of the neighbor's houses to the back to a degree. Small sense of privacy. I pulled her close by the ass pockets of her jeans so she could feel I was feeling the same, when OH LORD….what's this? I pulled out a piece of paper in her back pocket. The mail hadn't come yet. Unfolding the weathered piece, even I could see the format…stanzas, ancient lyrical fluff…. A fuckin' poem!!

Laurel had screeched at the discovery in desperate defense, her right hand swung out only to meet my bulky forearm. (I used to work out more, but the Pummel Down 2.0 gel tabs started coming a year ago, and muscle just kind of comes in the mail now…HAAAHA.) So I asked her politely to sit her cute ass down, in her tight jeans on a plastic deck chair. Sighing, she did, though those blue almond eyes went wider with fear now and some sweat beaded her brow.

Oh…this was going to be juicy!

OVER THE MOONBOW
Darkness and Shadows fill my surroundings
I listen to my heart pounding as the silent night
Creeps in. I smell your hair, even though you're
Gone.
Gone with the mist that rises past the mountain tops
and into the glow of the moon.
Your soul is flying high with the midnight clouds
Racing for tomorrow
Reflecting off of ribbons of soft light
Against the moonlight your image smiles at me
As a Moonbow appears and says she's safe
She's here beyond the Heavens.
Here high above the Moonbow
Where souls rejoice away from suffering
And pain where only souls and love hide
And wait for thee
-JAMES

It was beautiful. Sweet. Made of a substance that I know nothing about. But I knew when someone was better than me! So, she kept a sheet of memory from her old lover on the outside, James. What a romantic he must have been. I supposed he was dead. Didn't care much. When they bring them in, very little was left for them on the outside as they were escorted to orientation (I've seen the vids) filled to the brim with premonitions of a better life in Hope Springs. These hopeful ideals are implanted through the courses. These classes were very similar to the distribution courses that Casey and Peter take on the inside. But those are hands-on work courses. Maybe James was still alive? This made me jealous and angry. She knew someone better than me that I could not compare to.

Laurel missed her old life. I hated that she gave me doubts about my own future. What could be so great out there? I mean now that they got a handle on things again. Cholesterol? Commuting to work? Night clubs? Eccentric and self centered and all important baby boomers? Women with postpartum sickness even when their kids are growing up in their own damn house? Dinner Dates and needy relatives....WHO THE HELL NEEDS THAT! She'll learn. They do sometimes. She was a smart one.

Kasey, my mate prior to this one, who was also my Casey's mom, aptly named of course, suffered from that postpartum shit. She came here half out of her wits anyway. She was taken away. Good riddance. Take her back to the outside and let her flourish into madness.

So past disturbances aside, Saturday morning was upon us. Block Association Day. Laurel and the kids could meet their social outlets while I drank sufficiently enough to talk to a few of the neighbors. Alcohol and Steady Gaze was a good ole buzz when staring at neighbor's spouses in tiny summer time shorts. And don't worry, guys like Franklin Hoffman stare right down the blouses of your women too. I met him outside, two houses down on the street setting up a fold-out table to serve some shitty salad that his little girl made. Or maybe his dumb wife Valerie prepared that slop? There he was! That Playboy in his tennis shorts and polo damn shirts, big horse teeth falling out of his clean cut face. His thick brown hair trimmed to one side, paved like an origami scarf. Made me glad the only hair I had left was my red brillo pads on the sides, like one of those clown vids I saw. Kept my head cool.

"Hey....lots a new folks this year Franklin?"

"OH HEY.... Mason, how are you today.... HOT as hell huh?" Franklin Hoffman said.

I hated his fake exuberance. We hated each other, but that was ok, cause Saturdays during the summer and sometimes spring were the only times we crossed.

"Neil, that fat little retarded kid next door's been staring at my Casey again. Didn' he get caught peeping in your windows last fall at Valerie?" I wanted to make him equally uncomfortable. It worked. His perfect teeth were enveloped by his pursed lips.

"Well yeah, Mason, he was looking in the back windows. I dunno if that Neil is gonna go the distance. Just his Mom in the house now right? Dad was taken away by an ambulance last summer...that was him right?" Franklin queried, but he knew the answer. No one wanted the ambulances coming for you.

"Hahaha, yeah *SIRENS IN THE NIGHT*.... " I sang a tune that I heard my dad sing a few times back in the outside. Not many memories out there though, but "Strangers in the Night" was the real song. *"Sirens in the niiiiight....* Just like those old people's homes in the vids. You don't want those sirens coming for you Franklin." I poked his chisel toned chest under the green colored shirt with the dumb alligator on the nipple, pretending to be playful. I could see he was afraid of the idea of an ambulance coming for him.

"See you in a few." I walked away from him to see the other folks coming out of their Cape Cod homes that lined the winding neighborhood. Women carrying various bowls covered by cellophane while their men handled the chairs, tables and coolers of Bisners Choice. There was a light version of the beer. Lighter? Really?

I thought better of wearing my damn sandals on the hot newly paved street, and was about to turn back to the house for some PRO-JEK Skids when Edward the Skinny Mailman came up to me from across someone's yard.

"Hey… Mason… question…" He was in a hurry, sweat making his thin hay-like blond hair turn browner by the second as it flopped on his cheeks. His nose and chin pointed out almost seeming to meet each another. His thin eyebrows seemed nonexistent over bulging green eyes in hollow gray sockets. He looked like a scarecrow approaching me. "Did you see it? Our new Gutter Crew?" Edward said.

"Not yet. I thought PRO-JEK was holding out on that. So they fired Jack Landis?"

We were referring to our personal Trash Pickup service in Hope Springs. One guy had a mini-rig and drove around by himself to pick up our trash on Wednesday mornings. He hadn't been around. Nice guy that Jack Landis. Graying in humor as was his salty hair and beard, but he took better care of himself than most. He also had to take it easy on the Steady Gaze to operate machinery. Hmmm? Maybe that was the problem? He was too functional? Too Aware.

"Fired? FIRED? You can say that. On his normal route on my block I watched as he was taken by his replacement Gutter Crew. Right in front of me! I mean, I was outside early, but didn't expect to see his damn retirement happen in front of me. Bloody Mess." Edward the Skinny Mailman was chuckling while he said this. Then he popped two thickies. Another name for Soft 03's. We take those blue 900 milligram babies to calm us down. Good boy Edward! Now you have a good day ahead of you! I thought. Then he continued, "AND, I have this to provide for today's festivities." He produced a jar of what looked like honey. It was.

"Edward, put that away remember the Montville's? Last summer?" I says to him, and I can feel my fat head twitch with shock and anger at him.

He shoved the small jar back in his uncomfortable looking trouser pocket. I was referring to the fortunate and unfortunate tale of Mick and

Brenda Montville. They lived across the street. For a while anyway. Honey bees were extinct in most of the world per the vids, but some-fuckin-how, Mick Montville had kept bees thriving in a bee keep in his backyard. A whole Honeycomb and shit! Well, it was a hobby, and it may have been planted by PRO-JEK when the Montville's had moved in just to test them. The idea, you see, is to *TELL THEM* when you see something suspicious. Win their trust. Well, Mick and Brenda were scientists in another life, white lab coats and all. She was pretty, blond, tall, glasses....legs that could reel you in all nice-like during those intimate moments....ahha. Not sure what she wanted with Mick the Mole, as the kids called him. Thick glasses, bald like me but he grew his sides stupidly, and had nose hair hanging out to match his ear hair.

Stupidly, they hid the honey comb in a semi-enclosed area of their basement when they thought folks were on to them.

Well, maybe it was the hum of the bees or the honey itself, but a swarm of our Blue-Backers (wasps about two inches in diameter with shiny blue armor) penetrated a basement window and went to war with the bees for supreme authority. The Blue-Backers were brought in occasionally to moderate the spider population in the trees. Natural enemies. Hope Springs was full of natural equilibrium, testing the finer points of nature and man in gleeful symbiotic grace. SHIT, that's funny.

So, I do remember being on my front yard with my son Peter when the Montvilles had come screaming out their front door swinging like that monkey KING KONG in that vid I saw where he was fending off those spit fighter planes! Man, at that moment I was on some serious Steady Gaze and a bit of Soft 03's. The scene looked as though blue lasers were zooming about the two folks in slow motion, their jaws wide, and their screams loud. I saw a Blue-Backer go right down Mick's throat, and he held his neck. It was so cartoonish, I had started laughing. Peter tugged at my open shirt, saying something about helping. I slapped him in the head. Probably too hard.

Mick Montville was on the ground, surrounded by blue lights. The wasps were humming such a relaxing chant, that I could have slept right on my yard. The bugs were pretty far away, after all, the Montville's house was adjacent from mine, a good enough distance to watch. Brenda meanwhile, running in her adult pajamas with some kind of cartoon sponge character from what seemed hundred years ago on them, had attracted an ambulance. Or someone had called? I looked over my shoulder and saw in my bay window, Laurel, with a phone in her ear. Bleeding heart bitch!

Here's the thing, this ambulance did take Brenda Montville away. The siren had scared the wasps away from the basted body of Mick Montville, who appeared to be like a human sponge himself. Haha...dummy. Everything here has a button. Turn on. Turn off. Cameras? Sure. No idea where they are ….don't care. But just as quickly as those Blue-Backers showed up, they were gone. I looked up at my towering maple overhead and smiled at the unseen spiders, hiding up there. "Lucky day fer you guys huh…?" This time the Blue-Backers found new meat.

So that memory of the Montvilles being aside, now I turn to Edward the Skinny Mailman. "Yea, hide that honey. You got bees?"

"Yes. I found some that day …. Delivering mail to the Montville's. They were dying on the grass so I collected them. I ain't never seen them before other than vids…and you know what Mick was doing…."

What my nervous friend was referring to was, Mick and Brenda had found a cure for stomach cancer using a mixture of Soft 03's grinded down with bee honey. Brenda, like myself was one of few folks to be taken away by ambulance only to make a better life for themselves. Brenda was now made a highly paid CEO up at PRO-JEK's corporate office just outside Hope Springs. On a clear day you could see the loaming building over the gates. She made announcements and sent us gifts on the vids. She looked good. Her pulp of a husband was left for the Gutter Crew. Jack Landis at that time was still the Gutter Crew. He's gone too now, per Edward.

"See you later Edward, gotta get the family." I just wanted an excuse to walk away. Street was getting packed. I needed a Bisner. Thinking back about my own trip in an ambulance bothered me. Yep I was carried out once. It angered me that I did not end up like lucky Brenda Montville. Sure, I got some notoriety, and they brought me back. But what a day that had been.

Couple of years back I had turned on the sprinkler system for the front and back lawn. Sundays, in the summer we had to start them early morning to nourish the soil for *them*.

Spouting gently, it was so relaxing to see that blue water spit mini fountains that shot five feet in the air all around you. I stared too long, maybe….stayed too long out there. The water had gone red, the smell of copper all around me. No one was outside, just me, and every house on the block had their sprinkler systems running….. But RED!

In my own Steady Gaze comfort, I thought, "Rusty pipes?" I knew better. The rich water landed in my mouth and coated my arms, painting my wife beater shirt with its coppery stickiness. Something new? I had heard about this fountain of nourishment *for them*, but thought I missed a memo somewhere? Steven, the older neighbor across the street would tell me later that there was a mailing regarding the change in the sprinklers on that day. Laurel had conveniently hid that from me I guessed, just like it seemed as though I was a couple of doses ahead on my Steady Gaze. That Bisner she gave me the night before tasted more lemony than it should'a. I was on to her. She was setting me up. Interesting turn of events.

Now at that time, I thought they were coming for me, and it was my time to provide. It wasn't! My life had suddenly become like that horrible oldie Manfred Man song, "Blinded by the Light." Nothing was making sense. I saw a swarm of Blue-Backers fly overhead, buzzing by like a small jet that we could hear every now and then up there….. The spiders were chittering applause with their mandibles above me, oddly and audibly in the towering maple tree and the ground… oh man, I felt the ground tremble. Was this happening? Had I overdosed thanks to Laurel?

I remembered a siren in the distance and everything halted. Even the sprinklers on *everyone's* lawn had stopped! Someone at PRO-JEK had hit manual override, I guessed. Casey had run out to hug me, but Peter and Laurel pulled her free as the blue frocked EMT's pulled me onto a stretcher. The disdain in Peter and Laurel's eyes turned into somewhat of gleeful gleam. She won. I had thought.

I fought the EMT's but knew that I was incapable of moving, but could not remember why? A blood vessel had burst from my left nostril with pressure from my combination of Steady Gaze, (had Laurel od'me ? Thinkin yes) some Soft 03's and my Pummel Down pills!?! I mean, yeah, I was trying to get rid of the belly fat and put on some muscle!!

The blood had coated my throat to the point that I had choked, sat up and spat up what was a congealed tomato of blood that had clotted in my throat, slapping the floor of the ambulance. Gross. Looking out the ambulance doors I saw more people than usual on my block all peering at their unfortunate neighbor. Mason, the overweight, obnoxious pervert was finally out of their midst! More folks had gathered than on Block Association Day! What a goddamned honor! Fuck them.

It was clear I had overdosed. However there was no memory of being treated at PRO-JEK's HQ. Soon I was out of PRO-JEK's infirmary, being driven outside the gates of Hope Springs and brought back. I remember passing these two maintenance workers outside the gates while the ambulance brought me back through. The look on these two young workers' faces taking note that someone was actually coming back was beyond shock, and I'd say envy. I recognized one of the guys as my produce delivery driver, Mr. Sellers. He had clearance to go to the outside. PRO-JEK had to approve some folks to go to and fro. Mind you, they were watched more closely than most.

Life sucked on the outside after the big war. It was all hard labor or delivery service like these two dolts in their blue khaki uniforms and hats. I flipped them off! They just stared as my escort brought me through the iron gates of the high brick wall, and home.

That was then. I'm still bank rolling on the distribution programs. I must be a good provider for the resource department because no one ever comes back like that when the sprinklers spray you all copper. NO ONE comes back! Powers that be must like me and sent the EMT's to get me out of there before…

Casey is my faithful assistant. That last Block Association Day had gone well. Out on my front porch that night I reflected on how we sat as a family on someone's yard, all cozy like a *REAL* family with soft blankets underneath our boney asses. Some dumb Kansas song was talking about "dust" on several boom boxes. (Boom Boxes? They still have them with the cassettes? Weird. I remember thinking. Nope. These were digitally issued radios. We all had 3 channels.) All eyes were on the maple trees in front of the houses. Everyone had willows and maples. The spiders liked those best. The smell of grills was ceasing with the night and sure enough the show was beginning. As they spin the glowing webs, a silence always sweeps over the crowd, yet some douchebag almost always says "amazing" to ruin it. Usually Franklin Hoffman with his dumb polo shirt and his wife, Valerie, were the cheesy folks responsible for the obvious comments.

Sitting there as a family, every Fourth of July (fell on a Block Association Day for once!) I have to admit it was nice. We had heard a rumor (or maybe a memory) that gun powder and explosives used to be involved? What the hell? The natural order is so much more thrilling.

Thick strings of blue, red, yellow and green spiraled, circled and angled just below the lowest branches in a light show beyond any fireworks display. Who needed the loud explosions anyway? In silence the plum sized night crawling spiders worked their colorful magic in the dark. Occasionally you could make out the shape of one of the larger ones when the light of their glowing webs bounced off the shimmering yellow or green hue of their bellies. If you got close enough, and you never wanted to, believe me, you could hear their chittering mouths and scurrying legs in the trees. Sometimes one would jump from tree to tree up high, leaving tracers of blue, green, red or yellow striping across the night sky. This still was amazing to me. My Bisner was cold in my hands, so I became annoyed when someone came between me and my buzz, but Peter had tapped my shoulder. Sitting next to me on the blanket, he looked up to me and asked "Are my spiders going to be big like that too someday?"

"Yes, keep tending to them, and they may never bite you, and sure…the buggers will grow nice and provide the colors and the shapes ….like those…." Not their only purpose, but why spoil the kid's night right? He'd seen enough anyway. Spiders were part of the equilibrium of course.

Then business came up. I could see several blankets of families away, sitting among the strips of front lawns, my neighbor lady and her "special" kid, Neil. The woman was in her early thirties. Pretty little hippie type. Straight light brown hair, well-shaped in her flowery summer dress, her knees were up by her chest as she motioned for me to come over. "Laurel, bring the kids in the house before ten." I told my wife, and she nodded.

No one would be out here after the web display and past ten anyway. No one ever was, unless you were friggin' stupid.

OH…the tracers were amazing as I got up and made my way past Franklin and Valerie Hoffman, and almost tripped over nervous Edward the Skinny Mailman. My old neighbor Steven nodded to me with a sad smile, eyes glowing with the web show across the street. Maybe he missed his wife Margaret? That would be weird, but possible, he seemed attached to that one for some reason. I plopped down next to my neighbor….Rachel, that was her name, Rachel! Almost saw two Rachel's. Steady Gaze kicking hardcore. I could see she had a similar circle of comfort in her realm too. Something different too.

"Hello Mason."

"Rachel."

"Go play Neil." And little Neil, speechless and indifferent went over to where I formally sat, so he could stare at Casey some more…. I bet. Fat little retarded kid. Yeah, she ain't wearing a bathing suit tonight, ole' limp dick. I thought.

And then Rachel says, "Tonight … Talk to Peter ok?"

An understanding permeated between our own here in Hope Springs that most folks in those vids would not understand. She continued, her pretty pink lips drew me right in and I could not help but wonder how they tasted and those exposed legs, that went all the way the fuck up…. She continued, "There's no way around it, he won't learn things about distribution, he won't, he feels its wrong…. "She began to weep into her bony knees. "He just wants to look at Casey, and play…. Keeps asking for books….I dunno where he got the idea… I can't handle him anymore."

"Books? I think I know…" I felt my own glare back at Laurel. "Ok, Tonight."

The shimmer of the spider webs began to fade. Getting late now, and the arachnid workers themselves had retreated to their hiding places among the higher parts of the maples and willows. The show was over. Left behind, on every front yard, nets of spiraling webs were hung and drooping in every manner of hieroglyphics that man never created. Brilliant, but I got bored. People too, now, retreated to their houses, with some waving hands and vocalizing a "goodbye" or "see you next week". Shut up, go home, enough of you, I laughed to myself while herding my flock back home.

"I'm going to work on the computer a bit dad." Casey flapped her lips up to me through her glasses before going through the front door.

"Do you think my spiders will be ready next year dad?" Peter said as I held the door open for him. Laurel traipsed by, blinking at me.

"Actually buddy, go get your tank. I need you to help me out in an hour." I said with a smile, and not even a forced one, I felt really good that night! Laurel gave me a pleading glance, and a tear ran down her cheek. I showed my teeth, mouthing to "SHUT IT."

Around 11:00, I had sent Peter out the door in his pajamas with his plastic tank with about six of the moderately sized spiders. They had indeed grown, and damned if I knew just how capable they were but I've seen the juveniles provide for the cause, as well as the adults.

"Dad, is it safe to go out there?" He had asked before going next door.

"Yes, as long as you have those guys with you, but make sure you stay with Rachel and Neil tonight. You can't come back without those guys in your presence. She needs them for an experiment tonight, and don't worry…but still you know better than to venture out late…"

He looked up with puppy eyes of surprise.

"….she is not going to hurt them." I assured him.

Running to the bedroom where Laurel was crying in the corner chair, sobbing in her hands, I had to be sure this went down with some sense of smoothness. Oh man…the Steady Gaze was going away, as the lights from the webs disappeared almost entirely outside. I opened a steel heart shaped box with my Soft 03's and popped three. Oh yea, I would need three on this night! Our bedroom window faced the house of Rachel and little hopeless Neil.

My Peter was at Rachel's door. She was there, and glanced my way, but I knew she could not see me in my window with the lights off. Holding the screen door open, her sad eyes and pretty face turned to a viscous animalistic mask, suddenly turning toward Peter she yanked the small tank of spiders from his hands, kicked out with one of her strong sleek boney legs. She had caught Peter in the chest, and the little boy tumbled backwards.

Closing the screen door and swiftly shutting her steadfast oak door quickly I could hear the locks turn from inside my own bedroom. Man, I had wished to see that kick again, I got the best look of that leg all the way up to her rump! What a sexpot!! I will have to look more into this neighbor of mine, and soon. I remembered thinking, "I hope she digs some Seals and Crofts." Summer Breeze, that damn song, came in to my head while I watched my son get up from the wet grass in a frenzy. Panic was in his eyes as he scrambled frantically to get to his feet. Right then a thought came to my mind.

MUSIC!

In my state of comfort, blood warm with euphoria, I flipped on the house surround speaker unit, and pressed the menu button on the bedroom wall next to the large mirror. Laurel had run out of the room as expected.

I pressed "S" and sure enough Seals and Crofts "Summer Breeze" came on throughout the house. Showtime! And oh I was buzzing strong.

Laurel had run out the front door. I locked it behind her. Didn't really have to. This happens fast usually. At least the initial part happens fast, the rest….eh…notsomuch. Hahah… "Summer Breeze…makes me feel fine….. blowin out the jasmine in my miiiiinnnnnd…" I sang softly, opening the front curtains by the bay window.

The full grown mature spiders had already descended from our maple out front, falling onto little Peter, and Laurel was inches from him by the tree trunk when about eight of the shiny green bellies flashed with moon light, legs gripping and mandibles biting. The beasties dangled from their cotton candy neon webs for the offering!

It's known that they hurt, but soon the body shuts down, and there is a throb where the bites are while the body gets immobilized. Almost as soon as the plum sized sonsabitches came down on Peter and Laurel, attaching, gripping and penetrating their flesh, they ascended back to the highest reaches of the tree, getting their fill of the human blood, and always just enough to keep the victims very much alive for the second act.

Remember that balance that Hope Springs purveys? Lots of little learning tools and experiments in this here community, bugs, reptiles and even some mammals (people included) and drugs, lots of illicit sex (keep the numbers going, dunno how Casey is going to feel about that part) all of which makes for an interesting place. Man the Soft 03's were kicking in good! Casey stood next to me watching out the bay window to the front yard as that oldie "Summer Breeze" was still making me feel fine!

"I want to watch this time." She muttered. I nodded. Put an arm out to my little doll. She was nothing like her mother had been.

Time for *them*. Did not take long after the tenderizing immobilization from the spiders above for our friends below to make their appearance. Laurel was on her back, weeping, looking directly at me, but not seeing me through the window's glare. Then she looked up at the ceramic moon on the tree that she had put there, weeping with streaks of tears shining with the real moon's brilliance. It was getting harder for them to move at all. Peter was on his back but managed to get one arm up, fingers spread, pleading for me to come and get him. "Let me get Peter…..Laurel is enough for now…." Casey looked up to me and asked quietly over the music playing loudly through the living room and the entire house.

I smacked her hard enough that she fell to the ground. She got back up though. Quietly she regained her stance, watching with me.

Peter was shouting "HELP… Please….DAD" Choking. I knew that had to take an amazing amount of strength after the siders venom was in your veins. Shame. Maybe his talents were wasted?

Laurel was just weeping, lifting her neck up enough to see her surroundings. Then the first albino worm head broke the surface. No one knew just how long the things are or how big they actually got, but they came out after 10 o'clock for feeding. When feeding was offered, if ever. The idea with these new blood sprinklers pumping life fluid, was obviously to keep them nourished enough to baste inside the soil for weeks sometimes but now and again a necessary pulpy fresh feeding kept things rolling in the natural course. What they provided after the feeding was the very essence of Hope Springs.

"Here we go!" I cracked the Bisner in my hand. Sipped tall and smiled. "All spider basted and smelling attractive!" Yeah, the venom attracts them like stink on sex.

A half dozen breached the soft soil of the turf, winding around, seeking prey, they crawled about but never really come completely out of the ground. White, glistening, eyeless oh but how those sucker like mouths can open wide when they find what they came for! All at once, they hit Laurel, three of them! Peter had four bite down on him, two on his legs one on his belly and another had his left shoulder. The size of a radon pipe, here's what these guys do; attach, suck, and break off pieces of you to bring down below for a slow digestion, and then a fine excretion into our soil.

The screaming did not end for more than twenty minutes. Not efficient killing machines, they had a purpose equally, if not more prominent then that of the spiders. But like that honey and Soft 03 blend the Montville's had developed, the spider bite and the digestive tract of the albino worms created miracles! They say dinosaur carcasses gave us oil? Well this was purer and even more efficient than photosynthesis. Dumb plants could not do this. Though I've heard talk…

Both Peter's legs had been pulled slowly from his body as his shoulder was crushed and partially swallowed by the giant worm on his left. It was the giant white hose of a worm attached to his stomach that eventually did him in! I watched that white worm go red with the boy's entrails gulping through its sinuous muscles. His screams ceased while four more worms broke through my lawn and dragged him below as quickly as they had emerged. Laurel was not *that* lucky, dumb bitch that she was!

"Hey…how about your boy James writes a poem about this one? Huh… or how about me…. Mason's THE MOONS' CRYIN"…. Huhuh… bitch?" I yelled at the window, not caring if she could hear. "It will be a best seller!!"

The last I saw of Laurel was her glazed eyes staring at me blankly and one out- stretched arm seeking solace that would never come. Then she was pulled into the soft earth alive. The remaining three or four worms went down with her, biting and dragging. You could feel the rumble under the ground for a bit and then nothing.

Morning had broken with those loud-assed birds, and I made sure I was up to meet my sexy next door neighbor, Rachel. "Missed you last night." I smiled, after 8:00 a.m. and my first beer of the day in my hand. Only one small Steady Gaze dose to get the humming in my blood while I sat in my metal lawn chair with the vinyl straps. I thought to help her, so did Edward the Skinny Mailman as he walked up my driveway, but this is family business.

She was busy. She was dragging her fat, limp and young Neil down her walkway to the street. He was still in his PJ's from the night before. Oh and WHAT a night it was! Right? What Rachel would tell me later, when she stopped mourning, was that she did not have the heart to put Neil outside after she snuck the spiders into his room in the dark of night and let them loose on his bed while he dreamt about his action figures. He was supposed to have been outside as an offering with Laurel and Peter. So Neil just ended up immobilized all night. She did not have it in her to make him suffer. Dummy thought the spiders would end him. That's not what they do. They're prep chefs.

When she plopped him onto the curb by the gutter, you could see he was starting to get his motion back and the young boy was very much aware he was being thrown away...hahaha. They were juvenile spiders of Peter's. Their potential capabilities were still in question.

Edward sat on the broken chair in the front yard next to me, one hand had reached into my cooler, "Mind?"

I nodded, watching. Odd, that she did this for her own convenience and not for the sake of distribution. I guess not everyone is born to be a parent. But damn she missed out in soil credits!

Rachel's backside in those tight shorts poked through to say "good morning" to me, while she got back up from dumping her immobilized but conscious son on the street. She smiled at me, briefly and it was at that time I sensed a merger coming between houses! Woohoooo! Not bad for an old ugly fart like me!

Her face went serious suddenly turning away from me while she traipsed into her front door, not even closing it behind her. She looked depressed. Why? You got rid of your problems. What did they call them in the outside? Dumpster babies? Good riddance.

Edward grabbed my arm, nervously excited. "HEY... it's Sunday... you suppose they do special pickups?" What does a mailman know about pickups? Ha. But maybe.

"As a matter of fact, it was in a vid scroll last night. Rachel made a call this morning." I said, sipping my beer. "New thing since Jack Landis got fired. What we talked about."

Doors shut. Locked. Windows closed. Curtains swept, but left a crack to see out of every house on the block.

Me and Edward? We were just too curious.

No other sounds this morning, except a few birds and they ceased when the slap and patter of multiple clawed feet tapped their way around the bend in the road. The new Gutter Crew was making a special call. The same crew that not just stole our old trash man, Jack Landis's job, but actually had stolen the man himself, alive!

Something blackened and green with scaly skin flecked with gold wound its way down the road. The reptile was the length of a moderate boa constrictor, yet flanked with eight to ten legs on either side that rotated rapidly to keep the iguana type beast moving gutter side with precision and speed.

In seconds it opened a mouth filled with yellow teeth, bit down on young limp Neil's immobile left foot. Dragging the heavy child past my house, front bushes, driveway and ever forward along my street, you could see the scream in the boy's eyes. A scream he was not capable of letting loose. His tongue was probably numb, but his mouth open...eyes almost wider than the dumb kid's mouth.

Kind of a hideous a scene, this new gutter crew by PRO-JEK! Their latest creation rolled past us toward a sewer grate in the street in front of the house next to us. Now, I could be sure about ordering the special pick up calls! Someone hidden from view must have flipped a switch and the reptilian beast that only stood a little higher than the curb itself, was next directed toward an opening grate in the street. The grate had slid to one side. Old Steven, across the street came out to watch now too. We all watched the thick squirming body supported by all those little hideous legs disappear into the sewer door, dragging the silently screaming Neil with him. When the last of the tail end of that fifteen foot long Gutter Crew creature was gone, I belched and smiled at Edward, "Well, let's hope the fucker doesn't learn to deliver mail....HAHAHAHAAH."

Two days later I checked our soil meter outside by the street. It peaked with a red line upward. Walking inside I pointed to Casey to immediately get on the distribution program and start the process.

Laurel and Peter's counts were richer than some others. The worms had produced some of the best ore that we had yet. Maybe because it was the first time we had two go down at the same time. Now I can get those shoes for Casey that she wanted and move our movies up to 8 a week. Also I can get the Steady Gaze 3.0 that some of the other folks have been boasting. Maybe get some Haze too.

So our pipeline underground soaked up the rich ore. The ore we could only thank the culmination of the spiders, worms and our passed family members for. Now it was on its way to the corporate PRO-JEK HQ for export. Casey did a fine job. She even opened an account overseas for the next time. Someone must have liked her. Maybe Brenda Montville? She was up there in the bureaucracy somewhere, god bless her.

I had to go retrieve the spiders from next door. They bit Rachel when she went to bed that night after she had put Neil out for the trash. One less liability out the door, and the poor slut had got bitten to all hell. No luck for that bitch. She's got some itchy multicolored welts appearing now. Lucky for me, Peter's baby spiders had gathered back in their tank, so that *much* that was easy going for me. I had my way with Rachel on her kitchen floor while she slept off the two day hangover those guys can give you. So two days later Rachel woke up at the same time that Casey and I made our distribution to PRO-JEK, celebrating with some steaks from the Sweens truck. Rachel came over too and sat at our kitchen table with us, holding her head, staring at me, knowing what I had done to her. She glared at me holding a hand by her crotch with a recognition of flinching pain. She wanted to share that pain.

This going to be interesting.
-MASON

OVER THE MOONBOW
-poem by James Clark

- 4 -
DEMONEYE

When people ask me if I know fear or whether or not I am shivering in my boots, frightened at our current state in this damn sandy abyss they call Texas, I have to say no. I'm the alpha male, I'm the one to fear. But I had to learn that. My hair shot gray at the early age of twenty five, practically overnight because of the very fear that broke the wager. Since then, I'm a new man. I keep my brim low as I tend to the gray hair that tends to hang just on the shoulder below my sombrero. Can't hide it. Shields the back of the neck when the sun is beating down. Rare do I have my back to anything else but the sun. Learned too, never to have your back to any blokes you come about these days.

In some towns that I've recently come across they pick up on the fact rather quick-like that I 'm snappier with my Colt than most riders can pull their dick out for a piss after a long stretch of sand. This is true. Ha ha... Not saying much really. Everyone has met someone quicker than them at one turn or another. They just ain't all around to talk about it anymore.

But over in Caravass Pass, that town that you may or may not have come across in your travels, there was a little tavern called Paven Stone, coincidentally where I did some residency, and where I came across some thick-headed wrangler type who just did not see fit to leave me the hell alone. Y'all have been there. In that position I mean. Some hunk of snot that just cannot learn when to back off and let a man drink. Screaming for attention, these folks just need a bullet in the head and no more wasted breath.

I had been in the town for two weeks, but seldom could I stand more than one swig of their house rotgut whisky. Of course that was why I had Ole' Clacky the barkeep blend my own swill. This was important to me. Something I had to learn in ways I'll do not feel like explaining at the moment. I made sure when my own well ran dry in my flask that I could hit a small town that was capable of brewing me some more.

So when I arrived at Caravass Passs, the town was full, mostly of passer-bys. But along the walls of the cavernous rocky shale stones was this slit of a town. You had to walk through a nice little trail through a caustic cavern to find the town, which may have kept it safe from the hordes for a while. I do say, there were other things dwelling in the dark that should make a man (or army of men) steer clear of rocky outcroppings, especially at night. There were things coming out of the deepest depths of the desert that I've seen. Spirits or otherwise, these were the days that man stood on trial with the putrid stench of hell.

I must say though, the gracious hand of god did shine through all blue-like from the heavens now and again, and the debauchery of man (and woman) continued on. A town like Caravass Pass pursued some hot times during gold rush- now sex and drunkards make me envious of the hardasses that made their cash and got the hell out. It seems sex was the main source of income in towns like this.

So, I took residency. I drank. A lot. My own brew just waiting for when the rotgut shit that Ole' Clacky served ran dry now and again.

Of course all shit drops south eventually and the day came when this dolt walks up to me after my first sip of that foggy glass of swill, knocks my sombrero off, mistaking me for a Mexican. Mistake either way, mind you! Those bucks can fight!

Now old drunken puss, with his flab and limp jab (he swung and missed me) had true gray in his beard and not much else but age to earn my respect.

But my hat came off... and the gray hair fell to my shoulders, and then the giveaway. My shock of black hair on top that fell over my left ear did show itself. You see, this may appear as a weakness to blokes like this old fart pick'n a fight with me.

"WHO"RE you... looks like you got some yello-belly'in you...." He muttered, grabbing the attention of all those around. Even the teenager playing the piano, a kid named Weaver, stopped his jovial tune. The bordello girls that had swooned about the young piano player, well, quit their swooning. The bartender walked somewhere I could'nt see. Card players turned.....eh.. you get the damn picture!

I stood taller than the old drunken coot. He was new in town, and apparently still human, if he did not know who Dekker Collins, the *Dead Shot* was. "No qualms with you sir, but that black streak I got on top, is the only part of me that survived the things that scare normal folk like you. Now it's a beacon to the rest of me, reminding me to put fear away, and put you in the grave. Now, can we finish our drinks?" I said this calmly, looking down on the shaggy fellow.

I never had to touch the Colts at my sides, this time, cause when he went to swing I had him by the elbow, and broke it the way that elbows don't bend. There was the usual shout and fall to the ground. Bobby Kin, last of the deputies in town, came over to attempt carrying the man out of the Paven Stone Tavern. He struggled at his job, not fit to be a deputy or any law enforcement for any town. But this was Caravass Pass, and trouble came here because that said *trouble* wanted to make a name for themselves and strip me of my insidious reputation. Dead Shot Dekker.

Poor skinny Bobby Kin came running up, frantic-like, in his form fitting brown uniform, complete with vest and that silly badge that may have just as well said "target."

"Come on Dekker, didja have to break it... Doc is still sewing up the Brewster kid. He doesn't have time..." Skinny Bobby Kin whined as usual helping the old angry coot out the door.

I could have said something typical like..."And that's what you get...." Or "maybe next time he'll think twice..." ugh.. makes my stomach twitch at such bravado when things are creeping out of the earth and nipping up settlers like ....oh dammit... "fish in a barrel..." There I said it!

Bobby Kin was the first of the townies I met when I strode in. On the day I had arrived he came out on the road while I hitched up my poney, Stoney, basically interviewing me to see what the hell my business was. When I told him my story, showed him my gold coin for spending, he had bowed his hat down, welcoming me to town. He knew he might have one more gunslinger in town to scare off the other types, if they did show up. Who am I kidding, they always showed up. Bobby Kin was a bit younger than me in his late twenties. Too young to be in charge of a town, but smart enough to know not to call himself sheriff. I supposed the actual sheriff was long gone.

Calling himself deputy could keep him alive a bit longer if some dark ones came along looking to take out the town's alpha.

Deborah, a beautiful brunette with curls down her back, swaddled in foreign scarfs of purple and pink, was the second person I met in town. Also how I spent half my gold in two days! It gets lonely in the desert too, with nothing but spiders for company, and not good company!

Deborah came up to me after flirting with the teenager piano kid. She thought she had made her money for the night like I had thought I always had enough swig in a jar. She didn't. Weaver, the kid with the braids through his long brown hair, and suspenders was half injun and completely not interested in the beauty that is Deborah. She was clean too. Not all the girls that worked the upstairs of the Paven Stone kept themselves as well. You could not blame them when you considered the clientele. I monopolized on that situation. Claimed her as mine, almost nightly. It got expensive.

Bandits, farmers, wranglers, Indians, families- it never mattered how hard you thought life was or who you crossed unless you met one of these dark ones. They were somewhat new to our world, unless you had religion like some of the church going folk that I've come across in some towns. Lets not forget the Indians. They saw this coming almost as soon as white man pilfered their country.

You see, all it would take is one time for you, one chance to see what they are capable of and you too would be as calloused as those that now lived in Caravass Pass. Most locals here that were just passing through, now stay because of me. Those that leave, we don't usually hear hide of again.

Deborah narrowed her beautiful wide eyes at me, smirking at my handy-work once again, "New one came in yesterday Dekker. A pretty one if you don't mind his ragged skin. Tall like you but blond. He's upstairs with Loreen right now." Deborah's dark brown hair was up in a bun on the back of her head, and curly up top and front. She seldom let it down while working, always ready for a brawl. I liked her. She wore a pink puffy skirt with a tight white top to it that held her bosom at bay. Oh hell, they all did! God how I love them whores!!

She sat down next to me smelling of powder and some soap that injun kid Weaver had sold her. It was nice, compared to the whisky before me. "Guess I need to turn off the house whisky for a bit huh?" I said knowingly, placing my hat back on my head. GOD, I could feel the new wrinkles on my own dry skin. Skin stretched tight on my face, but not as tight as our friends that rolled in to town smelling like burnt chili and molten flesh.

"Did he turn in to town looking for me? Make any mention?"

"Not yet. His eyes are wild though. Looks right through me and poor Loreen. Hope he doesn't go for the full blown ending with her. I've grown attached to her." Deborah said, motioning for Ole Clacky to bring down my private stock. Bald, long eyed, sad and not much for conversation, we referred to the old man behind the bar as Ole Clacky because the bad smelling evil ones had torn his right leg off at the knee a couple of years before I even knew this half-assed town existed. His peg leg made a clackity clack sound. Funny…

Ole Clacky brought me my jar. I poured the whisky into my now empty glass fogged with resin, and downed it quick, warming my belly and my smile for the lovely Deborah.

What a good girl. GOOD GIRL. She slipped me a rolled up piece of paper, immediately getting my gratitude with a kiss on her upper cheek. She works fast! Always good to be ready. The remaining resin in the jar that Clacky had behind the bar would not be enough without some fresh ingredient. Deborah had somehow seen to that.

I had asked her if this tall and blonde newcomer to town had asked about me since I did indeed have a reputation for talking *them* out. Whether he had come to town looking for me or not was irrelevant.

*****

So let me explain something. And I'll keep it current. No use for backstory. Like I said, I aint scared, now, I was scared *THEN*, when I watched my family die…HELLS, I went gray overnight and emotionless in a day. A need to vaporize the land of this scourge grew a cancerous hatred in my stomach and mind.

When I first rolled into town with my black and white Shetland (good story where I acquired that ride, but little Stoney only carried my gear. I was too kind to ride him) it was goin' on dusk. I could see the cavern that sheltered Caravass Pass from the glassy dunes I was traveling, for quite a ways, even with the glare. The desert cool was setting in and I had come from just more of the same trouble elsewhere. Bored with it now, but when I saw those damn X's in the dark standing upright I knew it was time that I stop. You see, when you learn the things I did, early in the game you feel responsible to do what you can. As much as possible. These "X's" stand upright, tall as an average man because normally that's exactly what they were meant to hold.

I pulled Stoney over another hill that may have been a mile from the town itself. The sun was on its way to its desert pillow, yet shimmered just enough so that I could see the dozen or so bodies (some fresh) hanging on the wooden planks shaped in "X" fashion. This was their way of showing off, and an attempt to keep the likes of me out.

I stepped forward.

Like I always did now. Seems like years-which it may have been, that the land had cracked and given way to evil, like a boil popping and spreading its fine wine staining the sand with blood. Funny to say, the tide was turning. Maybe this demon spawn had not realized that starting out in the plains where everyone was armed comfortably was a poor choice!! Haha.. But not so easy mind you, they are cunning and merciless. Standing there looking at their methodology will remind a man what needs to be done. And what they have done to my own family.

The human casing that houses the demons becomes bonier, harder, like an exoskeleton, bones poke through like weapons. Most have yellow eyes, long and moonlike, only shining at night when in a feeding frenzy. Their teeth get sharp, growing out the old human teeth only when need be. As I have witnessed it takes a long time for their teeth to look human-like again. As I said, their numbers are diminishing so they like to stay incognito as long as possible. Erupting in the form of spirits to take over a corrupt human host was not working as they maybe had set out.

The day I arrived at Caravass Pass, it just so happens that one young boy that was posted on those "X"'s that day was Deborah's young brother Harris. He was only fourteen. They like to use the hard shell of their nails, like claws to poke into the temples and pull the arteries and veiny stuff like bird beaks nab grub worms. All the while, the poor slobs are kept alive and one or more of these possessed human carcasses peel the straws of life free from the skin and suck down the life fluid that God gave us all. The screams go all night usually, so the town can hear their beloved's final throes.

AND they look like you and me. For the most part. Till you get close. Hideous.

If you talk to the Indian tribes they will tell you that they saw the spirits come through the larger canyon cracks in the earth, those holes in the Earth that seem to have the most exposed surface area out West. The Indians know to stay away, so the pickens were weak. Human bodies don't hold up too well with all that malicious intent and physical ability that the demons have.

So I'm here to trim the numbers down a piece even more-like.

Sometimes it feels like peeling briars from a bush. However, I have an edge now.

******

"Loreen's screaming…. Ms. Deborah!!" that injun Weaver kid came running up to us. I could hear Ole Clacky grab his rifle under the bar. "UPSTAIRS!!!"

Deborah ran behind the bar to the staircase as I got to my boots upright.

"NO..Dekker. Stay. Lets keep the game rolling." She pointed at me before disappearing up the staircase behind the bar.

I had to respect her business. She was in charge of twenty odd women, and most were still alive, so breaking the chain would lead to ...well, I always said "STICK WITH THE ORIGINAL PLAN" so I do.

There was some thumping upstairs, I heard a woman or two gasp, and then someone was "thunking" rider boots rather hard, down the stairs. Hand's ready, I could smell him before he rounded the bottom of the staircase. Burnt chili and molten flesh.

He was taller than me, thin wisps of blond hair to his chest, face long with the skull peeking through. Those blue eyes were big rounded almonds that I knew would turn that lantern light yellow in the moon light or sooner if he got real cankerous with me. Luckily I had dispatched with the contents of the roll of paper that Deborah had given me before she ran up to check on Loreen.

Ugh…there was a smear of blood on the right corner of his mouth matching his right palm. I had hoped he had not killed Loreen. These beasts like to torture more than kill. Killing is not their only game. To simply kill would provide no satisfaction, and one less shell to crawl up into, ya'know? They do have a penchant for the blood and flesh, a lust that cannot be harnessed with the strongest of mesh.

Oh damn, the smell of his dark brown long coat was that of a cattle carcass that was pecked by carrion crawlers for a week. We stood face to face for a bit before I sat down, motioning for Ole'Clacky to bring me a shot of house. Why not?

The inside of the tavern was dense with the scent of this lanky bitch of a man while he seated himself next to me! He put his rifle on the bar.

"Dekker Collins? Dead Shot Dekker?" Smiling through human teeth shaped like horses teeth, square and ready to fall out when he needed to show some real chompers.

"Dirty Smoked Chili man?" I harassed, smirking wildly.

He smiled back, tipping his brown hat. They love a challenge but rarely gave a name. A challenge is pretty much all they got for their little time given to them in the plain of the living. He spoke with a smooth rasp, "Gametime. Smoking too many of my friends of late. You good? You *that* good?" The thing in the man-suit had a voice that rattled like gravel down a washboard.

I swigged down my second glass of my own hooch. Some resin that had remained in the glass may help me a bit. Of course, the whisky itself eased me into good spirits. "Good enough for you, and whoever you got, stinky."

"Marvelous." His thin gray lips showed his horse grin of teeth as he got up from the stool. I smiled back over my shoulder while he walked away. Sure he could have whirled around and tried to smoke me then and there, but I knew already that he would not. His main of blonde hair swished behind his back under his hat. That hair, that swagger, his height and that smile reminded me of an old traveling buddy. Haunted me for a bit, but no, this creature was not my old friend.

"Ran into an old friend of yours in the desert, not far from here. You shouldn't leave a trail to your snake hole friend." The thing hissed as it got up.

Yea, there had been a friend or two, maybe a loose end or ten, but these things lie. You're wasting your own time letting them inside your mind. Besides, that was my job now!

Everyone was already outside the Paved Stone when I set foot on the gravelly sand. I nodded to old Stoney across the way, tied to his post at the Sheepskin trader shop. (Did we really need that? I never got *that* cold that I had to wear that shit). Poor pony sort of knew what was about to follow, though I doubt he had any hearing left after the last two towns we had wandered to. Lots of rifle fire power on those goes! But not a one had my edge.

The whisky hit me harder than usual. Worried me for a bit. Maybe three large glasses was too much? Or was it four? Yep. The demon posse always thinks you're too drunk to fight, and even will tell you on an occasion that their boss downstairs supplies us with such spirits to make us weak. Gift of tolerance may or may not help the old gunfighter.

It did me good. Righteously fine with blind hatred pulsing with fiery memories. My extra ingredient provided the focus.

Almost at equal with their tolerance for blood, violent sex and ripping flesh which knows no bounds but fills them with pleasure.

So, Mr.Tall and Smokey Stench, was there on the other end of town, approaching. Only I could see the bright yellow of his eyes, like pools of gold, and with that, my focus carried on breaking through his thin dead mucousy cornea ....thwap....thwap the sound it made in my mind's eye while I poked into the gray matter being puppeteered by evil. That was when I could really see. NOW, I was in his gray matter, the fool. Another dead eye fool! He had others with him. Five of them lay in wait. The closest were behind a wagon to my left about 8 paces.

"I BELIEVE IN A FAIR FIGHT, SMOKED CHILI MAN! NOW, GET YOUR BUD'S OUT FROM HIDING BEHIND THAT ..." I motioned to the wagon. The demon's credibility was shot, and he stopped walking. Pride makes up for their lack of hygiene.

He snarled, glanced to the two henchmen with rifles to emerge. And they did, and down they went, in two shots from one of my colt's chamber. Two men with beards, dressed in black, snarling through their demon teeth had just received brand new orifices in their skulls.

My smelly lanky friend at the other end was in disbelief that I had drawn and downed them. The edge- I knew he had no plan to draw, at that moment. Back to focus.

"THREE PACES DEKKER COLLINS...and ..." It snarled, already its human teeth were dripping down its chin, while steel needles poked their way through. Eyes, yellow. The crowd to the left by the saloon were gasping in horror.

"OK.. back to basics ...I'm good on three..." I replied.

I knew when he would move- I knew the angle, the speed - I knew to inch one step to the right, I also knew that when we drew, this creature would have a colt souvenir drilled fresh through his rotting piñata noggin. Done.

Made a nice sound though! This bud had a thick skull! Flack shattered out the back of his head with bits of blonde hair.

There were cheers, but I was already blowing four more shots above the other saloon down the way where two more of his cronies had rifles at the ready pointing over the fenced- in porch.

Got'em! One fell to the sand, bones broken, and I had missed his head, so he was lurching on one leg, dragging himself, lurching toward me. BLAMO! His head went back and flying hunks of hair went out the back! That one felt good. Now, earlier, old Stinky Chili man's gray matter had also told me there was one more outside the bank, in the dark behind some crates by the door. Oh Lucifer in the grass!! He had drawn on me before I could turn. Lost track of him…dead Dekker!

But no sir! Bobby Kin, that skinny bastard had come up behind him and blew his head to shards of chalk and hair.

"How'd you know Bobby?" Turning around, I asked him.

"I grabbed a shot of your hooch on the way out. I'm the law…" he smiled riley, "Got to do my bit for the team now and then."

I nodded, thankful, but not terribly happy. I mean, yea, Skinny Deputy Bobby Kin stole my thunder a bit, but there was more to it than that.

I ran back into the Paved Stone and up the stairs. It smelled of sex, musty wood and dead flesh. Demon flesh. Deborah was outside of Loreen's room. The pretty little dark skinned lady was dead on her bed, blue dress soaked with her own fluid; that which the creature had not finished apparently. He had pulled the veins from her right wrist, underneath, where it is soft, straight out about a foot and sucked her like a straw in a child's malt.

"I should have known… I should have known.." Deborah cried in my arms while a dozen or so other girls gathered in the hallway to see. "Loreen gave me the roll of paper after their second….*go around town earlier…* "

What Deborah had told me was that this bloke that I had just killed outside was a repeat performer today and Loreen managed to dig some of his skin under her fingernails for me. A good bit actually, and these things enjoy pain as much as they like to give it. He went for the happy ending with Loreen. Not good. But she did her part. That dead skin was handed over to Deborah. In turn it got to my hands before the fight, but not before we lost Loreen. Damn, she was too young.

****

I remember how Weaver cried that night. The kid had a crush on Loreen, like I did for Deborah. That's tough on a kid. Dunno if we'd hear much piano after that.

You want know how I came to "*see* " things as I do? My edge? You guessed by now, silly me, I'm sure you did.

As I write this down for you, I had just had some of my hooch. Demoneye we call it. Weaver, Bobby Kin and even Ole' Clacky call it that, but only in certain circles.

I'm gonna label it Dekker Collins. But we'll see.

These tales are meant to be shared. Stories are told to open the mind to problem solving as much as entertaining folk. There was this old fairy tale book that I used to read to my boy before he was brutally taken from me. A writer by the name of Daniel Foytik, or something said, "What is life without a good story, but a dead man's soul disappearing into the never."

True. I do not think my kid got that idea behind those bedtime stories. Hell I did not till now.

There was this horrible incident a while back, before Caravass Pass, when I called on my first lady of the night. Some place in Rushdale Arizona. It was quite the digs! Beautiful girls everywhere! Some clothed, some not... some on tables while a crazed group of bandmates strummed multiple banjos, a piano and some washboard device...it made a ruckus and the place was packed. FOUR BARTENDERS!!! Now that's some drinking!

My family had been gone for a while, and other than my Stoney, I traveled with this Cedric Bodnatsen guy. Tall and lanky like that demon you just heard of. They shared the same long blonde hair (that's what made me think of my old riding pal, Cedric!), but this guy was deadly with just about any weapon you gave him...and funny as all hell! He had campfire stories that made your skin crawl and your guts burst with laughter.

Just don't get too personal, or out-do him in any way, cause then you'd lose your traveling buddy. We found each other in a tavern like this months before; got drunk, had laughs and stuck together. He knew a lot about the demon epidemic and did not blame the Indians as some had, with their magic. He joked sometimes and said his own evil ways may have conjured up the depths of hell!! Oh that Cedric- killer of comedy sometimes. Miss him.

Anyways...we were eyeing up our own women that night. He picked some scrawny blonde thing with scraggly hair and smelled like yesterday's rotten potatoes. Dunno what that was about but Cedric had said she reminded him of some witch he had bedded a lifetime ago.

I have stop for a second. Look at my audience, assess some thoughts I previously blackened. Cedric rarely even looked at women, because like myself he had lost emotions along the way. He was an old soul, mind you, and when he said it was a lifetime ago that he had found love and lost it, you kind of believed him when he said he would never even look again. Just keep it physical.

During our nights around campfires, if he had shared too much wine with me, we both gave up stories. Between taking pot shots at the big nasty shiny desert spiders and shots of whisky and wine, we laughed like children. Those spiders became more common of late, and I trusted my friend to find safe campsites, away from the rocky outcroppings they seemed to migrate too. After we pelted a few a way, Cedric would move our camp to somewhere a tad bit safer as he claimed he had grown accustomed to where these eight legged monsters tended to nest.

When all else was quiet, on some nights I found that the man was lonely. Usually the good stories revolved around his pension to be himself-normally a conceited gambler with a mind for trumping the next town's card playing stud. His melancholy only set when he talked of his past and what seemed his only love. There had been friends too. Traveling partners, adventure seekers alike. Cedric admitted to using them to his advantage.

Why he told me that, I only now understand. It was a warning for me to put my trust aside as it would make me weak, again.

Back to my story though, with me and my pretty blue eyed companion, Cedric - So upstairs they went after the money was exchanged Cedric and the lady he favored disappeared for a bit. I followed a red headed harpy up the stairs myself. These were big stairs, with flocks of cowpokes and busty young ladies goin' to and fro, so this pretty waif did not see me follow her. Young in her twenties was this one I had practically stalked, with her long red hair to her waist, dark brown eyes, and a maroon skirt, with white under-all leggings. A bit shorter than me, I took to liking her immediately. She had clothes on the whole time, so the mystery was the *GET*!

She turned and smiled, stopping short in front of a door that led, more than likely, to her temporary chambers. Along the hall there were broken bottles of whisky on the floor, and a sticky substance I did not care to identify. "Oh Hunny bunn, you have to wait, I have a man waiting for me inside …wait your turn cutie, I'll come holllerin'!" Her smile was amazing, her eyes dazzling. My mind, drunk. This could work fine.

I saw what waited for her behind the door as she opened it. A most unpleasant, pock faced lug of a wrangler with skin browned from hard work and eyes… well the eyes locked on to mine before the door shut.

Desperate as I was, I had watched Cedric leave a room with that girl in tow, nodding to me with his hat on his back and a shit eating grin. One of us was having fun. The blonde girl he was with had looked exhausted.

OK, two of us were having fun.

Then the door opened, and the red head came out, grinning with her mouth closed tight. All I could think about was the heap of a man in there and how I could take her away from all this. Whisky talking of course. Without any concern of those party folks surrounding the hallway, and the man still in the room (I wanted to incite him anyway), I planted my lips on hers and forced my tongue in her mouth to kiss her… She struggled a bit, and fought me off, shaking her head and her hand was out as if to say, "No no…not yet…"

That's when I tasted the copper in my mouth and saw the bit of red fluid drip from her mouth. I gagged. Their transaction was not quite complete yet. I am so stupid!

I spit out the brackish fluid to the ground, gagging and hating myself for my desperate ploy for affection. Then, her customer, with his thick brown mustache surrounding a huge angry jaw, emerged from the room into the hall, while I wiped my mouth with my sleeve.

"Enjoy that?" He rasped, a bit of blood coming from his mouth. "She's a biter if you pay enough. Hahahaha."

With that I turned back down the stairs to where we had left our glasses. They were gone... I threw some coins on the counter and downed one more whisky to clear my mouth. The salty taste of the blood and whatever else was happening on the other side of that door washed down my throat.

The dark skinned man, now wearing his black hat and vest was coming down the stairs, smiling at me, but then turned away. That was the moment...

Cedric, with his handsome, yet sturdy features, barreled into me, mocking me. "So...dontcha know to let bordello girls clean up before you try to ....." He made a kissing gesture..."HahahahHAH!" He punched my shoulder. Disgusted as I was, something new had happened.

Looking past my friend, I focused on that pig of a man whom I just shared spit with. I saw the rugged man's yellow demon eyes from the stairs. More to it, I saw inside his head. He was a demon, alright, but he also had planned on shooting my friend Cedric and stealing his horse when we left. I *HEARD* his mind say so! "Damn long-haired fool took my favorite bitch... I'll take his..." Referring to the young blonde attached to Cedric's hip.

"Stay here Seed..." I said to him. I called him that because it was easy.

"WHY...Dekker what the hell..."

"That man wants to kill you. You got his girl tonight...and ...he's one of THEM! Don't think he's alone either...." The man's voice in his own head said something about telling *Gordy*. Theres another man out there!

Cedric knew what I was saying, but evidently there was some disbelief there, so the fool followed me out the door, young blonde girl in tow, right into the fray.

The man was there, just untying Cedric's black stallion, so we had the surprise on our side. Before he could whirl, I had shot him dead in the back of the head, just as his gun was pulled from his holster. The man called Gordy, this partner I did not see, had already shot at Cedric, missing but taking the young blonde wench out with a shot to her throat. She held herself, gurgling with futility and gobs of blood bubbling forth. Poor thing.

Cedric shot him full of holes in the chest. "WANTED ANOTHER ROUND WITH HER....!!! PAID FOR IT!!" Seething, my blue eyed friend shouted at the fallen man named Gordy.

"Calm down Seed...but put one in his head...his eyes are yellow to me....and I can hear him still thinking." I told my friend. Cedric was a little angered with me and more envious that he could not see the demons for what they were as clearly as I could. Hearing their thoughts was a new one for most gunfighters.

As soon as Cedric turned his back, the man (that was not a man at all) named Gordy sat up and reached for his gun on the ground. I had already triggered the shot to his head.

My friend turned around, thankful, but angry too. Leery of me perhaps. I know now that it was jealousy mostly. If it came down to it, I could beat him in a gunfight. This was not a man that traveled with an equal nor be partners with a man that could possibly best him. Or was he hiding something else? If he had shared bed with a real witch, what did that make him?

We parted ways that next morning. I lost a friend to trust and my taste for red heads forever.

******

Deborah came over to me and handed me a small roll of paper. She sat next to me, smiling but sadder than when we met weeks ago. We had buried Loreen two days ago, and that's all that it took for more scum to roll in to Caravass Pass. Sadly enough, she was not the first of the bordello girls to hand me a roll of paper with some bits of flesh that day. I was handed a small vile of some fluid I preferred to not identify, from a young girl earlier in her workday. I had poured the fluid into my jar, mixed it, poured a shot, and promptly went upstairs and shot a horny demon that waited for her to return. Its funny, I do not always have to look them in the eye, depending on how much of their body fluids, flesh or otherwise I consume. This last bloke I had shot right through the door, for I knew he was flanking the left side waiting to jump the young lady as she returned. One shot, through the door on an angle and his head was all over the girl's (was her name Tiffany?) bed.

She had thanked me.

As did Deborah now.

"This one is smart. I had to scrape dander from his hat while he relieved himself. He never let me touch him. It may not be enough."

I took the paper from Deborah, opening the wrapped scroll I began sprinkling the tiny pips of scalp flesh into my jar of whisky that Ole Clacky had put in front of me, right on cue. You'd be amazed how much skin falls free of these stinky beasties.

"Two in one day, Deborah, I dunno…its taking a toll on my soul I think."

She kissed me. "You're doing God's work."

So she said. I never took her for a religious girl. I suppose it was God's work more than the Devil, but for how long? You see, I told you I ain't scared no more, because I'm the alpha. Though you cannot help but wonder for how long one can remain on top?

She removed my hat, pushed the gray silver hairs from my face to kiss me and noticed the black shock of hair was gone to gray. She blinked, after another hug "This one is already outside waiting for you," she stepped back and went up the stairs.

"Out in the Daylight...?? Cocky... like that last one with the posse. Are they bearing the sun better?" I said to Weaver and Bobby Kin to my right. They looked to each other, like frightened squirrels, and they nodded. "DOWN we go..!" I downed the big glass of Demoneye, the whisky hiding the rank taste of the dead skin mask. "Showtime." My confidence waned, my stride slowed. This sumbitch wanted a gunfight in the daylight?! High noon?

The town was outside lining the sandy road that led to and from Caravass Pass. Folks I had never seen outside their own windows lined the street. All the girls followed Deborah outside the Tavern, as did Skinny Deputy Bobby Kin, and Injun Weaver. I noticed Weaver had Stoney by the reigns. "I'll take care of him for you Dekker Collins. I promise." He looked sad.

Cedric Bodnasten waited on the other end of the street.

I could not see into his eyes. They were not yellow, but still diamond blue. No demon sense about him. Or had he learned to hide it? There was a slight glimmer that was even bright in the daylight to those eyes of his.

"Seed." I breathed more than spoke.

So as I write this, Deborah is by my side, crying. We are in her room. My old long haired, blue-eyed friend by her side, gun drawn on me. DAMN! ONE OF MY GUNS!! Cedric had handed me a scroll and ink to get this down. There is a bullet hole on my left shoulder. Yea, that hurts. Guess I lost that fight. How about that! Dead Shot Dekker lost....to a demon?? Or just an old jealous friend that used my new friends to thwart me because I had become...

"You did good my dear, you really did....for as long as you could." Deborah said. I could smell her powder fresh skin, and the blood pulsing in her veins, that I began to lust for. Her blood smelled so sweet under her skin, that I could barely...

Cedric is wanting me to log as much of this treasure trove of information that I can, so I am, but that damn long itchy finger of his on that trigger tells me I will not have to fear what I will become much longer.

- 5 -
WORLDS APART

Metal clanked against metal echoing down the limestone tunnel. Two men walked side by side, each with a wooden torch in hand. Their leather boots stomped the dust. The dank and narrow cavern pulsated with their footfalls off the brittle earth between them. Sharing a common direction and a most determined goal bonded the men, dragging them deep into this journey into the dark. Trust held no bearings here, for each gripped their sword hilts tighter as they moved deeper toward the thickening dark. Every other step they turned their heads, sneaking side glances at one another.

"I never imagined in all my years that I would have to go to this extent to find an answer to any such argument," stretching out his broad back, cracking some tired bones, the dark skinned man named Herran Malx taunted the man next to him. His booming voice startled the slighter, younger man beside him. The disbelief of the extreme measures they found themselves in was inherent in his voice. Herran was as surprised as he was distraught.

"…where death is imminent," Herran's withered chainmail armor rattled about his chest as he spoke. Turning his head to the thin pale man walking beside him, he was waiting for a reply. He remembered how much more talkative the young man beside him had been the night they had met, wishing that he had never sat down next to his younger counterpart at the bar or better yet had just never stepped foot in the tavern that day in the first place.

Yet, as it seemed now, it was fate that brought them together, thought Herran, as it was an unavoidable broken stitch in time that tore them apart. "There are worse things than death, you know." He continued to insight the young man, to the lick of the torch of the flames in their hands.

Pride, blind faith, it seemed that farmers, hunters, magic seers, no matter what clan in the caste system of the world one found oneself in, the insidious argument was all too common among the humans of different clans in these strangest of days, after the cataclysm.

"All I wanted was a drink and a bench to rest my duff," Herran's mind drifted back to that day, trying hard to ignore the current circumstances, as a musky limestone tainted breeze blew past him, soothing his skin but not his mind.

The moisture rich air had been similarly temperate, the same as it was that day when he met the young man on a humid afternoon some time ago, at the Drylock Tavern. The old stone building was the center of activity between the plains and the city of the Shydling. All races could meet there and usually be without a hassle. The farming clans of the plains and the Mara Cromaire (Herran's own magic practicing background) clans of the forest both drank from the same spouts.

Whether it be a watering hole portioned between Mara Cromairens, plainsmen farmers or simply shared by both of their cattle, the land and its ores were for sharing. Be it a natural hole in the earth or a tavern, like Drylock. Herran Malx, a Mara Chromaire frequented the tavern, mixing well with the likes of the hard working farmers. Even nodding at the Shydling Swordsmen that policed the lands outside of their castle walls. The Shydling were always happy to see currency and wealth being spent in the very taverns they squelched for percentages.

The oppressive Shydling Warriors came about in their silver armor enriched with crimson adornments, flanked by even more crimson robes of garb underneath. Rich, protectors of the realm, or how they saw fit to project themselves.

Rather than sit with a lowly mage or farmer, the Shydling normally could be seen at the Drylock sitting among the stout and hearty mining dwarves who drank their mugs fiendishly with glee, ignoring those around them anyway. Even the dwarves knew that men made the best mead this south of the borderlands, whether they all got along well with one another or not. Most of the judgments were drowned in faulty memory anyway. For all they cared, the human tribes could just wipe each other out and leave the mead for them, or so a Dwarf Chieftain told Herran Malx once.

He thought on that, chuckling to himself, seated not far away from some shaggy bearded dwarves on that same day that he had met the plainsman, Kylor Raven. Just a hunting season or two ago, the tavern was full of pot-bellied merchants, drunken dwarves, and mead drinking mercenaries from the Highlands beyond the ravaged borderlands. There were some lowland plainsmen too. Herran seated himself next to the young plainsman, who at that time was not so pale. A farmer with toned tan muscles under his long black braids. Still, more of a boy than a man was this drinking partner next to him, muscles or not, Herran picked the spot at the bar next to the handsome fellow, tired of drunken dwarf talk.

Smelling of beer, sawdust and more than likely rich cow fodder after a day in his parent's fields, the young man did not seem to be much of a threat, considering the reputation of such taverns in the Wildwood Trading District. The Shydling Castle was only miles north, standing like a sentinel of guilt and power before the plains.

Yes, incidents did occur, but most of the men were too travel weary or tired from the heat during harvest season. Still, a darker skinned Mara Cromairen in a place like the Drylock was sure to attract some attention without the asking.

Herran remembered why he had chosen that resting post at the bar. Letting out a breath, he remembered what *ease* was, and why his elbows could fall easy on their own flat lame plane of relaxation, for once, without rising to fight. He had come to the common tavern to forget his family, his awful little sister who left long ago writing off the family's magical practice, all of his past, his regrets. Herran Malx just wanted to have a drink. The man next to him at the sticky oak bar had looked to be just out of his tender years, completely harmless.

"I can just drink and not think."

Herran let out a breath of relief, remembering why he went to the Drylock that day. The poison of the cave's scent squelching his memories of possibilities. Of hope. Still he thought back.

Dressed in a thick brown tunic belted at the waist with fine leather, he noticed that the plainsman farmer seated next to him must have some sort of income to afford a heavy belt (was that a sword hilt on the other side too?) fine enough for a commoner.

And bold enough to be questioned by the Shyd.

A long thick mane of black hair hung to the man's lower back. Thin wispy braided hair locks grown from his sideburns that reached the young man's shoulders had assured Herran that this young man was a farmer from one of the clans of the Lowlands; a place where he, himself was from, but Mara Cromaire Clans distanced themselves to the forests of Lowlands.

Respectful. Sad. A transcending lark of a routine, this trend among the denominational classes of humans that had been prodded and wrangled like cattle to quadrants that could be monitored by the Shydling Warriors. The Shydling, human as well, but only barely by a thread of flesh in the eyes of the Lowlanders, had made unnatural pacts with ill born inhuman entities throughout the lands.

Abhorrent of his born identity, he dealt with the card drawn for him. Belief in the higher gods of magic, the silt that assaults the blood, the sap of blood that taints the Earth, he knew he was to be born of chemists of stone. His clan was practicing in harnessing man, nature, fluids, crust and sand to deter the evil of the land.

Why? Because it exits. Evil was incarnate. Man could overcome. Thus was the Mara Chromairen. They would not succumb to the fall of tomorrow as the Shyd had so contracted themselves.

Herran was of the mage practitioners. The materials needed for such a life had to be taken from and to the woods of the lowlands; cork of trunk, blood of frog, venom from snakes, air blown off of oleander or be it a simple well spiced poison blood from a fallen ligorath tree; these were barely some of the prerequisites of the mage's life.

Both the Mara Cromairen's and the plainsmen farmers lived off the land, but in very different ways. It was accepted, controlled and as long as the guard of the Shydling and their very inhuman leaders could keep uprisings from occurring, the silent dictatorship functioned as normalcy. Fighting amongst the magic clans and the farmers was of no concern to the Shydling, syphoning the surplus population of course.

"Thinning the dragging horde," was the term that Herran had overheard a Shydling Chieftain say to a fellow chieftain one time while he attended a plainsmen market. As for the braids in the hair, it was the farmer clans who wore them as some kind of branding, separating them from the other mage-types, or Highland Warriors, a now defunct lineage. The warriors disappeared into the wilds of Wilkyus seeking fortune, never to return, similar to some of his own clan. Wilkyus, just north of the plains was the hopeful source of many a hopeful nursery rhyme told to young plainsmen's children, as it was rich with resource, game, hidden treasures and danger. The Shydling let those brave enough pass their Castle to search the land to the north, for none had ever really returned. They had allies in various tribes of creatures that parents dared not include in their children's bedtime stories.

Still, farmers turned into overnight warriors and adventurers disappearing into the wilds of Wilkyus.

Some Mara Chromairen sought that ill-fated route too.

Keeping his mind in simpler terms, easier times, Herran preferred his hair short cropped, understanding that the braids of his friend at the bar next to him, was an inspired insult to the Shylding's perfectly over-spiced powdered and hygienic ways reflecting their life within the confines of the castle walls. As for his own nice trim that he had so adorned, he now wished he covered it with one of the thin, worm-drawn white scarfs that his mother had sewn for him, his head felt cool. He was used to the sweat of the day that would pour off his head and not stick to the scalp too long. They did share the similar toned bodies of heavy laden farm work, unlike the surrounding bar weasels. Herran was not afraid to tend to his clans labor in the fields, since it meant food in the winter time.

Normally preferring conversation, eventually he tried to get the attention of the plainsman next to him, of course after several rounds of mind clogging mead. Herran ventured to ask the man his name. At first, the man turned to him, and quickly looked down to his drink again, unsure if Herran had addressed him.

"Excuse me, are you not of the Lowlands like myself?" Herran persisted. This time, the man nodded, smiled and held out his right hand, after placing his drink on the bar, spilling some on his wrist and splashing a bit on the bar resulting in a scowl from the barkeep that resembled more of a pig than a man.

"Kylor Raven, and yes I am a farmer of the Lowlands. Low and Lands. So outstandingly poetic? Huh?" The young man chuckled at himself, like a child who heard a joke for the first time.

Herran was reminded that this was no place for a boy to waste his time as the raunchiness of the drinkers ensued behind them. Ignoring the melees of idle challenges under the gruff mutterings of loud boasting surrounding them, they talked of farming and the challenge of growing up fatherless (for the most part), finding little difference between them.

"I never much understood why our clans were kept apart, I mean, there could be much more production if we made a joint action," Kylor Raven seemed to wonder aloud, in a soft, smooth voice.

"Well, your race has a certain fear of the dark magic that the Mara Cromairens dabble in, at least that is the way your people look at us...Your religion believes us to be devils,"

"Pour me another drink then, Devil!" Both men laughed as Kylor held his mug in the air. "But really, my friend..." he placed his hand on the broad man's shoulder, "the real argument lays..."

The shadow of a bulging man towered over their conversation. He wore the red plated chainmail armor of the Shydling Guard, not just a warrior, this was the most affluent of mercenaries in the opulent Highlands. When a Shydling was hired for mercenary work, it was a rare thing; a dangerous thing. They already were born with the belief that they had the gods given right to police the entire realm, a trait of all the Shyd, burned into them by the dark magic of a long dead witch queen. This queen of the Shyd made pacts with dark mages, and the vile Sythgorak Reptilian Race of the North, who would enslave men. Over privileged, born into entitlement, the Shydling only knew one mother, the Queen, who seduced all the men behind her castle walls, enslaving all the women that she found more beautiful than herself, eventually signing treaties with a bastion of horrific creatures of the borderlands so that her Shydling would prevail above all else as the only human horde accepted in the realm. She had even banished her own husband, a Mage named Malkyre' who was said to walk the lands, as a powerfully vengeful renegade mage who sought opportunity in others' moments of lassitude.

Having this background as your fortitude provided a single Shydling Warrior the preamble to always take what they felt was theirs upon the first notion that someone wanted it more. Fumbling with a needle in the dark to prick the weakness of others was a game that played out on a daily basis.

So, when the giant man in the crimson chainmail of the Shyd Guard lurched ever too close to Herran and Kylor, they knew death had not yet knocked, but noticed that their door was a tad bit brighter than the other tavern patrons.

"Damn," Kylor whispered.

The man's large scarred face speaking of the brawls that he had been a part of and more than likely, thought Kylor, the man *had caused.*

"What is this here... A Lowman (hiccup) farmer getting far too intimate with a burnt skinned forest urchin?" He rumbled in a drunken slur, waving a crimson gauntleted fist between the two. Herran and Kylor exchanged nervous glances as the tavern became still. Even the annoying minstrels were stifled, after several mugs were used as missiles, erupting about their heads. A grumbling mixture of inebriated faces closed in around them. "Such debauchery you may keep in the Lowlands, boy," hot sour breath spilled forth onto Kylor's cringing face.

Be it the beer, or experience with a drunken Shyd, action came faster than words, as Kylor leapt onto the bar agilely, and booted the bruiser knight square in the jaw. Herran hopped to his feet, grabbed his barstool and swung the heavy wooden stool to the back of the Shydling's already off-balanced legs.

Herran smiled as the man went down, hard, with a *SLAM* on the sticky wooden floor.

The crowd was closing in around them, awakening him to his immediate danger, and Herran unsheathed his long sword while his young counterpart simultaneously bared his short sword. Bent-kneed on the bar, crouching down as a wildcat, Kylor swung with viscous speed, fending off the drunkards with swoops of his blade.

Fighting was an overreaching option, and they both knew it. The patrons would stand behind the mercenary Shydling Guard, for fear of reprisals, while the other Shydling Officers were getting to their feet after gathering their swords to back up their fallen comrade.

Herran took action though, swinging his broad sword over his head in a wide arc, he warned the advancing line. As the creeping dipsomaniacs ducked or fell to the floor, Herran shifted to the right and swung at the painted window on the wall. It smashed into an oblivion of blue crystal shards. Turning toward the bar where Kylor thrashed, warding off the slobbering horde,

"Kylor! Come On!" Herran jumped onto the sill, and then out. Hurdling over several pursuers, Kylor was out the window, in two leaps and a jack rabbit bound off the bar.

They ran into the night like children, giddy with exhilaration. There were shouts behind them, but no pursuit followed. Darting down the road with their swords sheathed, they went to find their horses. "We could have lashed them all!" Kylor boasted with adrenalized glee, grinning like a goblin in a gold mine.

"It was possible friend (gasp), but they were not worthy of such a keen death," with that sarcastic reply, they both burst out with childlike laughter and stopped running. Herran clutched his chest as he sat on the ground. "I'm getting on a bit too much for such midnight antics." It had grown late since he had entered the bar. Time disappeared while drinking.

Kylor crouched beside him, "Where's your ride?"

"By the wayside trees, not far, tied to a farmer's post," he pointed to the trees along the road. The night air felt good on their sweaty bodies, the humidity finally lifted.

"Well, I guess we part here friend, but we'll drink again some night," the black haired boy ran further into the night like a demon, and soon was beyond sight, shouting, "Just not at the Drylock Tavern again! No…"

"Yes, we will," the man chuckled to himself, realizing that the young man did not have a horse to take him home.

And they did meet again. For a full season they met at bazaars, and hunted boar on two successful occasions. Theirs was a friendship looked on with disdain by the majority in the surrounding villages. Old white maids wrapped in shabby brown scarfs scowled at them as the two friends passed their tables at the marketplaces. Mara Chromairen Farmers, mostly male, muttered their disagreements under their breath whenever the two passed them on the crowded streets of the Lowland trading posts. A friendship that seemed unable to wilt was theirs, until one night at a tavern just on the outskirts of their Lowland villages. Human nature would challenge their bond.

*****

The Boar's Gut was slightly friendlier than the Drylock and was common ground for plainsmen farmers and Mara Chromairen clans to drink, yet it was uncommon for them to drink together. Even women occasionally sat at the bar, but the clans seldom shared the same table.

Several of Herran's clansmen had accompanied him that night, as did some of Kylor's. The two clusters sat just a mere couple of splintered seats away from one another.

They had casually ignored each other for the first hour they were there, just throwing back the thick mugs of mead with their cronies.

"Kylor?" Herran moved over several stools, and sat next to his friend. It was always expected when in certain company, that personalities would be warped and radically changed as the comfort of friendship is tested under a new pretense. Being older, Herran expected the silent rift between he and his younger friend when in certain company. This was taught in the Mara Chromairen gospel.

"Huh? Herran, we drink again, eh?" The boy's brain was quite drowned or he had pretended to be more far gone in front of his friends and Herran knew that this was possible if not probable. The two longhaired youths accompanying Kylor pretended not to notice the dark, broad farmer as he found his seat all too near to them. They became quiet and tended to their drinks. Herran, smirked at their backs and turned to his friend.

"Little soaked, are we? Your friends intimidated by an older man? Hey, recall you that night at the Drylock?"

Mead shot forth from the boy's nose, as he erupted with laughter. Kylor's cronies joined in, laughing as well, for he had told them proudly of his escape, leaving out the fact that a practitioner of magic had helped him to do it. Collecting himself he replied, "What of it?"

"During our conversation, or should I say, as our words were interrupted so rudely by the Shyd, you were to tell me of the true argument between our races. I've been intrigued for several months, but never bothered to inquire," the Mara Chromairen drank generously from his own mug, hoping the boy would remember. "You surely had something interesting to say, hmm?"

"Oh, that." The boy's eyes widened with hesitation, but, "Well, the slavery history." Sober, he would have avoided this topic.

This caught the attention of Herran's friends as they quieted and glanced over. One had tapped the other on the shoulder, in order to get him to listen in too. "And what history is that?" asked one of them, who was about Kylor's age, staring with very accusing eyes.

Herran raised a hand to shut his friend up, and looked back to Kylor, intrigued.

"Surely, you do not mean..." Herran narrowed his eyes at his friend.

"The fact that long ago, when our world was young, the farmer plainsmen, of the lowlands enslaved the Mara Chromairen nature lovers...they were given certain privileges after a day's work in the fields."

"That is myth! Mara Chromairens rose when the selfish plainsmen strove to reach this pointless notion, and we enslaved the weak farmers before the Great Cataclysm!" Herran lashed. "Do you really think an army of men with pitchforks held back the slime of the reptilian Sythgorak Armies without the help of Mages? Impossible. Your youth betrays your knowledge of truth."

Kylor scoffed, standing to meet the man challenging him, as openly bold as a Shydling Guard. The two stood firm, facing each other, their eyes met in an icy glare. A familiar silence fell over the patrons. Only the sound of final big gulps of mead could be heard over the clunking of wooden mugs on the tables. All eyes focused on the two challengers. This was a safe fight, a quarrel between lowland plainsmen and mage woodsman also of the lowlands. No officers of the guard, or Shyd involved, so a fight could ensue without fear of an entire village being burned to the ground for repercussion sake.

Herran seethed, spittle shooting between clenched teeth, "I thought you were different from others in your clan, but you believe the same narrow minded foolishness! What do they teach in those ramshackle cabins you call schoolhouses? What..."

Kylor's cronies hissed obscenities in return at Herran.

Herran Malx also became aware that they were the only game in town. Onlookers smiled, sneering, waiting for a fight, ravenous for blood. "What is wrong with the minds of you plainsmen... so starved for entertainment that you forget who the real enemy is?! I actually saw the reptilian beasts in your markets buying *your* food, *your* weapons that *you so pride* yourselves in forging... How could you let this happen? Sythgoraks in the plains! Your ignorance has become desperate preachment on wet parchment. Sad." He shook his head with genuine disgust.

"It is not foolishness!" Kylor was surprised at his own shout resonating through the hall catching the attention of the mass of drinkers. "That *was* the way. Learn you nothing from the elders schooling?!"

"Elders schooling is nothing! Nothing but pale plainsman myth!" He turned to his own cronies. "Come on, we go." Silent turning of heads and stares of interest followed the Mara Chromairens as they gathered their robes from the back of the chairs, now making their way across the sticky floor to the double doors.

There were whispers of, *"Go back to your forest"*

And, *"Go make some soup out of pine needles."*

"What good has your magic done for our lands?"

Just before reaching the doors, Kylor's voice bellowed through Herran's back, "This is not over, *FRIEND*!"

The boy's pronunciation of the word welled an icy pit of premonition in his stomach and Herran closed his eyes with fear because he knew what was to ensue. Whether it was pride, the crowd, the drink, only one tragic rebuttal could follow an argument that could stab a man in the heart worse than a sea siren's bite.

The very thing that Herran had tried to avoid, became a very real beast. He knew it was time to walk away, get out, through the doors before evil pride enveloped the room in a shroud of ignorant bleakness.

Leaning against the bar, holding his drink in the air and grinning, while his friends nudged him in the back, Kylor growled, "To the Cave of Council with it, *FRIEND*!" A wave of breath drawn in all at once, as if a hill troll was about to blow on his own bowl of soup, had silenced the crowd.

Herran half-turned, and looked into the glazed eyes of the black haired boy, sternly, "To the Cave of Council," he replied with vivid melancholy. The defense of his people's history blinded his common sense. An age old argument, taboo among the Lowlander clans alike, had surfaced again like a bug in a blanket. This was a subject rarely policed by the Shydling Officers, for they did not pay mind when the lowlanders fought amongst themselves and decreased their surplus population. This was to be dealt in the fashion of the law of the poor folk. The Cave of Council was the only answer, for honor sake.

*****

Now, with the crowd's waiting outside the rocky outcropping, a judgment would be made, once and for all. An argument in a tavern, would lead to someone's demise once again. Here they were in the Cave of Council where one man would stand correct, the other would never leave. His imprint imbedded on the rock within, forever.

"It could have been avoided, but yet, here we are in this damnedest of places," thought Herran Malx shuffling down the trail. Still awaiting a reply from Kylor, Herran walked on, down the damp limestone path laced with dust, flattened by those before them.

"I believed myself to be stronger than to succumb to the will of a drunk boy's aggressiveness."

"I'm more a man than you. Besides, there is more to this than drunken wisdom, FRIEND!" Kylor stopped, and pointed a finger at the bigger man.

"Do not refer to me as friend, or I'll bleed you here and now!"

Both gripped their sword hilts fiercely, looking away from each other and re-embarked on their mission.

"Not only will I be the one to hold the correct answer to this quest, but I will also be the one to see the light of day again, while you wilt away with the other souls the witch has engulfed." Kylor boasted.

"If only one of us is to emerge, as this game is played boy, you should merely ask the witch to have your soul. It will save me the trouble of releasing it to her!"

The witch. Herran went on, picking his brain with thought of the history of her in his mind. The Queen Witch of the Shydling resided in these walls now.

Too much time to mull about, too much time to turn around. Disappointed in Kylor and how quickly this person could spin on his heels to dispense with accusations that would ultimately kill one of the two men, he could not wane from his own guilty conscious.

This was a plan ultimately. There was purpose in every action he had made since meeting the young man whom he was now as much in debt to as he was ready to watch die.

You can hide the feelings from those around you, he thought; Kylor, his tribe outside, your own tribe of Mara Chromairens, the elder mage, the farmers who waited in the dustbowl arena for one of the men to step outside the wall of the cave entrance in victory, but never in this life can I dismiss what I have lattermost accomplished.

Reasoning with his emotions, the man thought back to his plan of one year ago, while traveling to the borderlands outside of the Shydling Keep with his older brother Caleb. A stronger mage, Caleb Malx had decided on more than one occasion to travel alone (he trusted no one other than himself and his younger brother) to the dangerous wilds of Wilkyus, the land of rich forests of twisting ligorath vines the size of sea serpents. The vibrant green and brown twisting sapsixt trees with their thin twirling branches were just one of the many pure resources that the Mara Chromairen mages sought to gather for healing potions as well as soil enrichment oils. Only the mages of their acolyte clans knew the proper boiling method to cure such oil, culling the poisonous nature aside to provide a much more potent usefulness.

Yes, he knew that Caleb sold these potions too at the bazaars to Shyd as well as the human hating Sythgoraks. Trying to persuade his older brother from sharing such rare accoutrements with races that wished to destroy their own tribe was impossible.

"Do not test my nobility Herran, father tried that once. He now lives alone on the rim of the desert, afraid to even come back to the village." Caleb referred to their home just south of the plains, to the cover of forest where they built their cabin under the cover of the shading pines. Their father had overheard his boys, approaching middle age themselves, plotting to kill the witch of the Cave of Council. By firelight, after a lesson in Mind Silence with a dozen of the others in their vastly expanded village, Caleb had forced his brother to sit, stay and listen to a plan he had been developing since they were children.

"Herran, the witch must die."

The fire cracked with a pan filled with some sizzling sap, filling the air with a syrupy smell, while the men inhaled.

"Clear your head. You will need to practice this potion, and the Mind Silence spell, both of us better had, if one of us is to approach that bitch in the cave. She can read minds, she can make you believe untruths, but worse, so much worse, younger brother is her ability to manipulate men."

Staring deeply into the dark brown eyes of his brother, Herran became frightened by the fire dancing on the man's brown face, highlighting his tight bone structure, shining off his smooth, bald head. "Caleb, you look possessed yourself." He joked.

Caleb threw an arm out from under his brown robe, slapping him in the shoulder, "I'm serious. Soon, one of us may very well find ourselves inside that cave, and when we are deep in the confines of the Queen of the Shyd's lair, we had better be prepared."

Rubbing the stubble of curls on his head, Herran shivered at the revelation. Yes, somewhere in all his years, living with their paranoid father he had come to realize that the very fallen queen of the Shyd, the same bitch that had most of the Shydling women destroyed for their looks alone was now in exile in the Cave of Council in the plains. Hearing it from his older brother now drove spikes in his chest.

"So, it really is the Queen Witch that polices our lands. Father was not fighting dementia… as our own sister thought before she left us."

"Yes it is indeed the Queen of the Shydling. A pestilence in our pure lands. She needs to die. A Mara Chromairen will be the death of her." Caleb removed his robes, revealing his muscled arms and chest beneath his leather vest. He appeared disgusted. "We will make the first push. I know some of the lowlanders, farmers, yes, hard workers but not harsh with the blade, many are still good people who will follow suit, rise up, and we will take the Keep on the borderlands. The Shydling Castle can indeed be taken once their leader has fallen. First. The Witch must die. She provides eyes to the north for *them*, somehow keeping a watch on the Sythgorak Armies, similar to her unnerving ability to monitor our behavior in the plains, or here, under the veil of our forest. It's *INFURIAITING*, Herran. Infuriating."

The fire snapped, as if replying to his brother's frustration and anger. "Caleb, we cannot do this alone. Maybe, just, well, her magic is of such an ancient nature... maybe perhaps," Careful with his words, he knew he was dealing with a steam pot boiling over, "we should just gather father, and leave."

Caleb had glared at him over the fire, pulling his long sword from his back strap, to brandish it over the fire. Of all the memories going through Herran's head now, inside this loathsome cave on his way to seek death, the retained vision of his brother's contempt at his words struck him hardest.

He remembered his brother's next words, "Any creature that has lived as long as she, wielding spells of affliction... molding the very essence of an army with vile speeches, preaching of empirical strength, must be vanquished. Even the Shydling Warriors, with their weapons, expensive armor, and overflowing bellies knew this… Of course they would use her as they see fit, but their leader at one time was a strong mage too…he could not best her, this Malkyre', they called him, whether that was his true name or not. He too is gone, she cast him out, but not before he was able to have her harnessed, and placed inside that cave where she can no longer leave. Powerful magic, Herran, of the type I want to learn to use for our benefit. How was this Malkyre' able to do it? I want to go one step further. Until that bitch is dead, and her overseeing eyes, moldy with crusting death, she will forever put out our flames of hope."

Caleb went on, "Why do you think our healing spells fall short? Our weapons never forged from the powerful ore needed to penetrate Shyd armor? Why in HELLS WRATH, do you think a reptilian magic user is able to fire a missile weapon of affliction at a human, and yet our feeble attempts at such aggressive necromancy fall short of lighting a lantern!?"

Herran turned his head sidelong, warily taking in his stoic brother's face, only to quickly look back down to the fire and the smoking pan, breathing in the soothing steam.

There fell a crackle of pine needles and leaves behind them in the small clearing, close to their cabin's door, someone approached. Smelling the dusty sand of fresh runes, they both knew it was father. He had been meditating by the dry rock quarry again at nightfall. The same quarry that had the carvings of their ancestors doused with the ash of their fallen.

"Boys, mitigating by firelight again?" Their father had his olive hood up, his gray beard poking down to his tight brown tunic. His black skin was ashen from the stony sacred ground of the quarry on the edge of the village. A day of prayer had come to an end.

"Conspiring a certain demise I take it. Caleb, must you bring your brother into this circle of hate." Exhaling, seating himself on a wooden bench opposite his two sons, Velann Malx, was at his own wits end. His sons knew this, though it only showed in his deep breathing. "If you continue on this route, the reprisals will be countless upon our people."

Their father rarely was at their home, only to come for an occasional visit, he also had exiled himself from the tribe to venture the border lands.

"Not if we are victorious." Caleb snapped back.

"At what price, son?"

"What say you about our endeavors, this is not your home anymore old man." Caleb spit through his teeth. "Gave in years ago."

All the men knew that the only way to see the witch was to beg a question of morality amongst their own, or other plainsmen. Someone would also pay with their soul, scraping fingernails maliciously against all the Mara Chromairen religious gospel.

"Manipulate an argument with an ignorant second party, to gain entrance to seek an audience with ...."

"FATHER PLEASE! Do not speak openly... she has ways, she always knows..." Caleb hushed their father, snarling.

*****

Herran wished he could go back to that night, possibly talking sense into his brother, or maybe, leaving alongside their father the following morning. In the end, it would be he, not Caleb that would provoke an audience with the Queen Witch, almost by accident.

Could he possibly follow through, kill the witch, save both their souls? Was this too far reaching a quest for a mere Mara Chromairen squire?

The young man to his left cleared his throat, throwing echoes down the chasm.

His throat suddenly dry, Kylor looked to the ground for solace. His feet shuffled forward, almost unwillingly dragging him to some unknown doom.

"Is pride worth all this? Am I defending my own selfish pride, or the prowess and reputation of my people?" A man before his years, Kylor wished his father was still around to see him emerge from the Cave of Council. Remorseful thoughts clouded his mind, as did the memory of a successful boar kill he shared with the man next to him. Strange how the mind wanders to places to escape an uncontrollable situation. It was only a month ago that he and Herran had sat next to a snapping fire on cool clear night, together feasting on fresh roasted boar that they had killed earlier in the day. This had been the young farmer's first successful hunt.

Kylor had spotted the grunting beast from a tree top, immense for a boar in this particular forest corridor, the boar was the size of a cow! Its skin was gray and rippled with leathery muscles, and it stood taller than a normal sized man. Sniffing the ground beneath them, the creature seemed oblivious to their presence. Herran had taught him this hunting trick, hiding away on a tree branch, smothered in a mud basted stench.

He found that this was no easy task as his feet had nearly slipped from a smooth branch underneath him. Kylor's sweat had dripped from his body, mixing with the mud that they had smeared on their skin, creating a more slippery environment than he was comfortable with. His young impatience rattled the nerves with exhilaration, now that they had actually spotted an animal worthy enough to hunt.

Herran had told him that the Shydling Wilds forested the best boar in their country, but he disbelieved, hearing that the rich Shydling Warriors had picked these vast woods clean of fine game. In due time, with the passing of the afternoon, there it was, through the brambles above, dense with red and green leaves, Kylor caught sight of the grazing beast.

"Of the Gods! Look at the size of that!" Eyes wide with excitement, and maybe a little fear, the boy's voice cracked. A calloused brown hand went to his shoulder and tightened, signaling him to silence his wonderment. Though they were thirty feet from the ground, the beast would turn and flee at any unusual sound, becoming accustomed to Shydling hunters in the area. Unless, of course, as it would turn out, this intimidating creature was hunting as well.

Herran had explained the procedure to his counterpart, and prayed now that the boy remembered, for if one mistaken slip took place it was common knowledge that someone could end up with teeth and tusks in their soft belly.

He was not happy that his hunting partner considered him a boy in his late teen years, unconsciously condescending the arts of hunting to him again and again, but as the man explained, he himself had started hunting giant boar when he was Kylor's age and there were scars on the small of the man's back to prove that a tusk surely had ensnared him when he had not been careful enough. Kylor chose to respect that.

Then, it happened. With a crack! The branch under Kylor snapped and he began to plummet and bounce from branch to branch, descending to the ground, screaming all the way down!

"DAMN!" The man rolled his eyes in frustration, then looked down in time to see the boy finally slump to the forest floor.

Sucking for air, Kylor rolled onto his back. The wind had been knocked from him and judging from the pain on his left side, several ribs were cracked.

It was then that the initial terror struck him; he had fallen to the same ground that the boar was ever so recently standing on.

The surrounding forest was suddenly quiet. The only sound he heard was the sandy dry "gulp" at the back of his own throat. His breathing had regulated. Sitting up, he raised himself slowly on the pine needled carpet. Pain erupted in his ribs, and he squawked while gritting his teeth, trying to remain as quiet as possible. Where was the creature? Looking up to the tree above him, he could not see his friend, who surely was still up there, somewhere. "I wish I was still up there." He thought to himself. Then decided to try and stand.

A hideous wrenching screech came from behind the boy as he stepped one foothold onto the lowest branch of the tree, *thinking* to regain his safer position above. Cold fear flooded his body from his stomach to the back of his neck. The boar had appeared from the brush beside him, only five feet away. Looking over his shaking shoulder, his black hair caked to the side of his face, acting as a sweaty shield, almost as efficient a blockade as a child's blanket, protecting him from a darkened bedroom. Only, this monster was *real* and when its eyes met Kylor's, the young man knew it was going to charge. Thick clear saliva oozed down its chin, the maw opened wide for the attack.

An attack came, but from above!

Herran Malx had dropped from the tree, only feet from above. He fell onto the massive creature's back, throwing all his weight to his arms jabbing the spear piercingly through the bucking beast's scalp, somehow slicing the tough skull. The struggle ended in a heap of dead boar in front of Kylor.

The melee that seemed to last for ten minutes was over in seconds.

"Help me up, Oh lord and king of gracefulness," The sardonic mutter came from under the dead boar. Herran's legs were pinned under it, and he lay face down on the earth.

Smiling, the boy held out his hand and helped to pull him out. "Much thanks, that was impressive," He slumped to the ground again, next to Herran who held his right knee in pain. The dead weight of the creature had landed on it.

Kylor in turn gripped his cracked ribs, searing with the heat of internal bleeding.

"I've had easier game. I've never had a hunt mate that decided to become live bait, though. I'll have to remember that graceful procedure for next time!"

The boy glanced at him with slightly wide questioning eyes.

Herran tapped him on the back, "Just playing my boy, just having a way at you, huh ha ha!" They both smiled and laughed, but simultaneously they also cringed and grabbed at their wounds, moaning dramatically.

Shuffling the dust of the Cave of Council's winding hallway, Kylor came back to the present situation.

That was indeed a fond time. When do I let my pride back away to regain what we had? When do I turn and shake this man's hand again?

Too late. A voice told him in his head. The voice droned, rattling off the vocal chords of the old mage he had run into in town, only days ago prior to this dreaded day. The mage had worn a ragged crimson robe, walking with a brown staff carved adeptly, showcasing a snake wrapping around the entire cane. Cane? That was no walking stick that Kylor had ever seen. Had the man spoken to him inside his mind, without moving his lips?

It had been just after the incident at the Drylock Tavern, Kylor was sent to pick up goat's milk from a farmer's market just outside of their ramshackle town. He hated going there since Shydling Guard's preferred the tasty milk of his farming folk over whatever substance they purchased up north from questionable resources.

Still he preferred going to the markets than allowing his mother or his young brother to go, risking their lives venturing beyond the dirt roads of their own village. At least in their own village, they had the eyes of their own peering through the cracks between their own walls to witness any malfeasance that took their folks away from them.

Slavery was accepted. A family could live if they donated a member to the Shyd, who in turn either put them to work far into the mining realms of Wilkyus or...

His father had left long ago and he wondered, and would forever wonder the man's fate. Leaving of his own recognizance to venture north to bring back wealth for his family, Jekk'Iva Raven had decided to embark on a mission, as so many others before he, to chance that salvation could be found in Wilkyus. Traveling up north, avoiding Shydling forces, Sythgorak Strongholds and any other manner of beast that Wilkyus offered to find the treasures of the wild or at least a better way of life.

More terrifying were the rumors that slavery no longer was an option granted from the Shyd, begging the question, what exactly did they do with the many captured lowlanders, plainsman, and woodsmen alike?

"Rumors grow like tumors when not sprayed down with calming elixir," The old mage before him was tall, lanky, with a pointy nose and chin. His diamond blue eyes were shining under the veil of the crimson hood. He remembered standing roadside, next to a farm stand waiting for a man to retrieve his jug of goat's milk when the mage-looking man, with the frightening tongue for linguistics had approached him, snake staff in hand.

"What old man? I have to be going..."

"Kylor Raven. Yes, you do have to be going." The man had long graying blond hair that fell out from the hood to his chest. Narrow, perfectly square teeth seemed to break free of his thin purplish lips as he opened his mouth to talk freely to him, no longer melding his thoughts inside Kylor's aching head.

"You worry about your father, and how your mother and brother, Kren will survive, you wonder, what exactly do the Shyd do with the women and children they steal in the night? You wonder, dear boy, should you sacrifice yourself to the Witch to ensure the safety of your family, village… Killing her is a rightful choice though you embellish your fighting agility to a point of uselessness. You could indeed win this quarrel, Kylor Raven, but if you were smart you two could work together and kill that wretched bitch for the good of all!" The mage rasped in his face, bending only slightly to meet his eyes, almost equally as tall.

"Who are you? What business do you have? I know Shydling wager on these Cave of Council… endeavors, like it's all a game! Pride is not a game..."

"Pride is the biggest game." The old man smiled. "That is why the witch tried to banish her husband, after vanquishing most of the Shydling women. She was beautiful too once. Pride, greed, evil, quotients of the purest deviations within the human soul. Soon that too, is gone when such a potion is drunk."

"I have no idea what you say…." Kylor took the jug of milk from the farmer, who quickly ducked back into the stand, away from the conversation, as if he knew this mage in the crimson robe and wanted nothing to do with his presence.

Kylor began to walk down the dirt path, several wagons were creating a slight bit of traffic, slowing him from stomping forward. The old man put a hand to his shoulder. The fingers felt like snakes made of ice, fingernails scraped his skin. A very unnerving amount of strength pulsed from the long hands of this arrogant mage.

"Do you know what orders she gave the Shydling? Do you know why the reptilian Sythgoraks, who insult us by walking upright…" (The man was losing his composure, getting louder, and more abrasive) "…why the Sythgoraks do not break from the wilds up north and destroy the Shydling?"

Kylor gritted his teeth, placing one hand on the hilt of the dull bladed short sword hanging by his waist in one of his father's old leather belts. Holding his ground he stood eye to eye with this insistent man who persisted to buy his attention.

"What is it you would tell me, old man?"

"Food. Your people are traded to maintain order among your richer Shydling folk who reside in the safety of the castle walls, while your lowlanders are sent to the swamps of Wilkyus to line the gullets of our reptilian friends. Those mines you hear of are not mines at all, Kylor Raven, they are gathering encampments for the use of processing." The man smiled a wide grin under his pointy nose. The teeth were unnaturally white, gleaming a tight snarl of mockery.

"You insight me. Is this what this is? I know the rumors. What gain have you, if the witch was killed? Why not do it yourself?"

"Her many eyes forewarn her. Be mindful boy, keep to your Mara Chromairen friend, he may have the ability to fool her. She may already know that I have now spoken to you… So many eyes… so many eyes." The man began to walk away.

"What is your name mage? Where is your allegiance?" He shouted at the man's back as he made his way between the farmer's market and the white paneled schoolhouse, down the main road. Wagons were being pulled by horses on either side of the man.

A reply resounded within his skull, hurting at first, the mage's raspy old voice became a younger man's voice. "I assure you, my allegiance with the Queen ended in bitterly sanctioned divorce years ago. Kill her for me. For your clan. For the realm."

There was laughter in his head. Old man's laughter meshing with a young man's giddy chuckles. Then the man disappeared in a crowd of farmers and patrons alike.

*****

Kylor felt the old familiar laughter in the back of his throat, but one glance over at Herran's serious glare reminded him of the situation at hand.

"I hope you are prepared for this, boy! It's almost time." Came the icy whispering reply to his gaze.

"I would not have spoken of the Cave of Council unless I was prepared for the risks involved!"

The pitch of their echoes were becoming less pronounced, ceasing in repetition. A hideous stench gnashed out with a dying dank breeze.

Their boasts had come to a halt as did their leather boots, standing still now under the torches that brought an orange pronounced hue to the mouth of the witch's lair. At least, what they thought to be her lair. All their prior knowledge of this place revolved around stories of the other survivors; fellow clansmen, and in some rare cases, clanswomen. This rupture in time however was the first inter-clan counseling in an era.

"After you, child," Herran motioned, bowing cynically toward Kylor, who acknowledged with a sheer look of disgust from his big hazel eyes, and proceeded with mock bravado.

"How do I know you won't dare to stab me in the back?"

"Not my killing style, boy."

Herran could faintly taste and smell the syrupy residual scent of the bowl of Sapsixt sap. An hour before their clans met outside the cave, in the sandy clearing, he had been inundated with his Mind Silence potion, in order to keep the witch out of his head, and away from his true intentions. Destroy his motivational will of intent, killing his own thoughts, crumbling the rabid viscous hate in his own blood to better the state of the poisoned land they shared. A spell, a taste, a scent, and a potion he cooked up with a strength beyond the knowledge capacity of the average lowland plainsmen or mage squire.

The plainsmen beside him was another question. On first impression he was not the killing type, but his angry youth mentality, agility and sword capable hands told volumes. Could he have overlooked the vague possibility that a farmer, a handsome young lad, this tall man just peeling free from the naiveté of youth, was capable of killing in cold blood? Would Kylor strike out to save his own life, attempt taking down a grown man whom he had once called a friend? Could he deliver a deathblow even with such childish innocence and trepidation in his own counterfeit eyes?

The limestone cavern opened up (audibly with a rush of evil breath) before them in the form of a round dank spheroid chamber adorned with an incredibly flat black soot-like floor.

Webs hung from the high ceiling, thick like wool. Spiders with shiny yellow, green, orange, red and blue shimmering shields on their skin were retreating up the webs by the dozens, rushing up to a ceiling that turned onyx like a void of beguiling reverence.

The chamber was abundantly heated by a bonfire lit in the center. The only fuel was a cross of wood shaped in an "X" that did not seem to burn, yet pink and red flames burned on nothing at all. The fire pulsated with a new color every other second. Blue, red, green, yellow, orange, then blue again.

As Kylor looked up, he noticed dozens of winged black and red demons crouching on rocky ledges, high up on the walls, looking down on them with eager yellow eyes. The men had seen statues of these demons on the edges of the Shydling walls. Imagining, as most plainsmen and woodsmen did, that these statues were to pay respect to the lineage of gargoyle shaped deities whom the corrupt human Shydling seemed to owe some dark debt to. The winged creatures merely kept watch, moving only their yellow eyes with a tilt of the tendons of their necks.

Years of burnt flesh caked the men's nostrils and swirled in dark misty air as they advanced toward the flame. A heavy pulsing beat hummed through the chamber, as if the room itself lived. The bonfire seeming to be the heart.

"Such deviltry," Herran whispered, looking in all directions at once.

"Ayuh," the boy peered about nervously.

"*Deviltry indeed, sweet ones,*" A shrilling woman's voice reverberated all about them, echoing in three different deep octaves. A skeletal woman with a white flowing gown appeared dancing about the fire. Long tendrils of gray-white hair streamed about the scraggy living dead atrocity. The men knew that this was surely the hideous witch of legend. She danced, wretchedly displaying her bones that twined and bent like muscles, gray, and sinewy dead. Deep black eyes pierced their hearts with each turn of her head in their direction. Then the dance ended, and the dead witch stood before them, with a gaping grin of gnarled teeth. Yellow pupils shone in the recesses of her eye sockets of pitch.

"Oh succulent, succulent souls, one shall have pass, the other is ...*mine.* What quibbling altercation has brought thee to seek my beauty?" Her eyes were empty sockets of black, those yellow pupils appeared to be more like tiny lanterns, rather than a working organ. The beams struck both men's chests with a ferocity that was as accusatory as much as they were unavoidably looking deep inside their very souls.

"Let's finish this quickly, Lich!" Repulsed, Kylor swallowed a sandy gulp. Throwing aside his torch. "He claims....."

The thing laughed. The wings of the demons above clattered their glee.

"Do you not find me attractive, worthy of your time, handsome boy," She curtsied, pulling the ends of the long torn bridal gown up. "My husband's gift to me, long ago, when he still loved me, when the land was fresh with opportunity. When he still found me to be beautiful. He did this to me, cursing me here with his envious magic!"

The witch was still across the chamber, but her angry words became snarls on their spines.

"Do you think I do not know why you are here boy? You met my husband. I *see* all he *knows*. I own this land still, even from afar; he knows no safe place from me, for the watchers above are my eyes… oh and so many eyes do they wield for me." A chittering noise above from the spiders applauded the witch, cheering with glee, proud of their work throughout the land. "I never have to leave my exile to control this realm, my husband failed, as did all of you, at being human. Or…"

She stopped, whispering now,"…are we witnessing what humans are now to *become*. Selling their own kind for food to other hideously inferior races… fighting to the death for some drunken argument. Ha…hahah…. Huh? Is that so?"

The witch laughed at her own pride. The spiders continued their chatter so that even the gargoyles above seemed to cower, lowering their heads away from the wool drapes above the towering ceiling.

Herran threw his torch aside and interrupted, "This young corrupted soul begged a question of historical value to my people. The answer to this question will hold significance in the coming millennium of all our peoples. The question of who shall rule who…."

"And who *did rule* who!?" Kylor, erupted, his fear of the hideous witch replaced by anger.

The witch's head turned from Kylor to Herran and then to the fire. Back turned, she broke the silence as the fire crackled in a hazing red whirlwind.

Bones glittered white with the fire's light beneath her pale withered flesh. Blue glistening organs hung wetly under her gown's bodice. Her jaw hung low when she spoke, loose, like a snake ready to swallow its prey.

"I feed off of your societies' lack of faith and knowledge. I use your veins to syphon out the ignorance, so that I can continue to evolve and grow with the strength of others. Always one right, always one wrong! With that, the witch whipped around and pointed a bony finger at Herran, who was taken aback with dreadful fear.

"Finish him, young one, and you shall leave." She hissed.

"Me? I'm to finish him?" Kylor stuttered.

Herran Malx's confidence returned as he unsheathed his sword. "Come 'on boy, you wanted this, now one of us is going to Hell for it!"

Both men stole a look around the wide chamber for the witch's whereabouts.

Kylor Raven unsheathed his short sword slowly. He looked to where the witch was standing, but she was no longer there. Sweat trickled down both their temples, as they stared with perplexed wonder into each other's eyes. Then their swords met in a clang of aggression.

The gargoyles above howled with approval. Herran's strength pushed Kylor to the ground after the initial clash. Then the boy leapt up and waved a mislaying arc over the bigger man's head, who parried with a swing that gnashed the boy's flimsy and dented chainmail armor slightly on his chest. This was a way of compelling the boy to back off. With an upswing, downswing and upswing, their swords clashed, but no more words were said, leaving the conversation to the weapons and their rapid steely phrases that promised pain.

Herran caught his breath and swung up. Kylor ducked the third upswing, and kicked the man in the back of his left knee. Howling in pain, Herran fell to his previously damaged right knee, yet managed to swing with the last bit of adrenaline he had, catching the left of Kylor's ribs, penetrating the armor scarcely.

The boy went down.

"This is not how I wanted this…" Herran whispered through clenched lips.

Putting a hand to his flimsy armor that had been once his father's, Kylor felt the hot wetness of his life fluid begin to spill. The pain would come later. He hoped he would have the chance to feel it. A chance to go home and see his mother again, her face framed comfortably in his mind, wishing he was home and not dying in this most wretched of places. It would be up to his younger brother to take care of her now, and be the man of the house. Could Kren handle that? He was nearly a baby….. "NO, Not here... not now!" Kylor found inner strength from the pit of his abdomen.

Herran strained to get to his feet, but the flashing fiery pain in his knee told him it had been snapped.

"Damn you boy! Don't you know?"

Kylor stood up, pulled back his sword to swing a blow, but loosened his gritting teeth and lowered his weapon as he approached the man. Herran looked up at him and whispered, "All this, for an argument. Could you help an old friend proceed with the righteous plan?"

The boy reached down to take his held out hand, but was immediately thrown aside by an invisible force. The witch was once again upon them. She stood over Herran, grinning.

"Do not look the glum, what it is done is done. One has lost, the other....WON!" A child's rhyme, Kylor remembered from school. Kren still said it now and then before they wrestled.

He watched as the witch's clawed fingers extended and thrust out, piercing Herrans chest. The boney fingernails had extended before his eyes into black tipped talons. All the while, her hideous head was turned, looking at him with her yellow pupils.

"NO!" Kylor tried to get to his feet but was held to the floor by slick black tentacles that had burst through the floor from some hell spawned beast to embrace his entire body.

Igneous fragments exploded in all directions from the crumbling ground under Kylor. Wrapping their foul rubbery muscles around the boy, they were squeezing, but only to hold, not to kill. Their burnt death stench intoxicated their desperately struggling captive. All of his muscles tightened, leaving Kylor to watch Herran's terror unfold before him.

The same tentacles that held him back seemed to be seeping out from the floor of the chamber. One was crawling up to where Herran and the witch stood. She had performed some sort of scraping motion on the man's heart. Black soot appeared on his open vest, below his failing frayed chain mail.

"His heart is pure, he is yours, bather of the deep." The witch stepped back. The tentacle bared up, like a snake about to strike. Kylor could not move, held down by these giant tubes of flesh that stunk like death.

A mouth appeared at the end of the brackish, oily tentacle.

Not a tentacle, but a worm from the depths below.

With razor sharp swiftness it struck Herran in the abdomen, attaching itself.

Herran's whole body shook as his eyes rolled to the back of his head. The man's teeth chattered until they shattered against each other in a bloody crisp mess that oozed down the sides of his face. The witch's overgrown fingers turned a crimson color as the tendril from the deep sucked the very life from the pain-stricken man. The crimson trail seeped all the way up her arm, to her now visible and beating heart; crimson and now plump with life. Herran's life.

Somehow, she managed to share the wealth of Herran's life force fluid and spirit symbiotically with this hideous pet of hers.

"We share. We survive. I have no choice, but to survive. You learn nothing, boy." The witch whispered.

For an instant, Kylor could see the beauty return to the Shydling Queen of old. Her hair was a beautiful brown, wavy, her cheeks warm with healthy skin, eyes of blue. The long needles of teeth dissipated to the perfectly white smile upon pink lips.

Her thin eyebrows braced in a welcoming look, as if she wanted to kiss the young man before her.

She approached, her breath smelled of roses on his face.

"If you find love, friendship, anything in this world worth fighting for, choose the path that turns you to the light. Your dead friend here…" There was nothing left of Herran but burnt flesh on smoking bones. "… Had planned a coup of sorts. Had you given him a chance, maybe you could have overtaken me. To think, after all, the Mara Chromairen was adept in the ways of magic."

She smiled seductively, beautifully with healthy high cheekbones, "No, instead you are left a poor pathetic boy with one less weapon against me, the Shyd and a realm full of hate. *Regret* is my gift to you today. Let it fester in your heart, ripening for me to take away one day."

Crying, Kylor turned way, helplessly weak, he picked up his fallen sword, waving in her direction.

"Too little too late." She hissed, her body transforming back to the undead lich that he had initially met. Her laughter filled the chamber.

Several of the gargoyles left their ledges above, and flew to him as the tentacles from the earth slithered back to the depths. The melee of evil had ended. Lifting him up, the winged creatures dragged the exhausted and screaming human out of the archway entrance. Looking over his shoulder, fighting impotently to pull away from the repulsive creatures, the boy caught a glimpse of the swirling fire. He wretched as he heard Herran Malx's outcry of pain echoing from the fire itself, hollow and fleeting. When he was released of his hold, he turned, only to come face to face with a limestone wall. A wall appeared where the doorway had been. It was done.

Daylight swept across the boy's face prickling with the hope and warmth of forgiveness. He exited the cave. Sweet, vibrant air and sunshine struck his sweaty arms, neck and scalp under his thick locks. The tundra before him was crowded with Mara Chromairen Woodsmen and his own plainsman farmers. The world opened up before him at the very place where he and Herran, his former friend, had entered together.

Two separate crowds had gathered. The many representatives of his own clan erupted with cries of triumph and cheer. Most of his own villagers were there, as were villagers of Herran's clan, dressed in robes, holding staffs, they stood straight up, staring ahead at Kylor from the other side of the clearing.

Upon his exit the two dozen or so mages turned their backs and began their slow journey home. There were several women that had screamed outcries of desperate protest, denying that they had lost one of their own. The tallest member of the clan, a gray bearded one, "the chieftain," thought Kylor, approached him. Reddened sad eyes shrouded by thick gray eyebrows met Kylor with a stern wisdom. A taller man was beside him. Kylor could not meet their eyes, but assumed these were family members.

"You've won today. You must feel as a man," The bearded elder dressed in layers of robes, turned his back and followed his people. The taller man beside him stood for several seconds longer. Kylor could feel his icy glare from beneath his robe, yet refused to look up at the man seething with hate. He had Herran's eyes and facial features. Then, he too fell in with the elder, walking away towards the forest on the outskirts of the tundra.

Some of the younger plainsman boys shouted obscenities at their back as they approached, making their way to Kylor, champion for the day. His peers, elder clansmen, and even whole families that he had never spoken a word to, encircled the dazed and emotionally spent fellow Lowlander.

One man in a crimson robe stood aside from everyone. Graying blond hair blew in the breeze from under the darkened hood. The familiar staff carved with the snake twirling around it was in his hands.

The head of the robed figure was shaking from side to side, as if in disappointment, "Your father left for noble reasons, a journeyman at heart, willing to rid the land of the vile disease that walks it. Jekk'Iva Raven was a man of principle. His son is one of ignorance, with much more learning to do before he ever moves on to make better for his family than a life of slavery and death. A rotten pit makes for a formidable tree of impending abominations."

The raspy insipid voice of the mage whom he now knew to be the once husband to the Queen Witch and to be Malkyre'for certain, emanated inside his head. Then he too turned and also made his way from the sandy plain outside the Cave of Council to disappear into the shade of the surrounding woods leaving a trail in the sand from his staff.

Walloped on the back with unexpected congratulations, jeers of pride surrounded Kylor Raven as his people lifted him to the air. Painfully empty, and feeling more like a boy than ever in his years, he glared back over his shoulder at the wall where the cave entrance had been. The crowd celebrated in ignorance to his feelings and he was carried off to the carriages. A painful grimace tightened across his face. Holding back tears he thought, "What have I done?"

- 6 -
THE COMMUNE

Devon put the book down on the counter. The rough red cover sickened him, reminding him of the rows of library books back at UCLA that he would never read after dropping out. This one was special. Exhaling, placing the yellow phone handle back in its cradle on the wall, he played with the twine of yellow wires hanging from the phone in Nancy's hallway. He was sure Nancy and her young boy toy were smoking and screwing rather than packing their bags for the trip to Pennsylvania. Back home for him. He wondered when she would tell her young lover that she was pregnant with his child. Keeping high all the time was an easy job, necessary to self-medicate when the world was coming to an end. Equally effortless to avoid talking about serious issues, like marriage, pregnancy and income. Rebuilding was still in question as the world tried to even out the interrupted equilibrium of rationale.

He scratched at his beard, agitated with the conversation that he had just had with his older brother back in the Pittsburgh area. Never wanting any part of his brother's arcane interactions with authority, he left the commune in Zelienople a year before the "big happening" and all the atrocious shit went down. Long gone were the simple days of selling his brother's popular strain of acid throughout Butler County Pennsylvania. Of course when the unthinkable becomes the new reality, the only positive aspect was that he and his brother had been exonerated of all their charges in Evans City and Zelienople. Devon and his brother Neville had already moved to California to avoid being arrested right away a couple of years before the madness went down. Death, blood, riots all provoked by a supernatural force or disease released by the government. The latter excuse Neville used when he moved back to southern Pennsylvania to start it up again, feeling he could feed off the negativity of a broken kingdom.

"It went down." Chuckling to himself, Devon was still rubbing his unkempt brownish-red beard, now resting his head on the phone box itself that hung on the wall connecting Nancy's parent's kitchen to the hallway. He could hear Nancy and Peter banging the headboard of her mom's bed against the wall. "How in Pete's sake can you two even be in the mood...?" He picked up his knapsack, containing all his belongings, threw it over the shoulder of his army jacket that normally he only wore for protests, but those were dying out now, being that *everything went down.*

"Come on. We have to get going. It's a long walk to Pennsylvania if we miss this last bus out." Not knowing whether he was more perturbed by his numbskull friends' ignorance to what was happening around them or the disturbing conversation he had just had with his older brother Neville. Devon slapped the red hardcover journal on the counter with an open hand. Placing it into the pocket inside his army issued "protest" jacket, as Nancy referred to his favorite coat as, he made sure it was secure, tightly close to him. If they were to get robbed, or worse, attacked by the "new forms" he knew that he could give up his knapsack with all his underwear, weed, socks and his scrap book that he had made on his own with clippings of Porky Chedwick and that crazy radio personality with the great voice, Wolfman Jack. Devon loved music. He wanted to be involved somehow, and now that things "went down" he had to find ways to preserve what he remembered, what everyone forgot, and what he loved. Music.

The Hollies were playing off of his transistor radio in the kitchen, singing about a bus stop during his phone conversation with his brother. Neville was dictating as he normally did during his one sided conversations with his younger brother. This time it was about finding the book for a second time and buying it back. Devon hated when his brother was right, and this time, book and all, he hit the nail on the head. Neville had tried to start up a following out in California, promising once they became popular at "sit-ins" and concert gatherings that he would buy Devon a guitar and let him begin to perform. Make a name for himself too. As it turned out, Neville did not have what it took to get into the girls pants out east. They were savvier, progressive and more prone to follow some of the more practiced madmen, who had better drugs and accommodations. Before the world changed.

As for charismatic fellows with shitty accommodations, Devon found a few. The place that Devon met Nancy "the future movie star, like Barbara Parkins" as she would say and the young former mechanic, Peter, had just escaped from what had been an acid fueled desert nightmare. Peter and Nancy were glad to leave with him.

Come to think about it she did resemble Barbara Parkins, he thought to himself.

Nancy's parents were gone. She was sure they were dead with the first wave that hit California. With the overgrown influx of population heading to the east, when it really hit California the wave would be even more deadly than the initial frays in the outskirts of the nation. The radio warned to evacuate major cities till the National Guard had a grasp of things. So when they had heard about the busses heading back to the Midwest they left the commune out in the desert hills; that nightmare in the making known as Spahn Ranch, in order to go back to her mom's place in Orange County. Things were a bit under control, temporarily, but per Neville and that book of his, the situation was far from over. Most of the activity had happened on the eastern seaboard and if not for folks moving westward, this disease, virus, or whatever in hell it was may never have gotten this far. A ghastly and inconceivable invasion had swooped in but was somewhat under control by local jurisdictions and now his tumultuous brother wanted Devon to head back into the fire.

"Living out in the woods, desert or mountains secured your chances to survive. Less people, more landscape to see the chaps coming." Neville had said on the phone to Devon on the first night when they broke into Nancy's parent's house. He sounded tweaked out on speed.

Devon mulled over his brother's words from that night a couple of days ago, almost as clear as Neville's desperate ramblings rasped in his ear just now. "Did you get the book back? Devon, we need it. You will not believe until you see." Devon could hear the dope crazed voice of his older brother, while some new hippie chick giggled with over-stimulated sensual whispers, more than likely sitting in Neville's lap. Clearly on the other side of the phone, some girl named Marly was groping him, stroking him or whatever sex fueled frenzy he managed to get his followers into.

"Yes, I went to San Francisco. Found the old shop. I got it. It was dangerous, so many people, so many "*new forms*" man, I can't believe you would make your only living relative do that Nev, so uncool man, so fuckin' uncool." He knew Neville only heard the words "*I got it*" referring to the unpublished book with the strange markings inside, no copyright, or discernable date. Neville had sold the journal to a pawn shop on Haight-Ashbury when he was unloading all his belongings to head back east after failing to fit in with the sophisticated western hippies who merely seemed angry at their rich parents and limitless sunshine. He had told Devon, two years back, how he could not handle these condescending pricks pretending to like The Doors because someone said just how "out of site" the music was. Neville just saw Jim Morrison as another alpha. Competition. At the same time, Devon started to see a frightening parallel between his brother and others he came across in these unsettling times.

"I'm *out of site*, bro. I'm leaving. You'd be smart to follow. You aint getting laid out here, face it. You got looks over me too, but you getting' none." Neville had slapped his brother in the face, awakening him from a dope infused stupor and left soon thereafter, leaving their squatter's paradise.

The small red hardcover book that read "People and other Misconceptions" by some unknown pagan preacher that only went by the name Malkyre', had made the rounds all about the beatnik scene for a while. Devon could remember going to see Strawberry Alarm Clock at a small club in L.A. with his brother, who broke out the book at the bar deciding to recite some excerpts during intermission between bands. The words got the attention of almost every stinky patron, beatnik, and hippie alike. He had to admit, the words were alluring. More often than not the words from this self-proclaimed *"Seer"* came to fruition. Some predictions had materialized throughout the years that Neville owned the thing during the Beatle invasion when they were kids, consulting it up until that war in the Nam that they all knew as a waste of human souls. How this book told certain tales ahead of time was something that troubled Devon as much then as it burned now while he was staring at the yellow phone on the wall, waiting for his friends to stop screwing.

"Malkyre'," He said the name aloud. What kind of name is that? He knew somewhere in the book the dude revealed his name, but in his own cloud of pot fueled forgetfulness, he never committed it to memory. No one had known who the dude was back then anyway. Probably some fascist hiding behind his own made-up propaganda. Cedric? Nah. He could care less about the made up name, for the words within were the meat on the bone.

They were kids just going through an old book shop on Carson Street in Pittsburgh when Neville fixated on the journal. Obliged, Neville felt he must have this book. Devon looked at it as someone's old family cookbook sold at an estate sale. Yet, the red hard covered curse had made it all the way to California with them.

"Guys, let's get a move on, huh? We do not know how many busses gonna be doin' this trip huh? I don't wanna get crass, you hear?" Devon lit up a cigarette, stepped outside to the front yard of suburbia. Smoke filled the air, cars piled on lawns, bodies…

Devon's stomach fired up with acid at the thought, looking at the bodies torn into contorted shapes with clothes like crumbled paper and entrails staining the grass and streets like red ribbon candy. Fire, police and EMT personnel scrambled to pick up the pieces left behind by the local posse. He had no fear of lighting up the joint outside the foyer of the ranch model home. He heard the Dave Clarke Five's "Because" come on from the kitchen, cooling him down some. "Someone was still spinning records, even now." He thought, "Fukkn California."

Peter must be in the kitchen, he thought, hearing the radio turned up a notch. Tons of pirate stations were popping up in light of the devastation. "Vultures," thought Devon.

Then the younger man stuck his mop of brown hair out the screen door scratching at his pork chopped sideburns. He was shirtless and smelled of sex. "Hey, man, we goin? Can I grab a hit off that bro?"

Devon removed his orange tinted sunglasses, rubbing at the rectangular lenses nervously wiping them clean of the steam rising from the burning bodies in the makeshift bonfire in the front yard to the left. Firemen were dumping bodies onto it, careful to be sure none of the victims were still moving. Live or dead.

"Get Nancy. Two of you, clean up. Tell her to change her threads, no more of that brown flower print dress that stinks like you now, and you, please, a clean shirt. I'm not traveling for days with you two skuzz buckets in close quarters, and friggin' you two smelling like each other." Devon took a drag, meeting the slight young man's stoned gaze and middle finger. Annoyed, he cynically tapped on the book in his inner jacket pocket. "Fantastic."

*****

"Route 80 had been the best bet for sure," Nancy shouted with a smile, hopping out the side of the blue van. Peter caught her in his boney arms. They shared a smile. Devon waived to the man in the driver's seat, saying thank you for the ride. The man with the paisley collar that hung to his chest, open three buttons down, nodded, after watching Nancy's tight ass in the pastel green slacks when she stepped off the chrome.

"Good luck. And stay off of the turnpike. Lots of unfinished business there. There's a gravel road that will take you to a lodge, if that's where you're heading. I'm not prying but there ain't much else out here." The man with the wide rimmed brown sunglasses held out his hand for payment.

Devon did not want to tell the man where they were going, though a road would be nice, he decided it safer to follow his brother's directives, so not to get shot by Neville's own scouts.

"Pay the man Nancy." Peter giggled, still high from the hits in the back of the van.

She promptly smiled, looking up at the driver seductively and flashed him with her head turned to the side, sticking her tongue out at her friends.

"Jesus." Devon shook his head.

Peter danced about in a frenzy of laughter, tripping over his own bell bottoms.

"Seen plenty of those miss. Fifty miles since Ohio. Twenty smackaroos, friend." Louis Armstrong's "What a Wonderful World" hummed from the passenger side window. They had listened to that and the Rolling Stones the entire way. Not many radio stations were playing music again yet and the middle aged gentlemen named "Just Dan," owned only two 8-Track cassettes. He had approached and offered them a ride outside a bar in Elyria, Ohio, where the bus driver claimed he would go no further. Also happened to be a place where Neville informed him there would be many drivers for hire at said bar.

Devon handed him a twenty and the blue van with the bubble windows and grim reaper painted on the side in purple took off in a cloud of exhaust down 40 east. They had come south of Pittsburgh on Rt.70 and then by way of 119. The closest "Just Dan" would take them was to the sign that read Ohiopyle State Park, agreed upon by Devon, as his brother Neville's campground was somewhere outside the park near the Youghiogheny River.

There were few border patrol stops, as most public and government workers alike were busy trying to clear the highways of abandoned vehicles or brush aside some of the "new forms" that still scattered along the roadsides.

"He was a real creep." Nancy twirled her braids that hung down to her chest in tight knots. Big purple bubbly plastic hair ties held them in check at the end.

"Hey Dev, how are we supposed to find your bro from here? It's going to be dark soon. Man, what if he's just as batty as the last buckaroo we stayed with...? He's just east coast/mid-west crazy and not California Jive, right?" Peter was tightening his boots under his light blue bell bottom jeans. He wore a matching denim vest that did not cover his skinny waist. "I'm stifled." Taking off his vest, he began to place a red bandana about his head. "Friggin' humid."

"We hike about a mile into the woods, just about where that park sign is. He said we will meet one of his guys there. They are armed, so stay together. This is how he managed to keep his people safe during this mess. Staying out of the major cities, or populated towns, and keeping scouts out around the clock. Some straggling dead may still be wandering the roads so we stick to the woods for now, per him." Devon adjusted a blue bandana around his tight reddish brown wave of hair. Removing his sunglasses, he lit a joint from the top of his army pocket. His thick brown eyebrows were dripping with sweat, irritating him slightly more than the two goddamned love birds he found himself in the company of.

"So, Neville, he's a bit more hip than he was back when you were in the service, Devon? We can trust him...maybe trust his smoke a bit more than the skunk we are used to?" Nancy had been nagging him the whole way on the bus to Ohio about the possibility of high quality pot.

"Hey, tweaker queen, keep it cool. He didn't last this long by being stupid. Before it all went down he was selling his shit for a good price. Sold some good trips too." Devon turned on the pretty girl who rarely acted their common age, just pushing thirty, Nancy tended to digress to her younger boyfriend's age bracket.

"Yea, Nance. Don't be a drag. How could it be any worse than staying with that Charlie guy in in the desert? Whether he did something really bad, or was about to do something really, really hairy, remains to be seen." Peter, wise for his eighteen years referred to the commune they had previously holed up in, then promptly left due to the foulness of the company they had found themselves in.

Silence fell between the three travelers, proceeding onto a very narrow trail that broke through the dense forest before them. Night was indeed coming and the trail was only the size of a single bicycle tire.

"Listen you two." Devon turned to look at the young man and the pretty brunette behind them. He liked them better when they were frightened. Seemed to keep them focused. They had all abandoned the last commune together, fearing that something dreadful was coming, even before the "new forms" began walking about. All they had heard, initially, were radio rumors of the horrors out here, before it spread west.

Now they were in the thick of it.

"Walk quiet-like. Listen for crunching brush, listen good. No more talking. We will be found by Neville's guys. If something else finds us first, I want to be ready. He shifted the 45, loosening it from his belt in case of a quick encounter. Each of them had one. Nancy reached for her backpack to get hers out now. Peter had his drawn, almost always, when they traveled on foot. This made Devon nervous. "Neither of them had looked at a gun before this petulance rocked the scene." He thought to himself.

"Keep the guns pointed down please." Devon whispered.

Taken by surprise several shadows emerged out of the gloom of the forest on either side of them far too quickly for them to respond.

*****

"And so it I tell you, decades under my feet through many guises, I leave these thoughts behind, to not only boast of my many lives and the sizeable tastes of cloaks I wore, but to warn, because it is only fair? Right? Of course. *Natural* occurrences; hurricanes, volcanoes, monsoons and more commonly subduction zones that open a wound in the earth to bleed a malignance on the land are as much to blame as otherworldly projectiles penetrating your skies to fall foul upon your family outing. It happens. (I'm snickering now, for I have seen it).

I am damned. Therefore I have been given such liberties to see disasters first hand and survive. A purveyor of the dark arts in life, married to a self-proclaimed witch, I was provided more than a glimpse into the netherworld that you fear. I'm a Seer. In life, my name was Cedric Bodnatsen, a long forgotten moniker.

Of course, I'm not without a sense of humor, tinkering in the dark for the precise genre of art to personify and entertain myself. Yes mostly myself. Watching humans squirm into and out of a situation that was beyond their scope of their very existence also provided decades of loneliness of the type that teaches one how to entertain oneself professionally. Decades of impatience and evil." —Malkyre'

Neville closed the book, his pointy chin willowed with wisps of a beard he could never quite grow in properly. Dressed in a brown velour leisure suit, he stared at his brother and two loyal friends by his side. "This man was brilliant, and see, he does say his real name brother Devon, you just never read it all the way through."

"I did. Just did'nt care to retain it." Devon sneered.

"I missed this book. Thank you Devon. How much did you have to buy it back for?" Neville paced in front of his new crowd of disciples.

"Thirty bucks. The same turkey you sold it to. Apparently it was a hot item that kept getting sold back to the old San Fran Peddler. Now are you going to read the part..."

Ignoring his brother, Neville pranced about the center of the common room in the lodge. His men had ushered his brother and guests into the lodge, offering some Schaeffer's and water bong hits of his weaker blend for guests.

Two men with rifles, long hair under biker hats and open button down paisley shirts stood by the frail white door. Twenty or more folks surrounded the room, like wallpaper, they hung onto Neville's every word. One girl was completely naked in the corner with the exception of a pink scarf on her head holding her red hair back in an unruly bundle.

Some giggling blonde dude that had to be just out of his teens snapped his fingers like an exclamation after every last word their leader said. Devon and his friends had learned that the young surfer looking dude's name actually was "Snappy". The kid was dressed in trousers that his mom had bought him before the fall, cowboy boots and a tight big collared tan sports shirt. Smoke hung down two feet from the low ceiling, concealing the brown wooden paneled walls that encircled them. The nude pink scarfed girl made Nancy nervous, visibly, so Peter held her in his arms tightly, with a fake smile on his own face. To the two of them, this was equally as creepy as the last place they had found residence.

The furniture was a bit better. Couches lined the walls, with big fluffy cushions. Some of these cushions were used on top of the many area rugs for Neville's followers to lay down upon to listen. The sound of a lighter somewhere constantly wisped the air of the room while bongs were lit or joints were passed.

Several of the long haired bearded men sitting around a table drinking beers were eyeing up Nancy's tight pastel pants, noticing the natural beauty, now making Peter very uncomfortable. He had reached around her to button up her white blouse. Her cleavage was too welcoming to the creeps from across the room. He knew he was too small to protect her from *that* many grown men.

Neville was as giddy as a kid on Christmas. Devon knew this about his brother, that indeed the end of times as the rest of humanity saw it was Neville's dream come true. He saw himself as more powerful than the average man left standing, for now his foreboding sermons had rang as genuine.

"The fascists have lost the god war man. What have I been saying?! Yea, sure, the sheriff and his boys in the burgh have things under control, for now…." Silence hung in the air as Neville twirled on his platform shoes, all for show to catch the little surfer boy, Snappy, off guard, mid-snap. They smiled at one another and then laughter filled the lodge common room. Neville of course making it clear that it was fine to laugh at that moment by over compensating his obnoxious volume.

"*For now.* Yes." The theatrics began anew, tossing the suit jacket onto a couch of onlookers, he raised his white sleeved arms in the air under his tight brown vest. Gold chains, with crosses hung gaudily about his veiny neck, shaking when he began to dance about the room, grabbing the attention from all while showing off for his own brother. "….NOW… local boys in blue and war mongers have control of their own tiny jurisdictions but for how long, really? Cause they're out there! You saw them brother?" He was in Devon's face again. Ripping a joint from a tall handsome man in a green pea coat seated on the arm of an orange couch, Neville took a drag and blew it into his younger brother's face.

"We share here. We have food, running water….the river will continue to provide for us…..Shhh listen…" Dramatically, Neville put a hand to his ear, some ash from the joint still hung on his thick moustache. "You can hear the precious flow from here. The river is right down the hill. She will provide." He motioned to the round wood card table in the corner where the tougher looking men were. They were larger, muscled, armed with belts full of visible ammo, and rifles on their shoulders. "And they will protect… As long as Marly keeps them fulfilled." Smiling widely, Neville looked to the nude woman smiling with bright yellow teeth, stone faced in the corner.

Snappy snapped his fingers, grinning through his thick blond locks on his face.

The naked woman stood, her pink scarf falling to her shoulders with her red hair, making her way to the table. In less than seconds, the sound of a zipper "unzipped" while the woman named Marly bowed head deep into the lap of one of the guardsmen.

Devon tried very hard to ignore the moaning in the corner in succession to the slapping of mouth on flesh. Looking to the eyes of every one of his brother's followers he knew there was not one among them that flew in a straight line to the rational factory.

"Neville, please read *that* section to them. Let our trip here at least make sense please." Devon smacked a joint from Peter's mouth just as the tall dark haired man in the pea coat came over with the dropper to douse the end of the joint.

Peter looked disappointed. Nancy however already had a fag from Mr. Pea coat man, who was now blotting some of Neville's secret ingredient on the joint. She shared with Peter.

"Are you certain your woods are safe here...? (Cough cough cough...)" Nancy's eyes watered up, feeling the effects."

"No. My pretty Cali lady of the braids. No one can be certain. That is why we take precautions. Scouts out there all the time... well cared for." Neville waived a hand to the round card table with the men and that Marly girl hard at work while new zippers opened. "However, none of my number have perished. The river to one side, mountainous woods of the Laurel Highlands surrounding the other... So my boys, my own posse, can see the *new forms* coming, these, oh what do they call them now on the radio, monster marauders? Ha ha-ha. We are fine as wine here my foxy lady. Even Snappy over here feels safer here than he did in California. Yeah this hodad came from the same place you did!" Neville poked fun at the teen.

"Hey, I surfed, that's not fair..." Snappy laughed back.

"Well not anymore. No one will be surfing for very long if they stay in those overcrowded cities. Here. Well here, brother Devon and friends, bringers of the feast... " He held up the little red hard covered book. "...you will be safe."

Devon prepared himself for the coming reading. They had not been in Neville's commune for longer than three hours and already he could see the brainwashing take hold on his friends. Peter was looking uneasy, taking a beer, sharing a grin with another pretty blond girl in white go go boots that climbed up her sexy knees and a purple form fitting mini dress. A purple headband striped across the top of her scalp showing off her impish face and blue eyes.

Peter walked behind Devon, whispering, "At least it smells a little better here."

Devon did not see them leaving here anytime soon. Maybe it *was* safer.

The commune consisted of a cluster of lodges formerly belonging to a catholic summer camp, (*The Chariot's Comin' Boys Camp*, read the broken sign in the Courtyard by the driveway entrance) just up a steep incline of rocky outcroppings above the Youghiogheny River, deep in the woods.

Vividly it seemed that the guardsmen truly did not mind their work. Like himself, Devon could see that some of the men were ex-military, unless the dog tags around their necks belonged to persons long gone. It worked both ways when he had had attended the Vietnam protests, consisting of both heroes and villains. All of it sickened him.

So did this show that his brother was putting on.

Now tall Mr. Pea Coat dude came by with two gorgeous young ladies, also in go go gear, hair down to their backs and bedroom eyes. They all had trays of what had to be the window pane formation, crystalized to Neville's standards that he and his brother used to sell up north of Pittsburgh. Soon the tiny crystals were wrapped up, mixed with the buds in a pile on a small TV table near the kitchen unit of the large room. Devon knew what this stuff could do, postulating a euphoria that could put you out for days with its potency.

When it was offered to him by one of the pretty go-go girls, he responded, "No, trying to cut down." The girl tilted her pretty little head like a confused puppy. Someone across the smoky chamber had put a record player on and the tune, "Rain, Park and Other Things" by the Cowsills filled the room with happy pleasant vibes. Some people danced, especially when the music shifted to The Grass Roots, "Lets Live for Today," there was not one person who could not smile. The music deterred Devon's mind briefly. False comfort, perhaps, but so welcoming.

Peter was beaming now, dancing with both Nancy and the pretty girl in the purple dress and white boots. Devon had not seen the boy honestly happy in months. Maybe his brother had it right? Was he really the only "jive bully dulling the buzz in the room?" Nev would say to him.

No. He was not. There was another girl standing by the window, next to the front door. She was wiping her tears on the fringes of the orange, green and white checkered curtains. Was she disturbed by Neville's reading from "Humans and Other Misconceptions?" A book that was more than likely written by some beatnik hipster who sold it for weed money at Golden Gate Park, than a prophet that Neville truly believed it to be.

"Are you ok?" Devon touched the girl on the shoulder.

She flinched. "No." The girl was wrapped up in a wool coat that clearly did not fit her. The mascara ran down her face in rivers. Blue eye shadow caked her eyes too. "Are the contents of that book true? Like, how your brother told us? Was that Cedric guy a prophet, lay it on me... please!?" She looked up. No older than twenty, this girl had genuine fear in her eyes. Maybe she had lost family members to those things? There's no telling what an individual had witnessed. Hiding behind the veil of drugs and alcohol could only hide everyone's past for so long before the memories came back, tenfold. In a commune, such as this, however, most of the folks had already left home, leaving family behind to forget anyway.

"Um, I can't deny the truths that I have read. Not now. We had that book for years before this happened, and, well, crazier people than my brother saw it as truth, so I was not prone to believe a lot of the supernatural stuff. I mean who is going to believe some surf Nazi swag dealer claiming to be a warlock from centuries old, preaching about end of the world shit… but then, some of the things happened."

"Who would dare bring a child into this world?" Her tone was threateningly deep. Pushing away from Devon's touch, the girl ran out the door across the lot between the lodges, disappearing into the confines of one of the smaller cabins to the right next to the woods.

"Don't trip on Lara, man, she'll bum you out till the end of time, bro. She was quite the disappointment. Post natal syndrome they call it, this was different though. Born stillborn." Neville had come over, straining an arm around his taller brother, high as all hell.

The brothers watched as her cabin door opened. The curvy woman, healthy by comparison to the thin waif girls surrounding the room they were currently in, threw a white cloche on her head with a big crimson flower on one side then continued to run to the woods on the right side of the campground. Neville seemed suddenly sobered, shouting "WARREN!" to Mr. Pea coat, the tall handsome man with the greasy dirty dark hair. "It's Lara again. Go get her Warren."

Listening to the conversation, Nancy had come over too, very interested in Mr. Pea coat man, now known as Warren. Devon knew that this was just her attention seeking behavior that she performed when her boy Peter was straying with other girls, younger girls. "She's distraught. I'll go to her. Bad trip, right? You say she has a child?" With that Nancy was running out the door following Warren.

"No, wait… ugh… whatever man." Neville swiped one of his special joints laced with the speckles of window pane from one of his Go Go Girl waitresses. Firing up a match he took a drag. "Dev, take a hit. You'll need it." Neville opened the book again, picking through the pages, "Ah, here we go. This is the ditty that made you come all this way Devon."

Devon reluctantly took the roach clip, sucking in a drag of the sour smoke, staring at his shorter older brother puffing out plumes, fearing that maybe taking their chances out in the wilds or even Pittsburgh, a major city, would have had less risky results than staying with his wild eyed megalomaniacal brother whose delusions outweighed his intelligence.

Peter came over in a sudden frenzy. "Man, she shouldn't go running around like that. Why is Nancy going out in the woods after those cats? What's the deal? She's pregnant you know, two months."

Neville looked at the wild eyed boy, "You're young boy. But yeah, go get your woman. They have a better chance at getting pumped with some iron by one of my boys out there."

"Pregnant. So she told you Peter? You dumb skags." Devon took the roach again, snatching it from his brother's hands and sucked in a much larger drag.

Shaking off the interruption, Neville and Devon watched Peter almost fall across the gravel courtyard, gathering himself in his light blue denim vest, high as a kite, he ran in his heavy boots to the trail where Nancy and Warren had disappeared after the Lara woman.

Gathering around their leader, Devon was uncomfortable with how close the stench of cigarettes, laced weed, beer and body odor had engulfed the air around him. His knees were buckling a bit, nauseated too with the site of his brother in his brown vest again and brown polyester pants (did he think that made him look powerful?) waving around in front of him to get everyone's attention. Devon noticed that some of the armed biker looking types had also gone outside to pursue the distraught Lara chick.

Neville was not one to overtly show concern for another person. No. He was ostentatiously looking out for this Lara's welfare, so something was amiss. Devon stopped caring about it, just trying to get his bearings, shifting in his boots from side to side with the wicked buzz of the window pane strain that had supplied his brother's living expenses up until the dead began to rise from their graves. Yet, he had a fortress of solitude, soldiers that obeyed him and women…

More women removing their clothes. Boots slid off, one piece dresses slid down, giggles with tantalizing teasing come-ons echoed around the open common room as bodies fell to the many shag area rugs placed just for such an occasion.

Snappy was rolling around with the cute girl still wearing her purple dress, purple head band falling to her neck so that her golden blond hair fell to her face. Marly, already naked was snaking her hands up the back of the girl's dress, having her way, while the pretty girl in the white go go boots continued to ride Snappy the young surfer.

"Jesus, Nev, what is in this stuff…?" Devon was trying to take in the sights of the orgy beginning around him, striving to keep his own focus on his brother standing in the center with the book before him, open for a reading. Others stood clothed, drinking, smoking, and watching. "Set me free why dontcha babe…" Blared off of the record player.

"Simpler times revered simpler means. Pirates, nautical experts, sailors… even the best were all misguided when looking to the stars. The blanket of diamonds above their voyages were not telling stories. No. They were all idiots overlooking a mere map for an existential canvas! Fools. My contrition for those before me was in their ignorance. The fear should not come from the stars above themselves weaving tales of honor and brutality. Their true concern should have been what those stars shall bring down upon the Earth!" Neville smiled up at the ceiling to the delight and hollering of his followers grinning over exuberantly with his pointy features like a court jester. Then he continued to read from the pages.

"A light would explode about the stratosphere, an inconceivable gift radiating from another world will illuminate almost just beyond the naked eyes reach..." Neville, high on his own window pane laced weed, equally as his love of himself, was feeding off the attention of the women on his legs, groping for him to just look down at them.

******

Peter wished he had listened to Devon and not taken a hit. Eventually he caught up with Warren the Pea Coat Man and Nancy. They stood in a clearing. He could just barely see the other woman, who had gone running into the woods, yet there she was. Lara was standing in the center of the clearing but the gleam off the river below, a fifty foot ravine, was shimmering bright behind her. He could make out the cloche hat that she was wearing when she had gone running off. Nancy was backing up, getting closer to Peter. Just before them was a makeshift grave, adorned with a wooden cross. Broken pieces of a tiny coffin were strewn about the pine needles next to the hole in the ground appearing to be three feet deep as it was across. A name was carved into the cross. Peter's eyes had not adjusted yet.

*****

Neville was spitting with exhilaration, "The dead shall rise, reminded they are merely a house to those recently released from the lonely dark, tapped on the shoulder by the claws of Hades, AWAKE, dear ones... there is a new shell for you... In the cloak of their coffins a knock came, in the form of radiating heat cast from above and the recently dead...."

*****

"Nancy, what's going on?" Peter asked, the woods lit by the moon illuminating the mist into a frothing blue. A boulder had either fallen on this pine needled splotch of woods, smashing in all directions or a courtyard of rock outcroppings had formed from below as natural run off created the clearing. Objects were shimmering on the ground. Appearing like rocks with the exception that they were moving. Apple sized silver, green, yellow, orange and blue metallic glowing spiders with an odd armor were retreating to holes in the ground by the huge shale stone broken boulders.

"Come here..." Concerned for Nancy, Peter grabbed her hand. Were they all seeing this? He wondered. The trip was intensely bad otherwise.

Eyes adjusting to the dark, Peter looked to where the form of the woman stood. Warren was bent over now, there was a gargling sound in between whimpering. A sound like a lion humming. He could see the name "Cedric" on the wooden cross of what looked like a tiny grave that had been dug crudely.

*****

"Devon…." Neville looked away from the book, to his brother. "We watched the TV…KDKA had everyone's attention, talking about The National Civil Defense headquarters in D.C. Remember? That jive about a satellite that was circling Venus… The brass, claimed they destroyed it! Big Daddy said NASA destroyed the incoming satellite due to high levels of radiation. You'all dig?" Now he addressed everyone in the room.

The crowd was shaking their head, whether in the throes of coitus, drink, or like Devon, watching, listening for this to make sense. Most were shaking their head "No" disagreeing with the television reports, and agreeing with this sermon by Neville that they had heard before with prolific certainty.

"The Man Lied. . Maybe it was a comet and not man made. They say it may have been a comet that knocked NASA's baby off course. Who knows? From what I gather it was one of our satellites corrupted by the riches of space itself." A small chant began in whispers, indicating that what was reported on radio and television had been incorrect. A prophet from long ago had written the words that Neville held dear. The book in his hands was the only proof they required after witnessing the actual Hell on Earth.

"…only the unburied dead were affected, the man on TV said….. But oh no… no. Boys and girls we saw with our own eyes… before the posse's took some control. We watched loved ones turn after a bite. We saw the dead rise with hunger from graves… There is more. Our own, *Lara was special.* She came to us with child… though it was never to be. Her child was born dead to us." Neville looked to the book with voracious eyes behind his thick lenses.

*****

The woman was holding an infant, newborn to be precise, though the light of the moon shone with inconsistencies. "Stand back, the boy is mine…" Lara looked crazed. Blood was pouring down her neck, her blouse ran with crimson. She was moaning with pain. Warren had fallen to the ground before her, blood gushing from a wound in his neck where something had gnashed at him, soaking the collar of his pea coat.

"No." Nancy understood now.

The *suck, suck, suck* sound coming from the infant in the woman's arms ceased. It turned its gray head, blue veins glowed vibrant in the moonlight now, with eyes blazing yellow at Peter and Nancy.

"That's her child. It was stillborn." Nancy whispered, shocked that the woman stood, dying, watching her own life fluid splash to the pine needles and mud.

"We have to kill it. Her too. She's crossing over." Peter noticed that Warren had ceased moving. It would be minutes before he too would rise. Instinctually, he reached for his belt where his 45 should have been, normally. Where were the other armed men that had followed them down here? He wondered. Both he and Nancy also wished their bags with their guns had not been taken from them when they arrived.

"PETER!!" Nancy shouted.

The woman and child began to approach, her eyes dead blue with moonlight, the baby's eyes yellow. Both mother and child hissed. The baby's arms outstretched toward them.

*****

"Only the watchers, the spiders, would emerge from their lowly depths. These are the scouts who will choose the freshly dead newborn that they would honor with their venomous bites. Messengers of the deep, they are sent to breach the surface to choose a leader, one that would bring wisdom one day in his new legion on Earth as they evolve. Look to cracks in the earth, where ancient outcroppings burst to conjugate with the sky. The watchers show themselves nightly after the comet passes your skies." Neville lost in his own euphoric state broke from the reading. Something moved out of the corner of his eye, just outside the window.

The moon bounced off the river below the campgrounds, hitting the widows of the lodge. "Just the river." He thought to himself.

Devon ran to the sink to splash water on his face, breaking free of the circle of followers committing all manner of debauchery. Neville followed him to the sink. "Do you see? Lara's baby was born dead. We buried it yesterday. It did not rise yet, but I saw the spiders Devon. I saw the watchers coming to deliver their message. They chose Lara's son. Full of wisdom, strength, he will lead them all. I will inherit it all, as his adopted father." Neville's eyes were crazed, glasses hanging off his face.

Devon exhaled, enraged with his brother's insanity. "Read the rest of it, *NEVILLE!* Finish that paragraph! You say I never finished the book but I did finish that chapter, you fucking fool!" He shouted at him, knowing the words of the last paragraph.

"Awright, man, chill, ok. I got this." He went back to the end of the page he was previously reading. "... And as I am reborn through the human child, *all my legion* shall come to me, beguiled, enthralled by my light…" Neville looked outside, to the river below, just past the cabins. What he earlier perceived as rocks that lit blue with moon glow were actually heads, and now they were rising from the river to join the other living dead emerging from the woods. Shadows moving thicker than the blackness of the trees.

"Oh Shit."

When the horde broke through the windows in the back of the room, knocking down the unbolted side door, very few initially had noticed what was happening around them. Reaching orgasm in the throes of passion, jamming to the music, or under the spell of Neville's new form of window pane, not one of them was prepared as the rushing horde burst into the large common room, able to overpower the naked defenseless cluster of revelers. Wet, dripping bodies, some clothed, some naked as their prey, barged into the common room in such numbers from all angles that there had been no chance to scream. Most of the intoxicated mass did not know they were dying until their own blood was splashing the person under them. Devon saw Marly dragged out of the front door by a half dozen creatures wearing business suits. Snappy and Go Go Girl were smothered, dog piled by gnashing yellow jaws growling for a piece. Then the gargled screams.

Devon and Neville turned to the window above the sink as the horde was concentrating on the mass of people in the center of the room that they had all but torn to screaming shrapnel.

Neville was out the window on his feet when he came face to face with Peter and Nancy in the courtyard. There were living dead feasting on remains of some of the scouts. It was evident to Neville that help was not on the way. Half rotting bodies were tearing people apart in the courtyard, there were some guns among the bodies but too out of reach among the feasting creatures, lumbering from body to body, sometimes consuming all but bone so that the body would never be able to reanimate.

Devon hopped out next, rolled to the ground on top of a man being eaten by three boys dressed in Catholic School uniforms with big patches that read *The Chariots Comin' Boys Camp* embroidered on their shoulders. The undead children were growling like dogs as they pulled at the open abdomen of the dead guard. Their wretched skin was blue and cracking. They dragged the remains of the man away from the rest of the fray to consume on their own, ignoring Devon, briefly. Then their eyes lit up with the moon, acknowledging the man. Devon swiped a rifle from the ground, praying it was loaded.

It was! He pumped out shot after shot. "Go… Run!" Devon pointed to the garage with the flimsy rustic door at the other side of the courtyard.

"What do we do? You have vehicles right?" Peter shouted into the Neville's face, holding Nancy's hand.

"Yes, follow Devon to the garage, there's a van." Neville stopped before keeping up with the others. He looked at the broken bodies shambling about, some lumbering in his direction, others still dragging his screaming worshippers out of the lodge.

"Wow. Huge oversight." Neville's mind was broken, eyes dilated and cartoonishly wide behind his glasses.

*****

The keys were in the ignition. "Get in Nev! Do it!" Devon revved the engine. Peter closed the side door once Nancy and Neville were inside.

"Recognize this van?" Devon tried to focus on the pedal and steering wheel, his mind still foggy with the window pane speckled smoke.

"Yea, it's *Just Dan's* van." Nancy held her own stomach with one hand, crying, unable to concentrate on their current dilemma.

The van bolted forward, knocking the approaching dead, crunching others feasting upon the shrieking living victims pinned and squirming on the gravel.

"Dan works for me. He was supposed to pick up more the day he got you three. He brought Lara to me. Got a bonus that day." Neville sat in the passenger side, holding his head. "God that stuff is strong. Certainly will make getting through this night easier, haha. Where is Lara? I need to find her."

"There she is..." Peter's wide eyes peered straight through the windshield. Lara loomed out of the forest to the left of the gravel road. Her white blouse, beneath her oversized coat was stained with blood. She turned her head adorned with the cloche now stained a darker hue of crimson than the flower on the hat itself. In her arms, the infant had its mouth of sharp yellow teeth open as wide as its little tiny hands. Unlike its mother, it had yellow eyes so ungodly bright that they cut the distance between it and the approaching van.

"...and there she goes!" Devon plowed into the living dead mother and child reunion, a thump pounded off the grill of the blue van with the purple grim reaper on the side. Under the wheels came a pulpy *Crush* compounding a *Crunch* from the back end.

There was a shuffle in the back of the van. Peter looked over his shoulder. Under a mess of blankets, ash trays and cans of beer there seemed to be movement.

"Guys..."

"So, you had *Just Dan*... our Dan, meet us to begin with? Was he roving the countryside bringing you people, Nev? I mean really..." Devon was catching on.

"Guys..." Peter repeated nervously.

"It's over now. Yea, he brought me Lara, and there were a few others, but they either left after a healthy birth... Not too many people getting funky these days." Neville turned to his brother as if he was talking about an old board game or favorite sports team they used to share, "You know, that guy that was interviewed during the early days, on TV, Dr. Grimes, that guy, talkin jive. He had said, and I quote, "they're just dead flesh," but they're not, Dev. Ole Malekyre' here, in his book, says it clear as blue cheer man." Neville was rambling while paging through the book. "No more room in Hell."

Devon was disgusted.

Neville was crying, feeling defeated. His head down in his lap peering at the book.

"Guys...." Peter's voice was quivering.

"Peter, *what*?" Nancy turned to touch her boyfriend's shoulder, rubbing his sweaty long hair.

Becoming furious, Devon shouted, "Did you abduct women for this ....purpose? If so, people are going to know this van. There's enough people still trying to turn this shit around Nev! What were you...?" Devon's head was clearing from the drugs. Now on PA 43, on the road ahead he could see police cars, men with large hats, red and blue lights flickering. A Posse.

"Timing! Looks like they were waiting for *Just Dan* to come back through." Devon could not help but smile at his brother's demise. He could sense Neville's defeat, feel him shaking in his shoes.

But how damn close had he come to his planned damnable future for the human race?

Then white hot pain shot from Devon's shoulder to his neck. He looked down to come right eye to left eye with Just Dan, only now his skin was pale going on blue. Dan's eyes blazed with hateful hunger. After the creature that was Dan leapt from the back of the van from under the blankets which he had died under, Nancy had pulled Peter aside toward the side door. Just Dan landed on the back of the driver's seat and on Devon instead.

Impulsively Devon's foot floored the van causing it to plow ahead. Chunks were being taken from his shoulder and neck while his ear had front row seats for the chewing. Within moments, the posse ahead opened fire on the van, thunderous holes blowing through the shattering windshield. Devon knew pain and then black.

*****

Nancy awoke to the sound of a policeman's megaphone. Moving shadows surrounded her. Men speaking. She felt around, sat up, feeling a body laying to her left. Peter was sprawled out on the road next to her. He had broken her fall from the side door of the van when it swerved off the road. He looked serene, beautiful, laying there with his eyes closed, if not for the fresh gelatinous red bullet hole in his head.

"NO PETER….NO!" She was screaming. Gasping. "Peter…. Oh no." Two officers picked her off the ground, dragging her away from Peter's body and the van. "I'll name him Peter, I promise, like we said." She wept in an officer's arms, before resuming screaming. "Let me say good bye…let me…."

Neville had his hands up in front of a circle of cops, while a man they all referred to as The Sheriff began interrogating him, shouting "Now why don't you listen when you are told to stop? Why the hell you traveling with one of these messed up goons? HELLO?! I'm talking to you." The Sheriff was in Neville's face. "I didn't like you in the days before the dead, Neville Cordry, mucking up Zelienople with your drugs! Well it is irony that we heard a mass of them were coming this way…and now I get to save your dumb ass this far south! Get him outta my sight." The Sheriff shook his head, taking off his hat, he looked into the van.

"Looks like we got two squirmers in there. Burn it!"

- 7 -
THE CRYPT OF EDGETOWN

David Wright unfolded his glasses, placing them on his face. Standing before him was the pointed iron gateway to the grand cemetery of Mountain Top, Pennsylvania. Beyond the maze of ancient gravestones, stretching for about a mile, lay the monolithic black hill that housed a single crypt. The onyx rock of the hill itself appeared to be carved up, depicting manmade shelves. The shelves were platforms complete with stone steps created for the newer additions; the stone memorial markings and tall silver crosses.

These plateaus formed a step ladder fit for giants all the way up to the black mountain of rock that sprouted with a magnificently intimidating single silver cross. This was the Crypt of Edgetown, a terraced mountain of insidious black crystal in the light of the super moon. The silver cross forged by human hands from an age beyond recorded events, had acted as a lightning rod. This cross was placed with purpose. Its placement directed power. This lightning rod absorbed the blast from above and never did a storm pass without striking the metal peak, radiating the small mountain crypt with a pulsing power that could be seen from the cemetery below. During a storm, the black hill glowed with an unnatural blue, but only when it was struck. The blue pulse of the strike could actually be seen, shaking the ground below, though very few had actually been allowed to witness the event.

David Wright savored the moment every time. Some of his friends did too. A cousin of his, Chris, saw this several times but never really wanted to come back in later years. David was alone now, approaching, without fear or trepidation that kept most of the past visitors from returning. There was a power here in Mountain Top, that few could explain. Yet, the Crypt was permitted to remain now that the local township recognized it as a historical site. And it certainly was.

"Should be going back to college, instead I'm here. Like some loser gatekeeper, I'm here, alone, again." David threw the empty Pabst on the ground then pushed the creaking iron gate open while taking a breath of the humid summer night wind. A mist hung above the rows of stones that was lit with a blue hue of derma outlined by the last bits of the orange skin of the sun. The glowing rays of the sun seemed to be absorbed by the stones themselves during the day. The surrounding willows and other shrubs also soaked up the sun so that a natural glow emanated about the cemetery even in the pitch of night. The blue mist and orange glow only lasted for the first few hours of nightfall and dissipated by the evil small hours of the night.

In his early thirties now, David thought back on how a night like this, with a warm beer in hand, would have been considered cool, endearing, and fun with some friends from summer camp or his cousin, Chris, that lived just past the border into New Jersey.

"Barley Hop Pop." Whispering the homemade term that he and his cronies used back in the good old days. "Before the dark times. Before the Empire." Laughing to himself now, he quoted the phrase from his favorite movie that now represented a dying, underappreciated piece of pop culture. He had been coming to the Edgetown Cemetery since he was a young teen. Having grown up on Long Island, he also had family in New Jersey. Spending his summers with his cousin at camp in Mountain Top, he had heard the tales of this particular burial ground more than enough times over burned embers and marshmallows on sticks handed to him by teen counselors.

Maybe he listened a little too intently.

It would not be until his early twenties that he realized he was not well. This had nothing to do with the fact that he misplaced his glasses to the point that he sometimes forgot that he even wore them. Nor did it have to do with the wet sheets in the night. Always awakening from nightmares that were more real than the normal dreams of being late for class or not knowing your own schedule.

David dreamt of drowning or being buried alive. Sometimes the "things" in his dreams were still at the foot of his bed when he woke, sitting up, there they were staring directly at him. Hideous apparitions that stared back before dissipating into his murky memory.

David was addicted to the dark side of human affliction. Not by choice. Horror, remorse, deep regret. These emotions dragged him in by the heart like a magnet. Could it be self-infliction? Of course all the cool kids were agnostic! They hate Christmas, they pretend they do not watch superhero movies, and everyone is in a band.

Old news. Boring. No originality.

This was different. A lifestyle; heavy metal leads to drugs, drugs lead to sex, girls lead to violence and death. He chuckled to himself again, standing on a trail of gravel between the rows. Aids was scary and very real. He had to be choosey and careful; everyone had to these days.

They called him prude. They are dead now.

Of course, there were worse things than impulse killing you. By far. He was aware of the other side.

"They don't know. No one knows what is waiting. These daily speed bumps are a gift! Our everyday gripes qualify as dread for the future?

Really?" He thought, rubbing his eyes under his glasses. He wished that all our problems could be summed up by too many dishes in the sink, forgetting to put the garbage out or parking within the yellow lines.

No, not quite. Try having *my* dreams, *my* visions *my* fuckin' reality! He said to himself, staring accusingly at the stones of the dead that he envied. His other pastimes were merely distractions. Sedate the mind, stay calm, and for the sake of others as well as himself, tell no one what you have seen and know!

He tried therapy once. Well, three times. Useless. If only someone would listen, then the coming wave could be avoided.

Oh please. It would take more than a shrink... one *damn* shrink to take his word for it. He exhaled, hearing his own lungs rasp on the damp air. He pulled his hair back, being sure that none of the well fed and engorged spiders of the graveyard had snared themselves into his long hair again. Driving home with a prickling at your scalp was more than uncomfortable. In these back roads of Pennsylvania, it could be life threatening to swerve along these narrow pot hole pocked excuses for paved pathways.

He laughed to himself, crunching the gravel of the path between the stones, thinking about the misconception that folks had about him. "If they had only known." He said aloud to the audience of stone with laughter on the wind.

There definitely were sounds and shapes moving about. Creatures, unseen, were hiding behind the stones. He could see their shadows. Their idle attempts at scaring him away made him smile.

"Save it for someone who cares." David sneered. He reached into his ragged black denim jacket, (from his high school days, it still fit) to find the butterfly knife he had ordered from a karate magazine in 1987. It was still there. He just needed to know it was there. Comfort in the dark for most, but for him, it subsided the need for blood. If only one of these creatures could cross over sooner and confront him now, it would redeem all that was rotten in his mind if he were able to lunge out and stab one in the gullet.

Even if it meant dying in this most god forsaken place.

Shadow people.

It had rained earlier. Watching from the dry safety of his 68 Cougar, parked just outside the cemetery, he had downed a six pack of Pabst. A little early Pantera was still twining in cassette form from his stereo, playing low, but enough to hear the grind of "Right On the Edge." No one had listened to him in high school, but he knew this band would be big. There was a great source of power in strong music. Confidence, strength, and assurance were all spoken of in the best of songs. Sometimes, before battle, or simply doing something that set your mind back from your comfort zone, the music provided fortitude when it was lacking naturally. Music *surely* was *Mother's Little Helper.*

Drums of war.

Earlier, just before he cracked his last beer to take with him outside the car, David had clicked the old cassette out of the stereo, and placed a disc into the newer CD player he had installed. A somber blues riff filled the black interior of his prized vehicle. Relaxing bass engulfed by the gentle voice of a woman singing "Find Ya' Love," floated in the air so that the tapping of the rain outside could no longer be heard. The rain was ceasing while he eased his head and neck back on the seat. The song reminded him of Teddy, his dog. He actually had called in to a radio station (he was obsessed with annoying radio disc jockey's. Ironically he would eventually work for a radio station for a bit of time. The only job that actually kept his prowess in check, his mind focused.)while the band The Bloody Nerve were doing an acoustic set in studio at WRHR in Pittsburgh to request that they dedicate the song to his dog that he had been forced to give away. The DJ obliged. The tender lyrics of the song meant more to him than anything in years.

Aren't you supposed to outgrow these attachments to songs after your twenties? He thought to himself. Most did. He found it sad how people forget their passions. That is, until certain passions were lost or taken away, everything before that was just taken for granted.

Like life without demons.

Lightning struck the silver cross on top of the crypt while he glanced at his own sad face reflecting back at him in the car's window. The patter of rain had stopped. It was time to go, so he had decided to take his last beer with him, proceeding to the cemetery.

Gravel shuffled under foot, David was making his way toward the crypt.

There were dogs here. Of course, he knew that. Eight years ago he was forced to leave his shepherd lab mix, Teddy, here, when a landlord said he could not have him at his college apartment. He was enrolled, and also had to quit school when the funds ran dry. He would go back to school someday.

David knew he had to go back, but leaving the dog here had destroyed his soul to a degree that could not be weighed in most human terms. The dog was a strong intelligent soul. David was sure that Teddy understood his conflict with the nether regions that surrounded this place known as existence. When David had his dreams, or woke with claw marks on his back, sweating, bleeding, screaming at the blurred void in the room, Teddy had also witnessed these visitations. Usually the dog heard it coming or smelled the vile stench that these visitors in the night had reeked of. The dog could sense it hours ahead of time too.

Someone that understood, David thought to himself with a smirk.

It was important though to rewind back to the idea that he knew Teddy was well taken care of by Mr. Grell, the groundskeeper. The dog would have a wonderful life with fields to run, a warm place to sleep surrounded by his favorite bags of food for the rest of his years. Beyond the mount of rock were acres for a dog to tire himself out for days on end. Tall, thin Mr. Grell with kind eyes that sunk into his frail skull, adored the dogs he took in. A smile, larger than his face, had provided David the comfort he needed on the day he brought Teddy here to say goodbye.

"No Bones though, hahaha, not for the dogs, hehe hehe." Mr. Grell snickered between his gummy mouth, vacant of front teeth. He stretched out both of his scrawny arms motioning to the ground below them that housed countless numbers of dried up bones. David forced a smile in return.

That awful day made him cry for the first time in years. Walking away from Teddy's brown eyes...oh those almost human eyes that were surrounded by his creamy tan- on- black beagle face nearly killed him.

Breaking up with a girlfriend? No comparison. All they wanted to do was go to the mall. He wanted to scream at them. He could not remember their names. Except one.

"DON'T YOU KNOW WHATS OUT THERE!?"

All but one. She was a good girl.

As for his dog. Leaving that wonderful face behind was one of the worst days of his life. Not *the* worst, just one of them. That happy little boy whose body never stopped wagging even as his tail did, especially when you were trying your hardest to just turn your back and leave... He could feel the love, the sadness and hear Teddy whine as he had made his way down the hill to the cemetery parking lot, to the car, turning his back to leave. In his heart he knew it was best for the dog's welfare, and to the welfare of many others, as Teddy proved to be quite a beacon of intense insight.

Animals knew what was coming. They tried to warn us.

That day though, his dog only felt sadness.

Almost the worst day of his life. He knew a much worse one was coming.

Awful. That dog had lived with him from his high school years to his first apartment and almost made it to college with David, and now he had to leave him behind, in *This Place*.

The years had gone by. Edgetown Cemetery was known among some of the locals during these contemporary times in Mountain Top Pennsylvania as bad ground. A tale told to children as an evil place to steer clear from. "Stay away from *The Crypt*" was heard as often as "go to the RX drug store for cough drops." In the same breath, locals also were aware of the love and care that canines received from the companionship of old Mr. Grell. When the folks of Mountain Top could not take care of their own dogs, or simply had to give them up, there was a place here for them at the cemetery.

A bright spark in the dim muck.

Mr. Grell loved animals. There was a need for them in Edgetown Cemetery. Animals, pets, beloved creatures accentuated a natural positive force for the burial ground itself. The presence of dogs, especially, lightened the spirits of the dank place for daylight visitors. They kept the groundskeeper himself from pulling his long salt and pepper hair out of his thinning scalp. Surely they had a stronger purpose than posing as therapy dogs for the living visitors. Something that David and Mr. Grell knew all too well about.

They're coming.

He had seen them in the shadows of his school hallways as far back as elementary school. Parents, teachers, doctors, whatever, whoever he told, well, they could not and would not pay attention to his ramblings but were glad to give him a hall pass to see the guidance counselor. Or worse, he would more commonly be sent to the nurse where he sat with female peers on their period. David's mind bled with visions; his permanent period.

Smelling the rancid ground amid the humid summer breeze, he stopped walking, torturing himself, reminiscing about a moment that stabbed his chest with a piercing knife of ice.

He really missed her. The one. Others came, but no one compared to her.

Memories are just painful and time is mean, he thought.

As he shuffled gravel under his feet, he could hear the pitter patter of the shadows' movement as they strove to surround him, grope at him. Deformed shadows of all sizes, disfigured mockeries of human beings trying to hide or cease their movements among the graves and the vines hanging low among the weeping willows. The shadows were never faster than his thoughts.

He smiled. "Gotcha." Along with their vile scents, the forms left a snapshot in his mind. Peripherally glimpsing them even when the specters thought they were quick enough to hide behind a tree, tombstone or bush.

It was hard to breath in the thick air that was making his hair twist with wetness around his own face. He would have to shave it again. He hated when his hair got too long because of his own forgetfulness. The managers at his job at the radio station did not mind his disheveled, aged, heavy metal rocker look, but to him it was just laziness. His appearance worked for photo shoots when media came by. Added realism to the spinning of Megadeth CD's.

Arching his neck to the sky, he looked up at the star speckled night, "I'm back. Lucky you. This is how I spend my Saturday night. Why? Cause I see you, I know who you are." He yelled at the top of his lungs, silencing the night birds in the distance. Crickets lost their bows in the mist for ten seconds, then resumed. The shadows that were shaped like distorted men scattered and hid behind gravestones, always peering over the tops with clear empty eyes. These specters sometimes glowed with a blue hue, with a tinge of yellow to the eyes. He had a sense these were the older, wiser ones. The younger, more vicious things had pure yellow eyes, sharper features, with quills for hair all over their bodies.

David did not need a light to see the entryway to the crypt. This was a chamber that no one was to enter, except Mr. Grell, the groundskeeper and his numerous dogs he kept for company through the years. Inside the crypt, somewhere, was living space where he could keep watch 24/7. There was indeed a need for this. The contract for such an obligation was obsolete unless you had a certain unspoken gift.

Approaching the broken stone steps that went down only about four feet, David stood at the oaken door. Everything was gray in the dulling moonlight here. One look over his shoulder and he could see the human sized shadows move about the maze of white brittle teeth that made up the ancient gravesite's lower jaw that now lay behind him.

"Nice try back there. You little bitches. Now you are just old friends of mine...keep scaring the locals. Keep the kids out." David flipped his middle finger straight up, making sure his thick silver ring's skull insignia smiled right back at the elongated dancing specters. He continued thinking, but not sharing "Claws and teeth do not scare me anymore. You already ruined my life, ruined me with the visions of your existence, now I'm just completing the barter." His toothy grin could not hide his amusement at threatening the insidious night watchers of the graves. Not many could see them. He was aware there were others. Someone other than Mr. Grell and himself kept watch on this intersection of the void, long before their internship. That was obvious.

He always could see what others preferred not to.

Ruined my damn social life. He thought, giggled a bit, looking at the oaken door with the rustic rounded top before him. Ruined my love life. Although, sex? That part was fun.

Taking a breath, thinking back on that one chance at a real relationship, he paused before the door.

Marianne was beautiful. Tolerant for about a year. She wore his rock tee shirts and sometimes nothing else. That was nice. Taking her to lunch after class for pizza and beer was a unique pleasure when the things in the dark did not show themselves.

Hitting the latest Argento flick at the local hipster theatre was his favorite. Marianne with her black eyebrows that pitched upward like batwings under her straight black hairdo, was more than a willing participant in his private world of escapism. God how he missed those drunk bowling nights (she would drink, he never drank and bowled. Nope. No drinking and bowling, after that arrest at Brunswick in Coram back in the day).

He thought he was falling in love at one point. Still working the job at the radio station, before he left for his late DJ shift on some nights , she would come to him at their apartment on Mulberry Street, (running in the rain sometimes) during her own work break at the Starbucks down the block just to bring him his chai tea. Vente? Stupid. Large, small. Vente? Either way, she was so sweet in her apron hanging limply over her thin pale white skin. He knew she hated that job where she winked at old men for tips while they stole looks at her ass in black stretch pants as she extended the opposite direction for more plastic lids. Wait, isn't that how he met her?

Older now. The memory stabbed deep. She's gone, just like that Hall and Oates song.

David thought about singing it out loud, to scare the shadows of the night. He wanted to chill the bastard horde of evil behind him some more while his hand was on the giant iron knob to the crypt! The pang of how he tortured Marianne for that year... well, eh, no laughter there. No. Not anymore. He didn't necessarily miss her. David missed the companionship. There was definite regret too. Hurting a good person never sat well, or went away. Still, he knew he made the right decision. There was that girl in his college courses that he knew liked him. Courtney. She had told him that it was the right decision, to leave someone that was hanging on for comfort. He should cease being selfish. He looked forward to the pretty blond girl's advice every time he ran into her at the campus radio station where they both worked a shift.

Squeezing his lips together he found new regret. That girl in his night classes was a good friend that he simply blew off for the very reason that she, herself had agreed that it was good that he broke it off with Marianne.

Irony.

He missed having friends.

Marianne had endured too much of him, night after night. He wet their sheets with cold sweat, soaking the bed with an alluvial plain that oozed onto her side too. It was not the wetness of the bed or lack of sleep she had lost that was slowly breaking down her affection and character. So many times, poor Marianne had to wash his old Star Wars sheets or her own hated New Kids on the Block quilt that she stole from her little sister before they could afford real bedding. If anything, she wanted to help him through his "night terrors" as she referred to them.

He hurt her feelings once, laughing at the artificial term. Night Terrors. Sure.

Initially there was nothing that could drive her away from David. Nothing natural anyway. She loved his work ethic even when it did not pay. She knew he was always driving for something more than the future of cubicle mayhem, pushing pens on paper and tapping keys. Marianne knew there was more to this dude she had fallen in love with and moved in with conveniently when her rent got a bit too high. No amount of anything trivial that he subjected her to could scare her back to the point of moving back in with her parents again.

The screaming took care of that.

"THERE! THERE! Don't you see them...? Don't you see them... in the street, behind the garbage cans...? Their hands on my shoulder... BEHIND THE COUCH! MARIANNE! They followed you into the bathroom..." Shouting with the seeping sweat of a summer night, over and over.

No. Marianne, in her early curvy twenties, beautiful in spirit as she was in appearance, was not going to put up with those banshee spouts for long.

He remembered the day she left. Wearing a yellow sundress with a packed duffel bag over her shoulder, she shared some crying kisses and then she was gone, back to live with mom and dad.

Family. Is that not what people say? Family is everything in the end? No matter how many girls or drinking buddies you have, it all comes down to family.

BULLSHIT.

Biting his bottom lip with bitterness, he still refrained from opening the crypt door. Could entering this doorway be the end of all that remained of safe reality? Was he on the road to insanity by entering this supernatural plane that not many folks would even want to believe existed? Decision time.

Clenching his eyes along with his fists, he stood apprehensively. David's boots were flat on the stone floor below the steps. Staring at the door, he thought back on his last attempt at normalcy. He was considering going back to school, live off campus maybe, meet new people, work part time at the radio station perhaps? Drink at the coffee shop with Courtney.

Contemplating going back to school many times, he had even driven up to the campus to see what extracurricular clubs were open and possibly re-enroll. While standing in the student union common room staring at the post-its and classifieds on a cork board, he came face to face with Courtney. Remembering why he ran from that friendship, now, he merely listened to the over privileged blonde beauty when she tried to recruit him for some writing contest. The conversation was one sided, so the only reciprocity he received from the pretty, nice smelling, intelligent cheerleader type was the knowledge that there might be other folks out there that understood, even if they were self-serving. If he went back to school as a non-traditional student, then he might share something with this Courtney girl, maybe, if he could get her drunk enough to shut up. She did say she still worked at the local radio station? Hmm? She had seemed interested. Also, she had seemed truly disturbed. David knew this look. She talked of night terrors. The universe brought them together.

He should have got closer with her, shared info and see just how much ….

Again, he spared her too. Maybe. Don't drag anyone else into this darkness. Or was she alone in the dark? He thought they would see each other again. Unless her night terrors were full of jock straps and proms.

If only his own family gave him the time of day. If only they would have listened.

With the exception of one family member on his mom's side, he was not taken seriously.

In their defense, who listens to a twelve year old at a family picnic at Eisenhower State Park during the 4Th of July who says he sees yellow eyed black skeletons hanging upside down from the monkey bars?

One family member listened. Good old Uncle Bill.

Still with one hand on the cold iron crypt door knob, he bowed his head, chin on his chest. His damp hair clung to his cheeks. Memories of Uncle Bill had given David's mind some temporary relief from his regrets about Marianne and so many others. Uncle Bill, through the awkward teen years, had provided creditability to his reclusive instability. Why? Uncle Bill and his dumb B.T.O. records that he blasted in his parent's living room, during family visits, was always a fun and welcoming presence.

Although the visits always resulted in ineffective talks on rock and roll symmetry and driving in his 78 hippie van, there was no one else cooler in David's young eyes. Tall Uncle Bill, his only human hero, truly was the only person in David's life that understood what was really happening around him.

Around them.

As a child, David viewed Uncle Bill as a renegade pirate, wearing his multicolored bandanas adorned with skulls. He loved when he showed up at family picnics joined by his entourage of cute hippie girls with their long unkempt hair, giggling and sharing stories about John Lennon and the revolution that never happened. Uncle Bill was the ridicule of the entire family, ultimately becoming the hero of one.

Sure, Uncle Bill smoked pot. Big deal! A lot of the folks did at the campground up in Lake George during the family reunion weekends.

David did not know, or relate to anyone out there during those trips. They all seemed to know each other, sharing inside laughs and tales of other family gatherings he had missed. He knew very little about his extended family. They paid him even less attention with their private jokes and stories that had nothing to do with him. Trips to Disney or Six Flags that he was not invited to or even previous camping trips, and weddings that he did not attend. No one paid him any attention other than Uncle Bill.

Fireside, beer in hand, girls on his shoulder, he thought about his hero, with those cuties in flip flops, giggling with big white teeth gleaming. There was shirtless Uncle Bill, trickling sweet Marlboro smoke into the air.

The last Lake George trip was a memorable one. Oh yes. A pinnacle point of his boyhood. A most predominant excursion. Lounging fireside with his uncle and the girls, David could remember a moment of clarity. His uncle met his gaze over the fire attempting to get his full attention. Creepy at first, but then invisible waves of consciousness opened between them. David sat on a tree stump meeting his uncle eye to eye, smiling. Uncle Bill wanted to tell a ghost story. Initially. However, there was more in his gaze than just one mere ghost story on that night.

Many fires were lit on the lakeside campground. Families were gathered around each other. Most of the hunched bodies were sitting with the folks that they willingly flocked to in comfort, comradery and of course false familiarity. They clung together in their safe clans after a summer day in the lake to share the day's events. Or past events. Mostly, in happenstance, the small fireside groups were together in order to roast marshmallows, hear dumb acoustic guitar sessions with even worse singers (family or adjoining campers) reveling in their *one* night of fame. David sat with Uncle Bill and his two gypsy girls that smelled alluringly of that store in the mall... Spencer Gifts?

Was he twelve? Fourteen? No idea. But damn if it was not a great memory even if he had to sleep in the humid drippy tent with his little cousin Benny who pissed his sleeping bag every night, it was wonderful to listen to Uncle Bill talk through that red beard of his, watching his glassy green eyeballs stare into his own eyes with a meaning that only someone *that knows* could understand.

The girls giggled. That was annoying. But David shut them out, just like he would when Uncle Bill's van, which was parked right next to his tent, shook a bit with even more laughter later that night.

Weed whiff wafted through the air, and the girls on either of Uncle Bill's shoulder snickered, sharing the burning roach clip chunk of skunky weed, but neither of them ever really paid attention to the words being said.

David did.

It was like Uncle Bill spoke without opening his mouth. Actually he did. The dumb girls in their sheer flowing sun dresses were so immersed in their smoke that they did not even pay attention to David peering up their....

"So, you hear me feller? Davey Boy. I know. I see inside your eyes. The fire is nice, but those shadows in the woods, outside the flame of our shit heel relatives... and their ignorance...yea they're real. I see'em too boy. See'em hard." Uncle Bill's voice penetrating within his skull hurt at first, like a stab from a poker searing his membranes, initially. Within a second, the pain was gone and the radio show between uncle and nephew began.

David wiped his chin clean of barbeque sauce onto his Han Solo iron-on t shirt.

Then, he thought. *Really, concentrated.* Clenching his eyelids, not shutting but tensing them, he kept them open slightly. He stared into Uncle Bill's eyes across the licking fire. "Yes. I see them. In my closet. In school. Oh god…." A tear streaked his cheek. "Shadow's, with finger nails and teeth…. Yellow eyes when they become strong, trying to prove themselves… younger…..hungrier…….usually the eyes are clear…..they tease me at the bus stop…… I got in a fight….thought Jeremy Gladstone was one…..the eyes are clear sometimes, but yellow when they become angry….. I kicked Jeremy's ass bad… I'm still in trouble for that …." David had said this to his uncle without moving his lips. It was like using his toy Star Trek walkie talkies.

Over and out Scotty.

Memories fade, though the ashen scent of that fire still filled his nose with pleasant wooden smoke, he thought back on that pivotal moment with his uncle. He could remember the odd and slightly painful burning feeling in his brain that flowed symbiotically with that stare from Uncle Bill that night, penetrating his soul. Knowing. Just knowing. Someone else was KNOWING!! And Seeing.

They are coming from the other side and no one knows… no one cares!

Finally someone else did. Another soldier.

Standing in front of the most forbidden place in Mountain Top, Pennsylvania, he had to laugh to himself at this most unlikely scenario even while his hand was on the iron knob turning it. He wondered if he should have called his cousin Chris to meet him this time. He thought better on it. Chris had a family. No reason to disrupt that.

Do not drag anyone else in.

David harkened back to that moment at Lake George with his uncle like most grandmas focus on a Sunday mass.

Uncle Bill had shrugged the girls off, removed his bandana revealing his red mane of hair. He then moved his shirtless midsection closer to the fire, glaring deeply into his nephew's eyes. "They are real my son. David, those shadow people are real and they are coming." He spoke without words.

David held that moment dear.

It would be soon that he would learn the concept of seduction by the use of a mere "idea inception." This was their term. Uncle Bill made it up and they used the term. It was a more tangible term than Marianne's "night terrors." Or that Courtney girl's "alien visitations."

Uncle Bill could get any cute girl he wanted. Sometimes two! And he did this by simply looking at them, and getting inside their heads. Idea inception.

How else does a pot smoking, jobless, two time loser with a hippie van, roam the country with two gorgeous girls half his age?!

I had a gorgeous girl for a time. One that loved me. David thought. She would do anything to be with me. Ruining that was just the natural order of being, *him*.

"I could have been happy", he whispered to the night air. He let her go. David purposely held back this new found mind warping, idea inception, power. He played with it briefly when talking to that self-centered college girl. This quite possibly being the reason that she had opened up so much to him while standing in the common room of the student union. Had he spliced her brain like peeling an avocado?

On that day that he ran into Courtney, David had just wanted to consider signing up for classes again and here was this blonde bombshell, by far out of his league, in her designer sweater, yoga pants, pink bow in her hair and a Coach Purse on her shoulder, spilling her intimate thoughts on alien abduction and nightmares. Strange, he had hardly tried.

Honing it would be essential for the coming days (years?) when it all came down. Uncle Bill could never answer the question, "How did we get this?" Not entirely.

Uncle Bill only responded to that question once, on a van drive to mini golf near Mountain Top. There had been a camping trip to Lake Harmony. Mom and Dad were more than happy to let David go for a week with Uncle Bill.

Fishing off a canoe, on a warm sunny morning, Uncle Bill had said, "Don't ever let people tell you its mental illness. It's a gift." They stayed in a campground, where they could go fishing just outside the rural town. That was when Uncle Bill introduced him to Mr. Grell. He fished at Lake Harmony too. It was a good time.

Before the worry of girls, jobs, college, losing dogs, friends and family.

Breathing in the dankness of the crypt, for one last time, he thought of Marianne again.

He could have kept Marianne in his life. A second chance emerged after she had left that first time when he had tried to let her go. He wanted to let her get away from his madness. She had come back after a week with her parents. She wanted to be with him.

Instead. Under tears, duress, and a grilled cheese sandwich, he told Marianne "It is a good time to leave. Go." While she was ironing her work clothes for Starbucks, with her back turned, he tossed his half eaten sandwich down on the paper plate and thought. Concentrated *real hard*. *Tell her to Go.*

Marianne did not deserve this.

She never came home after her shift that day. Never again.

David was not proud that it worked like it did, sparing this girl the ongoing grief that was his malfunction, nonetheless she was gone. Like that damned Hall and Oates song that persistently ran through his head. His tolerance was high, but the beer buzz still worked its magic when he thought back nostalgically about music.

Turning the bulbous iron knob to the crypt, "She's gone…." He sung pathetically with a droning whisper.

The oak door creaked open, alarming the spiders that there was a new guest arriving. A new intruder creaked his way in, possibly endangering the sanctity of their home. Like watchers over the realm, yellow, orange, red, blue and green bellied plum sized spiders sought refuge in cracks and crevices of the wood beams overhead in the musty crypt. There were rows of pews, about six in all, of the oldest wood hewn by man on either side of David as he walked down the aisle between them.

Upon entry, David turned his head to the side, rather than immediately looking at the wall of glass at the far end of the room and the horrors within.

Mr. Grell came to his side from a darkened doorway on the left.

"Good to see you boy. Things are smooooooth." The old skinny man in overalls whistled through his missing teeth. Beady brown eyes in wide sunken eye sockets welcomed his most common guest (though not often) while he scratched his long wrinkled neck of his gray and white hairs that grew off the back of his chicken skin.

He whistled, "HEEEERREEE BOY…"

There was a comfortable couch next to the pews on the left made up of the finest cushions of puffy maroon that David had ever seen. Two dogs were awakening.

"How did they not hear me open…?" David smiled at Mr. Grell.

"They have comfort here. And they play in the fields all day. They sleep so true here. Only two of them now. Tell the townsfolk there is plenty of room for more. Angels I tell you. Pure and sweet. Unbroken. They know only love." The old man smiled, leaning on his walking stick. The top of the stick had a tiny skull on the end of it, carved in wood. The forehead of the skull featured a gem in the shape of a silver cross.

"I see. Poor boy is getting old, losing his touch," David smiled with glee as Teddy, came running up to him with a tail wagging stronger than his forty two pound body could sustain! Tears, joy, hugs! "Love you boy. Love you. Good to see you. Going back to school, man… I'll be in the area again… See you more often!" David cried, hugging the only child he would ever know. He paid little mind to the black and white boxer lab that came over. She was bigger than his boy, seeking similar love from Mr. Grell.

"This is Jett Marie. She's a good girl, young, but she's mine. Someone left her in a box outside the cemetery a few months ago. She loves your Teddy. Good Girl." Mr. Grell arched his own back, leaning on the stick just to pour some more love on the pup. "Her senses are tuned well. She knows when they peak." He glanced up at the spiders in the rafters, gritting his teeth.

David forced himself to put Teddy aside, though the dog never would stop loving his old master. Mr. Grell whistled and both dogs sat still.

"Yeah, you see we got three in there." Mr. Grell's voice rattled like weak thunder. He focused on the glass wall and what was behind it, now indicating that this was still a working visit for his younger friend.

David's knees cracked in succession with his ankles inside his Doc Martins. He stood straight, pulling his hair back, wiping sweat from his brow. In front of the pews was a glass screen the size of the wall before him. The crypt itself was not that big. David never asked to see the conditions that Teddy was kept in. The dog's happiness was enough proof that Mr. Grell took great care of these little sentinels of his.

He walked up to the glass, impossible to dismiss the feeling of Teddy, Jett Marie and Mr. Grell at his back, watching.

Torches were lit on either side of the dank chamber. Six and Six. Mr. Grell saw to the torches when he knew he had fresh bodies and possible visitors in advent.

Beyond the glass barrier were three bodies that had been recently delivered to Edgetown Crypt. This was the contribution that the locals of Mountain Top participated in, occasionally (those in the *know*), after a beautiful ceremony, luncheon with some ham and cheese, speeches and whatever other rituals were performed to keep the surviving members in peace in the town below. Next, the bodies would be delivered here after they were wrapped in air tight cloth and placed on cold slabs in this very visible chamber.

David removed his glasses, folded them, placing them into a pocket in his denim jacket. Then he put his hands and face against the glass. Unaware of his own breath fogging his vision he watched as the bodies, naked under the sheer white cloth, writhed and twisted into the dance of the dead. Three bodies. Two men, one woman, limbs moving to the tune of some unheard jam band, twitching about endlessly in rhythms that the living tissues of these fine humans never imagined they could ever achieve, even in their prime.

The sight was most unsettling. Yet, he could not stop watching these people appear to be suffering even in light of their death. This was wrong. Death should be serene. A time to rest.

He thought of his nickname, "D.J." that initially only his beloved grandfather addressed him as. His Grandpa Joseph had lovingly given him that name when he was a child, bearing the middle initial of his own namesake. It caught on, and he thought of bringing that back into his repertoire to honor his grandpa's memory. Praying that his grandfather slept well, uninterrupted, spared of this atrocity after death, he exhaled with thoughts of that cemetery out in Long Island where many of his family rested. A very different type of resting place. Very few "soldiers" in death existed compared to the truly dead.

He prayed that his grandfather was not writhing in the dance of the dead too.

"Is there no peace within?" David spoke against the glass. His left hand was met with the cold wet nuzzle of his boy Teddy, who proceeded to lick his old master. "Good boy, Teddy. Good boy." The dog came to his side in response to his master's emotion. This was something Teddy was remarkable for at moments like this, emotionally healing the invisible, yet open wounds.

Of course he knew better. Opening his eyes after a tense couple of seconds, he knew that these bodies before him were warriors. The bodies behind the glass were volunteers who at the time of their death were placed in this sacred ground in order to defend the black hole of cancerous evil that opened up at the surface of the earth right here in Mountain Top, Pennsylvania. A pit that was covered by centuries of live and dead warriors before them. Evil spewed out below Edgetown Crypt years before the land had a name.

The mound was constructed. A cemetery was erected. Sentinels in spirit locked horns on an unseen plane, struggling and keeping the full form of demons below in their depths of ancient reek. For now only shadows lurk in the world of humans while the spirits of our valiant dead work hard in another realm with the strength of prayer supporting their arsenal, until their bodies rot. After the bodies of these unsung heroes break down, ultimately the final sleep ensues, they are given the "all clear" to pass on to the light, or so it is believed. With hope, new freshly passing dead are brought to the crypt to replenish the old warriors turned to dust. Guardians in the Dark. The very title of the ancient book that Mr. Grell shelved in the foyer.

Their dance would continue for weeks as they fight what terrors lay below the igneous mound of defensive rock. The spirit of these soldiers keep the darkness below as a legion tries to breach the surface. Only the mentally ill, (preferably the mentally empowered) like David, Uncle Bill, Mr. Grell and the many misunderstood people that are passed on the street every day could see the shadow people. The demons in the mist. Only those precious few knew that the terrible shapes in the dark were just waiting to take form to barrage our world with a bastion of gnashing teeth that were so evil that only our dead could comprehend.

David addressed Mr. Grell without turning his head from the shifting forms wriggling on the slabs before him, "How many more crypts like this exist? How many watchtowers do we have in this day of nonbelievers full of damned wastes of life?" He unclenched his angry teeth, bending down to hold Teddy closer than he ever did. The dog fell into his master with love.

"No one knows anymore. Even less care." Grell's voice echoed off the concrete interior bleakly. "I know there is another pore in Jersey…"

"Then a breach is impending." David spoke with the voice of a man that had witnessed three world wars and only returned to interrogate *you* and ask *you* what *you* thought of it.

"I'm a watcher and a keeper here. The dogs inform me when something is coming, or when the cemetery dwellers you can see, outside, become too joyous, pompous and proud. If the bodies stop their commotion, that is when my own guard is up, and I go to the church in Mountain Top or Malcom's funeral parlor in town and plead with the owners, nice family mind you, but I have to plead to have the next ceremony here. They understand, being in the business and all, how important it is. People don't stop dying, they are just more reluctant to bring'em here. And don't think I don't see those pudgy spiders in the rafters. They are watchers too, but for the other side. For now we have an agreement."

The thought chilled David.

Mr. Grell was scratching young Jett Marie's chest. She was wagging her tail, with such love. "Your Uncle Bill is the one on the right, but I suspect you knew that with his red hair showing under the zip cloth. He's a strong one. He'll fight them off a long time. The Seers, like you, him and myself always do, David. I, too, will stand strong until I die David, and then *Stronger.*" The old man nodded, leaning on his stick with the skull on the end of it.

David took his eyes off the pulsating dead bodies, sleepless in death behind the glass. He stood up, patted his Teddy on the head coming eye to eye with the groundskeeper on the other side of the crypt. "I know. And if those things beyond get past you… I'm training to do my part. Just like this beautiful boy will let us know when something unnatural breaks into our world. The best alarm system we could ever have." David bent down and kissed his dog on his tan and brown head, careful to be sure to feel the wonderful "knuckle" that labs and shepherds share on the top of their beautiful scalps. "My little knuckle head. Anything happens to you, Hell will pay."

David smiled sinisterly.

Excerpt from, "*The Fall of Tomorrow was a very real thing.*"-Cedric Bondnatsen

DEMONEYE PART II
DRINKIN' AIN'T FOR NUMBSKULLS

As I expected, at dusk they began erecting the wooden cross on top of the dusty hill. How many rough riders does it take to erect a wooden sacrificial "X" shaped killing device? The answer was four, apparently. I know there were at least twelve Numbskulls in the riding party. The rest may have went out on a hunt now that night was coming. Bracken was the leader, or so he thought himself as the leader of this broken pack of gunslingers. Raiders, marauders, no better than the red skinned native folk that they emulated. And Mutilated. HAHA. Yep.

The sun painted the sky pink over the sandy dunes beyond our campfire. K. Killoy, young feller in his late teens had the fire going to fend off the cold air. Normally the boy had the fire going just before dusk, a diligent effort at that, late in coming. A fire was of little use to thwart a pack of demons in flesh overalls. Fire attracted them, where other fine desert dwellers in the dark tended to steer clear.

My name is Cedric Bodnatsen. I'm dashing, fascinating and pretty. Ha, yes, I can attract the females (and men too, but that's not in my arena to judge a gift horse). Looking at our captive's leader, Bracken, was like looking into a mirror for me. That is, if you poured hot wax all over pale skin, cut some swiveled jagged etch marks into the parts of the flesh that you could see under his long overcoat, and turned the long blond hair of mine into a mess of dried hay. In a sense I got a gander into the future me. Still in my prime in a middle aged body, I had the strength of two normal men, mayhaps three, but to look at my thin elfin frame you may want to notch back a smack or two at me for stealing your significant other right under your nose.

Madness came in the form of manslaughter or man's laughter as I prefer to refer to this dark period of western civilization. Happened just a while back, adding the right amount of peppered flavor to your already spoiled pot roast.

When the demonic spirits broke through that Grand Canyon to the horror of settlers and native folk alike, these soulless specters began swiping up body suits so they could walk the plains. One oversight by the powers down below (of which I have much familiarity with) was that they did not contemplate just how quickly their stolen vessels would break down. So many men died young out west from hard living. So, on a nightly basis, the night sky filled with blue swishes of light that danced far below the diamond stars, floating about looking for a host. To the delight of the dimwitted and the horror of the wise, these blue demonic spirits were hopping from town to town possessing the best gunfighters the west had to offer.

It was an interesting time for Hell to cause a breach between realms. Maybe it was the violence of man, or the paltry sex trade, child labor, or attempts at completing genocide in a new land that drew their darklight powers more so. Personally, I knew that none of these factors were the number one monster motivation behind an invasion. Nope.

Guns.

Yep guns made life easy for the killing type running thick and in ample supply from one mining town to the next decadent gambling strip district.

Demons come in all forms. Unbeknownst to some of my past cronies or traveling companions, I knew a demon to see him, however outgunning their speed is still a challenge for me. I got better with more kills, but there is a blind motive inside those withering skulls that I just wanted to tap into. With the living, I had many tactics in order to thwart silly con men. As for the demon hoards and their types, there is a variety. The spiritual gliding type that meander the desert looking for a weak minded soulless slob who offered themself willingly by prayer to a sentient malicious lord happened to be the current stock inside this group of meatsuits that we found ourselves in ill company with. They penetrate during sleep sometimes, creeping through the orifices of these do-badders. Like here's one for you, even more fun, the ignorant bank robber, like the one I shot dead in Coppers Kilt, who decided that killing all fifteen witnesses in the bank two towns over was better than leaving a squeaker behind. Yea, those types were easily taken in their sleep. I shot that bloke down before he could be taken by one of these nomadic drifting spirits, but he surely was marked for the legion.

I've seen monsters. Truly, though, the full ranks of evil are abated by some unknown force, whether it be above, beyond or something I have not come across yet. It is surely hard enough, if not impossible to kill these things. Sure you can shoot them dead cold in the street in front of the Sheriff in towns like Caravass Pass or Tremblefoot. Do they really die?

No.

You merely shook down the host permanently, of course, everyone knows that. Those that can read have been hearing that noise since men have been carving up hieroglyphics in caves. The stronger demonic spirits get'on up and out. If no locals are deemed worthy of evil shenanigans then they make their disgruntled way back to some crack in the earth. I've heard tell of a crack in the sky too, but havn't really witnessed that for myself.

So here's the cow patty minus the flies.

I have this friend, old traveling partner I met along the way, Dekker Collins, (Dekker Dead-Shot Collins is his latest nickname I hear) who could gamble his way out of any saloon with his nose held high. That was until he met me. I don't like to lose. I made this clear. We made fast friends, shared several rides, popping demons along the way to save a family or two for a good meal if they could not pay us proper. That made me angry, but Dekker thought it was fair.

Seems, he found a way to outgun even the faster of the demon gunslingers. From what I hear, he never loses a gunfight no matter what the odds or how many of these diamond eyed bastards he faces. We parted ways as he had a family too, we'll say, to contend with. At least a memory of a family.

Not me. Not the marrying type. That was my excuse really. I don't deal in feelings and Dekker had delved too much into his lost past, dwelling in the darkness of his dead family, murdered by types like this rogue wave of demons we found ourselves in the midst of now. The real reason I left him was he had become a better shot than me. My competitive narcissistic nature could no longer travel with an equal much less than one more adept.

Dekker could see the yellow lantern lights behind the diamond blue eyes, somehow tap into the possessed gray matter behind his opponents and know their next move.

Impossible!

No, impossible for me to deal with.

So I left him.

And kids? Whats the fraggin' point? They drag you down. Except K. Killoy, in this new crew of mine. He's a good boy, fantastic listener and almost of drinking age. This is what I deem important. The desert is a lonely place unless you got good drink while sharing a fire with good company. I require stimulating conversation. I'm older than I appear, so the stories are few and far between that can spike synapses in my beautiful brain. K. Killoy, with his handsome features, two colts at his side, and a brown vest full of ammo that matched his dark brown skin, also had a finer tongue for telling wild tales around the fireside. So I kept him with me. The boy's listening skills ran deeper than most out here forging a bond more important since my stories span decades of interest. On some nights, I knew when he let his wide brimmed hat fall to his back by the strap that he was ready for one of my tales of absolute adventure in debauchery and history. The handsome young guy even asked one night, staring deep into my own blue eyes with his lusty brown, "How do you have so many stories?"

Decade's worth. That's all I said. Truth is, there are more than decades worth.

Unfortunately it did not seem that there would be a fireside tale told on this night. There were four in our party in all. Didn't matter now. The Numbskulls had our horses tied up somewhere beyond the ridge of the hill where they were constructing that damned cross. K. Killoy kept his cool under pressure. Maybe he relied on me too much? I'd get us out of this, sure. Always did. Even my old travel companion Dekker Collins knew I could get him out of a dilemma or two. Lord knows he had an eye for the whores, wife or no wife, he looked, always looked. Dabbled? I really do not think so. He was a classy guy, of the type this century surely was lacking. Dedicated to his family. This dedication may have gotten him into trouble back in Caravass Pass, the place where we were heading before this particular band of Numbskulls found us. Handsome, quick with a gun, and trusting. Sure. That part, the trusting part, would cut a man's life short at the nutsack. Poor Dekker.

For me there was much traveling in order to find myself some work, taste some gold, or just blast away at these drooping bags of flesh stretched over human exoskeleton. The latest member of our party was Collette, the black haired gypsy whore. Heh, mean that in the best way possible of course. K. Killoy and myself had just left Blinkpaw Shank, a mining community where we picked up Jo Jo Mince. Mince was a miner, recently fired for stealing another worker's lunch when he could not afford his own. Jo Jo Mince was only around for a week together before Collette came around. Spend a week in the desert with a man, be it a thief, drunk brigand or otherwise, you will certainly get to know the man. Mince's wife had died of that tuberculosis that seemed more than popular these days.

The new plague. Devils know, I've been around for a few good plagues.

Jo Jo Mince was a slave at one time too, who had migrated north, until his wife became ill and he had to stop roving about. She died in his big strong arms in a tent that he had constructed to keep her warm in her final moments, coughing up blood. Per, Jo Jo, his hair went gray overnight. Same thing happened to Dekker too. Fear, sadness, loss, I forget these passions the more I roam. As for Jo Jo Mince, not much scared him after that. He was always ready for death, or so he told me and K. Killoy. I sensed that my old friend Dekker Collins was going that route too, now that I was not around to distract him from his family's death.

Feelings. Who needs'em!?

So along came our gypsy, Collette. K. Killoy had led the way on his white pony who was pocked with black spots, sticking out like a piece of coal in snow on that cool desert morning outside Blinkpaw Shank. He had come to a complete stop, flipping his hat to his back, dark curls blowing in the breeze, hand up to "halt" us. Jo Jo Mince rode alongside me. I was glad to stop. My black steed hated me. All beasts of burden despised carrying my long body across the way no matter where it was. This had nothing to do with weight, to be clear, I'm rather thin. Scent. They know a bad man better than a whore knows about a fierce grip in the right place.

Speaking of whore, there was Collette, wrapped in a sheepskin hide, stumbling about the cool sand of the orange morning.

This is a fun time for lingo. The bumbling bubble mouthed words just kind of roll out of your mouth with pure laziness. Interesting time to be alive. Again.

Before long we were all stealing peeks under her sheepskin while she sat open legged across from us over a morning breakfast fire. We had soup to make, so we did. Chopped up some snake cuts, beans, some potatoes. K. Killoy took out a jack rabbit too. That meat was better to me, raw too, like I was used to in another time.

Skipping the soup since it seems the herb's we had in a small satchel had gone a stale dry, I stuck to the rabbit meat for breakfast while we listened to the runaway whore tell her tale of Caravass Pass. Her boots were high and tight to her knees, meeting some flesh colored leggings that gave her the false appearance of being nude beneath her long coat. A beige bodice below only made young K. Killoy steal more peaks at what he thought was skin. Poor desperate virgin, I understood his ploy.

Collette was polite, thanking us for the food. She claimed to have worked for a brothel in Caravass Pass, where I was heading, whether Jo Jo and the young man knew it or not. They seemed to trust my lead no matter what or where the percolating situation seemed to arise. The town was just the next partially prosperous town within a reasonable distance. Of course I'm not going to throw you a splintered bone, and lie, I was always heading to Caravass Pass! Dekker Collins more than likely was there, still hiding his trick for gunning down the devils breed.

As for the lovely curvaceous Collette and her ridiculously over pronounced lips (now sun baked and cracked) she had answered to a Madame named Deborah. I watched her lips across the breakfast fire. You can tell a lot from a person's lips when they told a tale. Personally I concentrate on lips and eyes, back and forth, flashing between the two looking for lies. Lies smell like hot copper, similar to blood if you are attracted to the scent of the life fluid. This comes with experience. As far as I could see this woman was not lying yet. Odd for a whore, right? I will say this, the middle aged beauty really stole my attention while she fiddled with a pink head wrap to pull back her straight black hair (almost so black it shimmered blue) letting if fall to her back. I knew that she was about to say something of substance now. Women get serious when they pull their hair back, all professionally committed to their next words and such. If you were ever married you'd know that. Yes, just because I stated that I'm not the marrying type should not fool your stinking membranes into believing I was never hitched!

It's impossible to hack down a harvest that you ain't never grown.

She spoke with a very sexy drone, delivering her name, looking all three of us in the eyes, one at a time, shifting back again as if we were three brer lappin racing for the last carrot. Here were three men, desperately (not me, not for the same reasons anyhow) alone in the sand sitting with the sudden scent of a woman on the arid breeze. We must have looked like salivating feral desert dogs to her.

"I could not stay there any longer and feel safe. Deborah, my lady whom I answered to, had commissioned a gunman that fights by most unnatural means. Though this, Dekker Collins, never loses, his very presence has now attracted the likes of more evil, more of these creatures of the night... all looking for a challenge. Seems they have a problem with a human that is not only able to quick draw on them, he can also put them in the grave permanently. The specter within dies with the host, if they are so shot by Dekker Collins." Shuffling her puffy white blouse under her sheepskin coat, she wafted a sweet perfume into the air. She smelled like roses. Odd for a whore. They must have gotten some bastard Frenchie passer-throughs in that town or they had some Indian to trade with that sold quality scents such as Collette's pleasant aroma. After the passing comfort of the womanly balm dissipated I remembered the scourge inside her words. My own personal scourge, mind you.

Jealousy heated my cold blood to a searing rage. How had he done it, and before ME?! This man she was speaking of, Dekker, an old friend had found a way to put a demon down, never to return.

Claiming to be on her way to Blinkpaw Shank, where we had just come from, Jo Jo Mince tried politely to change her mind. "Not much there if you were trying to escape the whoring practice my dear, but you could make your weight in gold with your looks, and fine scent... there aint much competition in that town anymore." He smiled like the gentleman he was.

That morning when the four of us came together had been cooler than most, comfortable for travel even if I had come up with a better idea to waste some time. Traveling to Caravass Pass was the only thing on my mind of course, more so at this juncture. This was high time to influence minds, win my little group's confidence, ultimately to get what I want.

This is what I do. This is how I lived for so long.

As the boy stared at the lovely raven haired girl, and Jo Jo tried to politely tell her she was ill fated making her way north to that old mining town, I rose up from our fire, traipsing casually between the rocky out cropping that hid us from the desert view. I was thankful for such an outcropping of broken brown rock in the light of day, in order to stay hid from other bands of rogues. At night though, I knew better than to stay too close to these shambling mounds where the sand beneath them were sometimes blessed with a sinkhole. More on this later, trust me.

Demons came in all shapes and sizes.

Stepping away from the three of them by the small fire, my black steed flinched at my approach, so I spit at its feet, making it dance a bit. Horses. Hate these damn things. A reciprocal relationship. Reaching into my saddle, ah, there it was. My private cask of the finest wine that no one could ever find again.

Like most whores do, Collette's eyes lit up at the sight of my square bottle with the copper outer covering. K. Killoy shifted his head sidelong like a curious puppy. "Morning drinkin' Cedric?" The boy said to me.

"Day drinking boy. Day drinking. We can take a day to ourselves, relax a bit. What's the rush. I need to hear more of Collette's town before I go there." I sneered at her. "Lets call this, *research*, ha."

"I'm not going back there." Her eyes as firm as her voice was deep.

"Your choice lady, but I can guarantee your safety. I can also guarantee, if you go with me, you may even move up in the ranks of your trade. Oh, hell, with my pull, we may open a competing brothel across the street from your said, *Deborah*. Your choice…. Here, have some."

She took the bottle and sipped.

"Sweet wine. Oh, this is marvelous." She smiled.

"It just so happens Dekker Collins is a friend of mine. Dead-Shot Collins." I sat down with them. "Heh heh, funny, *Dead-Shot* Dekker. He was always good, now I hear he never loses."

Collette passed the bottle to Jo Jo. "Far be it for me to pass up a drink from a fine lady such as you Ms. Collette." Jo Jo was genuinely smiling. Adorable for an old guy. Still, I found it pathetic.

I nodded to K. Killoy. He took the bottle next. He passed it back to Jo Jo. He wrinkled his nose.

"Nah."

It was alright. I needn't get the boy drunk or even slightly humming in order to win his favor. He looked up to me since I found him next to his dead family after an Indian scalping party took them on a road up north.

I had them in my grasp. We would be heading to Caravass Pass sooner than they could think of a second way to load a rifle.

Now, of course, the Numbskulls had all four of us forcefully in their possession, spreading out my work before me.

The wooden X-shaped cross was up on the hill. The sun was going down completely. *They*, of course preferred this. Not much for fighting in the daylight, though they could take up the task they just are not as adept in the sun's light as the humans that they sought as prey. Bracken, the long haired leader approached us in long strides. Collette was cozied up with K. Killoy. Not sure who was comforting who there. Jo Jo Mince was tied up next to them. The demon mob trusted the big mining man the least, so they tied him at the hands and legs.

"So, that guarantee… where is that lie now?" Collette stared daggers at me from across the fire that we had lit during the day, feeling that we would stay in the safety of this particular site for one more night. I had insisted on the fire being lit long before nightfall. Then, of course these bastards found us.

I could tell that Collette was holding me personally responsible for our sudden arrest by a demon horde, since I had decided not to keep on the move that day. Women are so one sided and fickle.

Of course I certainly saw where this was going. I stood to meet Bracken, again which was like looking into a mirror that spoke the future. "You are pretty a one, while the skin lays intact of course Numb Skull." Smirking with sharp words always inflicted such pain to their pride.

He hit me then, knocking the wind right out of my chest. I expected to be hit. Begged for it when my sharp blue eyes stared into your face, while I tilted my own high cheek boned grin larger than a lion's, I beckoned to be hit every time.

Proposition time. I knew Bracken better than he knew himself. As his posse fell in, surrounding us, the fire lapped red and orange glows across diamond eyes with the coming night. I was still so jealous, envying Dekker that he could see the "yellow" of their pupils! How can he know what they are thinking?

Well, I was not without similar tactics though my means were more challenging to ascertain.

"Cedric, is it? That the name you said? I have found myself obliged to provide you with the power of choice. Between the four of you, you will choose which one of the four will dine with us tonight. I give you an hour." Bracken's voice had a raspy echo, like a snake over a gravel road, moving at full pace. I know this. I've chased snakes across a broken gravel road many times.

"Fun."

"I can take two, if you wish Cedric." He stepped up, boot to boot. I really admired his brown leather boots with the crosses carved into the sides. His breath smelled of dried blood and moss.

"I have a better idea." Stepping aside, I approached the mad lot of them. I held my arms inside of my long coat up in the air, smiling at the grubby bearded faces and snarls of human teeth that hid the pointy silver blades beneath. Diamond eyes glared beneath hat brims. All hands were on holsters. "Bear with me... please, this can be fun. Have any of you gone through pillaging my saddle?"

Bracken despised my whimsy. "There was nothing of any value in the saddles.... Get to the point man!" He was leery of me now. A bit more than my comfort level could take.

"Actually sir..." One of his lackeys stepped forward, nervously rubbing his gloved hands together, then began to nervously scratch his beard. "The black steed does not like us getting close. It could make a run.....its tied down, but that horse is big... could break free when we come near..."

BABANG!!

Bracken let loose with his rifle, blowing his own henchmen's head to a broken mess of hair, hat, bone and blood all of which flecked the desert sand by the fire. A blue specter of ghostly light outlined like a floating skeleton flashed from the fallen body to the sky searching for a new host. I'm sure it may have thought to take one of us. Maybe none of us were keepers? More than likely the thing inside the dead henchmen knew that Bracken would just gun that host down too.

So, even Bracken did not know how to make permanent resin out of their kind?

Good.

"Oh, you should've been more patient sir. The steed doesn't like me the fairer either. Brilliant shooting though." I could not hold back my laughter. "Please, come with me, keep a gun at my back and I'll retrieve the best bottle of wine you will ever have. A scent of it can envelope your pulse in the warmest euphoria. Oh hell, even you might crack a grin, sir! Oh, but not too much. We don't want your face to crack and fall to your feet completely." The love of the drink enticed demons and man alike. Providing a challenge attracted them even more.

"All you need is to try and you may thank me for the best tasting batch of the last bit of nectar of its type. Besides, what else do we have out here in the barren waste?" I continued. I saw Bracken wince at the proposal. "All I'm asking for is a little symposium before we have to get brash with one another." The next thing I knew we were walking by the hill with the cross on it, passing it to the other side where they had our horses tied to a log.

A cool breeze blew our long coats open while we walked exposing my empty holsters and Bracken's ammo belt. I felt his rifle in the small of my back.

Away from the fire, the shadows on the sand stretched wide, dancing with the blaze among the mob of cowboy demons. I could not see my travel companions beyond the group of silent watchers by the fire, though I knew by the fire they would be safe from what I could now see (as my eyes adjusted) were scurrying about between us and the horses. The horses were roused more than usual that night, uneasily dancing about.

I turned to face my captor. "The funny thing about demons, my friend, that you may or may not know, depending on your age... there is a caste system, a bureaucracy if you will."

Bracken held the gun high with both hands. "You are not as you seem. Which makes me trust you less. Keep walking or your barter for your friends ends here."

"While you are inside that human shell, you become more susceptible to the same elements that humans are born at the mercy of. Your melting skin, rotting bones, are all haplessly accelerated as you cannot by any means maintain a human soul for the up keeping."

"Get the bottle Cedric." He growled at me.

"There is a large spider on your shoulder. More surrounding your feet. They are big, and all about us. Neutral if they are hungry enough. Mindless if they are starving."

He swatted the yellow plated spider off his shoulder with a brush from his long bone encrusted hand. The shimmer of the fire flickered off the belly of the spider. "I know of the spiders. I know of all of the unleashed beasts that will inherit the Earth in time." Hissing his impatience at me.

More scurrying below our feet. "What you do not know is that I picked this campground in particular. You are not the first batch to try and take me," I reached into my pocket, nodding for his approval, "A match, is all." I lit the match off of the leather of Bracken's jacket. Throwing the tinder to the ground beside a rocky outcropping so we both could see dozens of tarantulas embroidered with yellow plates scatter from the tiny light, retreating to a large hole beside the cracked boulder. "Fire keeps us safe. Darkness, not so much. Now, Bracken my friend, before we retrieve the bottle and move to the safety of the fire, were you aware that those hellspawn spiders do not discriminate? Flesh is flesh to them." He saw something in my eyes then, possibly recognizing me for what I was for the first time. I grit my teeth behind my pursed lips, hating myself for giving away my secret.

"Cedric....*Bodnatsen*. Your name is known to me. I appreciate your vile banter as well as the warning. But now. The bottle please." Bracken's deep drone became calm, vibrating the air around us with a comforting hum that would chill most good folks. He trusted me a bit now, glancing at the scurrying black legs in the sand around us, not at all at ease with the swarming movement in the shadows.

Bottle in hand, I kicked at several spiders that scrambled to climb up my legs. "Sorry boy. If only you liked me." I said to the black steed. Bracken and I walked back to the security of the fire to the sound of the horses whinnying their pleas for help.

"I don't need to hear that all night..... Tolson! Free the damned horses and tie 'em near the fire! We can use them. And get a fire going for our own damn rides, immediately." Bracken ordered one of his lackeys who jumped to action. Bracken looked at me again, nodding, thanking me silently for saving their own horses as well. The ridges of his chin and cheekbones began poking through the deadening skin of his host's once handsome face. Bracken had taken a handsome man during his prime.

If anything I had bought more time.

Collette's hair was pulled back from her face so that the glow from the fire lit her seductive features orange, her accusing glare under her dark brow could not be hidden though, piercing through the blaze. K. Killoy held hands with her, sitting as close to the fire as possible.

The entire party had been informed now of the spiders, keeping closer together around the fire. K. Killoy too looked a little put off at me hiding the spider thing from them, surely upset that I never explained why I chose this particular campsite, ultimately of course for the safety of all involved. Believe me? You may not. That would make you a tad smarter than some that have traveled with me. Truth be told, buster, the rocky outcroppings such as said property, always seemed to house these fist sized shimmering beasties lately. A situation such as this gave me power. Knowledge is power, right? I had that over Bracken, and now, I had Bracken's full attention.

Jo Jo Mince was still tied at the cuffs. So I uncorked the bottle of its silver tab. Taking a nice swig, I shuffled over to Jo Jo, pushing several stinky numbskulls out of my way. There were growls of greedy need. Collette took the bottle out of my hands, sipped then handed it back. "The boy doesn't' need any. Spare him some innocence on his last night." She smiled at K. Killoy.

The boy rolled his big beautiful eyes with sheer disappointment at being left out.

"A little numbness before dying couldn't hurt." He pouted.

"Sure thing boss, if I'm to hang on this night, make me numb as these dead things." Jo Jo strained hard to smile up at me. I poured a smidgeon down his throat. The bottle was mostly full still, assuring those around me that *all* they needed was a swig, I nodded, bowed, tipping my hat to Bracken.

"Pass it around, one sip'sall you need. Trust me." I sneered through my own perfect teeth.

Soon, they would have us all tied down while they were lowering their guard with the fine drink. Four of them were left to stand guard on the outskirts. The remaining eight to ten of them indulged.

The fire burned bright under the dome of desert stars. I sat across from Bracken. The bottle was going on empty quickly after the bunch of drones took their gulps. This was fine with me, surreptitiously silent, I was once again getting things done my way, fastidious and selfishly greedy, and this was going to end by morning. Obsessing inside, I had to get to Caravass Pass and see about this Dead Shot Dekker guy I used to ride with. All these folks were in my damn way.

I do not like being upstaged. Ever.

The warmth of comfort hummed in every vein of my body like ants in a feeding frenzy sliding throughout those wonderful tubes within me that shared the life blood. Bracken knew who I was now, eyeing me while smiling through his now pointy demon teeth. *His* gray matter was the first to connect to mine. I could see from his own eyes, his perspective, as his blue lit wings were gliding through the dark passages of Hell. Guided by a crack in the black and red sky his translucent blue wings flapped on either side of him while he swooped upward about the pyres and red brimstone below. Joined by other specters of light like himself they rushed to the hole provided to them from above to penetrate the world of humans, blinded by the sun at first, sickened by the fresh air of the earth, they broke through, looking for hosts, praying for night.

I watched the one called Tolson, seeing into his memory as he was taken while behind bars. His name was Tolson in life. The bastards were seldom creative enough to come up with original names. Suppose I'm guilty of that too, but I've had many nicknames.

Myself aside, sorry I'm extremely narcissistic to the point of chronic addiction.

Tolson. I was inside Tolson, the bulky bearded sweat stained and horny for rape Neanderthal with an appetite that could not be satiated. He was easily taken, invoking hell as his being was no different in life as he was in possession. The vision shifted. Seeing through the large man's eyes to memories before he was taken by the darklight spirit, he was in a schoolhouse, in the middle of a lesson…. Fifteen young girls and a teacher…

Then he was behind bars, being spat upon by the surviving family members. I could see the reflection of Tolson in their angry eyes, taste Tolson's blood run from his broken face. He was laughing back at them while the spittle of a dozen angry townsfolk ran down his bloody face. A comedy of horrors in human fluid, Tolson was waiting for his hanging to come at dawn when a blue light shot through the bars. A blue specter of evil light vaporized as it struck Tolson in his sweaty chest, creeping upward and below, I could feel the demon's light penetrating every orifice. A mirror inside the eyes of the onlookers shone back at me. His eyes went yellow, teeth elongated in a snarl of pins. I had just witnessed the night he was taken. Reborn.

There were others now. All of them. Sometimes, all at once, the weak-minded individuals with demon poisoned thoughts entered my mind as I tapped into their skull's threshold. Rapes, murder, mass graves, gunfights, blood, lust, and ultimately genocide. Waves of violence pulsed in my own veins at their memories. I watched an entire Navajo village burned to the ground while I stood on a hill in one of these demon's boots. There was laughter rumbling from the chest of the beast's head that I found myself in, one hand on the crotch, inspired by his own work. Others stood on the hill with him. Possibly some from this same filthy pack of hyenas.

Desensitized to the defamatory state of the damned, none of these visuals nor the smells and chills that came with them truly phased the likes of me anymore, sadly. I could care less what crimes these blokes had ruptured throughout the halls of justice that is the crux of human morality.

Nope.

"Bracken, take off my bindings. I know where there is another bottle." I stood up. Penetrating his decaying human mind, I felt my way through the sap and grime of the long haired leader.

"That was your blood in that wine, was it not, Cedric Bodnatsen?" He rasped, strands of his hay-like hair blew about his face down to his chest while he spat at me.

I could feel Collette and Jo Jo Mince both turn their heads to me, not needing to look at them to feel the flare of horror dropping with their lower jaws.

Bracken had his rifle in his hand and made quick work of bashing me in the head with the bottom end. It was the last thing I saw before wakening an hour or two later to screams.

Jo Jo Mince was hanging from the erected cross by his wrists. There was a line of numbskulls on either side behind the two that were taking their turn. Bracken stood at the bottom of the sandy hill, making sure that everyone was getting just enough before the next in line moved up. The older man was howling in pain, while a yellow eyed demon in cowboy leathers ripped and tugged at the veins that they so carefully peeled free from the temples and his forearms. They sucked the fresh blood that way so that each one could get some of the life fluid without annihilating the source altogether. Smart really. Grotesque poetry of the macabre in such an organized fashion. When feeding, they were no longer capable of hiding their needle teeth and yellow eyes. The bones of their knuckles, arms and face shone through, breaking the skin. Jo Jo was suffering.

I saw the weak minded one named Tolson standing behind Collette and K. Killoy, keeping guard. I did not let him see my eyes taking him in. I did not need my eyes open for the exchange. My blood was in his decaying veins and he was drunk on Jo Jo's blood. He had taken more than the others. Easy prey.

"Release me, cut the ropes." His skull was easy to nab. I was inside the rotting veins of the vessel that housed the being within Tolson, floating through crispy dry tubes all the way up to the rotting brain, traveling, not unlike the moment I flew with Bracken in his other form when he broke from hells gates.

With his buck knife, Tolson obeyed my command and ripped me loose. "Now, blast Bracken in the back of his head." The thing that used to be a serial rapist and killer named Tolson, fired two shots at his boss man. Both hit Bracken in his back, bolting him to the ground. "Dammit, son..!! I said

Head!" I got the impression, Tolson never was a good shot.

I sat up now, watching some of the other henchmen turn from their slow feast.

Focusing on the two that had just taken their bloody maws from Jo Jo's visible veins, I called on my blood that mixed within all the henchmen. "These men want the remainder of your captives for themselves, Tolson is a mutinous bastard! You must act!" Their minds were a pale flap of paper in the wind soaking with my intentions. Standing in front of the fire, I could feel my own diamond eyes burning into the numbskulls forcing their hands onto each other. They became their own adversaries.

"TOLSON!!!!" One of them screamed. This gray haired bloody faced gentlemen pulled his colts loose from his belt and let go with the bullets.

Guns blazed, lighting up the night. There were growls where talons were tearing apart flesh, ripping out organs. Bodies dropped. In some cases the specter of evil light was visible leaving the bodies in search of a new host. DAMN! If only I knew Dekker Collin's secret at *acing* these bastards dead for good!

I ran over to Collette and K. Killoy to cut their bonds.

My orders seemed to be a might of overkill. Four men ran for the horses, I could feel that one or two of them were so confused that taking horses and breaking loose was the best bet. I had hoped they left one or two horses for me.

One selfish yellow eyed bloke decided he would get some more of Jo Jo for himself during the fray. He seemed to be the last man standing. To torture him some, I picked up my belt that had been tossed aside, pulled my own colt out, releasing two bullets to the top of Jo Jo Mince's head, ending his misery. Mostly I did this to piss off the hungry confused and desperate being that lurched in front of Jo Jo's now lifeless body. Some would say I did it to end Jo Jo's suffering. That would be a mistake. I never once thought of the man's needs unfortunately. All I wanted to do was upset the demon that had been feeding on him.

I rely on a considerably diverse form of algebra.

Always being a fun seeker at the expense of others, I continued to do so, focusing on the last man standing again, "Before eating one of your own bullets, I need you to put a bullet through Bracken's skull." I could see Bracken lifting his large lanky body from the sand, growling angrily, garishly turning toward me with his jaws of protruding razors.

Bracken drew first, rifle in his hands, he blew the head off of his former foot soldier.

Now I remember clearly saying "Uh oh," aloud.

See, here's the true bite of the situation. I was scattered within the confines of about nine adversaries at once. When consolidated down to the mere one, Bracken, as it were, my blood within serves up a true pot of hot chili beans, peppers and all. Finding clarity within his own mind, Bracken found the memories that belonged to me. Only now they became more vibrant. Even with the focus on him, I could not control this old specter of the damned even slightly. Had he consumed more of my blood, perhaps? He knew what he was getting into when my blood hit his lips. Not the usual numbskull. He was experienced.

Tolerance. What a bitch!

I had scrambled for my belt on the ground with the remainder of our booty.

While Bracken got to his feet, and we drew on each other I was frozen solid in my tracks next to the dying fire. The sun was peeking over the horizon. That line of red across the desert, a bloody ridge behind the dangling body of Jo Jo transposed to a different time and place. The light of the horizon went from a deep red to a bright white light shining under a locked door. The door was slowly open. I can see my boots. Bracken's sweet expensive boots with the wicked etchings upon them. He was entering a room, a dank chamber lit with several lanterns on a card table. There were four men sitting at the table in religious garb. Missionaries, I was sure. I had come across the likes of those faithful types many times in my travels through the decades. I also now know there is a real reason for men to believe in something that provides hopeful strength against a bastion of evil that lays in wait for them otherwise.

There were books, crucifixes and wooden pews stacked up in the back of the dusty room. We were in the rectory of an old church. The four men were seated facing one another, gagged, dripping with perspiration, eyes wild with desperation. Three were younger men in their twenties. One may have been an Indian, converted in order to convert more of his own. There was a lot of that. To each his own. The man in charge had to be the older bald man with scars along his neck. My eyes, now Bracken's, were fixated on the elder.

"You do your work father. I do mine. You may have thwarted an entire town's descent, of which I commend you," It was Bracken's voice. I could see the hands in front of me holding a scythe, polishing the blade with a shawl embroidered with a gold cross as I moved closer to the men bound to their chairs. "With your presence disposed of, I can move on with my work. I too am a missionary. You have a few empty shells walking around your town that you never really got the message through to. This *good news*, as you refer to it." I, we, were whispering in the old man's ear. I could smell the salty sweat through his black robes.

Without warning the scythe was cutting through his neck, mercilessly slow, rubbing more than cutting. Blood poured down the front of the man's robes audibly while the slow cutting continued. I could smell Bracken's elation as the droning gag of a scream slowly became a pig squeal.

Horrific. Even for me this was too much, simply because I knew that there were three more younger men about to succumb to the same treatment and if I did not shut down I would have to witness the entire exchange. Now realizing that Bracken did not do this to feed, I was sickened at having to witness another being's extreme self-centered behavior when I had so much of my own to contend with. His intentions were his own. I was growing bored. I had things to do. Time to move on.

Pain pulsed into my back and out my gut as if I threw up all my nerve endings out of my belly button! On the bright side I woke from Bracken's memory, no longer subjected to the damned conceited engorgement of the malignant rascal before me.

I fell to my knees, noting that the shot came from behind me, not from Bracken who stood just feet away with his rifle drawn, but not smoking.

Falling to my back, I looked up to see K. Killoy's Colt pointed directly where my back had been. Collette stood next to him. The boy had done it.

Losing a bit too much of my satchel of life fluid, I began to black out. The last words heard this time were Bracken's "Don't even think about it boy. I got you dead where you stand. Woman, lower your gun."

******

When I came to I was face to face with Bracken's long pointy face. The yellow had faded from his eyes as night turned to dawn. "Your wound is already healing Cedric Bodnasten." He whispered. I was tied to one of those nifty "X's" so that he could hold court.

"Where is the boy and the woman?" I was quite hurt that it would be K. Killoy, the kid I took under my wing as a younger brother of sorts that would be the one to shoot me in the back, when I knew for sure Collette was the creature with the bona fide intentions to go through with it. Yea, I saw in her head too. She had several customers in her past that left her bed with a few less marbles in their sack, so to speak. Hurt to watch those memories. Ouch. Poor slobs.

"I let them go, seeing that we had a mutual game plan in gunning you down Cedric. Gave them a horse since we seem to be in surplus at this juncture. I saw potential there. After all you did free up quite a few of my boys. It's possible one if not both your friends may already have taken up residence with an old travel partner of mine by now. But something escapes me Cedric,"

He was having fun now. I know because we shared the same sense of humor. "And that being?" He was swiping a stick into the shredded bowels of Jo Jo Mince, laying on the ground.

"How did you miss that? How the hell did you make such a concerted effort to control my boys, but miss that one of your own had your number?"

"Truth be told, stinky," My stomach hurt, but the bleeding had stopped, "Collette drank the wine. I saw her for what she was, and true, she will be an excellent shell for one your kind. But the boy did not drink from it. Also, thought I could trust the bugger." I said.

"Spread yourself too thin." Bracken was smiling through his short whiskers.

"Perhaps. So what now?"

"I saw into your soul. Lucky bugger. You have one. You are merely a real human. But once, oh yes, once you were so much more. A king? Cedric Bodnatsen sold his soul for a woman, a queen with silver hair and penchant for killing all the women and young girls who threatened her allurement. Those that were more beautiful than her died at her orders. You've lived many lives. You are a monster. They tooled with you. Something about you keeps *them* intrigued enough to keep you in the realm of the humans. They let you keep your soul, damned as it were, yet you thrive through lives. What use do they find in you I wonder?" Bracken sounded like a child with a broken toy. "I'm soulless. Your life is not for me to take. There must be use for you here in this plane, because dammit man, they just keep sending you back!" Bracken was laughing now, removing his hat to scratch his brittle head. I could hear his nails scrape his skull beneath the rusting scalp. Bits of flakes fell to the sand.

All true. I had a human soul. This is what made me different than the numbskull specters that possess the living. I had a reason to change my ways and die by rightful means, or go on with my demon puppet strings providing whatever cause that the fellers below deem worthy. Hell had let me go to clean up some of their messes, Bracken now knew this. He was one of their stinky messes. The Demon Horde was lessoning now that people were fighting back with holy means like that priest and his missionaries that Bracken had destroyed. This particular invasion may have been too obvious, too blunt, too easy to thwart here in the barbaric west.

Never show your cards too early. Fail.

Then Bracken got up in my face, swiping the hat off my precious blond locks. "So the boys below have other plans? I can go with that ditty. Till then, I will have my fun. Make my marks so that someday I can be as famous as *Cedric Bodnatsen.*" He spit in my face. Needles scraping each other in his mouth. "Malkyre'." He spoke my hell given name. The one I strove to protect and forget.

"You were never human. It will never happen, *spuds for nuts.*" I noticed then that I had a bit more pain in my left wrist, than my right. Bindings tighter? Oh bugs in my sandwich! My veins were hanging out of my left wrist. He had been *at* me, having his way with me!! Dried blood smeared one corner of his mouth.

"I'm going to leave you out here for the sun to beat down on that pretty scalp of yours. Being that I can shoot you full of holes, and you will heal, that's not fun. Could blow your head off. Probably see you again anyway huh? Cept maybe you'd have a new head and I wouldn't see you coming. I'm jealous you get to come back in the same pretty body. Yes, saw that too. You have looked the same through centuries. A vampire too once? Unique. Not many get to enjoy such elegance. That stint you had as a magic user could really have been a lucrative career in this decade, selling snake oils and all. Rethink that career, Cedric you old drover." He was enjoying himself too much. He continued, "Oddly we have the same intentions, even right now in this uncomfortable scenario in the heat of the morning sun….whew… gonna be hot today!"

"What do you mean?" I asked, turning up the serious a notch.

"Seeing that I'm gonna leave you for the spiders tonight, which may or may not do away with your beautiful body for quite some time, though the suffering will be fierce, while I will find my way to Caravass Pass and *do in* your buddy Dekker Collins. Yep, saw that in your noggin too….heh heh…" He poked me with one of his long finger nails right in the middle of my small forehead. "Found a way to kill us permanently. Can't have that. Neither can you. Cedric Bodnatsen just cannot allow *a being* to have an edge over him in any way. So you are gunning for your old gambling pal. This will lead you directly to me in time. Perhaps, a rightful death for one of us. What kind of life is this anyway, Cedric? Hmm? Look around. Sand. Nothing but sand and murder by beheadings. Surround a man with sand, guns, ugly women, and what do you get? A dark spiral of murder. Fun yes. Short lived? Well, look at yourself Cedric. How long are we supposed to keep this up? Even that wife of yours was bored being a queen in a majestic land. And You? Sold your soul to try and save hers? What is that? Love?" He spat red goo onto the ground. My dried blood.

He whistled, and my black steed, came to him, reluctantly but even the beasts of burden wanted to make haste getting away from the spider outcropping of a campsite. I'll admit that I was jealous that that dumb horse came to him willingly and hated me spitefully.

Hated that horse!

"Do you know how your buddy is doin' it? This Dekker wrangler?" He was upon the steed, about to squeeze his legs to get the horse to begin a trot. Looking down at me, he knew I did not know the secret. He was just trying to spur my envy even more that someone was better at killing demons than me, reminding me that he was going to find out first.

"No. No idea. But I intend to find out. When I do, Bracken, you too will know. Oh hell, stinky, you may find out sooner. Dead-Shot Dekker, as he is known now, has not lost a fight." I smiled.

In cloud of dust, he was gone, my horse kicking up sand behind them.

As experienced as his specter inside was, Bracken's rashness might get him killed for good. Something he may actually be asking for, if not for the bloodlust within that called on for survival.

*****

I had an entire day in the baking glow of the sun to ponder the outcome of Dekker vs. Bracken. Ponder yes. Care? Not so much. More prevalent to me was the possibility that the shimmering desert spiders would be coming as the night approached. Without a fire I would be facing a horrible death.

Again.

This time, at the hands of hell spawned creatures such as these spiders, it was indeed possible that I could also be facing the most final of curtain calls. There was no way to know this for sure until you were in the moment. Sleep could be welcoming, if not for the halting aspirations of my soul in hell for eternity.

I would have to get out of this.

Chittering. I could sense them coming. They smelled like burnt breadcrumbs. With the sun almost completely gone in the purple sky I knew those hungry buggers were coming to chew me apart. The giant solid pieces of shale were down the mound below me, broken in about six pieces. In the center of the rocks was the blackened ash of our fire from the night before. No movement in the shadows yet.

My scalp burned from the day baking in the direct sun. The wound on my wrist had closed up unnaturally, with the gift of the dark ones. Nothing was left of my stomach wound where K. Killoy had shot me. I could not feel the point of entry in my back either. A slow agonizing death was approaching with the brisk of the night air.

Something else too. I heard the whinny of a horse just past the rock outcropping. I could see a shadow approach.

Her perfume was unmistakable. She wore it the day we found her and then some. Collette had returned stinking of that musk that the Indian's sold to the whores now and again. Pollen powder I call it, even though it could be pleasant at times. This was not one of those times.

Her gorgeously shaped figure rounded the corner of the maze of rocks, followed by the slighter shadow of K. Killoy.

"Come to make fun of me? Maybe shoot me in the back....well yer' approaching from the wrong side, dipshits." Could not resist the chance to poke fun, whether they were here to help me or not. "Get on with your business. Spiders are coming. Happens to be a nest below this campsite of ours."

Collette held a rifle up, pointing directly at me. She motioned with a tilt of her head to the boy. In this light they resembled each other and could have been brother and sister. Who knew? Both of their dark hair blew with the night breeze. "Go on, cut him down." With that, K. Killoy ran up the hill, knife in hand.

"You healed. So it's true Seed? You are one of them?" The boy looked into my eyes. Some anger, some disappointment there.

"No, I'm not like them. Different. More like, say… Collette. Only her demon is between her legs…."

PEOWWWW! The bullet from her rifle blasted the dirt next to my left.

"SHUT IT!" She screamed.

"AWRIGHT…Awright….. See kid, what having one of those between your legs will do to you? Heh heh." Spoke with boisterous confidence to both of them while the boy cut my wrists free. "Why the change of heart?" I reached around on the ground where I saw my hat. It would be a relief to cover my burned scalp with the cool leather of the hat's interior.

Never lowering the weapon she approached. "I saw you. I saw why you became what you are. I drank your blood in that cask, just like the rest of them. Right tidy trick you got going there Mr. Cedric. I did drink though, and a little more than I should have I suppose. Real question is why did you not try and control me…surely you did it in the past. Like that first night. Influencing me to go back to Caravass Pass." Collette stopped feet away from me. I was free.

"Didn't see the need lady. I was preoccupied." I motioned to the bodies of the dead shells scattered all about.

"We could not rightly leave you." The boy said, backing away to stand with Collette.

"And we cannot rightly take you with us. Go do whatever it is you do, but I ask you not to follow us." Collette could hear the spiders too. They were louder this time in anticipation for the coming feast. Plenty of meat lying about, stinking up the joint. Patter patter patter. Here they come.

"Go. I'm not going to thank you. You fukkn shot me in the back like a numbskull. Go on, get to your ride….move. Oh, and Collette, watch yourself. Bracken saw you as a potential host. You all that bad? I think he overestimated your vile intentions. Wrong?" I said to her, as she turned to walk back to the horse beyond the rocky outcropping. She stopped, turned, wind blowing her black locks in her face. I continued. "Yea, I saw your thoughts….memories… Collette…the murdering whore of Caravass Pass. You were forced to leave weren't you?"

"And you? You loved your woman, did you not?" She smiled, turned and walked into the coming darkness beyond the rock.

"K. Killoy? Hey you. You ain't no numbskull. Keep it that way. Stay clear of me and the likes of Bracken. Use your damn noggin. Go you little shit, I never want to see you again." I chuckled, but turned a bit stern towards the end of the statement to batten down the words.

The boy smiled a bit, then followed Collette into the darkness of the night. I heard the horse trotting within the next minute.

Gathering up a belt of bullets, a rifle, some satchels of water I pulled on my old long coat that had been thrown to the side of my would-be grave with the "X" in the ground. I wrapped my wounded wrist in the torn shirt of one of the dead shells. The bleeding had stopped long ago as the healing began to itch with heat.

Climbing two sandy hills to the southeast a bit, soon I was on top of a new hill with a bit of grass. No broken rocky out cropping. Good. I heard the bugger horde of spiders begin their feast in the dark before I was able to put at least two miles between me and that foul camp.

Caravass Pass, Bracken and Dekker Collins here I come.

The night air smelled sweet again. It was nice to remember what it was like to have someone to care enough to free you from certain death. Spared by enemies and friends all in the same day?! Maybe there truly was more hopeful substance among men as opposed to the hellish circumstances out here? One thing was certain, drinkin' aint for numbskulls.

- 9 -
BARREN

Captain Barren Polynski flipped on auto pilot, directing the ship toward the blue gem in the void. Stewart Hayes, his co-pilot, along with Virginia Pentrace were all going home for Christmas. The conversation between the three member crew, just hours ago during an anti-gravity session was full of jeers, in advent of seeing their families again. Virginia was going home to her equally gorgeous husband of thirteen years and their little boy and girl. She had a crag of comet rock wrapped for her up and coming little astronaut son.

These missions were redundant yet necessary. Since NASA ELITE first landed a remote unmanned probe on a passing comet, the new space race became a game of nabbing samples of the passing particles. Tracking them on their journey, the hope was to maybe find a cycle in their direction through space. Finding the source would be the most advantageous of course before another one of these bad boys hit the Earth. At least that was how Captain Barren fooled himself into justifying these sometimes fruitless voyages.

"I feel like we actually accomplished something this time. That was a big mutha of a comet! More of them have been striking Earth than I feel comfortable with. Smaller ones of course, but this baby that passed Earth was a monster." Captain Barren spoke to the console more than the man next to him. Stewart Hayes was not known for small talk.

"Only a matter of time before we go the way of the dinosaurs." Coldly he addressed his captain's attempt at cordial conversation. Hayes tapped a rear thruster motivator that flashed from red to green, indicating their coordinates for home were set and on course.

In his early forties, Captain Barren was jaded with the world, seeing enough of human hatred and disgust. Hayes was just one more nugget of bleakness. Luckily their time together was waning.

Without a family to worry about back home, the vastness of space with its empty quiet was welcoming. Virginia was better company. Stewart Hayes was just someone he had to work with now and again. What was it? Four or five of these comet tracking missions?

"It will blow his mind." Virginia had smiled with her beautiful gleaming teeth over narrow crimson lips, thinking about her young son opening the Christmas wrapping paper to reveal a genuine space souvenir.

Captain Barren fixated on her olive green eyes behind her shaggy brown locks that fell to her tiny bosom, thinking how lucky her polo playing husband was. What was the spoiled rich boy's name? Blaine or something? He thought through a fake grin.

Stewart Hayes had just rubbed his stubbly red head of fuzz, rolling his eyes, not connecting with anything that resembled emotion. Hayes was the youngest of the three man crew. Shrewd, cunning, a business man. He had what it took to be an astronaut physically but Barren knew he was an alpha in his own mind incapable of taking orders, bi-polar, (unproven of course, by the NASA ELITE specialists or he would never have been eligible) manipulating and strong for his thin stature. Virginia took orders well where Hayes questioned every motion inferred by Captain Barren.

Even erecting the Christmas tree.

Captain Barren's last order for them.

"Why are we wasting our time with this?" Hayes had said after they received confirmation from Air-Tech Base in Texas Province. Virginia had briefly put her hands into her tight jumpsuit pockets. This was her passive way of dealing with Hayes's negativity during their four week deep space excursion. As quickly as she had put her hands deep in her blue form fitting suit, she removed them, reaching for another hook from the console to wrap into the loop of a bright silver and red Christmas ball in order to place it onto their fake pine scented tree in the corner of the cockpit, next to the sliding door.

"We can be home for Christmas." Virginia's smile was infectious. In another life Barren saw himself with her instead of home with several empty Jameson Bottles.

It was *she* that dusted off the old box that Barren had insisted they bring with them, knowing that NASA ELITE was going to order them to start their return flight through space dust on Christmas Eve.

Was it hours ago? Time elapsed quickly when there was no difference between morning and evening.

Barren swirled around in his chair to face the cockpit window, smile fading as he put his back to Virginia. This was too easy. Every aspect of the mission had gone without a hitch, from meeting Comet B.N. 44 at the safe coordinates to deploying the laser tag dart with the tracking device. Some debris from the comet had come back with the remote sample scooper too. Part of which Virginia, with permission from her captain, had wrapped up.

It was a hollow rocky piece that was the size of a baseball. The rest would go back to NASA ELITE. As for B.N. 44, (named after the Bloody Nerve, a favorite band that Mission Control transmitted to them from home now and again. Director of Mission Control, Spencer Wray was 44 years of age and a fan of fine rock - n- roll, transmitting his own playlist now and again) the comet continued to roll on, missing Earth by 60 miles. That was good news to report back too. Captain Barren liked to deliver messages like that back home, almost as much as he thought it was great to get those radio signals playing new music once in a while to bring the comforts of home out here in the quiet of space. They could tune into some station called Society 13 or something like that, who boasted about playing new music all the time. Barren grew up on hard rock and it was nice to hear some good rock coming from home to remind him that he can be home again, sipping his scotch, listening to a little Mister Vertigo or The Bloody Nerve. Normalcy. Comfort.

It was the simple things that kept Barren moving through the dailies.

Then came the transmission.

Words spoken over the crisp crackling electronic feedback that blew the dust off their memories of anything they held rational and dear.

Before the haunting words flooded the cockpit, all was business as usual.

The arrow headed shuttle named MT1 spliced the pitch of space with Earth in its sight. Captain Barren was seated next to the robotic Hayes. Ignoring the coldness of his co-pilot, he continued to look at the seemingly small jump between their ship and their home, a bright white and blue marble on the infinite blackboard. Virginia had placed a soft hand on both their shoulders behind them. The scent of her long waves of brown hair was overwhelming; roses and honey.

How did she manage to maintain a wonderful scent in the bleakness of space? The captain remembered thinking. Barren adored her comforting tone too. Her voice soothed the atmosphere around them, blending in with the hum of the sifting oxygen ducts spewing out air.

"Look at the red and green lights off of the Russian Satellites, over there, left of the moon. Christmas in space. Do you think they did that on purpose? It's pretty." Her enthusiasm was contagious. Elated with the return flight, Barren longed for more of her touch.

"No. That's just their formational transponders. Nothing creative happening there dear." Hayes doused her flame as soon as he could. His tone was still resonating the stolid anger he had for the both of them. Breaking code, bringing a piece of the comet on board and not leaving it in the detainment chamber with the rest of the debris, was beyond regulations. There had been a small spat between Hayes and Barren about the subject. That conversation dissipated as quickly as Virginia could run to her cubby space in the drop room, to write out a card and wrap up the hollow rocky remnant for her little boy.

The strange hollow gray rock had passed the contamination chamber tests as well as the Geiger Meter when Virginia insisted that they test it out first. Protocol to ease her own mind.

When Virginia had returned from wrapping her little boy's Christmas present in the shiny paper, Barren was pleased to find that they had a private moment together. Hayes had left to his chambers to read or whatever the hell else the cocky little fucker did to appease his down time. Barren hated that the man seemed to bond with their other passenger. He even named the shimmering yellow spider "Zero" as the tarantula sized arachnid was the first test group of the comet tagging series of missions. Hayes was glad to keep it in his quarters and talked to it frequently, like an old friend. When Barren watched the recordings of Hayes' he was usually disturbed by his co-pilot's yearning to stare at the small tank with Zero in it. No more book reading. Just gazing at the Nasa Elite issued spider.

Since the approach of comets like B.N. 44 there had been odd, yet undeniably substantial changes back on Earth. This comet in particular resembled a similar beast that had passed Earth in the late 60's causing untold peril to the environment that most humans took for granted back then. Some disease had spread, but had been squelched, however, not without an enormous loss of life.

In turn, NAZA ELITE had to focus on the one species that were suspect, seemingly to sputter to levels of murderous inspiration, tantalized by these lights in the sky, like B.N. 44.

In the desert regions of Earth, waves of enormous spiders swarmed out of deep holes in the ground to chatter in the night at their passing god of light resembling a speck in the darkened sky above.

These shimmery plated arachnids were a new genus and species. Apple sized, aggressive, and seemed to be intelligent when congregating among their own.

Zero, assigned by NASA ELITE to Hayes, was to be analyzed closely when the MT1 came within a safe sample proximity of B.N. 44. What reaction would this creature have when within reach of the streaming comet that pulled its brethren out of the Earth from whatever depths that humans were never meant to see? How old was Zero? Were these creatures the first inhabitants of the planet? Barren assessed all of this as he queued up the video recording of Hayes in his chambers.

Eyes dazzling, hair bouncing, cheeks wide with elation, Virginia had reentered the cockpit with a "swisssshhhh" of the door next to their makeshift Christmas tree.

"Virginia, sit down. I need to show you this. I need your assessment."

"Captain, please, I'm not going watch that asshole play with himself in his room." She joked. Then thought about her words. Wait, if the captain watches Hayes, he must also....

"Just watch." Barren pointed at the screen above the console. Hayes was holding the spider's tank, standing in the middle of his room. Then he opened his door with a "swisssshhhh", walking into the hall. Barren pressed two green keys, entering his password and a new video popped up.

"What's he doing?" Virginia's voice sounded uneasy.

The video now showed Hayes in the drop room. He was placing his hand inside the tank, gently picking up Zero, gingerly, like a lover placing their hands on their significant other's chin. The spider stretched its legs out with submission, allowing Hayes to now place it on the piece of comet, after he released the vacuum seal, opening the container on the lab table.

"This was just before you ran down there to the drop room to wrap it up. He was frothing with impatience with you. If he was asked to do this, I know nothing of it. The videos of Zero, while we approached B.N. 44 only showed the creature transfixed. Completely still. Almost stunned. Have you ever seen Catholics visit the Vatican? Falling to their knees with absolute faith? That dumb spider was active the whole trip, I have the vids to prove it. When we approached B.N. 44 it was drunk on … I don't know what."

"He's placing it on the rock..." Virginia rubbed her body up close with her captain, unsure of what she was witnessing.

Zero was shaking. The yellow shimmering armor was vibrating, as if the spider was reaching climax. Without warning, it bit down on the rock, pincers penetrating as far as it could go, while into attack mode. Then it released its grip. Hayes watched from two feet away.

Zero became still again, showing the same behavior it did when they first approached the comet. Hayes picked it up, gently and then placed it back in the tank. Bringing the hollow rock back to the drop room, Hayes then disappeared from screen to return to the cockpit.

"Barren. What the hell?" Virginia looked deep into his eyes.

"I don't know. But I intend to call Mission Control and get Spencer on the line. If this was some weird experiment that I was not privy to, I want to know. Right?" Barren felt better that he was no longer alone with the information of this strange happening before him.

That was before the transmission.

Soon after, while the three of them were in the cockpit, the intercom had come on with a *BEEEEEP* followed by a *BLING*. Then the gravel laden hum of a very inhuman tone filled the cockpit, droning with forewarning authority.

"*WE ARE THE BOGWAHS.*"

Deep, inhuman sounds that resonated throughout the cockpit bounced off the white walls and rainbow pocked consoles. Barren had a vision of his childhood, sitting in front of his Grandma's fan, talking into it. It sounded like a child's voice filtered through a network of barbwire mesh.

"Where is that coming from? Look." Hayes pointed at the blinking blue light on the console. "It's not an outside source."

"That's an onboard intercom. The drop room." Glee turned to dread in Virginia's voice as the two men whirled in their seats to lock eyes on her.

"*WE ARE THE BOGWAHS.*" The tone was thick with threat. More growling than spoken the second time.

"Is this some kind of joke? How far are we from the Poseidon Space Station?" Barren asked Hayes.

"Captain. No. It is not a remote message. It's coming from on board." Hayes' deep blue eyes penetrated Barren's gray eyes with sincerity.

A red light blinked upon the vibrant green of the operations console.

"The two of you go. Armed. There are life-form readings. When you get to the door, wait for me. I'm putting a distress signal out, and contacting the Russians. This could just be a prank. It sounds like a prank…. Right?" Barren was nervous.

"This is impossible." Hayes had said in a huff, unstrapping the pistol from under the flight gears. Then he and Virginia disappeared through the sliding door.

They rattled the Christmas tree next to the doorway as they rushed out. The glass balls clanged together, and the fake pine branches shifted. Barren could still smell the old familiar scent wishing he was back home, in his parent's living room, safe, next to the glow of their Douglas Fir blinking with green and red lights in front of the snow covered window.

He wanted to go back to his living room with the wrapping paper strewn about the newly opened Tonka Trucks, BB gun, some dolls that belonged to his sister and the bowling ball for his dad. The smell of pine, from the tree with its starry angel at the top, would eventually blend with the waft of turkey from mom's oven. The doorbell would ring with welcoming faces entering their foyer. The bell that hung from the door would jingle with every new arrival. Grandma and Grandpa, who would bring the old trails of gold garland from their old decorations. Dad had always done well with the lighting, but Grandma insisted on the garland being added, every year.

The lights from the console woke him from his prayers.

The blinking on the console told him they were not alone. The only light not blinking was the communicom from Mission Control.

Why couldn't it have been a prank from the guys back home?

Something was wrong. Very, very wrong.

The distance between the MT1 and Earth had narrowed in the two hours that had passed since the hoarse vocals had haunted the cockpit. Barren stood with his back to the slanted window, his backside resting on the pilot seat. Sweat stained his blue jumpsuit to a darker shade, as did the urine that soaked and cooled in his crotch. His arms hung at his sides, waiting for the next order to come.

"WE GO WITH YOU. YOU PILOT. OR DIE."

Rolling his gray eyes toward the ceiling, Barren's mouth hung open. A brown slime coated a network of tendrils above him, connecting to a bulbous head with yellow eyes. The stinking long limbs stretched across the ceiling of the cockpit, dangling like some perversion of an octopus sprawling out its pulsating arms, claiming the room like a spider wields its web. The only discernable facial characteristics were the yellow eyes the size of golf balls. There were two of them, running their atrocious brown tentacles like roots around the ceiling, now creeping to the floors, vibrant with their recent nourishment.

Traces of the wrapping paper of red and green with Santa's and snowmen on it that Virginia had so lovingly prepared for her son now hung off of the fecal looking tendrils in torn shreds.

Barren glanced at the tree in the corner one more time before following orders from these beings that referred to themselves as the Bogwahs. There was no telling whose organs were who's now. Either Hayes's bladder or Virginia's hung in the center of the festive tree, gelling over the fake branches in the center like a deflated eggplant. Intestines draped like garland around the tree perfectly from the top to the bottom, just how Barren remembered his father had placed the old string of big green and red bulbs, later to be upstaged by Grandma's garland. Two human hearts were draped off of lower branches with fresh gore. What must have been bits of lung or possibly fatty tissue was shredded like tinsel, waving in the breeze from the oxygen flux. Was that a liver on top of the star? The scent of freshly cut meat was heavy.

Captain Barren's mind left moments before he noticed the tree topper.

The sounds of the creatures feeding was worse. Chewing, sucking through the very pores of their tree root-like bodies stuck to the ceiling.

Earlier, when the door initially opened, the two beings had slithered across the ceiling with Virginia and Hayes struggling desperately in the grasp of their numerous tentacles only to be picked apart slowly while screaming. Skin sizzled, hair burned, the suits vaporized while their vitals were stripped from the inside out. The two creatures only consumed the flesh and bone before Barren. Absorbing his crew into their elongated forms, leaving the organs behind to decorate the tree to appease Barren. He felt them in his head, reading his very thoughts. They wanted to make him happy now that they were given such a fond gift. Two gifts really.

The bells on the tree jingled through the entire melee, shaken by the creatures' movement, malice and violence.

"TRADITION? WE LEARN." From the ceiling, both the creatures hummed simultaneously, moving their molten heads to the side like children asking for a cookie. They gazed at him with their yellow eyes, waiting for a reply.

The ship continued its course for home.

- 10 -
RIBBONS

Tara Bennett rolled over to her left, pushing her overweight tabby, Belial, off the bed. The heat of early September always caught her off guard in the beginning of the school year. The air conditioner was set in the window, but it seemed to be blowing hot air with a tribal rattle resonating throughout the tiny bedroom.

"Dammit. Damn thing…. Dammit… oh… Belial!!" She stepped on her cat's tail sending his squealing chubby form under the bed. "Always, before the first day of school." Tara, in her mid-forties, was now nine years dedicated to the same school. Teaching elementary education had made her become accustomed to the nervous jitters of the Sunday night before the first day of class with the kids. Sleep never came easy with or without the crappy window unit air conditioner that was handed down to her from her mother in Philly, and held over from 1970-something.

Her curly brown hair was up in a bun on her head revealing the back of her neck to the open air of the humid bedroom. She rubbed a hand along her neck, feeling her skin dripping with cool sweat.

"Ew." Laying her palm flat down on the bed the sheet immediately became moist with her own dampening sweat. Tara threw the quilt over her sweat stained bottom sheet and mattress.

Stripping down to her panties with the Hello Kitty print on them (that no man had been allowed to see just yet) and her black Jane's Addiction tee shirt from a concert she had attended more than fifteen years ago with her college boyfriend, she hoped to cool down. She slid her only other bedroom window up for air to come through the lower screen, if a screen had been there. The day she moved in the screen was gone, and the landlord was less than responsive. Her one bedroom apartment was common in Erie Pennsylvania, not to mention affordable at a teacher's salary.

She tried to not use the window when her air conditioner failed her since there had been no screen to protect her from the elements. Mosquitos could be rough in the summer. More than likely it had been torn out three tenants prior to her, she was sure. The window actually already was open an inch or two at the bottom so that she could have easy access with her slender fingers, sliding them so she was able to move the rusty spring action upward when she wanted fresh air. On the second floor, Tara had no worries of a break-in, even in this shady neighborhood. There was no overhang below, covering the entranceway of the flat fronted tenement. She could hear the hum of the street lamp across the buckling road outside. No amount of tar could repair the winter beaten roads of her neighborhood.

"Nothing of value anyway, right Belial," She said to her large mirror across from her bed in the narrow room.

Have to call the landlord again, she thought, rubbing her sore eyes so she could look out at the street below lit by that single yellow streetlamp. Overcome with sudden loneliness, Tara was sickened with boredom at the typically bland view. That streetlamp gave her the shivers, reminding her of the overhead lamp at her dentist's office years ago, resembling a buttery colored heat lamp. Beyond the street light were run down ranches across the street, garden apartments beside them and a rusty green dumpster between the empty apartment complexes.

Right beside that was Mr. Seller's Hope Spring's Produce truck. He lived downstairs, making very little commotion when he left every morning to make his deliveries to some closed community that, in Tara's mind, must have fared better than anyone living in this suburban dump outside of the Casino district. She only ever heard the man hacking outside or smelled his morning cigarette come through her once working air conditioner. He was out there every morning smoking before driving off in his delivery truck and she did not have the heart to ask him to keep the noise down at 5:00 A.M. Even if she left the tiny bit of window open, she was still able to hear his throaty coughs of phlegm ritually through that barely open slot that she normally allotted for a bit of air. Otherwise she was not able to give a description of her one and only neighbor other than the fact that he was older, taller, skinny, and had wispy gray hair under this white delivery cap. On top of a very bad smoking habit.

She laid back down on the bed, staring at her bleak bedroom with the chipping white paint, hating the ugly bureau that came with the room. Her makeup mirror sat on top of it staring back at her, mocking her that in the next three hours she'd be staring into it dabbing her face to prepare for her first day with the kids.

"Shit." That was when she noticed the cold sore on the tip of her tongue. "Shit... man..." Sounding like she had just developed a lisp, Tara thought her nerves really had broken her down, getting to her now to the point that sleep would be impossible. "Damn hot pizza." Sticking her tongue between her thin pink lips, she rubbed a finger on the tip of her tongue to find the culprit. Sometimes she was prone to these on her tongue after some hot or zesty Italian food. She knew she would be rubbing the small bump against her lips all night out of pure painful instinct.

"Sadist." She laughed to herself.

"OW!" It hurt, stinging with an abnormally deep pang that resonated from the tip to the center of her tongue. "What the hell…"

The only positive thought that she had been dwelling on during her bubble bath in the earlier, more restful hours, was the thought of a new principal this year. Some of the younger teachers, like that hippie art teacher, Cynthia Main, had been stirring up the henhouse at the end of last June's session with rumors on the hot young principal. Tara was one of the only available attractive girls in the bunch, so it was more than a shot in the dark that she could at least rekindle that adolescent excitement over a new school year romance. She looked forward to flirting, in the very least.

Briefly rolling her fingers over the front of her panties, "It's been awhile. Too long…. Ow…" Her tongue stung. "Huffff…." She exhaled, got up, stepping onto the wood floor. Opening the bedroom door, then twisting to the right into the tight bathroom with the blue gingham wallpaper, it felt like it was time to take a look at this tiny blister that hung at the end of her tongue. "It's always smaller than it feels… yuck. All white….have to pop it if it's a pimple." She was talking like a toddler with a mouthful of M&M's, trying to not tap the pimple with her teeth again. It really hurt!

Seeing her pale complexion in the small medicine cabinet mirror above the sink, she rolled her bottom lip out, as if to say "Not bad." She still looked good without makeup. "Bonus!" She smiled.

Then she stuck out her tongue.

Expecting the white blistery beginning of a sore, what stuck out from the tip of her tongue resembled the tip of a pink ramen noodle. "Huh?" Her blue eyes went wide. A panic of cold sweat seeped down the center of her already sticky back. She put the bright pink tab between her index finger and thumb in order to touch it. The sting was the familiar prickle she would get from a normal cold sore, however the very unfamiliar itchy tingle that stemmed from the center of her tongue scared her.

"Whut tha' fa…" She then tugged on the small tab. Astounded at the itch from her inner tongue, Tara ignored the pain bursting from the very tip. The inside of her tongue was inflamed with a sudden overwhelming itchy tingle that she could not scratch!! Tears were welling up in her pretty big blue eyes. She stomped a foot in frustration.

"JEEEZUS!" Sticking her tongue out, she scratched the speckled surface of her tongue, but this only antagonized the inner itch.

Pressing her lips together, looking at her own desperate reaction she did not know what to do. Call a doctor? She could only leave a message for the Family Medical Practitioners. A message that they would receive in the order of the previous day's calls, perhaps getting back to her by Wednesday.

Tara grabbed the tip of her tongue again, hanging over her pink bottom lip. The tab was pinker than any natural skin color that she had ever seen. Unnatural, like the pink of one of those colored toothpicks.

Starting to hyperventilate, she took a chance and pulled on the soft pink skin-tag.

Like a splinter she had had once in the soft flesh between thumb and index finger it moved forward very smoothly from the depths of her tongue. To her horror, the small ribbon of flesh slid forward half of an inch, subsiding some of the itch within her tongue but now she had a pink flap of fleshy tendon protruding off the tip of her tongue.

It hurt like a pulled muscle, slightly, the itch coming back with some heat mounting in the center.

Then the itch became unbearable! She jumped up and down, panicking, like small child who had just fallen, scraping both palms of her hands, holding them open. "Oh Gawwwwwdth….."

Tara pulled at it again. It moved forward, almost orgasmic with tension, the sliding motion relieved her of the itch, until finally a ribbon of flesh the width of two toothpicks fell to the sink with a splash of blood.

"Oh….Oh…. gawwwwd……." She was hyperventilating, opening her medicine cabinet, grabbing at a tampon laying there. Unwrapping to the point of shredding the paper, she dabbed her bleeding tongue. Only a little pain, the itch was gone.

She pursed her lips down on the cotton, angrily peering down into the sink. Pinching the ends of the five inch long ribbon of pink flesh she held it up in front of her face. Too long. This was impossible. Had she fallen asleep, diving into a nightmare?

The pain was a little too real for that.

"What the hell. Really…." Talking out loud for the sake of Belial, who she envied now, never having such problems like humans do.

Thinking fast, Tara glanced around the hall outside the bathroom. On a small nightstand that was sitting in the darkened hallway was her purse with the little post-it of paper that smelled like bubble gum after sitting in there for the last five years. She immediately dug through, found it, ran back to the bedroom to sit on the bed, phone in hand. She dialed the emergency call off number that she still did not put on her cell phone, waiting for the automated system to find a sub for her for tomorrow. Removing the cotton from her mouth she could see, oddly enough, that the bleeding had ceased.

I cannot go in like this. Kids are mean, but how can I even talk, much less worry about the bleeding starting up again. What is this? What is that thing?! Her mind was racing, heart hammering in her chest.

Missing the first day of school was something she had never even dreamed of in all her years of teaching. This was something horribly out of the ordinary. A tumor? Had she pulled a tumor out of her bloody mouth?

Pressing keys, listening to the monotonously irritating female voice so that she could call off properly in the early A.M. to avoid getting in too much trouble, she felt like she was dreaming this. Must follow protocol, she said to herself, using her own cynicism to block the disgusting thought of what had just come out of her body. Tara became aware of a noise under her bed. Some tumbling noise. Belial must have found his cat nip. But why now? An itch on the back of her right shoulder forced her to reach around in front of her with her free left hand to scratch, while she held the phone intently in her right hand. "Dammit."

Completing her official call off, a call to Dr. Knicks was next. She left the message for the Family Medical Practitioners, planning on waiting outside the clinic doors whether they gave her an appointment or not.

Then the tears came! She wished her mother and younger sister were not so far away, in Philadelphia, knowing that she could not just call them and scare them in the middle of the night, nevertheless, she was needing them right now very badly.

BOOMF BOOMF BOOMF- the knock at the door downstairs made her jump off the bed.

"Wha?" She looked at the clock, 3:45 a.m. "Who the hell?"

Stepping into the hallway, she glanced down the stairs to the front door. "OH…." She put two hands in front of her panties, as if whoever was out there could see through the door. Putting a hand behind her bedroom door, she grabbed her black fluffy robe, wrapping it around her. The itch on her right shoulder was growing more intense, so she scratched at it while running down the stairs.

Her fingers scraped against three or four fibers sticking out of her own flesh under her shoulder blade, stopping her in her tracks at the last step before the door. Tara's robe hung open. The thing below her shoulder blade, almost out of reach, felt like a scab that was peeling in multiple places, though she had no memory of scraping her back. Throat dry with fear, she decided to see who was at the door. At this point, she wondered if she might need some help. Still, who the hell would be at the door at this time?

"Ms. Bennett!" Two more knocks.

"Who is it?" Her own feeble voice trembled. What is wrong with me?

"It's Mr. Sellers, from downstairs. Are you ok? I was outside smoking, heard you."

Opening the door with a sigh of relief to see another person, even if she had very rarely come in to contact with her fellow resident. The older man was very skinny, with sunken gray eyes, thinning gray hair that fell to his shoulders. The look of concern on his face was genuine. Mr. Sellers was holding his keys, wearing his white Hope Springs Produce jump suit. The white truck, not unlike a Good Humor Truck from the 1950's, was humming curbside waiting for its driver to make an unusually early start of the day.

"I was on my way to work...todays my early day. I was having a smoke, Ms. Bennett and I hear.....oh, honey, cover yourself, don't tempt an old codger with your cooter. Aw jeez..." The man, looked to the ground, stamping his cigarette.

More on her mind than exposing herself to the low income dying urban neighborhood, she closed her robe, briskly, stepping into the darkness of the small hours. "Mr. Sellers, please. Can you look at my shoulder...? I think I've had some kind of accident."

He turned to look down on her pretty blue eyes, seeping with tears. The woman was distraught. "Well awright, but I gotta go Ms. Bennet and frankly this is kind of weird..." He nervously continued to stamp out his cigarette, rubbing the permanent five'o clock shadow on his thin chin.

Tara dropped the robe. She peeled her Jane's Addiction shirt down, off her shoulder to reveal the flesh under her shoulder blade.

As if the concert tee shirt with the blaring red letters on the back shouting "SEX IS VIOLENT," was not enough to scare the poor old delivery driver off, now a younger woman was exposing more of herself outside the foyer of her soup whiff smelling apartment at 3:45 a.m. when he had to get to work!

"Thanks for doing this, I know you're in a hurry sir, and we don't talk much, but I'm desperate here. What do you see?" She tried to remain calm, her voice cracking with every other word.

"Um. Mam, you need to call someone. Call your doctor?! Did you? What did you do?" Mr. Seller's phlegmy voice was full of repose.

"What is it?" Now she panicked, whipping around to look directly in the tall man's face. Her hair became loose from her bun, falling slightly into her face. "Tell me..."

He licked his lips. "Do you need a ride somewhere? Why don't you get dressed Ms. Bennett, I can take you..." Straightening up his back, a new cigarette in between his fingers, he pointed at her with concern. "You got a wound... three or four pock marks... like open pimples... some kind of fibers, blue, red and green, coming through like hairs but thicker. Why don't you come with me...?" Mr. Sellers stepped onto the broken concrete walkway that led to his truck, motioning for her to follow.

Startled into a frenzy, Tara backed into her apartment, shutting the door, she threw herself against it. The unyielding itch began then. Her shoulder lit up with intense internal prickling. Running her nails on her shoulder blade gave her no relief, while her fingers slightly brushed the three or four fleshy tabs hanging out of her back. These felt bigger than the disgusting thing that still sat in her sink upstairs. Her fingers came back with blood on them. These wounds were seeping!

"Oh god, Oh god..." She tripped her entire way, barefoot, up the stairs, crying. On the final step she fell on her chest, her full breasts taking the brunt of the blunt flop to the wood floor. Her face was flat on the pink shriveled area rug that she had placed dangerously at the top of the stairs on the landing between the bathroom and the bedroom. At floor level, catching her breath, bending her head to the left, Tara looked directly to the floor of her bedroom, having full view under her raised bed. Some shoes tossed there, her slippers, a box of photos that she had meant to go through and Belial was laying there, rolling about.

"Belial?"

Something was odd. Movement. Several things that appeared to be the size of a quarter, shimmering like coins too, but yellow, green, blue, some orange were milling about. "Am I seeing things now? Sick? Fever?" Tara lifted herself to her feet, the itch unbearable on her back. *Scratch Scratch. Pull Pull.*

The scratching did not provide relief like the tugging on the fibers did. Almost total relief.

Traipsing over to the side of the bed, she turned on the light on her nightstand by the alarm clock. "Nightmare." She spoke aloud, not even conscience that she had pulled one of the ribbons of flesh from her back completely out. The relief was shockingly euphoric.

"Oh, three more…" She could feel a bit of blood pour into the back of her black tee shirt warm and wet. She knew she should probably not be pulling these scab things off of her (or out of her) without consulting a professional, but in her sleep deprived state, it felt so perfectly relieving when she slowly pulled this ropey substance out of her shoulder blade area.

"How could it feel so good….. For so long…" She thought. Removing the fiber birthed a humming sensation, briefly, soothing every ailment seemingly that she ever had. Her damaged derma layer hummed with a vibration stemming from the closing holes left behind by the vacating fibers.

Pulling the next fiber out, and dangling it in front of her, Tara screamed briefly before dropping the long blue limp fleshy ribbon. The sinewy blue fiber, two feet long, thick as a McDonalds Shake straw, dripped with her blood as it flopped onto the floor!

She fell to the floor landing on top of the fake Middle Eastern designed area rug on her bedroom floor, losing the strength in her knees with absolute disbelief, she sobbed. "Belial…"

The gray and black striped tabby was dead, eyes wide staring back at her, laying on its side as well. Spiders crawled about Belial, bodies the size of quarters, the creeping arachnids glowed with shiny colors, pink, green, and blue. A dozen or so.

The sight was beyond comprehension. Her itch was forgotten.

*****

Tara Bennett awoke in a wheel chair, dressed only in a white hospital gown. She was in a familiar waiting room in the hallway of her own doctor's office at Family Medical Practitioners. She had waited in this same room many a time for checkups, routine with poking and prodding. The room smelled of sanitizer, and she was surrounded by jars of tongue depressors, plastic drinking cups, cabinets with untold treasures and the paper covered examining table. There was blood on it.

Coming to her senses, Tara put a hand to her back, inside the white hospital gown. The remaining ribbons of flesh were gone, replaced by scabby bumps, larger than she felt comfortable with, though the itch was gone. Someone had removed them and not patched her up? She remembered her tongue and how quickly that had stopped bleeding too.

"BELIAL!!" Cupping hands on her mouth she began to sob, memories of those horrific spiders chewing at his frozen body triggered a gag reflex. "This cannot be happening." She pulled her wavy dark hair back from her face, gripping her hands on the arms of the wheel chair she attempted to lift herself up. Placing her bare feet on the cold floor, Tara slumped to the counter across from her. She held on tight, lifting her head up. Her hand swiped a keyboard and then the monitor to the left of the sink blinked to life.

Dr. Knicks, her own doctor, still used DOS. The screen was titled MORGELLON'S EVALUATION CHART.

SUBJECT: Female mid-forties. Single.
DOSE: Two to five Venom tracks. Tongue and Upper Back
WEB DISCHARGE: Two to three feet max. Colored.
ARACHNID AGE SIZE: Adolescent
RETAINED: Retention and recovery complete: Hope Springs delivery truck driver retained   escaped Morgellons Strain.
SUBJECT'S CONCLUSIVE VALUE: Further observation. Two weeks at Hope Springs Medical Complex under the care of Dr. Montville, Microbiologist and Dr. Richard's, Pharmacologist
SUBJECTS RESOURCEFULNESS: Venom not from adult spiders. Morgellon Strain only (Adolescent). Organs not congealed. No preparation for soil symbiosis initiated in this particular subject, yet.
SUBJECTS DURATION OF INFLICTION: One night. Adolescent bites. Multiple. Infection however completed in rapid succession. Potent Bites.
AVERAGE AFFLICTION FOR ALL TEST SUBJECTS: 15 Years subjected to Morgellon Strain Spiders.
CONCLUSION: Subject is either more susceptible to strain or escaped test group contained more potent venom.

Boots down the hall, then the door to the small examination room opened.

"What is this…" her body ached, knees incapable of bringing her back across the room to her wheelchair.

The door opened and Dr. Knicks walked in looking a bit surprised at Tara's mobility. For the benefit of his patient he forced a short smile, a politician's smile. Her mood calmed a bit, a grimace flashed across her pale complexion. She forced a smile back. Finally something similar to the word, *comfort*, had flushed through her entire body. He was very tall, broad, adorned with a mullet of white hair and glasses like Santa Claus. Dr. Knicks usually soothed her of her hypersensitive worry. Whether it was from the times when her flu lasted too long or a mole popped up out of nowhere. He was the only man in her life that had been around her longer than three years, so there was a false sense of confidence on her part.

Now in a white lab coat, (unusual?) the smile faded on his handsome face, dissolving her calmness. Those gray eyebrows of his were upturned in a manner she had never seen before on her doctor in the three years that she had been his patient.

"Tara. How are you feeling? Please remain sitting." He was quick to get her back in the wheel chair.

"How did I get here? I think it was poison…..did you see the things in my back? Did you remove them Dr. Knicks? There were these things in my apartment….killed my cat." Rambling and she knew it. There was anesthesia in her system or something closely resembling it, creating a fog in her mind and an imbalance in her struggled steps. Tara was relieved when Dr. Knicks put his strong hands on the handles behind her to wheel her out of the room.

"Your neighbor, Mr. Sellers was nice enough to bring you here." Dr. Knicks continued to wheel her down the hall to a room at the end. A room she had never been in, nor had she noticed was there.

"Really? I don't even know him… nice enough. Am I gonna be ok? What is this… oh God and those things… " Shivers of fear pulsed in her gut at the thought of those bulky bugs under her bed.

She became aware that when they passed the lobby that no one else was present there, nor at the front desk. "Where is everyone?"

"Technically honey, we are not open. There are some specialists that need to see you."

Now there is *something* that you never want to hear from your personal care physician! She thought, her face stiffening with fright. Then he did something erratic. He bent down to whisper, as if he was hiding from unseen security.

"I left the computer on and the door unlocked for three hours, hoping to let you slip out. You never woke up…. I'm sorry Ms. Bennett but now I have to do as they say." He flashed straight up again, increasing his speed for the door, as though he never had bent down to whisper in her ear.

Processing what he said, slowly, but then realizing the shadow of secrecy surrounding her was increasing, and whatever they had given her made it hard to focus her eyes- impossibly hard to concentrate.

"What? Dr. Knicks? What are you saying…?" Impending doom, she thought. Nothing is making sense. She was growing terrified while her legs tingled with pins and needles.

The door at the end of the hall opened from the inside. A nurse that Tara was not familiar with stood inside the room smiling with some larger male nurses in red scrubs. Dr. Knicks wheeled her into what appeared to be more of a garage, or hanger, with white walls, smooth cement floor and double doors at the other end.

Two other people in long white lab coats stood at the end of the room. One was a tall shapely blonde woman with her hair in a tight knot on her head, thick black rimmed glasses, dark red lipstick and a smile. A man stood next to her, looking like a news correspondent with his perfect peppered gray hair, fake smile, worry lines across his forehead and cheeks that were bashfully red. He had a weasely look about him that Tara immediately could not trust. "Who…are… you …people…?" A circle of other patients in wheel chairs all turned their heads to look at her as she was wheeled in to join them. "What is this?" Her nerves turned to ice.

"Oh Dear…another one." A woman who appeared to be in her sixties was shaking her head, hands going to her face to wipe tears.

"Friends." Said the pretty blonde doctor as she walked past the group of a dozen or so people, also in gowns and frozen to their wheelchairs.

"Where did they get'ya? In bed? Me, they got me in the bathtub. Fukkers can swim too!" A chubby man in a wheelchair to her left was slurring through big pouty cheeks. His face was scarred with lesions, open, still seeping on one side of it.

She watched as he pulled a pink and blue fiber, plucking it from a protruding scab on his cheek below his eye. "Eh…finally….even with the sleepy drugs they gave us, I could still feel the damn itch. Right? All of us right?" The overweight man was covered in lesions on his legs too, all protruding and seeping with clear blood. "That one was driving me crazy. No relief with those fibers growing inside you. Like something just trying to dig its way out eh? Right? Com'on you'all can't be *that* sedated!" The man was struggling to get out of the straps around his wrists. "You're young yet girly. You may survive this."

"SILENCE, please Mr. Rowger. We need to welcome our new guest with open arms, not scare her. She needs to know that this is a working group, all here to recover. Now, Miss, you are not alone." The younger, pretty blonde woman walked to the center of the group. "I am Dr. Montville of Hope Springs Medical Complex."

"What is this...?" Tara tried to speak, her mouth was as numb as most of her muscles. Through the fog in her mind she saw Mr. Seller's produce truck outside her apartment window.

"Shh, Tara. Just listen. It's for your benefit." Dr. Knicks shushed her, standing beside the wheelchair, he focused on the beauty in the long lab coat that was Dr. Montville. "Dr. Montville, Tara is different. It does appear to be Morgellon's Syndrome, however she was only infected last night. Several bites. Not the usual five to fifteen years of exposure like the others here. She's special. The fibers were immense too."

Dr. Montville approached Tara, her black eyebrows like batwings. "Not a local? Or not from here I take it? No matter, Miss...Tara. Hope Springs is a manmade island on the northern shore of Lake Erie. Unlike your doctor friend here, I am a microbiologist among the many other suits I wear in Hope Springs." The woman's voice was soothing and condescending at the same time.

"What she's sayin' girly is that we are unofficially part of an experiment...gone awry. All messed up!" The man, with the West Virginia twang, who had been addressed as Mr. Rowger continued. "Some of their buggers got loose and done this..."

"Enough." Dr. Montville hissed at the man.

"Why is he so coherent," said the other man in the white lab coat at the far side of the room.

Dr. Montville replied to the short shifty looking man, "The bite of the adolescent of the species that we found in this district has varying effects depending on the tolerance of the subject." Dr. Montville turned back to Tara.

Tara was becoming more aware by the second that all of this was really happening. She was not dreaming! Just hours ago, while trying to sleep before her first day back at work after a restful summer, her world was invaded by hideously metallic colored spiders that fed on her beloved Belial under her bed. Possibly, too, these things had infected her with some ailment beyond comprehension.

"What...what are you going to do with us...?" She was exhausted. "Why is this happening?"

"The venom of our test group that found its way into your home have a unique bacterium. When this bacterium combines with human tissue after a series of multiple bites, the normal outcome results in immobilization of that human for days. If these had been adult of this species, like we have in Hope Springs, your insides would be turning into jelly immediately. This is not completely out of the question for some of you." Coldly, the microbiologist turned to a young man, nearly in his twenties, who was hunched over in his chair, bile flowing from his mouth to his lap while he groaned in agony. The young man's skin was gray, but he still lived. "Dr. Richards..." She motioned for the other man in the lab coat, the creepy one, to come over. "Call the orderlies from the truck to come and take him first. Stabilize him, but load him up immediately."

The woman's manner of speech was too matter of fact for this to be real even as it unfolded. Sure enough, the short, news reporter-looking Dr. Richards picked up his cell to do her bidding. Tara could not talk. The muscles in her jaw taunt with pain and stiffness.

"This was an oversight by one of our delivery drivers. My apologies to you all. Now, we are under orders to take you to Hope Springs on the next ferry from Presque Isle, around noon. Until then we will keep you all stabilized. There is no telling how many bites you sustained but a body inspection consultation revealed that some of you are worse than others." She lifted the gown of a woman about Tara's age on the left. Open sores went from her legs to her shoulders. Blue, green, pink, orange and blue fibers were poking out of her flesh. Some were two to three inches long, and grotesquely visible to the naked eye. She was attempting to scratch them all at once, lifting more slivers of flesh off her body. The woman was only capable of moaning, her voice sounded raw as if from screaming for long periods of time. "Sedate her, and begin pulling the web spores out of her. We start with her after the young man." Dr. Montville said.

"Oh. Yes. Please...pull them out. I can't....sstannnnnd the itch...the pain." The woman's hoarse voice pleaded.

"Experiments? You experiment on spiders?" Tara forced the words. She could not take her eyes off the orderlies rolling the woman toward the double doors on the far side of the room.

"Come'on Docs...tell our newbie the story. Tell her about the Frenchies." Mr. Rowger was fighting the combination of the venom and drugs in his system like a baby trying to fight sleep so that it would not miss anything.

Dr. Montville and Dr. Richards converged on her, kneeling to look into her eyes. "Oh no, Miss. No. The spiders have been here long before us." Dr. Montville smiled, "You were just lucky it was merely adolescents that escaped from Mr. Seller's truck. He never should have made an unauthorized stop at home with them on board. Ever wonder why your neighborhood is so quiet lately Miss......is it Bennett?"

"Yes."

"Hope Springs is working to improve the human condition. The spiders, when they are just babies are born with venom that is capable of ..." Dr. Montville seemed so proud of herself.

Dr. Knicks interrupted with concern in his voice, "Is this really necessary doctor? We need to move this along. I have to open the office at some point before it looks more suspicious than it already does."

Resentful of the interruption, Dr. Montville continued, "...*capable* of peculiar abilities. One such oddity that we found was beyond our understanding, yet this strain was responsible for reanimating a dead human infant. Granted, motor skills only, yet, *Reanimation*! Miracles are coming!" She seemed to be bragging more to the insolent Dr. Knicks as if there had been some competition between them at some point. "The elder creatures, those that actually have controlled the use of their colorful titanium-type tendrils of webbing, have even proven beneficial during our refining and resource crisis." Dr. Montville could not hide her bliss.

She continued. "Dr. Knicks, your sloppiness back in her examination room revealed enough to Miss Bennett as it is. At least she can hear it from a voice rather than a computer screen." Dr. Montville poked a sharp red fingernail directly into Tara's shoulder. "What we have inside us, combined with the venom of our boys back on the island is a blessing in disguised. Symbiotically, a full grown member of this yet to be determined species of arachnid has venom that when amalgamated with the human interior design; congealed human organs; a multifaceted ore is created, transported overseas and beyond. You and our eight legged friends are providing an invaluable service to the world. You are luckier than most. You will be under my care at Hope Springs Medical Complex. Merely observation."

Was this her way of trying to win a patient's confidence? Tara thought, tears streaming down her cheeks. She just wanted to see her mother, her sister. LET ME WAKE UP! She screamed in her own head.

Dr. Richards stood by Dr. Montville's side. "What Mr. Rowger was referring to was Morgellon's Syndrome. A French town had entirely been infected with the fiber breeding lesions that came from no discernable trace on our planet. Some professionals thought the fibers were extraterrestrial in nature. They suffered chronic fatigue, bleeding from the bursting lesions, growing fibers that they had to have removed on an hourly basis."

Dr. Richards had the attention of all in the room. Even the most sedated of the surrounding inflicted listened intently from the confines of their wheelchairs, looking up at Dr. Richards with new found clarity. "I'm a pharmacologist. I alone tested twelve hundred known textile fibers against the multicolored threads coming from your bodies. No Match. These fibers..." He pointed down at a middle aged man with a gag around his mouth, straps on his arms and legs, and twirls of yellow and blue fibers falling out of the side of his neck, down to his lap. The blood on the giant wound was a dried crust, yet the ribbons were still growing. "... did not match a single organic compound when compared to one hundred thousand known organic compounds in the database."

Dr. Richards put his white glove around the threads hanging down to the man's lap, and began to lightly tug. With ease, bits of scab and white blood cells gave way and the ribbons eased their way out another six inches before the entire multicolored rope could be tossed to the wet floor below the tortured man's wheelchair. The muffled howls from the man ceased after Dr. Richards relieved him of the affliction from his neck. The man nodded, eyes blinked, "Thanks."

"Said to be a delusional infestation by doctors and scientists that work outside of Hope Springs, Morgellon's Syndrome was dismissed for years." Dr. Montville spoke in a softer voice. "But how are we supposed to ignore over twenty thousand victims of this infliction. We simply can't. And no, it did not come from space, Dr. Knicks, as you so mentioned in your doctorate presentation to the board of Hope Springs, but our spider friends come from the depth of the Earth itself. That much we have proven. Why their venom, when infused with human body tissue results in the discharge of their web-like material from the subject, is mysterious. That is why you are important, Ms. Bennett. Your immediate response to bites overnight from the lesser potent blend, adolescents, is baffling. Should you survive our study, you may be the most important human on the planet." She smiled, feeding off of Tara's face, a frozen statue of dread. A silent scream cracked from her wide open mouth.

A pink and red fiber, thicker than the previous from the night before, now the width of a pencil had begun poking out the tip of her tongue, with the slightest bit of blood running down her chin.

"Why....no ...Why.... peese ....no peese... no.... why me?" Tara looked up at Dr. Knicks beside her.

The back double doors opened and a delivery truck just like Mr. Seller's was backing up to it. This one was a bit bigger. Tara could see HOPE SPRINGS painted in blue on the outside of the doors before they opened to reveal a large interior with beds and metal benches along the sides. Four orderlies dressed in red scrubs began wheeling the dozen or so people to the back of the truck. They strapped them down onto the stretchers one at a time, then wheeled them into the back of the truck.

The redneck man, Mr. Rowger, began howling and hollering the whole way until Dr. Richards ran over with a syringe to quiet him down to a heavy hulking, slobbering mess. It took three men in red scrubs to get him onto a stretcher and into the back of the truck.

"No, peese. I just wanna go home. Dr. Knicks, peese, don't let'em take me..." Tara was starting to fight, desperately pushing her bare feet stiffly against the smooth cement in front of her while Dr. Knicks continued to push her.

"Dr. Knicks, do you want to tell her? Exactly? Why her?" Dr. Montville was smiling, flirting with the man, walking beside them, while he wheeled her to the back of the truck.

"Um... yes. Tara, honey. The ribbons are... when, broken down after several years of harvesting, um... well Dr. Montville and Richards have found them to cure almost every form of cancer." The fear, disgust and reluctance could not be hidden from his words.

"So far." Dr. Montville concluded.

The conversation was meant to be poignantly prevalent between the Doctors more so than for the benefit of Tara Bennett. Even in her state of shock, pain on her tongue, sedation, and the ever growing itch below the surface of her skin, she knew a battle of pride between Dr. Knicks, Dr. Montville and creepy Dr. Richards was ensuing. All of which were behind her now, throwing numbers at each other, shouting at one another about the figures that they deemed as facts.

"Four thousand cases of cirrhosis of the liver, diagnosed as fatal...cured, Dr. Knicks!"

"How many are still in remission... you have no real proof of the long term..."

"You have no room to speak, you will remain our provider on the rim... you just keep treating your flu and measles, while Dr. Montville and I cure the world."

"AT WHAT PRICE!!!??"

The truck had pulled away with the others. A new one had backed up before Tara, the size of a mid-range U-HAUL, with the blue HOPE SPRINGS insignia on the door. A very muscular man in scrubs and a blue Hope Springs ball cap ran to the doctors behind her, holding a clip board out. "Doctors, please you are my final stop today. Signatures please."

The itch below her forearms was becoming unbearable. The small of her back felt wet, as if something had just broken through. The new bulge on her neck felt like it had grown since she was moved from one side of the room to the other, and now her inner thighs... "Oh no..." She said to herself over and over again. There was a trickle of blood flowing down her left thigh, past her ankle and to the floor.

"Ok, let's move her in. Get her on a stretcher." She heard the man with the clipboard say, while the three doctors continued to bicker on about morals, numbers, pain, death, and success.

The foreman with the clipboard rolled the door to the back of the truck up. A stretcher was pulled down for her on a ramp. A smell like rancid meat soaking in copper wafted out to the horror of some of the men around the outside of the truck. "Damn man. I never get used to that ...." One man said to another who laughed, slapping his friend on the back with his paper bag lunch.

Tara Bennett had her head raised, chin resting on her chest as this was the only part of her not strapped down by leather bindings on the stretcher. They had prepared her for boarding. Now they rolled her up the ramp, bumping up into the back of the truck where the stretcher's wheels locked in place.

There were others in there. Some plastered to the walls by webs of blue, red, pink, yellow and green. The fibers that held them in place came from their own bodies, shooting from limbs, necks, torsos or any orifice that the thick healthy ribbons found access to breech. She found herself surrounded by men, women, children and some of the inflicted that were so deformed with long fibrous growths that there was no way to see an ounce of humanity remaining outside of wide terrified eyes that pleaded for death while others clearly wept. Still, some of the victims were wrapped in their own multicolored sinews of web, immobilized, and were placed on the benches along the sides of the truck's interior; a couple like herself that still had a human shape were on stretchers, while even more were wrapped up in the vines of fleshy tendrils growing out of their own bodies threatening to flood the entire storage area. The moans of the tortured droned into one complete cacophony of desperation.

She began to scream, cracking the new tickling fiber creeping up from the depths of her throat. Her shrill gag resonated throughout the hanger until the foreman rolled the metal door back down to lock it in place leaving her in the dark chamber of the truck. Soon the only relief from the growing itch and pain was the bump of the truck against the road that slapped her back against the cold stretcher. Tara Bennett prayed for a death that was not coming anytime soon.

- 11 -
RESIDUAL

Justin Deckland felt at home walking through the pines. He was smiling because grandma's house was only miles away off the path that he knew so well. Grandparents on his dad's side. His other grandparents were back home on Long Island. There was something soulfully settling that calmed the entire family when dad took them to visit upstate New York. The woods by the lake. The old fashioned downtown complete with post office, library, pharmacies, and souvenir shops based around the baseball hall of fame. The locals were charmingly behind the times. Justin liked that.

He was smarter than most kids anyway. Here, he could be king. With one theatre, not too many of them really knew what happened in the last Star Wars sequel. Especially the company he always found himself in. Dad would take mom, he and his little sister fishing on the lake. Justin liked the lake better than the ocean that he found himself by all too often in the summers back home. You can control a lake. The ocean can control you with its unpredictable force. Prone to feeling more keenly susceptible to the world around him, Justin accepted his role in nature.

Even if Special Ed. deemed him unworthy. In his own mind, he spoke well of himself; confident, powerful and even insightful. Others, like the dummies that grandma thought he could play with and be friends with granted him no ounce of respect. Justin went with the role he was dealt.

Matt and Kevin were behind him tossing pine cones at each other, as if the twins never had enough time to themselves. Sometimes, when they ventured into a clearing, the giant forest of the Catskills parted so they could see the town next to the lake below.

"Grandma's house is there." Justin's heart burned happily in his chest. Unlike the twins or big dumb Jeremy Faulk, who led the group through the woods, Justin's grandparents were all still alive and healthy. He also thought on his mom's parents back home on Long Island, looking forward to being with them. He spent a good part of his summers with his other grandparents, holidays too. So one week up in the Catskills, near Oneonta, sometimes two, his dad would make the six hour drive up to spend some time fishing, hiking and swimming in lake Otsego for the perfect getaway.

Justin was a year away from finishing the sixth grade and he knew middle school was coming. He had friends in the "special" classes that he found himself in, if you could call Josh Silverplatt a friend, who bashed his head on the desk after he ate half of Justin's peanut butter and jelly sandwich and complained about Jokey Smurf not having enough air time on Saturday mornings.

There was Benjamin too. He peed himself a lot, but Justin thought he was the coolest guy. No one else brought a Han Solo gun to school that actually had the batteries in it! No one! Oh and Keith Toleray was his idol. He had buckteeth that sprayed saliva every time he talked. It was the coolest thing ever. Keith also had sores on his bottom lip from his teeth digging into them when he was not talking. Justin would stick his perfect teeth out to look like Keith but it did not have the same affect. Keith thought it was neat that Justin found him so interesting. He even gave Justin his KISS 45 that had that disco song that he thought was good, even if the band hated it.

In the end, none of those guys really hung out with him. He played in his own head a lot, when not in the presence of other kids.

Still. It was all the same. He paid little attention to the insults where other kids in his special classes that got hit with spitballs by the other kids at school, really kind of lost their mind and cursed while kicking and screaming.

Justin reserved his power, harnessing the environment.

The fresh scent of blackberry bushes hunched on either side of the trail made him smile, even when big dumb Jeremy Faulk made sure that he held back and then walloped him purposefully with the branches that hung on the trail. It was so typical. Jeremy wore his Ked 's All-Stars, halting his feet, holding them together when he would stop walking, leaning on the folded branch on his chest only to let them go right into Justin's face on every turn that the pine needled path took them.

The dumbass would even turn, sneer, and smile with his horse-like block teeth and his perfectly short trimmed hair with cereal bowl precision.

Ugly.

Justin continued to smile each time, thinking to himself how ugly the older boy was inside and out, projecting his pride in such a small sense of power.

Justin was well aware of power. The real sense of the word. The real sense of the *world*.

In his world, he loved Benjamin for peeing himself while trading Star Wars cards (the blue series) with him in the recess area at school, as much as he loved Josh Silverplatt for stealing his lunch every day only to hurt himself at his own desk, resulting in a restraint from Ms. Debona along with the principal every Tuesday and Thursday (because these were non pizza days in the cafeteria, Josh said he could afford to miss those lunch periods, but not on a pizza day). He admired spit slinging Keith and his amazing buck teeth and feathered hair.

Control was a rare thing. Something you find in your mind, hold on to it and never let go if you know what's good for you.

It was very important that his school routine did not change. The same can be said for his visits with grandma and grandpa. Visiting grandma and grandpa for a week in the summer here at upstate New York was as valuable to him as his stay at his other grandparent's home who lived out on Long Island, very near his own home.

Equally important were his summers by the ocean. The beach never changed. Consistency. He loved that his parents had the summer house out on Montauk Isle. Just like the pine forest he found himself in now, it was so pertinent that the sun broke through the trees to beat down on his scalp once in a while to give him a brief warm lick to remind him that it was summer. It could be cold in the woods on top of the mountain, but not when the sun welcomed you now and again.

Justin looked forward at Jeremy, the bigger boy, already in the seventh grade, prancing ahead with his hiking stick he had found on the ground, marching like he was really leading the four of them on an epic journey. He was wearing fluorescent jam shorts and a blue and white striped shirt.

"No leader on a mission would wear that in the woods, especially on a secret mission," Justin thought.

Oh no. He said it out loud.

"What's that retard? What? Did you say something *JUSTINE*? Huh?" Jeremy turned his chubby body around, squinting his freckled face into Justin's.

Matt and Kevin laughed behind him. They were chucking tree bark pieces at the back of his legs during the entire hike up the hill since they left their bikes by the guard rails at Woodbine Street's dead end. He ignored their meager attempts at breaking his cool. Justin knew he could wipe them both out if he wanted to. There just was no need to slam both of the skinny boys together, bonking their little curly heads into one another's until there was blood. Useless waste of energy really. He would feel bad if he stained Matt's Mickey Mouse tank top with his brother's snot, or had to break Kevin's dweebish nose so that he had to use the bottom of his A-TEAM tee shirt to wipe the blood.

He pictured it though. Vividly.

"Not gonna make that happen." He said aloud, by mistake, putting his hand to his mouth, ceasing his own Converse Canvas Top All-Stars on the dry pine needled path.

"What? Retard? What? You still yammering? What're you... like Punky Brewster or something? That slut never shuts her trap! You'd probably *DO HER* huh....? HAHHAAHA." Jeremy blurted, parting the final branches before them as they entered the clearing.

He considered the twins and Jeremy his friends, knowing them for years now when he came to visit, they were as much friends to him as Benjamin,

Keith and Josh were. Justin enjoyed the familiarity of companionship. Jeremy was older, bigger, the twins younger (not even in the sixth grade!) and smaller. Grandma had introduced them at a church ice cream social.

Friends. Not friendly. Justin was used to this. Hurting them physically would only guilt him into a deep depression. He looked at scenarios from the eyes of all the players, never one sided. Sure he wanted to lash out and punch little Kevin or Matt, possibly kicking Jeremy in the face in the process but he thought of their parents and the horrible disappointment they would feel, looking at their young son's all bloodied up dripping with mucus stained Mickey Mouse and A-Team shirts that their mom and dad had bought for them.

It would make him feel bad to retaliate at their taunts. Besides, Justin had his friends.

Mom, Dad, his little baby sister were his real friends that he trusted. Both sets of his grandmas and his grandpas held final court in every ounce of his life. They all taught him to respect folks, be polite, and always say "thank you." Forgive, forget and be the best person you can. Of course, even his imaginary friend Charlie held deep roots inside his soul. It was so important to hold these people close even when they could not be standing next to you.

"It's what makes you who you are." Damn. He said that aloud again. Smiling.

"We're here retard. This year, it's your turn." Jeremy was too close to him. He could smell the onion scent of his underarms moist with summer's heat.

Matt and Kevin were chuckling like girls who just found out that Duran Duran actually could jump out from a poster and hug you. Justin considered them pretty pathetic, understanding the meaning of the word "pathetic" as he had heard mom say that about her boss more than a few times and knew it was not nice to say so. He knew what the word meant just by her tone in saying the harsh word.

Hating Jeremy's smell, he also held back the words he longed to spit out of his thin little lips, thinking, "Get away from me you smelly pathetic pussbag." He would spit like cool Keith's teeth would.

But he held on to his passion in silent repose.

Adjusting his Islander's cap he continued to smile. He loved an adventure.

Jeremy batted his hat off his sweaty head, releasing the long wispy bowl head of brown hair to fall about his face. Really, it was kind of a relief, so the urge to put his fingers into the bigger boy's eyes was sedated. His fingers could really feel the cushy gelatin of Jeremy's eyeballs while he gouged. The middle and index finger on his right hand were hooked, arched for the attack that never came, but oh, the elation in his mind while those eyes were plucked and sitting on the tips of his fingers. Charlie would chuckle at that, only to tell him later that that was "impulsive and bad."

Too hot to think such awful thoughts. Too much fun to be had. Guilt would beat him down to an early grave if he had followed through with the assault in his mind, knowing full well that the violence in his thoughts satiated the need for the real thing.

Dad said it was puberty. He was fine with that.

The sun beating through the tops of the forest at the clearing reminded Justin just how hot a summer day it had turned out to be.

"My own summer."

"What? Hehehe hehe" squirrelly little Matt said behind him, poking him with a twig.

"He mumbling again? You know its summer when we are hanging out with marble mouth again." Kevin kicked some dirty leaves at Justin's bare calves.

Justin bent down to pick up his hat. Placing it into the back pocket of his cut off jean shorts he then pulled up his knee high blue striped socks because he could not help himself. Hating socks, he always put them on because it made his sneakers stink that much less. Compulsively, whether in soccer camp or out at a park with his grandparents, he always made sure his socks were pulled up tight. He was missing hair on his shins from the burn, where the small stubble of puberty covered the rest of his legs. Not as bad as smelly Jeremy, who's unruly premature hair growth on his arms and legs resembled the twin's curly locks on their heads.

Justin laughed to himself with that thought. Most of his interactions with people resulted in a bit of laughter to himself that had been mistaken for arrogance. Really, he just felt misunderstood.

"Get moving boy, or I'll bring Theresa out here and..." Jeremy started to say something.

Something mean.

Smile fading, eyes narrowing, Justin turned on his heels. The mention of his five year old baby sister burned lava through his veins. His teeth squeaked audibly while rubbing together.

"NO." Teetering on his tippy toes, striving to get at eye level with the bully, Justin's hazel eyes blazed deeply into Jeremy's. He could smell the Pez on the older boy's breath. "NO." He repeated sternly.

Talk of his little sister, Terry, was off limits. These boys were not worthy enough to speak of the people he actually trusted. Back at school, in the playground during recess, Leonard had paid for his poking fun at his imaginary friend Charlie.

Don't pull his ear off. Don't pull him down by his nostrils. Don't keep.... Don't keep ... kicking him until his balls are broken, dripping down his legs and he is screaming.

DON'T.

Strength ran deep in his mind, of the type he had to maintain, or people could get hurt. He almost followed through with the visons, seeing them through completion. He did not give in.

Leonard was not in school for a week, spending his recess time in a hospital for the duration. Justin held council in in-school suspension.

Control.

"I'm going in. You're afraid." Justin whispered his retaliation instead of acting on it. He did not like to talk out loud normally, simply because there usually was nothing to say to most folks. Most folks were just dumb.

Deep breath.

Sucking in the sweet scent of the forest he looked at the abandoned house before him. The three other boys were behind him now standing on the fringe of the woods. Holding his chin up, he approached the overgrown front lawn, weeds hitting his bare knees gently above his blue striped tube socks.

"Don't chicken out retard... We all did it... ten minutes you douche bag! Matt did it last year!" Jeremy's fleeting words still held the residual tone from that one second of fear that he unexpectedly had felt from the moment that Justin had gotten into his face. This did not compute in Jeremy's mind.

Bullies seldom are ready for sudden confrontation that they did not control. Justin knew this, even if it did not stop him from shoving Leonard Mulligan's head into his own locker back home on Long Island. That little instantaneous affront had scored Justin that place in the SP'ED classes as it was. He knew better. Disappointing his grandparents hurt him deeply and mom had to bring the subject up at the last family gathering last Fourth of July at Eisenhower Park back home. Still, Leonard Mulligan should never talk to him the way he did at the bus stop, or in gym class in front of the others. That big bull-necked jerk with his endless array of Dallas Cowboy Jerseys was always in his face before school or in the hallway, showing off in front of his football playing buddies.

Mostly though, the one thing that bothered him the most about that kid back home was his personal shots at Justin, picking up on his most private time during recess when he would talk to his friend that no one else could see.

Leonard should never tell him things like talking to his imaginary friend Charlie was "insane". He was wrong. What did he know anyway? Justin knew for a fact that Leonard Mulligan, not unlike Jeremy Faulk, his summertime bully, had more imaginary friends than he, himself did. He just called them the Oldfield High School Football team. Ha ha. Justin smiled to himself, thinking also how Jeremy looked at the twins, Matt and Kevin, the exact same way. They were only his friends in his limited imagination. Surely they laughed behind Jeremy's back on a regular basis. Justin did not have to attend school here to know how the smarmy little boys probably snickered at the fat jokes that came Jeremy's way during the school year here.

Continuing to take his time making his way to the front door above the two cement steps, he listened to the three of them behind him, watching the rocks they hurled at him turn up dusty puffs in between the thick reeds of the grass.

Trusting in their horrible aim, he was slightly afraid of being hit by a rock, forcing himself to turn in a rage and bash them into.....

Still thinking of home, dreading the new school year, Justin just wished mom had kept his other life back at home. Grandma and Grandpa did not need to hear about his problems at school. It was bad enough that his mom's parents knew what he had done but now both sets of grandparents now knew he had done a bad thing.

"Summer is ruined." He said to the wind between himself and the flimsy metal screen door that rattled in the breeze. Not terribly sorry for the gash in Leonard Mulligan's head from the locker latch, but he felt bad that both sets of his grandparents looked at him differently now. This made him sorrier.

"Sorry Leonard." He said aloud staring at the weather beaten wood paneling of the split level house before him.

The wind blew the high grass around him whispering a smooth song of memory.

If those dummies can spend ten minutes in a haunted house without running away scared I can do thirty minutes. He thought to himself.

This was not a scary place.

School was scary. Here he had a sense of control, comfortable with the lonely house standing amid an unkempt lot clear of trees. Remnants of an old swing set rotted to the far left. Green paint had chipped to rust, no swings hung from the bar above and the slide had been removed.

Sadness. Inescapable nor explainable sorrow made his stomach sour with regret that he now sensed was not his own. He squinted his hazel eyes, pushing some of his bowl head of hair away from his face.

The only glass that was not broken was on the top of the front door that creaked open, moving slightly with the wind. Bay windows were shattered, falling like broken teeth to the right of the front door. A garage door was shambling to the ground, on top of the gravel driveway that swept up to the dirt road that paralleled the trail that the boys had taken to the orphaned home.

"GO ON… freakin' retard!" He heard Jeremy yell at his back while the twins laughed forcefully.

He pulled the latch on the screen door. It fell to the ground to the laughter of the boys now seemingly a mile behind him. This was Justin's world now, penetration was fruitless.

"Leave me alone." He said to the dust cloud that flooded the cedar scented foyer.

Welcoming the ghosts that supposedly resided here, he was far beyond driven with curiosity in what the ghosts had to say comparatively to the people he called his friends. Even his family did not quite grasp how deeply he saw the world around … them all.

He regrettably remembered (and quite often dwelled in the dark about) a moment when he had set up all his G.I. Joes for battle; tanks, jeeps and the entire Cobra force, supported by H.I.S.S. tanks, troops and all geared for a showdown; Grandpa (on his mom's side) walked in the living room and said "wow… what are you doing?" playfully.

Because it interrupted his equilibrium, playing with his own creative euphoria of the moment, snatching a blip of his conscious passion off guard, Justin had snapped at grandpa and said, "I'M PLAYING!!!" He was mad.

Grandpa picked up his step and said, "Oh… well I better go then."

He had hurt grandpa's feelings when he should have asked him to set himself down and play with him. Justin always tortured himself with his ability to whip snap a retort in those fleeting moments of time where he actually had formulated a plan that he needed to see through to the end. An interruption provoked a rash decision. Again, this is why he rarely acted on feelings or spoke his thoughts. He did not like to hurt people nor damage their emotions.

Justin removed his cap from his back pocket. Now, pulling the brim of his hat down tight, pressing his bangs hard into his forehead, he practiced one of his defenses against the world around him. This gave him the confidence to pull the white metal screen door ajar, creaking with rusty springs. He liked the sound of those springs. It reminded him of their own screen door at their summer house on Montauk.

"MOVE IT RETARD!" Jeremy shouted across the overgrown front yard.

He reached for the doorknob, turned and pushed with his shoulder to cross over the rickety metal threshold. Narrowing his eyes, peering under the safety of the brim of his hat, Justin breathed in the dusty air. Sunlight pierced through some of the windows and cracks in the walls, beaming through like orange lasers slicing bogs of floating dust. A staircase, fractured with pieces of banister, stood before him stretching up one flight, cascading into darkness. He stood on a crumpled oval shaped area rug in what must be the living room, judging by the decaying love seat facing a fireplace that would never be lit again and the two 70's style cushioned chairs rotting to his right. His own footsteps roused the dust particles from their sleep, hovering into the air thick as soup, threatening to make him sneeze.

"Like being inside an old book." He said to the shadowy critters that scampered away from him to the recesses of old baseboard heating panels, under torn living room furniture and something the size of a squirrel that ran into the fireplace to his right.

The twins ran out of there screaming like girls. Jeremy lasted five minutes, no matter what he bragged. As for Justin, he could not wait for his turn. The fact that he actually *wanted* to take his turn was enough reason for the other boys to delay his wishes and put his turn off till this summer.

Justin was not afraid of ghosts. He preferred them over people.

Rumors around downtown with the local kids spoke of snakes in the basement, rabid raccoons in the bedrooms upstairs and ghosts in the living room.

"But you had to open the coat closet under the stairs to make the ghosts come out..." Donald Bennigan of Bennigan's Straws and Sweets candy shop had whispered over the counter after Jeremy blurted out that they were on their way to the "old house in the woods," as local legend had named the lonely place just three miles in the backwoods of town itself.

Justin liked Mr. Bennigan alright. He wore a silly Styrofoam hat to match his blue and red candy striped collared shirt. When dad took him for a walk along Main Street when Grandma sent him on an errand to the farmer's market to pick up some vegetables, they would stop in Bennigan's as a treat and dad would joke and say, "Geez I thought he was going to sell us some Pepperidge Farm cookies." Justin sort of saw the resemblance to the old guy in those cookie commercials. He thought that that old man from those commercials would be a nice person to meet some day, even if that was just TV land.

A rattle and tap on the floor below him made Justin look to his sneakers. Something alive, running feverishly from his sight had just run across his feet above the dusty wood floor. While his eyes strained to adjust to the fairly dark atmosphere of the living room, he caught a glimpse of very small shadows about the width of pool balls, disappear under the high crevice of a closet door under the staircase.

Tightening his lips subconsciously, he breathed through his nose, striving to cut down on the noise he was making. He really did not want to disturb the wonderful aura of the house. It was beautifully lonely. Something he respected. There was a lot more to respect here than be afraid of for sure.

Justin shuffled over the dusty wood panels to his left. He saw the kitchen through the archway ahead with its white walls, sink shining with chrome reflections but this was just so uninteresting compared to his compulsion to the closet door under the staircase.

Matt, Kevin and fat old Jeremy no longer existed in this plane. For a fleeting second he thought to himself about the dummies standing outside. They could be cartoon characters on the Scooby Doo show for all he cared, with less credibility than that annoying Scrappy Doo character they introduced this season. Why?

He stopped reaching for the coppery knob to dwell on that topic longer than he thought he ever really cared about a cartoon. "Why?" Justin rarely was annoyed openly, but ruining one of his favorite cartoons was the pit inside the pear!

Shaking his head at his own pettiness he now yanked the knob. The door opened with a loud and unexpected *CRACK*, whining at the hinges to reveal emptiness with a shelf on top. Focusing on the dark to adjust his eyesight, he looked down. There was a box on the floor. He pushed one of his sneakers into the side of a box the size of grandma's T.V. It gave, a bit, so not too heavy.

HSSSSSSSSS

The resounding tone of a rusty air conditioner broke the silence, mocking the very sound of the box on the floor as he shoved it with his foot. Hot air hit the back of his neck under his hair.

The box did not make that sound. That was not wind on my neck, he thought.

Turning his Islander hat around to pull his hair back from his face, he whirled on his heels. Fighting was not fun but he knew he was good at it. His pretty babysitter, Erica, with her Rod Stewart haircut and leather pants would occasionally have her biker boyfriends come over against his parent's wishes. They showed him how to put his fists up, turn the hat around to pull your hair back to show your opponent that you meant business.

Nothing.

No one.

Something had changed though. Something disturbed the misty dust floating in front of the fireplace.

"Huhhhh......" He released a puff of air as if he'd been holding it hostage for an hour.

The dust disappeared slightly in the center of the room. Or rather, the dust enveloped the form of a man in reverse. Justin thought of those transporter's on Star Trek for a moment. It was like a man was trying to zap his way into the living room, but was failing, so the dust caked all around him. There were moments where he could see a tall young looking man with shoulder length hair, glasses, dressed in a white shirt, black vest, kakis and thick glasses. He was thin. Fading then back again. A wave of repetitive metallic bass rebounded off the flaking walls like a dish hovering on a table unable to land flatly.

"Justin." The voice was comforting, warm, friendly and knowing.

"Hi." Lowering his fists he acknowledged the handsome specter before him.

The presence glowed with a radiance brighter than the sunbeams that penetrated the room.

"You shouldn't be here. Ghosts you know?" The young man smiled. "That box does not belong to you." The voice became grim and deep. "Look close."

Unafraid, Justin did just that. He turned on his heels, looked at the box more closely. It was open at the top. He could see green Christmas garland that sat amid green, orange, blue, yellow, red, and gold Christmas balls, hooked for hanging on a tree. The light of the ghost reflected off of them, making them shimmer with a new glorious presentation.

"Everything else was stolen. All our memories, pictures, toys, trinkets from vacations.... And for what? What could these thieves do with our items? Bragging rights? This is all I have left. Twenty years ... all in a box." The ghost's warm voice was thick with regret.

Justin turned to the figure standing in the middle of the living room. The words transgressed to sadness. "Who stole your stuff?" He said to the glowing form.

The ghost of the young man seemed surprised, adjusting his glasses. "Are you not frightened, little boy? Not running like the others, Justin? You... *you can actually see me?*" He smiled on thin lips, his cheekbones pointed out. A real smile, not like Jeremy Faulk's devious grin.

"You're sad. I know." So much sorrow filled Justin's gullet, like someone had poured cement down his throat. It was a pleasure for him to actually find justifications for the emotions that he could usually not put a finger on. This place *was* sorrow.

While he stood listening to the ghost before him he became aware of a sound behind him, like tiny hands were shuffling the decorations in the box. This unnerved him more than the talking ghost that dressed like Han Solo but sounded like that guy that sang "Dreamweaver," Gary Wright or something. He was soothing.

The rattle behind him was not.

"I know your name. I know who you are. You gave that up when you came in here. Your classes proclaim you as "special." The wrong kind of special, child, you are beyond your years in wisdom. Forget those guys outside, if you haven't already, they are below you Justin Deckland. But you know that." The echo of the pleasant voice relaxed the air around them, reverberating from the semi-transparent lips.

"Yea." Justin could not help but reply. Someone finally understood him.

"Huh huh... yes. I do understand you. You have great things to do, and

I'm able to see that. Not because I'm smart, kid, but because I'm dead, and still feeling the pain." He paused.

Justin thought he saw a tear that shone like a star right on the young man's cheek.

"I'm not young. I just appear that way. I killed myself right here on this couch at the age of thirty five. You don't know what that is yet, nor the taste, the drive, the compulsion…. The self-hate. Whisky, coke, speed, some shrooms now and then all with a hit of weed... Yea, kid stay clean of all of it." The Ghost snickered, then raised its chin.

"No. No drugs. Dad said…"

"Your dad does not know my pain. Enough. Don't judge. Listen." The ghost's voice turned to a heavier foreboding tone. "Look here." The man's hand pointed to the mantle riddled with gritty grime and soot. There was a picture there. The specter puffed his cheeks and blew a visible wisp into the frame. "That's our boy, Taylor."

Expecting to see a picture of a child, Justin strained his eyes to see that the picture was of a golden retriever. His face, smiling, tongue hanging over white glistening teeth. "At least they left me this. I'm stuck here Justin. Forever." The man said. With each word he became less ghost and more human standing before the boy he now entertained.

"Why?" In his heart, Justin knew why. This was a gift he never spoke of, never wanted yet always felt tortured by.

Why couldn't he just play like normal kids? He said in his head.

"Because you can't, Justin. I hate to use the word special so I won't. It was so nice to feel you coming here today because I knew it was your turn. It's been so long since I had someone to talk to. Your gift pivots my self-pity. Look in the box. But please Justin, just look. Open the flaps, glance, but please do not reach in."

He looked again. Saw the pretty Christmas balls.

"Those are the first set of decorations that Lisa and I purchased… right down the road at Tinker's Dam." The shimmering man put his chin to his chest, sucking in some air. Justin could see the dust go into his mouth. "She was beautiful Justin. Tall, long waves of brown flowing hair, the biggest loveliest brown eyes ever and a smile…. Oh that smile. A teacher, an idol, a comforting soul unlike any comparison…any. She never knew how much she meant to SO MANY… I told her. She didn't listen." A pause, then the apparition looked eye to eye with the boy. "My name is Lewis, you can call me that."

I should be scared. I should run. I….

"No, don't be scared of me. Sure I slammed things around, shouted, and growled at so many others, especially when they took our things… our photo albums from Disney on our honeymoon…Really? The shell collection that Lisa made into necklaces from our time out at the beach…

our concert tickets?!! They took our concert tickets from the basement that we had framed! I can't even look at them now to remember those wonderful moments in time! Lisa loved music. WE LOVED MUSIC!" He was shouting now. The house rumbled as if an earthquake shook its anger.

"I do too. Don't shout." Justin stepped closer, putting his hands on the back of the couch, the only thing separating him from this ghost named Lewis.

"Sorry. Sorry." A loud aspiration choked the entire room. "She died here, in my arms, on this couch. I never was able to tell anyone that. Her family never called while she was sick, my own family were on the other side of the country... I sat, day after day after night after night, watching her sleep after the radiation. The chemo. You don't know what that is.....but..."

"I do. My uncle got cancer. I do."

"Yes... I see that now. Sorry. You should go Justin."

"No. Kids? Did you have kids? I saw the swings..."

"She couldn't. We couldn't. Taylor, our puppy, he was our kid. Not many understand that Justin, nor will they, simply because they did not ask." Lewis's tone was stern not scary.

"I have friends in my head. They are better. I'm sorry about the badness, Lewis, but Taylor looks like he was *better* too." The words came out of Justin's mouth quicker than he could think.

"Yes. He was *better*." Lewis chuckled. "Lisa and I would joke about how much better our boy Taylor was than people. We tried, man. This house, her teaching, my dental practice... we tried. You see that view out of the porch... on a good fall day you can see the lake between the trees. We had fires in the fireplace...even in the summer... hahaha... turn up the air conditioner, spill some wine...look over there on that shelf in the kitchen... you see those blue glasses? No one took them because of the thick-ass spider webs all around them. They're engraved on the bottom with our names. Had that done in California in Napa during a wine tasting trip on her birthday. She wanted to go to Italy. I took her to Napa because ....ahahah I'm an idiot."

You shouldn't put yourself down, Justin thought.

"You are correct." The ghost answered.

Justin turned his hat around. Not only did he feel the sadness, he could smell it too, like syrup over a coppery pool of blood.

"We got married for each other. Met in college. Twenty years man, we were together. Inseparable. Then a disease worked its way in saying "howdy do, got a little surprise for you." She suffered. Her last breath elapsed while her head was in my lap. I never saw those beautiful brown eyes open again. I'm glad it happened in her sleep."

There was another pause. Justin felt the air shift and knew that something angry was going to happen. Dad did this when he came home from work sometimes. Aborting a raging fit, dad would just suck it in and go lift weights in the garage while mom made dinner and silently prayed he would work it out, literally.

This was like water over rocks in a creek for Justin. He was aware.

"Awareness is you gift, your compass and your savior. Because you are who you are, Justin, your family will thank you someday. We wanted that. A family." Lewis spoke with humble guilt. "You have work. Your gift will help others. Your family..."

"You did have one." The boy became agitated.

"When she was gone, Taylor died six months later. He's buried in the back. You can see the stone with his name on it, under a pile of broken beer bottles and some bitch's panties that thought it was funny to....."

Justin cringed.

"Sorry, not for you. But see what they do? Disrespect, when all I want to do is go to her, see her... pet Taylor's head. Be with them."

"Why don't you?

"Can't. The door won't open. I'm alone here because I chose to die rather than waited to live." Lewis rubbed his nose under his glasses. He then pointed behind Justin. "Look. Justin. This is what fear is. They watch. They Judge. They report. Turn."

Justin turned around. Immediately he stiffened with absolute fright. More than a dozen spiders the size of apples stood rigidly on the top of the ornaments and garland in the box. He could not see their eyes but knew they were watching him with eight piercing orbs of malignancy. Green, orange, blue, yellow, red, and gold sinfully mimicking the Christmas balls they stood over.

"They emerge on spouts of darkness, pity and grief where it breaks free the strongest. Maybe it was the place we chose to build this house? The devil knows, they have been here longer. Or were Lisa and I predestined to not have happiness play out with the band at the end of mercy? Dunno, my friend. But yet, there they are, at a crossroads in the mind's eye. We never saw them while living, so the fact that you can see them, is part of your gift. There are things beyond our realm of perception Justin. Use your ability to warn others, or save them, like I couldn't."

Justin reluctantly put his back to the spiders watching the conversation. "I don't like them." He gritted his teeth, imagining himself stomping the spiders.

"And you shouldn't. They are purveyors of the dark, relishing its rich poison, biting and bleeding us while we sleep, creating children in masses that continue the fray, forever laughing at us in their quiet repose. Despicable."

Justin wanted to quote Daffy Duck, but thought better of it.

"You are right, that would have been funny. Just act on your thoughts Justin, it's worth it. Don't do what I did… and yet…. I still do not see a life without her. I can't forgive…."

"Yourself?" Justin said out loud. There was chirping behind him. The spiders were making an audible clacking sound. They may as well have been shooting spit balls at him like Delva Greer did along with her uglier twin sister Mavis, in the cafeteria. He could feel the spiders hating his very presence almost as much he could smell the horrible breath of those two awful twins when they made fun of his peanut butter and jelly sandwich that mom made him for lunch. Female version of the dummies outside.

"What did you say?" Lewis removed his glasses, dropping on his knees to the unseen floor on his plane. His hazel eyes blinked at the boy's words.

The spiders rattled obnoxiously, seemingly disappointed at the turn of events.

Justin felt something by his feet.

"They're getting aggressive. You should go. I have no reason to fear these puny reapers anymore, even though they feed off me even in death. They breathe in sorrow like they bite down on blood. Hateful bitches. I'm just relieved that Lisa never got to see these things….."

"Go to her. You should be together." Justin swept his feet to push the giant spiders away.

"I'm sorry if I ever scared you." Lewis said softly.

"I forgive you, sir." The boy said confidently.

The ghost that was Lewis was flashing with yellow, orange and white light.

Lewis spoke softly, "Something has changed. I feel like I'm not sick anymore… my fever broke…this is what it's like to not feel like I'm always about to throw up? My headache is gone…what is that?… Justin… look… do you see it?" Lewis was enthralled with the ceiling.

"No."

"Good. You shouldn't see it. You have stuff to do my little friend. My beautiful boy …that I … that we, could never have… you came after all, full of the forgiveness I could not give myself." Then Lewis disappeared in a flash of blue light.

Dust settled in the air. Beams of sun siphoned the silence. Justin turned his head around again ready to fight.

Spinning on his heels he wanted to stomp the hell out of the spiders. But they were gone. The box of Christmas ornaments sat alone in the closet. He smelled the scent of rotting cedar and closed the closet door.

The sunny outside air was welcoming when he walked down the cement steps, elated like the time he saw Star Wars for the first time with mom and dad and Theresa was still in mom's belly. Triumphantly he walked toward the three boys waiting for him at the edge of the forest.

Jeremy crinkled his nose and said, "So, retard... is it still haunted?"
Justin replied, "No. Not anymore."

ABOUT THE AUTHOR

David J. Fairhead was first published in *THE BIG BOOK OF BIZARRO* with his demonic apocalyptic tale, THE FALL, and his short story *DEMONEYE* appears in the horror/western anthology, *WESTWARD HOES*.

David's current novel, *THE FALL OF TOMORROW* is based on his *BIG BOOK OF BIZARRO* short story and is also published by Burning Bulb Publishing.

THE COMMUNE appears courtesy of the eclectic collection of zombie fiction in the legendary *RISE OF THE DEAD* anthology available from WWW.BURNINGBULBPUBLISHING.COM

David has also written two other novels. The horror novel, CHARLIE: A CHILD'S TALE OF TERROR and the fantasy novel BLOODBIND.

He is also the writer of the comic book series WZWA (World Zombie

Wrestling Association) in association with Dr. Jon Towers and Stigmata Studios.

The short story THE MOONS' CRYIN' was first published in The DarkRose Journal.

David is currently host of the radio podcast show, KETTLE WHISTLE RADIO, working with co-host Mizzdee Kwr and Heather Taddy of A&E's Paranormal State fame, where they talk horror, comics, music and subcultures. They also interview writers, directors, actors and many musicians of all genres. Check them out on Facebook under KETTLE WHISTLE RADIO or at SOCIETY13NETWORK.WORDPRESS.COM. David is co-owner of the podcast network SOCIETY 13 NETWORK with horror author Nelson W. Pyles of THE WICKED LIBRARY and author of DEMONS DOLLS AND MILKSHAKES. Now, there are seven shows that broadcast weekly. KETTLE WHISTLE RADIO, THE WICKED LIBRARY, TBA WITH MR. PINK and MOUTHING OFF, PROG-WATCH, RED HORSE RADIO and 9th STORY PODCAST, all available on Facebook and ITUNES.

You can contact David at KETTLEWHISTLERADIO@GMAIL.COM via KETTLE WHISTLE RADIO on Facebook and on Twitter @Fairlydark as well.

David grew up on Long Island but currently resides in the zombie capital of Pittsburgh with his wife Denise and their beloved dogs Teddy and Jett.

Now a preview of David J. Fairhead's next upcoming novel.

A small resort town
A child's imaginary friend comes to visit
Is he real or just a monster in the mind of Justin Deckland
Some people are missing

CHARLIE: A CHILD'S TALE OF TERROR

CHAPTER 1

The sand was cold as he grinded it between his toes. That was his favorite time to come down to the beach. Cold sand, quiet breaks on the shore and absolutely no other people around just yet, or they had already gone away with the coming fall. The gulls massed around some cracked crab debris among some dried brown seaweed that streamed like old cassette tape. The gulls, down on his right, continued squawking their monotonous cacophony of exultation.

Justin could care less. He left his house this morning, (just feet away up the dune behind him) for the same reason.

"Where were you last night?"

"Worked late, ran to the gym..."

"Took your time on the bay? Saw you come in on the boat...and then turn..."

Mom was accusing dad for being late again for... life in general. Terry, his little sister shouted at them to stop while smearing her pancakes around on her plate. She was eight now, and had stopped crying about their parents' squabbles for more than a year, bored with the redundancy of them. Terry had a hardened emotional shell too early in life. It made Justin sad when he had noticed this about his younger sister.

His own private resilience resided in his will to fall into his imagination. Playing with his action figures or the pictures in his mind preceding the wonderful canvas of Montauk Isle as his background, the young boy saw no end to his release from what ailed most folks.

When morning started with obtuse feelings or disagreements, Justin would just get up, walk down the hall, push open the screen door with that familiar twang of the metal spring, and head on down the front steps that always made a comforting crackle. The old wood spoke of decay from the salty air (also in need of a new coat of white paint, mom would tell dad over and over again) just before he made his way across the thin carpet of browning grass toward the second set of steps. These were the best steps. The steps that led to the beach below. Each step creaked loudly to his liking, reminding him that summer was coming again. Vacation from dumb school and even dumber kids. Now, however, it was the end of summer so these once comforting crackles were merely a dim reminder that it would be a year before another summer vacation. He and his family were here, at their summer home, at the tail end of the season. Mom would be closing the shop they owned, down the road, for the season. Terry and he would be helping mom pack up the remaining stacks of sun tan lotion, kayak paddles, beach tents, kids toys, pails and shovels of plastic and of course towels that had MONTAUK ISLE in some cheesy rainbow print. Most of the seasonal islanders had long gone. Very few stayed through the fall and coming winter. Even less tourists stayed at the various forms of villas and cabanas clustered on the southern and northern shores of the isle.

The sea air whipped his wavy sandy brown locks back. Some gulls were up early too but not even the birds in their rabble rousing fight to gain the largest bit of crab debris could faze him either. This was Justin's favorite time and place, outside of maybe grandma's house. That was always a good place too where he felt warm and welcome and important (not special). At school he was considered special, too. "Special." A word he came to hate especially when he heard his parents' friends or local Islander folks mention it with a fake smile at his mom while pretending to patronize the shop. People like old cranky Ms. Guildare who smelled like too much smoke dipped in lentil soup.

There were the occasional summer days when Justin or Terry helped mom at the shop. He could not stand when Ms.Guildare with her tight curls of fake red hair laced with gray, and her chubby bosom pushed its way into the tiny shop where she would then pretend to think he was cute. YUCK!

Not thinking about her now. Nor school, or mom and dad fighting back upstairs, at the house.

The smell of the cool late summer morning air with its salt and rich sea aroma woke him better than any cup of coffee that the stupid adults filled up on.

"Why don't you just come down here with me?" Justin thought to himself, but only partially meant it because he did not ever really want to be joined during *his* time. Well, THEIR time alone. Terry occasionally would come running down the crumbling driftwood staircase, shouting and yipping in her glee of youth. He did not mind that so much. Justin wished he could be *that* happy about *anything*. In his mind he knew he was too young to be upset all the time. This, of course being the reason he came

202

down to the beach by himself to meet his friend. His friend that would not always return the warmness of friendship to him, but at least "showed up for practice." A term Dad used to ensure that Justin (who did not really play anything anymore) and other kids that he had coached showed enthusiasm during baseball practice.

On *their* time, there was no actual practice with he and his friend. His friend was a good listener and capable of some cool tricks for sure. That was enough for him.

Justin did not care about baseball anymore. This *did* bother him. He was only 12 and he had loved the game. How does one lose complete interest in anything that quick? Toys, well, those he still loved. His G.I. Joes never let him down, but the kids at school (first day back was last week) had made fun of him for having his figure of "Clutch" in his pocket at homeroom. Nope, middle school was no longer a place for action figures. "They are staying home." Justin thought. "Not talking to those guys again either." He also thought, thinking about those other boys in homeroom.

For Steve and Dana Deckland, the summer dream was ending again. Closing the store, leaving their secluded home on the beach for the monotony of life on the mainland of Long Island once again. Indeed, for their children, Justin and Theresa, a wonderful summer had passed and so did the trips to grandma's house out on Long Island's eastern shore. Soon, they would all get in the boat and leave the summer home and go back to Port Jefferson on the North Shore, close to grandma's but not quite close enough.

They may enjoy one or two more weekends out here, but they would have the store closed. No money to be made off season. Mom ran the shop here on Montauk Isle for the tourists, but they were all gone now since Labor Day barbeques had ceased. No more beach excursions, no playing on the wooden jungle gym park by the ranger station, or late nights at grandma's or even fishing with dad. Cool songs that dad and mom liked, that made him happy like Bellamy Brothers "Let Your Love Flow" became sad instead of a beach radio anthem! The ferry horn became a sad whale song in the night that he heard from his bedroom window where he pictured troves of fun loving beach party people leaving to the mainland forever with sad faces, instead of the horn that used to provide joy and hope in the beginning of a day full of summer possibilities!!

In the post season the ferry went to and from Montauk Isle transporting some folks, but only for the few remaining Islanders, and only a handful stayed year around for the clippings of cash that could still be made off some rental boats, cabanas and tee shirts. As for staying, there was no need to really. Winter could be brutal. "So back to the mainland we go," Justin mumbled to the sand between his feet.

"HEY...who you talkn to? Oh never mind. Duh."

It was Terry. She had come crunching down the steps behind him in her yellow and white picnic table summer dress and bare feet. Her sandy brown hair in two pig tails flowed behind her as she ran past him and directly at the seagulls all minding their own business. In a mass swoop and squawk, they took to the sky and the waves crashed with foam behind them and around Terry's bare feet. She giggled at the cold water. This made Justin smile, but only for a moment before picking up a dried reed and stabbing the sand with it. "Write my name." He thought to himself. "Then he'll know I was here waiting..."

"Whatcha doin? ...stepped on crab guts...ew... they hurt. It's cold." Terry plopped down next to her older brother.

He smiled at her and then saw the smooth pearl white shale stones to his left, where the beach ended. Not far off his parents' property to the east, Montauk Isle actually ended too, giving way to the sea.

Looking left over his shoulder, the ocean stretched to the east forever, but even in the morning mist you could see the eastern most tip of Montauk itself on Long Island and the grand old lighthouse on the mainland. Montauk Isle had a lighthouse too, but it was on the western side, deep into the Sunken Forest Park. Forbidden to go to the lighthouse off season, when they were not giving tours, Justin rarely ventured out that way.

But where he was now, *"His"* island (what he called it) and where his family spent the summers. Montauk Isle acted as a barrier to the southern shore of Long Island, very similar to its sister island, Fire Island, to the south. The bay between Montauk Isle and Long Island was only a couple of miles, and Justin loved the boat rides in between. (Not the ferry rides though, too many stupid people and tourists).

Standing on the end of "his island," where his house stood on the sandy dune up behind him, Justin picked up more handfuls of the shale stones.

"Oh...skipping time huh... let me try." Terry nagged.

He put some of the smaller ones in his little sister's hands and they both proceeded to throw the stones. He marveled at how hers just plopped and dunked into the water. This was good, because Justin felt bad at how long it took those shale stones to strive to the shore from the depths of the ocean where they came from. All that travel just to be thrown back out again! When he tossed them, they skipped sometimes four or five times. He smiled at the last cast and watched as the piece of shale skipped the early wisps of morning currents.

Justin swore to himself that that last one took 6 skips! Then he felt bad, knowing how long it would take that stone to reach the shore again and would he ever see it again? He placed the other rocks in his bugle boy shorts pocket and stepped back before the foaming break could reach his

Nike hi-tops. He slipped them on as the sand was cooling his feet too much. Also, he knew he'd be called back to the house shortly.

Flip flops on the beach were okay to him, but he preferred to wear his hi-top sneakers when he felt the need to run fast. Run fast he could! Especially in that creepy Sunken Forest that his mom liked to take them to, too often. Pretty with its purple …what did she call those flowers? Wild Crane Bills? Purple and bright in the summer's beginnings. He would run around the planks of the wooden maze while mom tried to show him the pretty flowers named after…what? He had a Wild Bill action figure that he loved, and saw no connection to this flower and a G.I. Joe or even some weird cowboy? Terry enjoyed the Sunken Forest more than he did. She would pick at cat tails over the rails of the walkways, desperately trying to pull them out. He always knew it was fruitless and marveled at her tenacity and chuckled when she would fall to the wooden floor boards. That park was on the other end of the island, away from his beach, away from his shale rocks and away from the possibility of his friend showing up.

BUZZZZZ...

He looked over his shoulder at this new distraction.

Sighing, he saw that Terry had brought her yellow transistor radio (with the cartoon duck printed on the side playing with a hula hoop) down to the beach with her. Easily distracted she was dancing to some song in constant rotation this summer. Funny how they randomly got stuck on some songs over and over again, he thought. Sometimes not even a new song.

'West…end …Girls….'' What the heck does he say after that Justin?'' She screeched louder than the gulls. Even he knew lyrics better than she, and she now owned the 45 vinyl record that she had bought at Sam Goody when Dad took them there not too long ago. She played the record out, over and over again on an old Holly Hobbie record player. He preferred cassettes but had amassed a good music collection on 45 too.

Dancing around to the Pet Shop Boys' creepy ambience, Terry was enthralled.

Why can't she stop dancing once in a while? She's gonna keep the gulls, and well, *everything else* from making an appearance! He grew annoyed but then shook his head and laughed at her own delusions of Madonna moves in the pink lit morning glow on the sand.

"You're nutz." He muttered. She pretended not to hear.

The wind blew a little rougher than normal at this time of year, throwing his sandy hair into his face once again instead of blowing it back. The radio filled the air with summer sounds, and familiar voices of the local deejays and radio personalities. A good song had come on again. "Always somethin there to remind me..." A singer crooned. What was that band with the silly name? He had seen the video on MTV a dozen times before Grandma had shut off the TV. Naked Eyes. Dumb name. Good song.

Terry had ignored the good song to chase gulls down to the water again and Justin had plopped next to the radio to hear the tune better. It ended and Michael Jackson's "Rock With You" came on, and he got up again, knowing all too well how much Theresa loved this one! Soon as he thought it, she came running over writhing like a skinny dwarfin disco queen in her yellow checkered sundress.

"YESSSS!" She yelped, exaggerating her happiness, knowing full well how uncomfortable it made her older brother to start random dancing where people could see.

But it was not that, not really. Now, was his alone time, and he kind of hoped to be alone soon.

When the song ended with the typical rasp of a.m. radio, a disc jockey voice came on. There was a broadcast now and again about a young girl on the mainland who had disappeared. What was her name? They kept a consistent broadcast and here it was again. What the heck was the little girl's name? Oh it was Laura Lee! Justin could hear the voices of the news readers feign concern for the lost little girl. Justin *was* concerned. This made him sad. Here he was, safe with his family and some poor little girl was not going to make it home tonight to watch the Muppets with mom and dad. Losing his thoughts to his surroundings, the wind whipped at him and foam splashed his face.

"Brrrr...I don't know how you stand it out here... if you can't go swimming what's the use..." Terry threw her one last rock that "plunked" into the water, making its own little waves. "Dummy and Mummy are going to the mainland to get groceries... wanna come?" She had already started to run to the steep staircase with its rotten wood railings, dodging white splinters as she hopped. "Thought not." She proceeded up the stairs.

"THERESA DECKLAND!..you com'n?" Their mother called from the front door up at the top of the beach staircase.

He loved his sister, and knew that she understood his quiet. Most of all, he loved that she did not yell and scream at him for not talking. They always knew what one another needed anyway. Smiling at her reference to their parents, (Dummy and Mummy) he looked out to the horizon.

Not much there. For some. Yet for him, worlds opened wide. The pink and blue of the morning was dissipating a bit. A gray overcast sky with moving clouds that flew east with the wind accented by some sun glowing behind it, and then the wisps of the furthermost clouds greeted the green Atlantic.

Whether or not Terry had interrupted his attempt at meeting his friend today really had not frustrated him. Theresa had been his only friend before now. Oh he certainly admired some other older people, but he dared not call them friends, just yet. There was a girl ranger he thought was pretty, and of course the lifeguard security guy at the beach was cool for an older kid. As for his sister Theresa, he also knew that she was smarter than him at only eight. She did so well in school and he hated school, but she was already helping him with some reading that he just had become so bored with. "Make a game out of it… that's what I do…" Terry's advice was good advice. "See how many pages you can finish, and try one more page next time." He liked few people, but loved his sister.

And, on those small occasions when he did express himself, Theresa, Terry, really listened.

So, no, he could not find the anger in her little disruption at the beach.

There was a splash in the distance, and Justin looked out again at the water. Small breaks, but mostly placid. The wind was changing that now, shifting the breakers so that they accelerated and walloped the beach.

"Not as scary as the hurricane." He remembered last May, just before the summer, that terrible hurricane that hit. Luckily they were still in school on the mainland and had minimum damage to return to in June. Dad had to fix a few windows on the second floor and there was sand all over their wraparound porch. Compared to some unlucky folk here on Montauk Isle they had fared far better than some of their neighbors. Lots of folks were still without a boat. Those islanders lost their boats when they were sunk or smashed and they had to rely on neighbors or the local former New Jersey longshoreman himself, Captain Paul and his ferry.

SPLASH!

He whirled around again expecting to see a gull swoop off with a fish. Nothing again. No breakers at the moment. The water rippled in a larger radius than the normal fish or rock could produce, just a few feet short of the breakers.

Justin smiled. "CHARLIE's back."

CHAPTER 2 – A VISIT

Justin thought to the beginning of summer and how his life had changed three months ago. Back in June after the Hurricane was long passed, the Deckland family returned to their house on the east end of the Island. Hurricane Gloria had passed by leaving some rubble along the coast, yet their fears were subsided almost immediately. Dad had brought them back on his crude little outboard fishing boat that very next day. The Deckland was hardly a fishing boat, but it bared the family name crudely in turquoise, thanks to Grandma and Grandpa making a fun day out of a real bad paint job one summer afternoon with the kids.

Hurricanes can be choosey where they will wreak havoc, dismissing whole sections of coast entirely, then leveling the mainland. Some inland neighborhoods on Long Island had gotten wind damage, trees strewn across roads and wires were down, but Montauk Isle survived just fine this time. There was word further west along the coast, that homes on Fire Island were annihilated succumbing to the crashing waves brought up from the depths to meet human structures like anvils slamming on balsa wood. Justin's school lost part of its roof and a week of school itself, resulting in the fact that they had to make it up the following week, but any time spent outside of that place was ok with Justin.

"Not fair!" Theresa had yelled every morning that her older brother was allowed to stay in bed.

After docking that morning in the early summer, seeing that the light house on the far western end still stood by the Sunken Forest was a relief to all of them. However they did not know how their house fared on the southeastern most part of the isle till they got there. That morning was a glorious surprise. The damage had been minimal.

"Still there," Dana Deckland had joked pointing at the lighthouse that stood like a landmark signifying summer. There was no chance of the lighthouse tower ever being destroyed in a hurricane, unless the whole island went down, but she knew the kids would smile at this, and they did.

So picking up the pieces was necessary. They all expected more damage than what was discovered. Most of the Isle's homes were in good shape. Thickets were strewn about Sea Grass Lane and Point Road had a tree or two across it, so leaving the car home this time was smart after all. Dana gave her husband a "touché' motion at their argument earlier over waiting for the ferry to be functioning again so the car could be taken over to the Island. All in all things were intact for the summer tourists. The shop was still standing as well, when they decided to walk to the right toward it instead of the normal left toward their house. Dana had decided that she and Steve should see if their place of business was still there, since its structure was of lesser design.

"Bad news before worse," Justin remembered mom saying. But it was just fine. Some debris had to be swept from the gravel parking lot but that was it. Since the ferry had not been running on this day (to keep people off the Isle till the authorities could deem it safe) Dad had decided the boat would be okay to take over. Police would be too busy with clean up to mess with them. Who knew how long they would approve of the ferry to go across again. They had seen Captain Paul Mishurak bickering with Officer Rickon and Officer Mitchell earlier. He had motioned to his deckhands, Brenna and Jimmy to start loosening moorings when the K Boat with the two cops on patrol scooted up alongside the dock and the bickering began.

Steve and Dana both knew they could get across on their own, dodging the other K Boat patrol, that would be too busy to bother with them. Besides they had a place of business to protect or erect. Oddly enough, not much to fix on the shop after all. So after a quick once over of the shop, they walked a mile or two down Point Road to their house.

The gray siding of the two story custom Victorian structure was so inviting with its white wood trim around the upstairs windows. Seeing it standing up on the hill at the end of the eastern most tip of land that could still maintain a house, had been such a relief. All four had breathed an audible sigh. Beyond that was the forest below to the crashing ocean. In front was the small grass lawn that lead to where they stood at the end of their driveway. All with smiles on their faces. The wood stair case leading from the front porch to the beach staircase below was also intact. This was not expected, but welcomed.

Spending that Saturday picking up the pieces of driftwood and shale stone proved to be a bit tedious (maybe some sand on the wraparound porch) and rewarding. The Deckland family had dinner on the back porch, rather than the screened in front. Too much sand strewn about still. Dinner was nice, if just quiet. But later that night, Justin's twelve years in existence would forever change. For the better, in his opinion. At least for *that* night back in June.

From what he remembered, it was that Saturday night three months ago, at the beginning of Summer that he had run down the long staircase to the beach, tears streaking his pouty cheeks. His parents had bickered about the clean up, while there was minimal damage; more reason to celebrate really but they found some way to argue about the shop and why they were keeping it and money issues....

Terry was in bed, but he was sure she had heard the whole thing. Before he came down to the sand that evening, he had been playing with his G.I. Joes .(Cobra was losing the fight with his action figures. The G.I.'s were kicking it into high gear this evening!) Playing with his toys next to his bed, the conversation downstairs had picked up tempo and volume. His parents were a bit louder than his little boom box radio playing some Phil Collins song about "...feeling it coming in the air tonight." Justin remembered his friends liking the song. He hated this song, but he liked having the radio on for the company late at night when he played in his room upstairs.

"ENOUGH... Already...Dana" Dad shouted. Something pounded the kitchen table downstairs. (Dad's fist perhaps).

He heard his mom start rasping something angry in return, when he stopped his toy helicopter Dragonfly in mid flight before nailing the Cobra Command Center. His toys were strewn about the floor. Dad had joked about whenever he played, "all the soldiers look dead already...must have been some battle, " and he seldom set them up, sometimes he would not even put the weapons in their hands, because the toy weapons in his mind seemed cooler to him.

Justin had looked out his bedroom window next to his bed. The moon shone so bright, it was almost silver in the horizon above the ocean, casting a bright shimmering reflection. He became transfixed with the site as it was just so amazing with no clouds in the sky. This window overlooked the front of the house and the water beyond. The other window had a view of the driveway below on the side of the house and beyond he could see the southern docks where the ferry docked. But looking out the front window, hoping against hope, Justin always prayed for a shark fin in the night water to cut the sea in its wake. This never happened, in all his years he'd never seen a shark, or a dolphin for that matter. In the mornings around summer time there were plenty of horseshoe crab carcasses laying on the beach. Nothing really scary. The scary things he kept to himself, the things that his mind liked to dream up.

Leaving the confines of his room and the safety of his toys, he had put on his Mets windbreaker and grabbed his Islander's baseball cap and walked down the hall. He liked that they had matching colors. His grandma had said something about Pittsburgh teams all having matching colors and was drawn to the idea. Things should match when they come from the same place. Like people.

"But people never do." He was done thinking about people. It was late, so it might be chilly down by the water tonight;

windy perhaps. Walking past his sister's room he peered in while his sneakers shuffled on the wood floor. She was awake in her Strawberry Shortcake sheets, peering over at him with her giant blue glazed eyes. She was crying, but sucked it up just in time so he could not see. "Going outside again?" She asked, pulling the sheet up to her face.

He nodded.

"Can I come?"

He shook his head. "Late." He muttered. Justin really did not want to get his sister in trouble. Not caring about whatever trouble he'd get himself in, he had crept down the noisy slippery wood staircase, (newly finished).

"Please Dana, it's just a store…we are breaking even…"

"I can't just say 'SEE YA'… and walk away from it. I love that store…"

"Let someone else love it, and let us get PAID FOR IT! It would sell quickly and we could pay off this house and the other…"

Justin absorbed what he could from the 'conversations' that his parents had but really did not pay much attention when his focus was on his outside nightly excursions. They were down the hall in the kitchen and they could not see him open the heavy door, then squint his eyes in frustration at the slight twang of the screen door while he eased it shut behind him. He hated that spring loaded action of the screen door ever since he had gotten his hair caught in it when he was a younger kid. Smiling to himself he remembered why. After watching a Star Wars special effects show, he learned that laser sounds could be created from springs if you yanked them the right way. He leaned in too close and caught his mop of brown hair in the process. Embarrassing to have mom unhinge his hair from a spring on a door.

He stepped to the outside and then down the creaky flight of steps to the sand. A couple of gleeful pounces after that he was on the staircase leading down to the night air of the shoreline. Their closest neighbor, Mr. Kandish was already back on the mainland, but his porch light was still on in the porch of his red cape cod, as he always left it on when he went home for the weekend. This buttery yellow light was the only light outside of the stars and the moon above. The sand was glowing so cleanly by the moon and the stars creating an iridescence that was "better than daylight!" Justin thought to himself. And no one was around. Sometimes the annoying teenagers would be around, but further down toward some of the other residences, drinking, swearing and smoking. But no ferry, meant, *no one* else was here unless they had their own boat.

The waves crashed with solemn little "kurplashes" that foamed brightly under the moon. It was chilly but the boy paid no mind.

"Rocks…" He began crouching down to grab any rocks that may be flat enough to skip.

Thoughts of school ending soon for the summer made him even more excited. More late nights with his toys in his room and maybe mom and dad would get along once the store started getting some more business. Everyone needs towels and blankets for the beach right?! He smiled to himself. Maybe I should bring Terry down here some time to see the ocean at night. He thought about the idea and decided he would do that sometime this summer. Things were already looking brighter for Justin Deckland the further he left his problems upstairs at the house. He had a better outlook out in the fresh night beach air. Yes, he would have to share this with Terry one night.

SPLASH!

What was that...? He held back his third rock. After throwing the second, there was a splash in the water that could not have come from his small piece of flattened shale. Something had broken the surface. A brackish shadow darkened the top of the moon-glazed ocean surface, and then ducked under. And was that a green light? The boy swore he saw a light, or possibly two lights that seemed to blink at him.

Justin stepped back five paces and then fell on his butt in the sand, kicking up some more sand on his sneakers that went into his left eye. His hat fell off his head next to him.

Rubbing his eye, he was afraid to close them, feeling vulnerable on the ground to whatever he had just seen in the breakers.

It's a fish, silly, they can't get you, even if it's a shark.

What about a giant squid? His mind was getting the best of him.

SPLASH!! SPLASH... WUMP!

Struggling to get his eye open, he peered with the other directly in front of him where the foam pulled back to the ocean. After the foamy bubbles retracted with a crackle, he saw that the water had left something there, only feet away. It was standing as tall as *HE* was *sitting* on the ground.

Fear ran cold down his back, a scream was stuck in his throat and Justin's jaw hung down to his Voltron tee -shirt. Not a fish, not driftwood but something with green eyes lit like baseball sized lanterns plopped up on the beach with dark black and green leathery skin. Why was this *impossible thing* here? Was it here?

His teachers had scolded him for humming to himself in class on more than one occasion where he did not even realize he was doing it. Could he be dreaming up this creature while he was awake and not realize it? He tried to stand, getting up slowly, and was watching the thing in the moonlight cock its head to one side, like an oversized gecko, it was watching him right back.

It was sitting on what appeared to be long skinny reptilian legs in a crouch position while it began to extend two more skinny arms from its side. The thing shuffled a bit as the arms went into the sand in front it appearing to pull the creature forward slightly. Pointy daggers formed fin-like rows on the oblate head. Those same pointy features were formed at the tips of the creature's four fingered front claws.

Justin did not like the claws. The points were threateningly long talons. Terrified now, he wanted to run but could not take his eyes off of those green orbs. They were amazing, and somehow, *comforting*.

"What are you...?" He thought. "Sorry... if I hit you with the rocks...." He wished his dad would come down the stairs now. How fast could this thing be? Still, he was not as afraid as Terry would have been. He was more intrigued.

There was a sharp pain in his head that throbbed for a moment on his left and right temple, and then the middle of his forehead.

"*...won't hurt you...*"

Now he stood up. "You Talked..." Justin knew he was dreaming now. Must have fallen on my head on the steps. Cool dream though. Hope mom does not wake me up.

"*Lost...friendly. Friends?*" The creature spoke with a hollow rasp unlike any accent or voice he had ever heard, but its wide oblate head did not move. It appeared to have a wide mouth directly under two flat wide nostrils. (Like horse nostrils, the boy thought) The voice was clear enough for Justin though.

"What are you...where ...?"

"*Not here. No. Friends?*" The voice in his head was a heavy, dull rasp, deep and soothing. It heard him and responded, yet Justin knew he had not said a word out loud this time, though his mouth was hanging open wide. Was it reading his thoughts? He wanted his hat, and also really wanted to go back up the stairs. This was a little too much to handle.

Before Justin could finish his thoughts, the creature bounded twice and had snatched up the boy's Islanders hat with one of its horribly clawed hands and was now offering the hat back to him. Looking up at Justin with his baseball size green orbs glowing brighter than Mr. Kandish's porch light ever could, the creature only stood to the height of Justin's chest.

"*Take....Yours.*"

The raspy robotic voice sounded soothing, but it hurt his head a bit. He took the hat, careful to dodge those long nails at the end of (is that webbing?) its clawed hand. Its voice was like a whisper- very forced. If a kid on the playground had this voice he would not trust that person. He wanted this creature's idea of friendship to be genuine, but right now...

Placing the cap back on his own head, "What do you want?" He thought.

"*Friends... Lost... Found?*"

"Uh... Sure." Feeling more comfortable now, since the creature stepped back two paces by extending its bent froggy-legs, Justin felt like smiling. So he did.

It stared back at him. "*Happy.*"

"Ok... yeah....Happy..."

Then it was gone. It back-flipped with such brilliance and speed, that it barely made a splash.

Justin was sad then, and wondered if he'd ever see his reptilian friend again. Also he wondered when he'd wake up.

THE FALL OF TOMORROW

Hopelessness... How do you protect your loved ones when Hell itself opens its insidious mouth?

Horror... Nightmarish Creatures invade your world and there is nowhere to hide.

Blood... How long can you hold out before they come for you?

Pain... Where do you run to avoid being eaten alive by monsters with a voracious appetite for your flesh?

Screams... While you selfishly run for your own life.

Questions... Who is to blame? Where did they come from? How many people survived...and how does the human race find the means to fight back?

THE FALL OF TOMORROW is man's last tale of desperation told by those that are striving to salvage some hope against a ravenous bastion of evil beasts bent on ruling our world.

"David Fairhead writes compelling stories that offer very human characters and very inhuman monsters. There is no subtlety in Fairhead's imagination - he is simply dying to scare the hell out of you."

    - Nelson W Pyles - author of DEMONS, DOLLS AND MILKSHAKES

Burning Bulb
PUBLISHING

OTHER GREAT TITLES FROM

Burning Bulb

PUBLISHING

WWW.BURNINGBULBPUBLISHING.COM

DETOUR TO ARMAGEDDON BY SOLON TSANGARAS

"An all-pervasive breakout of ghoulish pandemonium related
with unbridled glee and terror."
—John Russo, author of *Night of the Living Dead*

WHO WILL SURVIVE? WILL THEY WANT TO?

Enter a world where your best friend, your neighbor, your mother
or father, just aren't the same people you knew. But THEY aren't the
real enemy...

Join groups of survivors as they make their way across this
once-great nation that has been devastated by a man-made plague
created by corporate greed and fed by self-serving men who are
hungry for power and control.

Burning Bulb
PUBLISHING

ANTHOLOGIES
BIZARRO AND TRANSGRESSIVE FICTION

THE BIG BOOK OF BIZARRO

The Big Book of Bizarro brings together the peculiar prose of an international cast of the most grotesquely-gonzo, genre-grinding modern writers who ever put pen to paper (or mouse to pad), including:

NIGHT OF THE LIVING DEAD horror writers John Russo & George Kosana; HUSTLER MAGAZINE erotica contributors Eva Hore, Andrée Lachapelle, & J. Troy Seate and established Bizarro genre authors D. Harlan Wilson, William Pauley III, Wol-vriey, Laird Long, Richard Godwin and so many more!

From Alien abductions to Zombie sex, The Big Book of Bizarro contains OVER FIFTY STORIES of the most outrélandish transgressive fiction that you'll ever lay your capricious and curious hands upon!

WARNING: This book may be one of the most controversial and dangerous books you'll ever read.

WESTWARD HOES

Nine outlaw writers rode into town from obscurity to pen nine tantalizing tales of horror and fantasy, and leaving once they branded their own personal marks on the weird western genre and became living legends of the American Frontier experience.

Like drunken Indian scouts, the writers fervidly tracked down and captured the Western genre, tore off its fashionable veneer and ravished its exposed essence.

So belly up to the bar with your favorite soiled dove and enjoy perusing these thrilling tales of Old West debauchery, danger and desire; compiled by the publisher of The Big Book of Bizarro and featuring the bizarro novella *Big Trouble in Little Ass* by Wol-vriey.

Burning Bulb
PUBLISHING

ANTHOLOGIES
BIZARRO AND TRANSGRESSIVE FICTION

THE BIG BOOK OF BIZARRO SPECIAL KINDLE EDITIONS

OTHER AWESOME COLLECTIONS

Burning Bulb
PUBLISHING

GARY LEE VINCENT'S
DARKENED
THE WEST VIRGINIA VAMPIRE SERIES

DARKENED HILLS

When evil descends on a small West Virginia town, who will survive?

Jonathan did not start out his life to become a rambler, it just worked out that way. William was a troubled youth with something to hide. Both were from Melas, a small town tucked away in the West Virginia hills... a town where disappearances are happening more and more frequently.

After the suicide of a wanted serial killer, the townsfolk thought the nightmare was over. But when a centuries-old vampire is discovered they find out the hard way it's just getting started. Dark secrets can only stay hidden for so long and when the devil comes to collect, there will be hell to pay. Can Jonathan and William find a way to stop the vampire before it's too late? Find out in *Darkened Hills!*

DARKENED HOLLOWS

In the heart-stopping sequel to the award-winning *Darkened Hills*, Jonathan and William must return to West Virginia to face possible criminal charges stemming from their last visit to the damned town of Melas, where both had narrowly escaped the clutches of a vampire seethe.

And as livestock start mysteriously getting murdered with all of their blood drained, worried farmers are searching for answers - leaving the local Sheriff and his deputy racing against time to learn the cause before a more violent crime is committed.

Burning Bulb
PUBLISHING

WWW.DARKENEDHILLS.COM

GARY LEE VINCENT'S

DARKENED
THE WEST VIRGINIA VAMPIRE SERIES

DARKENED WATERS

When the world goes to hell, the chosen must arise!

As Talman Cane orchestrates a flood of epic proportions in this third installment of the *Darkened* series the towns of Melas and Tarklin are caught completely off guard by the deluge. Hell-bent on finishing what they started, the evil brothers return to the lunatic asylum to take care of the witnesses and add to the ever-growing army of the undead.

Aided by Lucifer himself and the insane vampire demon Legion, the stage is set to channel all of the forces of hell to come forth. In an all-out race to survive, Jonathan, William, and Amanda soon discover they are up against impossible odds as Lucifer opens the Gateway to Hell, ushering in the zombie apocalypse and the End Times.

DARKENED SOULS

Melas and the Madison House are about to be rebuilt.
True evil is about to be reborne!

Young ex-priest and vampire-killer William is drawn back to the West Virginian town that almost killed him, where his vampire arch-enemy Victor Rothenstein still stalks the earth.

The town of Melas lies destroyed after the battle of the End of Days. But why is wealthy Jackie Nixon so eager to rebuild it using the bone dust of murdered souls?

Terrible evil has visited before, but the Gateway to Hell is about to be reopened in a horrific climax. And this time – it's personal.

WWW.DARKENEDHILLS.COM

Burning Bulb
PUBLISHING

NIGHT OF THE LIVING DEAD

Why does **Night of the Living Dead** hit with such chilling impact?
Is it because everyday people in a commonplace house are suddenly the victims of a monstrous invasion? Or is it because the ghouls who surround the house with grasping claws were once ordinary people, too?

Decide for yourself as you read, and the horror grips you. All the cannibalism, suspense and frenzy of the smash-hit move are here in the novel.

www.TheJohnRusso.com

Burning Bulb
PUBLISHING

"A sense of infectious fun, straight from the author's pen."
— Nightmare Library

From Legendary Horror Writer
JOHN A. RUSSO

LIVING THINGS

"Russo carries his talent for the horrific neatly over into the novel form."
— West Coast Review of Books

LIVING THINGS

Beneath the shimmering Miami sun sprawls one of the Mafia's biggest empires, a glittering world of lavish beachfront mansions, neon-painted nightclubs, beautiful women, expensive cars—and absolute control over the state's billion-dollar drug trade. But, one by one, its ganglords and henchmen are falling prey to a new rival. His powers are fueled by monstrous ancient rituals; his hellish undead legions slaughter mobsters and innocent citizens alike, his unholy lust for power is virtually unstoppable.

Now a burned-out ex-detective and a brilliant anthropologist must enter a gruesome, nightmare world to fight this master of malevolence and illusion. Their time is short, their weapons few, and they face an ultimate, terrifying choice - annihilation or the loss of their souls to the eternal torment of those who never die. . .

www.TheJohnRusso.com

Burning Bulb
PUBLISHING

SEA OF MEDIUM-TO-HIGH PITCHED NOISES

The zombie apocalypse is changing; the world is coming to an odd demise; and a serial killer tries to change his ways and redeem himself before it all goes away.

Now, Crabby has entered the world he left behind; the world of the undead. And things are changing. Everything will come to an end. In this new wave of the apocalypse, everything changes every five minutes. And death would be an absolute luxury. Psychological torment meets physical bloodletting in Sea of Medium-to-High Pitched Noises.

Burning Bulb
PUBLISHING

MAD WORLD BY ANDY RAUSCH

"*Mad World* is dark, twisted, no-holds-barred fun."
—Jason Starr, author of *Bust*, *Slide*, and *The Max*

EVERYONE'S PLAYING AN ANGLE IN THE CITY OF ANGELS

Mad World tells the stories of a black hitman who doubles as a
university professor, a Catholic priest who longs to be a gangster,
a would-be author from Kansas, a gay phone sex operator who
claims he's straight, a group of rich twentysomethings playing a
deadly game of life and death, a vicious Mafia boss, and a sleazy
Hollywood movie director. As each of their stories intersect, the
body count piles up and the action comes nonstop in this tense,
white-knuckle thriller by first-time author Andy Rausch.

"A wild ride. If you like it gangster, *Mad World* delivers."
—Daniel Birch, author of *Get Some*

Burning Bulb
PUBLISHING

WEST VIRGINIA-THEMED HUMORROROTICA

BY RICH BOTTLES JR.

HELLHOLE WEST VIRGINIA

From the heights of Mothman's perch high atop the Silver Bridge in Point Pleasant to the depths of Hellhole Cavern in Pendleton County, evil lurks within the shadows as the sun sets upon the haunted hills and hollows of West Virginia.

Bizarro author Rich Bottles Jr. blows the coffin lid off horror genre clichés with this tour de force cast of Eco-friendly vampires, beach-yearning zombies and sex-starved she-devils.

LUMBERJACKED

If you are easily offended or do not possess a truly depraved sense of humor, this story may not be the light summer reading fare you desire. As for the four feisty female freshmen stranded on top of West Virginia's third highest mountain, they have no choice but to experience the sick, twisted debauchery and perverted mayhem described deep inside the tight unbroken bindings of this horrific missive.

Lumberjacked takes the reader to a nightmarish world where character development and aesthetic integrity are prematurely cut short by the swinging axes of maniacal lumberjacks, who are hell bent on death and destruction in the remote forests of Appalachia. And at the climax, when paranoia crosses over to the paranormal, Lumberjacked makes Deliverance look like a family raft trip down the Lower Gauley.

THE MANACLED

What happens when twin brothers lease out the former West Virginia State Penitentiary with the false purpose of filming a documentary on supernatural phenomena, but their true intention is to make a pornographic movie?

Chaos ensues as the disturbed spirits of murdered convicts, along with the reanimated dead from the neighboring Indian Burial Mound, take their vengeance on the unwary and undressed trespassers.

Zombies, ghosts, mobsters and porn collide in this bizarro tale from horror author Rich Bottles Jr.

Burning Bulb
PUBLISHING